LITTLE BIGHORN

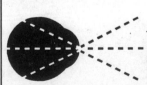

This Large Print Book carries the Seal of Approval of N.A.V.H.

LITTLE BIGHORN

JOHN HOUGH, JR.

THORNDIKE PRESS

A part of Gale, a Cengage Company

Farmington Hills, Mich • San Francisco • New York • Waterville, Maine
Meriden, Conn • Mason, Ohio • Chicago

Copyright © 2014 by John Hough, Jr.
Thorndike Press, a part of Gale, a Cengage Company.

ALL RIGHTS RESERVED
Thorndike Press® Large Print Western.
The text of this Large Print edition is unabridged.
Other aspects of the book may vary from the original edition.
Set in 16 pt. Plantin.

LIBRARY OF CONGRESS CIP DATA ON FILE.
CATALOGUING IN PUBLICATION FOR THIS BOOK
IS AVAILABLE FROM THE LIBRARY OF CONGRESS

ISBN-13: 978-1-4328-4843-9 (hardcover)

Published in 2018 by arrangement with Skyhorse Publishing

Printed in the United States of America
1 2 3 4 5 6 7 22 21 20 19 18

For Roger Lane

Prologue: Armstrong

The Custer Luck, he said, coining it in his letters to Libbie in the last year of the Rebellion. It had fallen on him at the outset like a blessing; God had touched his shoulder, had whispered in his ear. A promise.

He'd reported to the Adjutant's Office three days before Bull Run, coming straight from West Point, and inside of twenty-four hours had been chosen by General Scott himself to carry dispatches to General McDowell down at Centreville.

"You're not afraid of a night ride, are you?" said General Scott.

"I'm not afraid of anything, sir."

"Then I guess you'll do," said the fat old general.

He crossed Long Bridge at candle lighting under a rising moon. He found the Fairfax Road as ordered and cantered on into the warm, sweet Virginia night, happier than he'd ever been. The road was hoof-dug and rutted and milky-gray in the moonlight. Dark woods pressed in on either side. The horse was named Wellington; Custer had ridden him in cavalry exercises at the Point. He was jet-black with white socks and a forehead blaze. He had high withers and a deep chest, a good strong mount, and Custer cantered him along in a kind of ecstasy, as if the scented air and moonlight were intoxicants, drunk rather than breathed. Owls and night birds called in the blackness of the woods. Wellington's hooves thudded rhythmically.

Here and there, in small clearings, stood cabins of notched chinked logs with stone chimneys, and a few ramshackle plank outbuildings. The cabins were dark but inhabited, he knew, by the lingering smell of woodsmoke. He passed an abandoned plantation, its windows broken and a couple of outbuildings burned to the ground, and he wondered where the residents had gone, and where the Negroes had. He'd been told to keep an eye out for partisans, to get off the road if he heard horses approaching, but he knew that none would, as he would know, in the coming years, that he would not die in battle.

Here it was, the Custer Luck, and it held true and inviolate all the way to Appomattox: Brandy Station, Aldie, Gettysburg, Falling Waters, Yellow Tavern, Trevilian Station, Winchester. He was the Boy General, always at the front of the charge, always in the thick of moiling horses, slashing sabers, men shooting each other pointblank. He went straight at batteries firing canister, scattering the artillerists, shooting them down as they ran. The ecstasy of that first night ride would sweep him up, carry him into fights at the front of his men, who loved him for it. His hair rippled to his shoulders, and he wore a jacket of black velvet, gold-embroidered, a blue sailor's shirt, a scarlet cravat. He wore gilt spurs. Horses were killed under him, but no ball or shell fragment so much as grazed him. He never questioned this, never wondered why not. Because he knew.

General McClellan loved him. General Pleasonton did. General Sheridan. At Appomattox it was George Armstrong Custer who rode out to receive the flag of truce that ended the war. General Sheridan gave him the writing table — sent it to Libbie, with a courtly note of thanks — on which Lee and Grant had signed the surrender. He had, in the final days, captured four trains carrying food and ordnance, and when Confederate artillery tried to drive him away from the depot, he'd charged the guns and taken them too.

Then came the Grand Review. The day was perfect, a brilliant blue sky, not too hot, spectators clotted along both sides of Pennsylvania Avenue, patriotic bunting adorning the brick row houses and big hotels, which only a few days ago had been hung with black crepe for Lincoln. A two-day parade, upward of two hundred thousand fighting men, from the Capitol to the President's House. Custer wore his velvet jacket, the red cravat, a black hat with a gold cord and silver star. His hair, he well knew, was golden in the sunshine. Curls cascading down. On the first day there were seven miles of cavalry, it was said, and Merritt and Custer led them, moving at a stately walk, raising slow roils of dust. The spectators were in holiday spirits and well turned out, the men in frock coats, the women and girls in dresses in bright summer colors. Women fluttered handkerchiefs; girls threw nosegays and single roses. He could feel the women and girls watching him, the adhesion of their gazes. He could hear the men call out to him.

"Go it, General!"

"Looking splendid, General!"

"Here's to you, General. The Union forever!"

Then, where the Avenue bent at Fifteenth Street just short of the President's House, a girl darted into the roadway before anyone could stop her. She had golden hair like Custer's and wore an indigo dress, and she came running at him with ardor in her eyes, holding her skirt to keep it from dragging and in the other hand raising a nosegay of red roses. Custer checked his horse. The girl thrust the bouquet up at him, smiling, and as Custer leaned to take it, his mount — his name, providentially, was Don Juan — reared, nearly throwing him, and bolted.

He was past the reviewing stand — Johnson, Grant, Seward, all of them — by the time he stopped Don Juan. He'd lost his hat. Don Juan now was dancing sideways, nodding frantically, still aquiver with the fright the girl had given him. Custer held him, then reined him around and spurred him back to his place at the front of the column, checked him again, hard, and wheeled about to resume the parade, neat as you please. Applause, hurrahs, rose on either side of the Avenue, and afterward people said it was the rip-staver of the entire Review, both days, and some that he'd done it on purpose, but he had not. He had

11

wanted to have the roses and speak to the girl.

"George Armstrong Custer," he'd have said, leaning to take the flowers, "at your service."

But Don Juan had reared and run, and in that exhilarating minute or two when he'd checked the horse and calmed him and brought him back, the girl had vanished forever. He had never even known her name.

■ ■ ■ ■

PART ONE:
THE GIRL I LEFT
BEHIND ME

■ ■ ■ ■

ONE

The doorman at the Willard admitted him wordlessly, and Allen thanked him and crossed the columned rotunda with his valise and topcoat, his footsteps ringing hollowly on the tessellated floor. Two men on a leather sofa stopped talking and watched him pass. One of them leaned forward and tapped cigar ash into a cuspidor. The concierge straightened, brightened, and set his hands on the desktop.

"You'll be young Winslow," he said.

Allen nodded and put down his valise, his topcoat. The two men on the sofa resumed talking.

"Miss Deschenes is in the dining room," the concierge said. "You're to go right on in." He glanced at the two men on the sofa and leaned closer and lowered his voice. "She's in there with General Custer."

Allen looked at him. "Say again?"

"Think I'm joking you," the concierge said.

"No," Allen said. He looked off over the rotunda. Potted plants, the imperious leather furniture. It didn't surprise him. Nothing would. Buffalo Bill Cody. The King of England. "What's General Custer doing in Washington?"

"Testifying in front of Congress. I'm surprised you ain't heard. There's been a big stir about it. The general's been spilling some beans. There's crooks getting rich off the Indians and army both. Post traders and Indian agents and such. Cheating them. Paying big bribes in Washington for the chance. People'll go to jail before this is over. Friends of the president, I'm talking about."

"Good for General Custer," Allen said.

"Maybe not. The president's right huffed about it."

The concierge rotated the leather-bound register, dipped a pen, and passed it to Allen. Allen bent and wrote his name, wrote *Phillips Academy, Andover, Mass.,* and returned the pen. The concierge turned, hunted around on the wall till he found the room key in its cubbyhole.

"Come to see the play at the National, did you?" he said.

"If I'm here long enough."

"Miss Deschenes said two nights."

"Then I guess I'll see it."

"Your own mother in it, I guess you better. Room number four-thirty-seven, but you best go on in to supper. The bellboy'll take your valise up."

"I was hoping to bathe," Allen said.

"Miss Deschenes and the general have been at table over an hour," the concierge said. "You best go on in."

"Is there a washroom about?"

"Down the corridor, just past the barbershop. I wouldn't be long, I was you."

He was dressed in his uniform, Union-blue jacket with gold braid on the shoulders and gold tassels on gold cords dangling on his chest, light-blue trousers with the yellow cavalry stripe. His hair was neither long nor golden, as Allen had always heard, but reddish-blond and cut short and carelessly, as if he'd done it himself with a pair of dull scissors. The hairline had moved well back. He wore a bushy, untended-looking mustache. A slender unremarkable man but for the bladelike nose and deep-set agate-blue eyes. He had risen, smiling, as Allen approached the table, the smile implicit under the tuft of his mustache.

"I'm sorry," Allen said. "The train was late out of Boston and then . . ."

"We know," his mother said. "We sent a man around to the station." She pushed her chair back and rose. "Hello, darling."

Allen stepped into the tentacles of her embrace, her blossom-smell of powder and perfume. There was a sour-sweet tang of wine on her breath. Her shoulders were bare, and she wore a pale green dress of taffeta or satin, with white satin gloves to her elbows. The dress matched her eyes. She brushed Allen's cheek with hers and kissed the air.

"And now," she said, stepping back, "may I present the great Indian fighter . . ."

"Lieutenant Colonel Custer," Custer said.

"*General* Custer," Allen's mother said.

"My brevet rank during the Rebellion," Custer said. "I'm only a poor colonel now."

His hand was as small as a woman's and his grip easy, not insistent, something you could decline or accept, as you chose.

"Call him General, Allen," his mother said. "He loves it."

"It's a pleasure, sir," Allen said.

"Let's do sit down," said Mary Deschenes.

The dining room was oak-paneled, with maroon curtains and red and gold carpeting that deadened sound. Gas chandeliers

18

and wall lamps gave down a muted, churchy light. There were four or five other parties still at table, and Allen knew by their silence that they were watching Custer and the beautiful bare-shouldered woman, whom they may have recognized but would have looked at, anyway. Now they'd be wondering who Allen was.

"Have some wine, darling." She reached for the bottle.

"No, Mother."

"Oh Christ," she said.

"Quite right, Allen," Custer said.

She turned to him, still gripping the bottle, and their gazes met and they smiled. Allen wondered how long this had been going on.

"Armstrong doesn't approve of drinking," she said and lifted the bottle and refilled her own glass. Her hand was steady. The jade-green eyes were wine-lit but clear. "He won't even pour it for me," she said. She smiled at Allen, raised her glass, and toasted him wordlessly. Her shoulders were finely sculpted and very white. Her black hair was gathered above her neck in a chignon.

"Mother," he said, "what's this about?"

But the waiter had come. He handed Allen a menu bound in calfskin. Talk had resumed at the other tables, muffled and confidential-sounding.

"Try the oysters, Allen," Custer said.

"Allen doesn't like oysters," his mother said. "Tell Allen why you don't drink, Armstrong."

Custer eyed her mildly. He turned, winked at Allen. "The spring lamb, then," he said.

The waiter stood gravely by, and Allen wondered what he made of this and if he was accustomed to witnessing such illicit and blatant goings-on. He read the menu. He wondered if Custer was married and thought he must be.

"Chicken gumbo," he said. "Spring lamb."

The waiter scribbled it on his pad.

"Mashed potatoes. Lima beans. Maybe some stewed tomatoes."

"Did you not eat on the train?" his mother said.

"I bought a sandwich," Allen said.

"Try the sweetbreads," Custer said.

"Why not save time and order the whole menu?" his mother said.

"Bring him some sweetbreads," Custer said.

The waiter wrote it, then took Allen's menu and disappeared.

"You didn't tell Allen why you don't drink," Mary said.

"Maybe Allen doesn't care to hear it,"

Custer said.

"It's his high opinion of himself, Allen. He thinks drinking is beneath him."

"I think it's unnecessary," Custer said.

"Mother."

"What."

"Why am I here?"

She looked at him, her gaze canny, speculative. She'd been Mary Hennessy, then Mary Winslow. She'd come back from England, where she'd studied under Emma Brougham, with her third name. Allen's father had been alive then. Winslow, she said, sounds like a skinny virgin off the *Mayflower*. His father had smiled and made no objection, but Allen had never forgiven her. Winslow was her *name*. It was his. Theirs.

"Well," she said, "I've some good news for you. Marvelous news. Armstrong?"

"I hear you can ride a horse," Custer said.

"Well enough, I guess," he said.

"Darling, you ride excellently, and you know it."

"A farm horse," Allen said. "Just larking around."

"He has an affinity for horses, Armstrong, and he's strong and fit, as you can see. He disappears on the horse for hours. His uncle gets quite vexed. He *talks* to the creature."

"What are you two trying to put over on me?" Allen said.

"Don't you take that tone," his mother said.

"Be quiet, Mary." Custer set his elbows on the table, laced his fingers, and laid his chin on the top hand. "I have a proposition for you," he said.

"An *offer*," his mother said. "Do get to it, Armstrong."

And Custer told him of the summer campaign against the Sioux and Cheyenne in the Dakota and Montana Territories. Of the hostiles led by Sitting Bull and the three columns converging on them, General Crook's and General Gibbon's and his own Seventh Cavalry out of Fort Abraham Lincoln. He hoped to leave within the month, he said.

The waiter arrived with Allen's soup and Custer stopped talking. Allen shook out his napkin and tucked it under his collar and dug into the thick gumbo. Custer said it would be his last campaign. That he would come East then and write about it. Give lectures, maybe. He said that it would be a man's last chance to see the territories before the railroad went through and civilized them. He said it was beautiful country, vast and empty and unpredictable in its terrain and weather, a land of exhilarating extremes. The days are hot but bearable, he said. The nights are gloriously cool.

"Tell him about the beautiful Indian girls," said Mary Deschenes.

"They can be quite handsome," Custer said.

"Armstrong's a bigamist, Allen. He married an Indian."

Custer smiled. "One of those wild stories that go around. She was my interpreter. A Cheyenne. A captive at the Washita."

"She was your interpreter, all right. Why don't we get to your offer?"

"I think Allen knows what it is."

"Go with you," Allen said. "Fight Indians."

"Not *fight* them," his mother said. "Just watch. Think of yourself as the audience."

"You'll go as my secretary," Custer said.

Allen tilted his bowl, spooned up the last of the soup.

"My nephew's coming," Custer said. "Autie Reed. He's eighteen, as I understand you are. And my youngest brother, who's twenty-seven but more like eighteen. You'll fit right in with them."

"You'll be paid, darling."

"A hundred dollars a month," Custer said.

Allen looked at him. "To do what?"

23

"Nothing," Custer said. "My brother's going as a guide. My nephew's going as a herder. Boston couldn't guide you to your hotel room. Autie couldn't herd a litter of puppies."

"Is that ethical?" Allen said.

"Allen, *do* stop being sanctimonious," his mother said.

The waiter was back, one-handing a silver tray above his shoulder. He dragged a trolley up with his other hand and deftly swept the laden tray down onto it. He took away Allen's soup bowl and began setting out the dishes of meat and vegetables. His mother poured herself some wine.

"Another bottle, madam?"

"No," Custer said.

Mary Deschenes looked at him. Smiled. The waiter bowed and left them.

"What does the secretary do when the Indians show up?" Allen said.

"Darling, you'll be perfectly safe. Armstrong's promised me."

Allen took up his knife and fork and cut into the moist slab of lamb. "I can't go till after graduation," he said.

"You'll just have to miss it, darling."

Allen put his fork down. "Wait a minute," he said.

"You'll get your diploma. I'll write to Dr.

Bancroft, and, believe me, you'll get your diploma."

"Not if I don't take final exams."

"Really, Allen, you've the chance of a lifetime. This is General *Custer*, for God's sake."

"What about Harvard?"

"You leave that to me and Armstrong."

"The entrance exam is in July."

"I told you: we'll get around that."

Maybe she would, at that. Go up there and fuck the president of Harvard. Fuck the dean.

"Supposing you do rig it some way, I don't believe in putting down the Indians," Allen said.

"Oh for Christ sake," his mother said.

"It's their land," Allen said.

"They live on it, but they don't own it," Custer said. "Like the antelope. The buffalo."

"It isn't ours, either," Allen said.

"Do stop that nonsense," his mother said. "It's all been settled. I've given up the house on Washington Square. I've taken one on Gramercy Park, but the lease isn't until the middle of August. I'll be here doing the play till then. There's no place for you, you see."

"Why not the farm?"

"It won't do. You know Nettie was married and is living with them now. And then your Aunt Samantha's illness."

"Suppose I refuse to go?" Allen said.

"Where would you live, darling?"

"I'll figure it out."

"The figuring out has been done, and now stop whining and eat your supper. Armstrong, will you see me to my room? I'm suddenly all in."

She stood up, and Custer with her. There was a lax grace about the man, a lithe athleticism. Again a cessation of talk in the room, a turning of heads.

"Wait for me in the drawing room," Custer said.

"Ah yes," she said. "A little man to man. Talk some sense into him, Armstrong."

She leaned, shielding her décolletage with her arm, and kissed the top of Allen's head.

"Good night, darling. We'll breakfast together."

"Good night, Mother," he said.

Custer sat down and watched her go. Allen picked up his fork. He took some mashed potato. The supper had gotten cold.

"This wasn't my idea," Custer said.

"She wants to get rid of me."

"I know."

"Why are you helping her?"

"I thought I was helping *you*. I couldn't

imagine a boy not wanting to ride with the Seventh."

"I'm set on Harvard, sir."

"Rather than go with me."

"I hate New York City. I hate the theater. Harvard's my chance to make a different life for myself. I'll be a writer. A teacher. It's what my father wanted for me."

Custer had folded his hands on the table and considered them now, and the blue eyes softened. "You'll go to Harvard," he said. "Don't underestimate her."

Allen only shrugged, done talking about it. He ate his cold supper. Custer turned in his chair and looked into the drawing room, where Mary Deschenes was appraising herself in a mirror. A man and woman on a sofa, in evening clothes, were watching her.

"There's one other thing," Custer said. "One of my regimental surgeons has got a sister who wants to come to Fort Lincoln, see him before we go out. An orphan girl. She's quite a bit younger than George, and he doesn't want her traveling all that way alone. I thought you might come out with her. Watch out for her."

"I'm to be her nanny," Allen said.

"She's about your age. She might be a looker."

"I don't care if she's Sarah Bernhardt."

Again Custer smiled under the mustache. "You'll be getting a wire about her," he said. "Her name's Lord. Goes to some fancy boarding school on Manhattan Island. You'll hook up with her in New York. She's from up in Massachusetts somewhere, so you'll have that to talk about."

"You already told them I'd do it, didn't you," Allen said.

Custer looked again into the drawing room. Mary Deschenes was moving toward the elevator. He stood up, placed a hand on Allen's shoulder.

"A new destiny, Allen. It won't ever come 'round again."

And he headed upstairs, watched closely by the couple on the parlor sofa, to bed Allen's mother.

Two

She threw the covers back and got up and crossed the room, gloriously white in the darkness, her hair awry and thick on her shoulders. He turned his head on the woman-smelling pillow to watch her. Yes: crinolines, bustles, corsets concealed the truth of a woman. There was a decanter of whiskey on the vanity, and she poured some into a tumbler and drank it off. She poured again and brought the tumbler and sat on the edge of the bed with her legs crossed.

He'd met her backstage at the National two weeks ago. *The Lady of Lyons* was all the rage, a full house every night, bookings into August. Lawrence Barrett, down from New York, had introduced them. Lawrence had played opposite her in *The Seven Sisters* and *The Marble Heart* and might have given her a go himself.

"Why do you drink?" he said.

"Because I like it," she said, "why else?"

He placed a hand on her thigh. It was warm. Firm. "To annoy me," he said. "To get my goat."

"God you're vain," she said.

"I know."

She drank. He could smell the whiskey. A window was open to the balmy night, and a carriage rattled by below, a distant clop of hooves.

"You'll ruin your health," he said. "Your beauty."

"Risk is what makes life sweet," she said. "Where did I hear that?"

"I don't mean that kind of risk, and you know it."

"Risk is risk," she said and emptied the tumbler. He'd never known anyone who held their liquor as well as she did, and he'd seen plenty of drunkenness, including his own, once upon a time. She leaned forward to set the tumbler on the bedside table and looked at him and smiled.

Then she was in bed again. He was ready for her, and she sat astraddle of him, leaning to pin his shoulders. He smiled up at her. The covers had slipped down her back, and she loomed over him, shadowy under the canopy. Her hair fell like softest rain on his chest. Breasts white in the darkness. Whiskey on her breath. She held him down.

"Maybe it's because I don't want to grow old," she said.

"No one wants to grow old," Custer said.

"Then we won't."

He was going to disabuse her of this childish notion, but now she released him and rolled down beside him, yielding the initiative. He took it, had her till she cried out, and after a time he withdrew and curled himself against her and fell asleep.

She woke him some fifteen minutes later. She was sitting on the edge of the bed again, still naked.

"What time is it?" he said.

"Something past one. You'll be exhausted tomorrow."

"I can testify exhausted."

"This is what worries me, Armstrong. Your cavalier attitude. What'll I do with Allen if you can't go?"

"Of course I'll go."

"Stop riling your president, then. You needn't be quite so cooperative with the committee. Everyone else here lies, why shouldn't you?"

"I'm under oath," he said.

"So what?"

"The post traders and Indian agents are gougers, Mary. Cheats. Crooks. The whole business is rotten."

"I'd have to get Allen a room here at the Willard. Do you know what that would cost?"

"Allen's going to be with me. Does he like girls?"

"I suppose."

"A young sister of one of my surgeons wants to come out before we go. I'm going to have Allen travel with her."

"Is she pretty?"

"I've a feeling she is."

"If she harries him off the train, I'll have your hide, Armstrong."

Custer smiled and looked at her in the thin darkness. The curve of her back, the fleshy inner thigh where it was slung across her knee. The fruitlike profile of a breast.

"Get back in bed," he said.

Only Monahseetah was this beautiful, this ardent in bed. Monahseetah, daughter of the Cheyenne chief Little Rock. Her hair was blacker even than Mary's, a luminous silken crow-black, tumbling below her waist when she let it down. There was no trouble-some bustle or corset to unwrap, only a simple dress of gingham or calico, shed in an instant. She had tawny, almost clay-red skin. Eyes of black fire. She'd shot her husband in the knee with a revolver, crip-pling him, but no woman he knew — even

32

including Libbie — was as tractable in bed, as eager to please. As if she knew what he wanted before he knew it himself. The Custer Luck again, waiting for him in Black Kettle's sleeping village on the frozen Washita.

THREE

The girl got on the train a few minutes before it rolled out of the great glass and cast-iron shed of Grand Central Depot. She was carrying a Gladstone bag in a white-gloved hand and holding a beribboned straw sailor hat to her head, as if she worried a gust of wind might take it. Six o'clock of a May morning, the day coach not half full. She came down the aisle with her gaze shifting back and forth, looking at the riders, and about halfway she saw him and stopped.

He did not avert his eyes, nor did she. She brought her hand down from the crown of her hat and stood looking at him. Assessing him. She was thin and stood very straight. Something prissy about the thin mouth and face. Her hair was a pale honey-brown and fell straight down her back. Her eyes were the gray of the sea on a sunless day. She wore a green tartan cape. Navy skirt with a flounce in back, no bustle. A cloth purse

34

hung from her wrist. She came on down the aisle and stopped at his seat.

"Mr. Winslow?" she said.

She stood holding the Gladstone in front of her with both hands.

"You would be Miss Lord," Allen said.

"Addie Grace Lord. I've looked for you everywhere."

"Looks like you found me," Allen said.

"Perhaps you'd put this bag up for me," she said.

He stood up quite slowly and took the Gladstone from her and swung it up onto the brass rack beside his own valise.

"Thank you," said Addie Grace Lord. "You may have the window."

"You take it."

She eyed him coolly, then slid past him and sat down by the arch of the window. She set her purse between them. She took her hat off, lifting it gingerly with both hands, and placed it in her lap.

"You might have waited for me," she said.

"I did wait for you."

"On the platform, I mean."

"I didn't want to miss the train."

"You wouldn't have."

"As it turns out."

A baggage carrier had come in lugging a large leather valise and carrying a gray wool blanket. He was looking for the girl.

"You led me a chase," he said. "I thought you maybe got off the train."

"I was looking for somebody," she said.

"Done found him, it looks like."

"No thanks to him," she said.

The baggage carrier heaved her valise onto the rack. He stashed the blanket on top of it.

"Put your hat up, miss?" he said.

"Yes please," she said.

The baggage carrier took it from her, tucked it on top of the Gladstone. Addie Grace had opened her purse. She found a nickel and handed it up to him, and he thanked her and headed quickly for the nearer door.

"I might have stood waiting for you and the train left without me," Addie Grace said.

"How old are you?" he said.

"If you don't want to travel with me, say so."

"All right."

"All right what?"

"If I don't want to travel with you, I'll say so."

"You aren't funny."

"It wasn't supposed to be. How old are you?"

They'd unbraked the coaches, and they

began to creep down the grade, out of the giant shed into the morning brightness of the switching yard, where their locomotive would be waiting. A few tracks over, another train was waiting under steam. Red drive wheels on the locomotive, fittings of polished brass. The coaches were painted in soft hues of olive green, plum red, mocha, with gold scrollwork on their side panels and NEW YORK CENTRAL in gold under the clerestories.

"If you must know, I'm sixteen," she said. "And how old are you, then?"

"A wise and enlightened eighteen."

"That's not as old as you think."

"I think it's older than sixteen."

They were coupling the locomotive. The impact traveled back, a shudder echoing from coach to coach. A moment, some shouting from down the platform, and the train lurched and was moving, couplings straining, holding. The switching yard narrowed, tracks converging, and they entered a brick-walled cut. The wheels rumbled beneath them. The coach swayed.

"This was my brother's idea, I hope you know," the girl said. "He wouldn't allow me to travel alone, or I would have, willingly."

"You'd have willingly gotten yourself in a fix or two."

"So you say."

They entered the Park Avenue Tunnel and were lost to each other. They were moving faster now, rumble and clatter, and the tunnel walls threw the racket back at them. A red lantern winked past in the blackness, a green one. They came out of the gloom into another sun-washed cut.

"I know who your mother is," said Addie Grace.

"Everybody does."

"They say she's very beautiful. America's most coveted widow. I read that in *Godey's Lady's Book.* I wonder she doesn't remarry."

"She found someone rich she might," Allen said.

"Is she so venal?"

"With a capital V," Allen said.

They came out of the cut and climbed the Harlem Flats Viaduct. The land on either side below was crisscrossed with rutted dirt roads with brick buildings set at irregular intervals along them; breweries, coal yards, a slaughterhouse with its empty pens. There were fields, too, with four-story brownstones set randomly along their edges, misplaced-looking, as if they'd been transposed here from the cities where they belonged. They crossed the Harlem River on the steel bridge. Along its banks a hodgepodge of mills and shanty towns that looked to be spilling downhill on their way to tumbling into the river. They went west along the river.

"You're from Salem," the girl said.

"I used to be," Allen said.

"I've been to Salem. Saw the House of Seven Gables and where they burned the witches. They burned them in Boston, did you know that?"

"Can't say I did."

"On Boston Common. Witches, pirates, and Quakers."

"Quakers?"

"There's a sign that says so."

"Sounds like bull to me."

Addie Grace looked at him. "I don't care for that expression."

"You're going to hear worse."

"Not from you, I hope."

"I'll work on that. You're an orphan, Custer said."

"My father died in the Rebellion. At Ball's Bluff. I was a year old. My mother passed a year later. My aunt and uncle raised me. They're my guardians."

"In Boston, where they burned the Quakers."

"Cambridge. Where all the poets live. Mr. Lowell. Mr. Longfellow."

"Cullen Bryant. Holmes. I know all about it."

The two rivers met and they were climbing north now along the Hudson. The coach swayed side to side in quick, short jerks, racketing along, *click-clack, click-clack*. On the far side of the great river the Palisades rose sheer and black with the greening brush and scrub trees clinging to its cliffside crevices and ledges. The clerestory windows were open, and the air moved through overhead, pulling in an acrid breath of coal smoke.

"My aunt and uncle sent me to school in New York when I was thirteen," Addie Grace said. "Chartwell. It's on Forty-Eighth Street."

"They turn you loose early?"

She turned and spoke to the window. "I left," she said.

"Before finals?"

"What of it?"

"They won't pass you," Allen said.

"I'm quite aware of that."

The conductor came by lifting tickets. Addie Grace fished hers out of her purse. Allen pulled his pocketbook from inside his coat. He was wearing a cutaway and a four-in-hand tie. The conductor took her ticket in a yellow kid-gloved hand, punched it, and gave it back to her. He took Allen's and read it.

"You folks traveling together?" he said.

"Yes we are," Addie Grace said. "We're on our way to Chicago."

Allen looked at her. Her gray gaze shifted, avoiding him. An overdone nonchalance smoothed her face. The conductor punched Allen's ticket and returned it to him and shuffled on.

"Chicago?" Allen said.

"There's something I haven't told you, Mr. Winslow."

"You're stopping in Chicago."

"Of course not. But our tickets say Chicago, and that's what I'm giving out."

"And why is that, if I might ask?"

Addie Grace glanced around, then dropped her voice, though there was little need in the rumbling clamor of the moving train.

"I've run away," she said.

"From Chartwell."

"Didn't I say so?"

"You said you left."

"I walked out this morning, before anyone was about. Left a note. My aunt and uncle will wake snakes when they hear. They'd forbidden my going to see George, you see."

"What does your brother think about this?"

"George doesn't know. I didn't want to bother him with that part of it."

"The running away part."

"It would only worry him."

"And I don't suppose Custer knows."

"Of course not."

"So not one person here in the East knows you're on your way to Dakota Territory."

"Except you."

"And no one in the world but me knows you're a fugitive."

"I'm not a fugitive."

"You will be soon enough," Allen said.

He looked out past her at the broad sun-glinting river. The telegraph ran alongside the tracks, the poles shuttling past the window in quick rhythmic succession, the wires looping threadlike from pole to pole to pole.

"I'm worried my uncle will wire ahead and have me put off the train," said Addie Grace. "That's why I said Chicago. To throw them off the scent."

"I don't think it's going to work," Allen said.

"I know something that might." She met his gaze, held it. "You could pretend you're

my brother. It would make a kind of disguise."

"Your brother."

"Where's the harm?"

"I'll tell you where. They figure out this
so-called disguise, I'd go to jail. What do
you think they'd make of it, you running
away with me, and me telling some lie about
you being my sister?"

"I must see George. I think something terrible's going to happen out there."

"It isn't," Allen said.

"It's not like the Rebellion," she said.
"The Indians will kill a doctor quick as they
will a soldier. Do you believe dreams can
foretell things?"

"No."

"I do. And I had one about George. It was
right after he wrote that he was going out
against the Indians, and how this was going
to be the last big fight."

She looked at Allen. Something of age and
sadness in the sea-gray eyes.

"Go on," he said.

"He'd come to see me in New York, as he
does. He sent me a note to meet him at the
Fifth Avenue Hotel, and when I got there it
was on fire. It was nighttime. The fire
brigade had arrived, but there was nothing
they could do. I started to cry, and then I

saw George leaning out of a window. High up, you know. He was smiling. He told me to go find General Custer. General Custer would fix everything. 'Go get him, Gracie, and I'll wait here.' I ran off looking for him. The streets were strange to me. I was lost. The buildings were all locked up and dark. I never found General Custer. I never found anybody."

"It was a dream," Allen said.

"I *know* it was a dream."

She stared out the window. Rugged tree-clad hills. The wide river twisted lazily, and where you could see ahead to the north the hills were smoky blue.

"Listen to me," Allen said. "There are going to be three armies out there, something like three thousand men. The Indians aren't going to have a show."

"You're not frightened?"

"Just angry."

"At whom?"

"Mother, mainly. She didn't know what to do with me this summer. This is Custer's favor to her. They cooked it up together. They're good friends, if you know what I mean."

"I do not."

"Think hard."

Addie Grace looked at him. "How would

you know such a thing?"

"It'd be pretty hard to miss."

"Why, General Custer's married. Elizabeth Custer. She's said to be quite beautiful herself."

"Married doesn't bother Mother," Allen said.

"It should bother *him.*"

"It doesn't seem to."

They rode awhile, looking out at the hills and the river, where here and there a white sail drifted.

"Was your father no better?" Addie Grace said.

"He was everything she isn't. I still dream about him. Dream he's alive."

"Killed in the Rebellion?"

"In a way. He lost a leg in the Wilderness. He died in seventy. An infection or something. Mother said he didn't want to live a cripple, and for once she may have been right."

"You've had your troubles too, haven't you, Mr. Winslow."

"Why don't you stop calling me Mr. Winslow."

It grew cooler, and the brakeman came through and closed the clerestory windows. Addie Grace opened her purse and brought out a clothbound edition of *Eight Cousins* and began to read. Allen sat, looking out, listening to the iron grinding of the wheels, the lurch and groan of the coach. He'd brought a couple of books, and he got up and opened his valise and dug out *Great Expectations.* They read awhile, until Allen felt the girl's eyes on him.

"Do you like Mr. Dickens?" she said.

"Most of it. What do you read that junk for?"

"Miss Alcott is not junk. She's wholesome. Are you going to help me or aren't you?"

"I don't know," he said.

"I don't know what I'll do if they put me off the train."

"You'll go back to school where you belong."

"I have to see my brother. Can you not understand that?"

A little before one o'clock the conductor opened the door and announced that they were coming into Albany and that there would be a half-hour stop for refreshments at the Delavan House. There'd been stops — Poughkeepsie, Hudson — and the train had filled up, and as they crossed the steel girder bridge over the Hudson and came into the city, the passengers got up and

46

moved to the doors, crowding up against one another.

"Stay close to me," Allen told the girl.

She pulled on her gloves and took up her purse, and she and Allen stood up and moved into the aisle. The train came in alongside the granite, cathedral-like station and jerked to a stop. The passengers poured out onto the platform and moved like a mob through the high archways and on toward the street on the other side. Allen told Addie Grace to take his arm, and she glanced at him and then obeyed, and they followed along through the vast, echoing station and out again onto a wide city street bustling with carriages and pedestrians.

The Delavan House was a white-brick hotel. They climbed the steps and went in past the desk down a hallway to a big room labeled LUNCH ROOM, where a man behind a bare pinewood table was selling tickets, tearing them off a roll as the people pressed in on him. The tickets cost twenty-five cents. A pasteboard sign was propped against the wall by the door: SCOOT FOR THE TRAIN WHEN THE GONG SOUNDS.

Addie Grace let go of Allen's arm.

The first people to arrive had begun eating. White-clad waiters were taking their tickets and setting down plates of food. The tables had been placed end to end in long rows. There was a strong smell of coffee. In front of Allen and Addie Grace a broad-shouldered young man in a tailored suit wrapped an arm around his pretty wife and pushed his way forward, sheltering her against him.

"Wait your turn," a man said, and the younger man stopped and swung around to face him.

"Look at her, you son of a bitch," he said.

The man did. She was pregnant. The crowd stood back and let the couple through, then closed in again. Allen pushed forward and stepped on a man's heel.

"That's okay, I walk on them too," the man said.

"Excuse me," Allen said.

"Hello, missy." The man smiled and tipped his hat, a bowler, to Addie Grace.

She looked away.

"What's your name, sweetheart?" the man said.

"What's yours?" Allen said.

The man looked at him. "What did you say?"

"Ignore him," Addie Grace said.

"Leave the girl alone," Allen said.

"Meaning what, exactly?"

"Meaning what I said."

"Fancy Dan, are you. I'll whip your ass."

"Go on try it."

Then a woman's voice, sudden: "Ain't you inside *yet?*" She took the man's arm. She was blond and pale-skinned, and her face was painted up with rouge and red lipstick. She turned her smile on Allen and Addie Grace, both her hands now on the man's arm. "I'm two minutes in the little girls room, this one can't keep hisself out of mischief."

"I was just passing the time, waiting on you," the man said.

"Was he bothering you, honey?" said the blonde.

"He was saying hello to my sister," Allen said.

"I'll bet he was," said the blonde.

"You got good taste in sisters, pard," the man said.

"You keep your eyes to yourself now," the woman told him and pulled him around into what was left of the crowd, perhaps a half-dozen people.

"I thank you," Addie Grace said.

Allen looked at her. She glanced at him, then looked quickly down, as if frightened by what she'd seen.

"Sure," he said.

The half hour had gone fifteen minutes by the time they sat down. A waiter took their tickets and put down plates stacked with buckwheat cakes. They poured molasses over them from a stoneware pitcher. There were stoneware mugs on the table and pots of coffee and bowls of overripe pears. All around them, the dull chink of cheap tableware and a collective mutter of conversation. Addie Grace sat up straight and ate with deliberate propriety, as Allen supposed the girls must do at table at the Chartwell School. Their neighbors across the table — two men in frock coats, a woman in furs — ate silently.

"Coffee?" Allen said, reaching for the pot.

Addie Grace shook her head. "I don't take it," she said.

The woman across the table had been watching her. "Where are you from, dear?" she said.

"Salem, Massachusetts," Allen said.

"They're from Salem, Henry," the woman said.

"I've got ears," he said.

"We grew up on Essex Street," Allen said.

"Brother and sister, are you?"

"Yes ma'am."

"We know Essex Street," the woman said. "We once lived in Marblehead."

"And I wish we still did," Henry said and looked glumly around at the diners bent to their food, the long tables laden with cheap thick crockery, the surly waiters, as if all of this had been instrumental in depriving him of some palmier former life.

"Never mind," his wife said and patted his arm.

"Are meal stops always so rushed?" Addie Grace said.

"No they ain't," said the second man, who seemed to be alone, "they're *more* rushed. This one here's what I'd call leisurely."

"You folks traveling far?" Henry said.

"Chicago," Allen said.

"You'll see some meaner eatin' houses than this," the second man said. "This here's the lap of luxury."

Someone struck a gong in the hall, and there was a scraping of chairs and a general rush for the door. Addie Grace hadn't eaten half her hotcakes. Allen took a final mouthful of his and snatched up two pears and pocketed them in his cutaway, and he and Addie Grace pushed their chairs back and rose, and again she took his arm.

They got to their seats, half out of breath,

and in another minute the train was moving. They were quiet awhile. The brakeman came in, and they watched him kneel and lay a fire in the woodstove at that end of the coach. He came down the aisle and laid a fire in the stove behind them but didn't light either one. They passed the warehouses and factories at the city's edge, and then they were in the country again. They'd left the Hudson behind, and soon another broad woods-bordered river appeared to their right. The Mohawk.

"Allen," she said.

"What."

"I don't suppose we could eat in the dining car. There is one, you know."

"How much money have you?"

"Seventy-five dollars. George sent it to me."

"I have about a hundred. Forget about the diner."

"It isn't so expensive."

"It's a dollar. We've more tickets to buy. We're going to have hotel bills. Chicago. Duluth."

The conductor stood over them, burly in his dark-blue frock coat, double row of brass buttons, gold watch chain. Albany was a division point and he'd just come on. "Tickets," he said and lifted Allen's. "Chicago," he said, reading it. "I'd have bet money you two were going to the Falls."

"What falls?" Addie Grace said.

"Niagara, sweetheart. Ever hear of 'em?"

He punched Allen's ticket, handed it back, took Addie Grace's. He glanced at her, then punched the ticket and returned it. He turned to the woman across the aisle, punched her ticket, and went on.

"What was he getting at?" Addie Grace said.

"He thinks we're eloping," Allen said. "That's where they go, Niagara Falls."

"Maybe we should pretend we *are*," she said.

"You have no notion how much trouble I could get into, do you?"

"I have got to see George," she said.

The sun moved over, and the brakeman came in and lit the two stoves. There were more stops. Rotterdam Junction. Fultonville. Fort Plain. The locomotive took on water. The depots were of brick or fieldstone, with chimneys the same and sloping gray or red slate roofs. You might see a handcar in the yard, a water tower, and there was always a semaphore. Sometimes a postmaster would come out with a sack of mail and toss it up to the agent in the baggage car, and the agent would sling another one down to him.

"How long do you think it'll take your aunt and uncle to find out you're gone?" Allen said. He'd been reading *Great Expectations* and now closed it and put it aside.

"Any time now, I should say," Addie Grace said.

"We'll stay on the train next meal stop," he said.

A news butcher had boarded, and at about four o'clock he came through calling out his wares. Newspapers, tobacco, candy, sandwiches. He was lugging a deep basket, which bumped against his knee as he walked. Allen stopped him and took a slab of brittle wrapped in stationer's paper and three ham sandwiches on white bread. He asked the boy what he had to drink.

"Orange soda pop, but I ain't got but one left."

"We'll take it," Allen said.

"You want a cigar?"

"No."

"Soap?"

"Not today."

"Got a tin of sardines and one of peaches. I'll give 'em to you and call the whole thing a dollar."

54

"What do you call it if you don't give them to me?"

The boy grinned. "Seventy cents."

Allen paid with coins from his trousers pocket. The boy went on and Addie Grace opened her purse.

"Never mind," Allen said.

"I won't be in your debt," she said.

"You already are," he said.

The evening meal stop was Utica, and they took their supper in the quiet of the empty coach, watching the station platform for policemen. The brakeman had thrown more wood into the stoves, and Allen had removed his cutaway and Addie Grace her tartan cape. The sandwiches were wrapped in bakery paper, and they opened them and laid the paper on their laps like napkins. The bread was buttered. Allen unstoppered the soda pop and handed the bottle to Addie Grace, and she took it and drank. She took another drink and wiped her mouth with the back of her wrist and offered it to him. The pop was warm and sugary. He drank again and returned the bottle to Addie Grace, and she drank and handed it back. They cut the third sandwich down the middle with Allen's pocketknife and ate the halves.

"Is Addie for Adeline?" he said.

"Addison. It's a family name. A great-great-aunt or somebody."

They ate the hard, sweet brittle. They ate the mealy pears Allen had picked up at the eating house in Albany.

"Maybe they'll leave you alone," Allen said.

"You don't know Aunt Ruth and Uncle Gordon. Finish the pop."

"You sure?"

"Go on."

The train whistle blew and the passengers came scurrying back. Some carried food hastily bundled in newspaper, some pushed hunks of bread or pie into their mouths as they hurried along. They funneled aboard the coaches and had not all sat down when the train shuddered into motion.

They went on, straight west now, chasing the sun, in an endless-seeming pale yellow spring daylight. They'd left the Mohawk River behind, and all rivers for now. They passed through deep forests, wove among forested hills, caught glimpses of random towns and farms. They stopped at Syracuse, and both sat silent until the train was moving again.

"Three years ago," she said, "a veterinarian went out with General Custer and was killed. He wandered off to look for fossils, and the Indians shot him full of arrows and scalped him."

"Don't wander off, then. You bet I won't."

"George is very insouciant. I think it makes him careless. Trusting. It's funny, because he was twice engaged to be married, and both times the girl broke it off. You'd think that would make him wary, but it didn't. Now he says the West is his mistress, and a lot more dependable."

Twilight caught up with them, and behind it the lilac spring dusk. The brakeman lit the lamps, which hung chandelier-fashion above the aisle and gave down a drab oily light that would have been hard to read by, though neither tried. The wicks were bad, and after a while they could smell the black smoke.

"Aunt Ruth and Uncle Gordon are against fighting the Indians," Addie Grace said. "They say we are the savages, not they."

"We go pretty hard on them," Allen said.

"Don't they go hard on us?"

"When we provoke them. Steal land from them."

"Aunt Ruth and Uncle Gordon are so *preachy* about it. They never shut up. They were abolitionists, and now Aunt Ruth is all for women's suffrage. They can't abide anyone who doesn't agree with them."

"George, for instance."

"George doesn't get excited about such things. He goes his merry way. It annoys them. And they certainly don't approve of General Custer."

"He helped win the war against slavery," Allen said.

"They've forgotten that. Do *you* like General Custer?'

Allen thought about it. A town slid by, scattered lights in the bluing dusk. "I don't *dislike* him," he said.

"That's all? You don't *dislike* him?"

"So far," Allen said.

The washroom was lit by a smoking wall lamp that embittered the close and foul-smelling air. A public comb, brush, and towel hung from tethers. Allen had brought soap but no towel, and he washed his face and neck and hands and dried himself with the sleeve of his shirt rather than use the public towel. He brushed his teeth.

There was a line when he came out. Men in their shirtsleeves, women jacketless, shawlless. They stood silently with their travel kits and towels, bracing themselves against the insistent rocking, and did not meet Allen's eye as he passed. It was quiet in the coach, just the jolt and rumble and rapid *click-clack* of the train, and now and then the shrill cry of the whistle, flying past the coach and gone, like a wind-chased ribbon. It was getting on toward ten o'clock.

He pulled Addie Grace's blanket down from the overhead rack and let it fall open, and sat down beside her and covered the two of them. He reached down and pushed the iron lever that freed the seatback on its pivot, till they lay back as in barbers' chairs. The blanket was of undyed wool. Addie Grace pulled it to her chin and drew up her knees and lay facing Allen.

"You ought to have waited for me this morning," she said.

"Are you going to keep at that all the way to Dakota?"

"You ought to have."

"I was in a bad mood. I didn't want to be here. It wasn't personal."

"Apology accepted."

"It wasn't an apology."

She smiled.

"Go to sleep," he said.

"Nothing will happen tonight, will it."

"Nothing," he said.

"Good night, then," she said.

"Good night, Addie Grace."

FOUR

General Terry regarded him across his desk with a sort of troubled solemnity, as a schoolmaster might look at a wayward pupil. Dark-eyed, dark-bearded. Custer moved in his chair, shifted a leg forward and the other back. He sat tensed forward, with his elbows on the chair arm and his hands clasped.

"The president refused to see me," he said. "He humiliated me. I sat outside his office from ten until I don't know, three or four, and the bastard wouldn't see me."

"Colonel Custer," Terry said.

"My patience is about used up, and so's my vocabulary."

"He's your president," Terry said.

"I know who he is. People are going in and out, and I'm sitting there like a nobody. Like a fool. Finally I sent a note in with General Ingalls, very humble, and his secretary steps out and looks at me like I'm some vagrant off the street and says, 'The president will not see you, sir.' "

The office was austere. Drab. A conference table, maplewood chairs. The flag beside the general's desk adroop on its staff. Pinned to the wall a map of the territories comprising the Department of the Missouri, which was Phil Sheridan's bailiwick.

"You oughtn't to have left Washington," General Terry said.

Custer threw his head back and closed his eyes. Sighed. Looked again at Terry. "I had permission," he said.

"Not from General Sherman. Not from the president."

"From the adjutant general. Sherman was out of town."

"I know that. And you should have waited for him."

Custer rubbed his eyes with a knuckle, thinking. The sky in the windows of the second-story office was a fine morning blue. St. Paul, Minnesota. Building tops across the street, stone facades with arched windows. The street below was unpaved, and the hoof thud and clatter of traffic came up dulled, lazy. His train had gotten in two hours ago, and he had not slept in forty-eight hours. The chronic problem of money: he could not afford a sleeper.

61

"This will destroy me, Alfred," he said.

"I very much doubt it," Terry said.

"To watch the Seventh ride out without me? I couldn't face my family again. My friends."

"I wish it hadn't come to this."

"Well, hell, so do I. But what could I do? I was under oath."

"The Democrats were using you."

"I know that."

"There are ways to muffle what you say. Truth without so much bluntness."

"They're thieves," Custer said. "The whole Indian Department is rotten top to bottom."

General Terry eyed him almost sorrowfully. "I don't know what you're asking me," he said.

"Yes you do," Custer said.

Terry turned his swivel chair and looked out at the sky over St. Paul. He had never fought Indians. Nor had Major Reno. Custer had fought Indians all over Kansas and up along the Yellowstone. He'd fought the Sioux and Cheyenne.

"God, Alfred. Please," he said.

"Don't," Terry said and spun the chair again to face Custer. A melancholy man. Quiet-spoken. The Sioux would outwit and attack him, then scatter before he caught them.

"You want me to get down on my knees? I'll do it."

"Stop it."

"Then help me."

Terry brought a hand up and stroked his bearded jaw. His thin shoulders rose and fell. "Send a telegram to the president," he said.

"I'm damned if I'll apologize for telling the truth," Custer said.

"Be quiet and listen to me," Terry said. "Appeal to him as a soldier. Ask him to spare you the humiliation of watching your regiment take the field without you. Of not sharing in its dangers. I'll send a second wire requesting your services."

"My services as what?" Custer said.

"Commander of your regiment. The column will be under my command. You've lost that."

"Have I?"

"Irretrievably."

"But the Seventh will be mine."

"It'll be ours," Terry said.

FIVE

Allen slept fitfully and woke for good to the motion of the train and to another clear morning. Robin's-egg sky, the new leaves silk green. The girl slept beside him with her head tucked birdlike to her shoulder. The blanket had slipped down. Allen pulled it up, and she woke and squinted at him curiously, as if surprised to find him here.

"Hey, brat," he said.

"What time is it?" she said.

"About five-thirty. We'll be in Buffalo soon."

"I was awake half the night. All that bumping."

"I was too," Allen said.

The stoves were cold and it was chilly in the coach. A woman came by on her way to the washroom. She nodded, granted them a sleepy smile. Allen felt down beside him and found the lever and jammed it down, and the seatback sprang up to the vertical.

"We'll have to get off if we want breakfast," he said.

"Let's don't," she said.

He looked at her.

"Please," she said.

"All right," Allen said.

But it didn't matter. Two policemen arrived, led by the conductor, fifteen minutes after everyone but the two of them had disembarked for breakfast. One of the coppers had a broad, clean-shaven face. The second wore a dark walrus mustache.

"Here they be," said the conductor.

"Miss Addison Grace Lord?" said the first policeman.

Addie Grace glanced at Allen.

"Why do you ask?" he said.

"I didn't ask you, I asked her," the policeman said.

"I'm Allen Winslow," he said, "and this is my sister Adelaide."

"No she isn't."

"They're going to the Falls," the conductor said. "I knew it the moment I saw 'em."

"That's ridiculous," Allen said.

"Miss Lord, you're going to have to get off this train."

"I won't," said Addie Grace.

The two policemen looked at each other. The second one smiled under his mustache.

"You want her arms or her legs, Sully?" he asked his partner.

"We'll both get off," Allen said, rising.

"You aren't any part of this," the copper called Sully said.

"She and I are together," Allen said. He took down Addie Grace's hat.

"They're sweethearts, I tell you," the conductor said.

"Let the boy come, Tom," Sully said. "The girl's underage. Maybe we'll charge him."

Allen had pulled down Addie Grace's valise and her Gladstone bag. He hauled down his own valise and while everyone waited put *Great Expectations* and *Eight Cousins* in it and closed it again. He picked up the two valises. Addie Grace bundled the blanket. Tom took up her Gladstone. She rose, glanced at Allen.

"It's going to all right," he told her.

"It is, sure," Sully said.

The conductor led them down the aisle, past the woodstove, into the vestibule, down the steps. "They ain't et yet," he said.

"You go on about your business," Sully said.

The station was a two-story brick building, small and plain for a big-city railway station. Allen and Addie Grace walked side by side, with Sully leading them and Tom behind. Allen with the two bags, Addie Grace in her sailor's hat and tartan cape, with the bunched blanket clutched to her chest. Heads turned as they passed. They followed the policeman up a stairwell and down a corridor to a door with a brown and white enamel sign, Stationmaster. They went in.

It was a warm room with a coal stove in the center and a bank of windows overlooking the train tracks. A counter ran the length of the wall by the windows, and there sat the stationmaster in a swivel chair, writing in a clothbound ledger. A shrunken sallow man in a vest and shirtsleeves. He spun the chair, smiled.

"Found her, eh?"

"Found her brother too."

"What brother?"

"Got us some shenanigans going on here."

Allen had set down the bags. At the end of the long counter was a telegraph machine. Ticket box on the wall with tickets drooping off its shelves. A Rosewood wall clock. A calendar.

"You children sit down," Sully said.

The chairs were varnished and the varnish worn and scratched. Allen and Addie Grace sat down side by side near the middle of the room. The policemen stood with their backs to the windows. Their shiny black billyclubs hung from their belts.

"There's a southbound train due in a couple of hours," said the first. "You'll be on it, Miss Lord."

"I am not Miss Lord," she said.

"You want to eat some breakfast, you can."

"I am not Miss Lord."

The policeman Sully looked at Allen. "What's your story, bub?"

Allen looked at Addie Grace and she at him, and her smile was faint, defeated, and her eyes tear-filled. Stationmaster and policemen all saw it and were silent. Allen came forward in his chair.

"I told you my name was Allen Winslow, and it is. I'm an aide to Colonel Custer, Seventh Cavalry."

The policemen looked at each other.

"Rubbish," said the stationmaster.

"Send a telegram," Allen said. "Fort Abraham Lincoln, Dakota Territory. Tell Colonel Custer you're holding me here, see what he says."

"It ain't me holding you," said the stationmaster.

"What about her?" Sully said.

"Send another telegram. Dr. George Lord, Seventh Cavalry. Tell him you've got his sister here."

"That would be Miss Lord."

Addie Grace looked at Allen. She wiped each eye with the heel of her hand.

"Tell him the truth," he said.

She drew herself up. "I'm Addie Grace Lord," she said, "and I'm going to see my brother. I want to see him very desperately."

"The regiment's going out against Sitting Bull in a few days," Allen said. "She's worried about what might happen. Dr. Lord's the only real family she has."

"Sully?" Tom said.

"I don't know," Sully said.

"It don't sound like gum to me."

"Send those telegrams," Allen said.

From below came the first heavy chuff of a locomotive and a grinding of wheels. "There goes your train," the stationmaster said.

"When's the next one?" Allen said.

"You hold on," Sully said.

"We'd be ever so grateful if you let us go," Addie Grace said.

"You hold on too," Sully said. "It was your uncle put the word out on you. He's your guardian. You denying that, Miss Lord?"

"No sir," she said.

"He didn't mention Sitting Bull nor General Custer nor any of it. Said you were running away to see your brother out West."

"So I am."

"Colonel Custer asked me to travel with her," Allen said. "Watch out for her. We never met before yesterday."

"He's your guardian, Miss Lord," Sully said. "I'm obliged to send you home."

"I'll get off, turn right around, and go West again," she said.

"Will you, now."

"I've made up my mind about it," she said.

"An orphan, are you?"

"Yes I am."

Sully looked at Allen. "You say you're going out with Custer against the Indians?"

"Yes sir."

"I hear it's going to be quite the frolic."

"Yes sir."

"Dangerous."

"Yes sir."

"You mean to let them go?" said the stationmaster.

"Shut up, Sam," Tom said.

"You've told the truth of it, haven't you, son," Sully said.

"Yes sir, we both have."

"When's the next Chicago train, Sam?"

"Noon," said the stationmaster.

"If it was your parents, Miss Lord, I couldn't bend on this," Sully said.

"I'm very grateful," Addie Grace said.

"What'll I tell the uncle?" Sam said.

"Nothing."

"He'll wire again when he don't hear."

"Tell him we're still looking."

"I'll catch hell for this, Sully. We all will."

"Better'n catching hell from General Custer," Tom said.

"Just what I think," Sully said. "You children run off, get some breakfast. And you be on that noon train, sure."

They left their bags in the stationmaster's office and went across the street to a hotel and ate breakfast. The meals went for a dollar, but they were very hungry and in a triumphant and reckless mood, and even Allen felt no hesitation.

"My mother says, when all else fails, tell the truth," he said.

"You were magnificent, I must say," Addie Grace said. "And didn't you turn the tables on that awful stationmaster?"

They'd ordered eggs, ham, fried potatoes, biscuits. The dining room was pleasantly warm and noisy.

"Of course," Addie Grace said, "one *should* always tell the truth. Ideally, I mean."

"Mother does, when it serves her."

"Only then?"

"Pretty much."

"Your poor father."

"He forgave her everything. She moved to another bedroom when he came back from the war with the leg gone, and he said he didn't mind. He said he didn't mind when she changed her name."

"Maybe losing the leg took the tuck out of him."

"Maybe. We had a cook, Bridget, lived up on the third floor. Took advantage of Father to beat the band. The kitchen was a shambles. She'd go out of a night anytime she pleased, leave a cold supper. Or leave nothing. Father would smile his smile, tell her it was fine."

"I wonder your mother didn't skin her," said Addie Grace.

"She was almost never around. When she did come home, Bridget would reform herself. She could keep a clean kitchen when she wanted. Cook a good meal. It was kind of funny."

Addie Grace put her napkin to her mouth. A trolley went by, a passing racket of clopping hooves.

"A fine house, was it," Addie Grace asked.

"Very grand, but dark. Oak paneling, dim hallways. My grandfather built it. A sea captain. Made his fortune in the China trade. We moved in when he died. I was six."

"It must have been lonely for you," Addie Grace said.

"I had friends," Allen said. "And my cousins down on Cape Cod. After Mother moved to New York I spent summers at their farm. Spent the rest of the year at school. Mother didn't care. Half the time we didn't spend Christmas together."

"The Rebellion cost us a fortune in fathers, didn't it."

"Father told me not to go to war," Allen said. "He said no matter what the cause was, it wasn't worth it."

"But you're going, after all."

"Not as a soldier. I won't carry a gun."

"Do you think that's wise?"

"It's what Father would have wanted."

The noon train was late, and they took supper at an eating house in Cleveland and afterward watched the sun collapse into Lake Erie, molten red in an amber sky. The lake appeared ocean-vast and was as blue and wave-scalloped as Buzzards Bay or Nantucket Sound on a brisk day.

Her Uncle Gordon Ruggles, Addie Grace said, taught Greek and Latin at the Boston Latin School and wrote essays and verses that appeared in *The Atlantic Monthly* and *The North American Review,* though many more were turned down than accepted for publication. He was, she said, a pedantic and thin-skinned man whose long, bent, angular figure reminded her of Ichabod Crane, though he did not have the fictitious schoolmaster's sly and fawning ways. The opposite: he was overbearing. Outspoken. Intolerant of views not his own. He was a deal older than her Aunt Ruth, and Addie Grace had never seen them kiss, or hold hands, or embrace.

He'd sired two daughters nonetheless, four and five years older than Addie Grace, and these two cousins were nearly as high handed with her as the wicked stepsisters in the tale of Cinderella. It couldn't have been the meanness of jealousy, as in the fairy tale, because Addie Grace had been a skinny, ungainly little girl, while the cousins were quite handsome. When she was little, they were fond of frightening her. They told her that a wolf lived back under the loft in the barn, and Addie Grace could see its fangs and yellow eyes and for some years would not go in on any account and dreaded even going near the dim square of the open door. They threw her dolls out of windows and put snow down her back and played keep-away with her books and playthings, laughing while she lunged and leapt for them and

74

wept tears of frustration.

And then the cousins grew bored with persecuting her, or perhaps now had too many other interests to leave time for it, and Addie Grace was left to herself in the big yellow clapboard house near the Charles River. From the time she was eleven or twelve, the older girls hardly took notice of her. They would pass her in the hallway or on the stairs without speaking. They conversed with their parents at table as if she weren't there. Her aunt and uncle sent her away to Chartwell, and it was heaven when, upon her return at year's end, Annabel, then Martha, had gotten married and were gone.

Aunt Ruth alone took an interest in her and showed her some affection, but her aunt was so taken up with women's suffrage and the freed slaves and the Indian question that she was out much of the time, at meetings and lectures, and distracted and irritable when she was at home. She seemed oblivious of her daughters' meanness, and Addie Grace guessed she lacked the grit to stand up to her husband, supposing she wanted to. Addie Grace outgrew Cinderella and thought of herself as akin to the unloved and put-upon heroine of a Charles Dickens novel. Esther Summerson, perhaps. Amy Dorrit. The difference was, they forgave their tormenters, while Addie Grace Lord never would.

"I vex Uncle Gordon, as he does me," she said. "I've never been able to help it." Beside her now, the window was dark, the night landscape flying by, invisible.

"I doubt he'll ever forgive me for running away," she said. "He'll have to pay for me to take the year over."

"Maybe you should have thought of that."

"I did think of it," she said.

They slept again side by side, waking often to the cry of the whistle or a jolting stretch of roadbed and discovering each other in the dark. Waking for good in the gray predawn, Allen found her sound asleep with her head on his shoulder, and he drew a hand up and gently stroked her hair, which was as unsnarled as if she'd just brushed it. He put his nose to it: sunshine, summer flowers.

She woke an hour later and sat up. She blinked, and her gaze found Allen.

"Morning, brat," he said.

He reached down, brought the seatback up.

"I had another awful dream," Addie Grace said.

People were waking around them. Sleepy

voices. Several rose and got in line for the washroom.

"You were in it. You and George. We were looking for General Custer. The streets were all empty."

"What streets?"

"It might have been New York. Indians were coming after us. They were going to kill us if we didn't find General Custer."

"Indians in New York City."

"It was a dream."

"That's my point."

"We couldn't find him. George said we would, but he wasn't anywhere. There was no one in the streets, just like in that other dream, except that it was the daytime. George was cheerful. I was terrified."

He lifted his arm and pulled her to him. She turned into the embrace and laid her head against his chest, and they rode like that, not speaking, until she sat up and dried her eyes with the heel of her hand.

"Crybaby," she said. "My cousins were always saying that. They'd make me cry then call me 'crybaby.' "

"It's going to be all right," Allen said. "When you meet Custer, you'll see that it is."

"Why couldn't we find him?"

"They were dreams," Allen said. "They were only dreams."

SIX

It was late afternoon when they pulled into the cavernous shed of the LaSalle Street Station. Chicago. They'd come halfway. They collected their baggage, and Allen led Addie Grace off the train, carrying the two valises, while she brought her Gladstone and blanket. There were no policemen on the platform. They moved with the crowd into the station still looking for policemen, seeing none, and Allen left her on one of the varnished benches and went to a ticket window to buy tickets to Duluth.

"Wrong station," the man said. "You want Wells Street."

Allen swore under his breath and looked away. A handsome woman in a basque coat came strolling through the archway to the train shed walking a poodle dog on a leash.

"Do you have a timetable for Duluth?" he asked the ticket clerk.

The clerk turned from the window and

studied one of several schedules tacked to the wall. "Your train leaves ten in the morning," he said. "You of a mind for a hotel?"

Allen said he was.

"You want luxury," the man said, "there's the Grand Pacific on LaSalle and Clark. Then there's the Palace, next block from here, which ain't a palace but it ain't bad, either. Washroom on every floor. Bathtubs."

Allen thanked him. Addie Grace sat surrounded by their bags, hunched forward with her arms folded, and he saw that she was cold.

"Did you not bring an overcoat?" he said.

"Just the cape."

He sat down beside her and told her what he'd learned.

"The police will have all night to look for me."

"They aren't looking for you," he said.

"The farther we come, the farther away Bismarck seems."

"On your feet, brat," Allen said.

The desk clerk at the Palace Hotel told Allen that they should lock their doors when they turned in. He said there were "undesirable persons" about who occasionally got in at night and made mischief.

"What kind of mischief?" Allen said.

Addie Grace was sitting on a leather sofa

across the small lobby. A bearded man in a sack suit sat with his legs crossed, reading a newspaper in an upholstered chair diagonal to the sofa. Allen glanced over and saw him eye her over the newspaper. It was a dark room, dingily gas lit. A double door opened to the empty dining room.

"A year or so ago," the clerk said, "a fellow got inside a man's room and stuck a pistol in his face. Took all his valuables. Knocked on the door, said he had a telegram for him. Don't you fall for any such."

Allen said he wouldn't and asked about a bath.

"Washroom at the end of the hallway. Tub's got a sidearm gas furnace. Let us know, we'll send someone up to light it for you. You from the East?"

"Massachusetts."

"You'll want to reset your timepiece if you have one. We're an hour behind you."

Again Allen turned, looked at Addie Grace. Her neighbor had put aside his newspaper and was talking to her.

"She's a pretty one," the clerk said.

"Can I sign for her?"

"Sure."

The clerk found two keys in their wall cubbies then turned the register for Allen. He wrote his own name, then thought a mo-

81

ment and wrote, *Abigail Smith, Taunton, Mass.*

"I'll ask you to plank down now, if you don't mind," the clerk said.

The rooms were two dollars. Allen paid and took up the keys and dropped them in the pocket of his cutaway. The door opened, and a couple came in and a man behind them, the men lugging valises. Addie Grace had risen. The bearded man watched Allen come toward them.

"No bellboys in this low place," he said.

"I guess we'll survive," Allen said.

"I was telling her that if you want a decent supper, you should hoof it over to the Grand Pacific."

Allen looked down at him. A big, slow, round-shouldered man with a salt-and-pepper beard like President Grant's.

"This'll do us," Allen said.

"You'll eat cheaper here, it's true. I'm Phineas Higginbottom. Providence, Rhode Island."

He extended a thick white hand. Allen gave him his hand, and Phineas Higginbottom grasped it, eyeing him the while, smiling. His grip was warm. Moist.

"Allen Winslow," Allen said.

"Winslow. Descendant of a *Mayflower* Winslow, I'll bet." He let go of Allen's hand.

"Indirect," Allen said.

"Perchance I'll see you later. At supper, perhaps. I can tell you what's good on the table d'hôte. I know this place well. I pass through here often."

"Nice to meet you, Mr. Higginbottom."

"Likewise, Mr. Winslow."

Their rooms were on the second floor, adjacent to each other. Allen unlocked Addie Grace's and followed her in and set down the two heavy bags. He locked the door. Addie Grace put down the Gladstone and sat down on the bed. The room was small and square, with papered walls and mocha-brown trim boards that fitted with the dim and color-dulled feel of the place. Brass bedstead, dresser, bureau, one high-backed Windsor chair. A single gaslight wall sconce. A steam radiator, silent and cold.

"I didn't like that Mr. Higginbottom," Addie Grace said.

"What did you tell him your name for?"

"It was out before I knew it."

"It's no matter," Allen said. "We've outrun the law."

"He's going east, at any rate. He works for the company that makes the pistols. Colts. Goes around arranging contracts and so forth. He said he knows General Sheri-

83

dan. Said he's been to see him today."

Allen stood at the window, which looked down on LaSalle Street. The street was broad and unpaved. Across it was a weed-grown expanse where a building or buildings had stood before the fire.

"He told me to keep my door locked," Addie Grace said. "Said there are thieves about. Plug uglies."

"No one's going to bother you. Do you want the first bath?"

"I would."

"I'll go down and tell them."

"And Allen?"

He turned from the window.

"Will you sit outside the washroom while I bathe? There are chairs in the hallway. You could sit and read your book."

Allen smiled. "The girl who wanted to travel to Dakota alone."

She looked down, into her lap. "It's ungentlemanly to throw that back at me," she said.

"I'll go down and order your bath," he said, still smiling.

"Colonel Custer," said Phineas Higginbottom, "went down on his knees before General Terry and wept."

Allen and Addie Grace looked at each other. Higginbottom had been at table when

84

they'd come in and had waved them over. No help for it. He'd urged them to order the loin of beef, and they had. There was a bottle of champagne on the table and he'd filled Allen's glass. Addie Grace had declined. Higginbottom had refilled his own glass and sent the waiter for another bottle.

"This would be General Terry's version," Allen said.

"Do you doubt it?"

"Yes I do."

"Terry's a man of enormous integrity. Everyone respects him, including your Colonel Custer."

Allen sipped some champagne. "It doesn't sound like Custer, that's all," he said.

"Know him well, do you," Higginbottom said.

"I know he's no baby."

Higginbottom smiled, lifted his glass, and drained it, watching Allen. He had black little eyes. He reached for the bottle. Addie Grace was nibbling at her food. Her beef, her soggy potato. The dining room was a third full. Quiet. The three of them were at a window table, and in the light of the cool spring evening Addie Grace's brushed hair shone more red gold than brown. She'd put on a clean high-necked pale-blue summer dress. Allen wore his cutaway and a clean shirt and the same four-in-hand necktie. He'd only brought the one tie.

"I happened to be in the party of the secretary of war, Mr. Belknap, when he visited Fort Lincoln last year," said Higginbottom. "I wonder if you heard about that."

"No," Allen said, eating.

Higginbottom drank. He picked up his knife and fork and cut into his beef. He'd consumed a bowl of green turtle soup and a beef tongue.

"Colonel Custer didn't come down to the river to meet us," he said. "He greeted us at his house, then went inside and left us. Snubbed us. The secretary of war."

"Wasn't he impeached by the Senate?" Allen said.

"That's neither here nor there. He was the secretary of war, visiting a military post."

"He resigned in disgrace, I believe," Allen said.

"He was hounded out of office by the Democrats."

"He was selling licenses to the post traders and Indian agents, as I understand it. Taking bribes, in other words."

"Accusations by bitter, disgruntled men," Higginbottom said.

He stabbed a piece of eggplant and washed it down with a gulp of champagne.

Allen and Addie Grace again exchanged looks. There was a flat, uneasy brightness in her eyes.

"Colonel Custer, as I say, turned his back on us. Left it to his wife to entertain us. She's a looker, by the way. Very gracious and charming, she was. 'I wouldn't mind knowing her better,' Belknap says afterwards. Between us, I wouldn't, either."

Allen ate and said nothing.

"Later we found out that the post trader, fellow named Seip, sent him a case of wine to entertain us with. Custer sent it back."

"He doesn't drink," Allen said.

"No one said *he* had to drink it. The man makes me sick. His sanctimony. Have some more champagne."

"No thank you," Allen said.

"Miss Lord?"

Addie Grace laid down her fork. "I believe I'm done," she said.

"Don't drink, do you?" Higginbottom said. He was drunk himself now. His voice had thickened, turned mulish. "You and Custer, eh?"

"I'm not opposed to it," Addie Grace said.

"Have a wee sip, then."

"No thank you."

"Mr. Winslow."

Higginbottom had lifted the bottle. Allen

87

covered his empty glass with the flat of his hand. "No," he said.

Higginbottom topped off his own glass and put the bottle down. "If it's money you're worried about . . ." he said.

"It isn't," Allen said.

"We're tired," Addie Grace said.

"You've hardly eaten half your supper, Miss Lord."

"I'm quite full," she said.

"You'll take some dessert with me."

"I don't think so," Allen said.

Higginbottom regarded them both with a crooked smile and dark eyes gone blearily luminous. "Such beautiful children you are," he said.

Addie Grace smiled a thin smile and looked thoughtfully out the window. Allen turned, found the waiter on the other side of the room, and summoned him with a raised arm.

"Going to leave me, are you," Higginbottom said.

"We have to," Allen said.

"It's hardly gone eight o'clock."

"I'm sorry."

"I thought we might step out after supper, see the sights."

Allen smiled. "No thanks."

The waiter arrived and stood over them

with his pad and pencil, totting Allen's and Addie Grace's bill. He tore it and handed it to Allen.

"By God, you *are* leaving," Higginbottom said.

"Thanks for the champagne," Allen said, pulling his pocketbook from his breast pocket. He put two dollars, a quarter, and a nickel on the table. He and Addie Grace stood up, she with her purse on her wrist.

"Good night," she said.

"Good night, Mr. Higginbottom," Allen said.

He looked up at Allen, and his little eyes brightened. "I hope the Indians cut your gizzard out, boy," he said.

She took his arm as they climbed the carpeted stairs, lifting her skirt with the other hand.

"He's just a lonesome drunk," Allen said.

"You don't know the way he looked at me."

"He looked at me the same."

"The more reason to be frightened of him."

They turned at the top of the stairs and moved down the hallway with its bled-out carpeting and sallow gaslight and stopped at her door. She opened her purse and dug out her key.

"Allen," she said.

"What."

It was very quiet here. No sound, either, from the floor above. A distant gabble of voices from the dining room, where things seemed to be livening up.

"I want you to sleep in my room," she said. "I don't want to be alone. I shan't sleep a wink."

He looked at her. She held his gaze, then looked away. Allen reached, took both her hands between his and held them like a nosegay at his waist. She glanced at him, then away again.

"Do you understand what you're asking me?" he said.

"I don't mean *that,*" she said.

"I know you don't. But what'll it look like? This time I really could be arrested."

"Please," she said.

"Mr. Higginbottom doesn't know what room you're in."

"He could find out."

"He's already found someone else to leer at. And he's drunk."

"It's not just him. There are thieves about. Please, Allen. It'll be just like on the train."

He still held her hands, enfolded between his. She waited, standing erect and still with her head bowed. It was the moment she became beautiful to him. Past all doubting, ever.

"It's nobody's business where you sleep," she said.

"You can tell that to the police."

"I shall, if they ask me."

He locked his own door and tapped four times on Addie Grace's. She opened it with her eyes shyly downcast and stood aside, so somber that he guessed she was having second thoughts. She was wearing a peach-colored cotton nightgown that buttoned chastely at the neck, and he thought of an angel on a Christmas card. Dusk had come down, and the gas jet burned white-yellow in its glass chimney. Allen pulled the chair from the dresser and turned it and sat down. Addie Grace sat down on the bed, straight as ever, with her hands folded, gaze on the floor, like a penitent. The window was closed, and the street sounds came up muted but clearly audible. A man shouted, shouted again. *Hey. Hey, I said.*

"It's early to go to sleep," Allen said.

"I'm very tired," she said.

Footsteps in the hallway, men's voices passing. *I don't give a good goddamn what she said.*

Addie Grace looked at Allen. "You see?" she said.

He smiled and got up and sat down beside her. The bed sagged under him. A rustle of straw. On top of the straw mattress was another filled with cotton or feathers. Allen put his arm around her. She let him pull her against his shoulder. She felt very light and thin under the gown, almost weightless, and there was a second garment beneath it. A chemise, he guessed.

"The place frightens me," she said. "I can't help it."

"It's only Chicago. Wait'll we get to the Wild West. Gunfighters. Indians. I hear men are shot down in the street in Bismarck."

"I don't know much, do I?"

"About as much as I do."

"But you seem so . . . *calm* about it all."

"Because one of us has to be. If I were alone, I'd be scared every minute."

She smiled. "Liar."

He moved his hand up her warm, thin arm, down again. *Now, if this were Katie Doyle* . . .

If this were Katie he would turn her, and she'd lift her arms around him and look him in the eye and smile. She had bad teeth but he liked her smile. It was bold. Insolent. Happy. She was twenty-four or -five. He had found her sitting on a park bench with her silk parasol on the Lawrence Common on a Sunday afternoon and had sat down beside her, intuiting her profession. Reckless, his mother's son. He'd have been expelled from Phillips even for sitting there. "And what do *you* want?" she'd said, scrutinizing him with her chin uplifted, proud and saucy and curious.

"What are you thinking about?" Addie Grace said.

"Nothing," Allen said.

It had grown noisier in the dining room, a festive-sounding clamor that rose through the floor and traveled up the stairwell.

"Where do I sleep?" he said.

"Beside me. Just like on the train. Where else?"

"The floor," he said.

"Don't be silly."

"Get in bed then," he said.

She did, and lay on her side with the covers drawn up to her chin, watching him. Her wool blanket was folded on the dresser, and he shook it open and threw it on the bed. He stripped off his coat and tie. He sat down and took off his shoes. He extinguished the lamp and lay down beside her and covered himself with the blanket.

"I should have brought a pillow," he said.

"Take mine."

"Don't be ridiculous."

"Go on."

"No."

They lay awhile listening to the traffic below, the faint din of the dining room. Liquor must be flowing down there. It had gotten dark, and the sky above Chicago was star-speckled and not much softened by city lights. Again Allen thought of Katie and her warm garret room and how she would linger with him, let him have her again if he wanted, an exception, she said, because he was quality and so young, and hadn't been spoiled yet and treated her like a lady. He would ride the train into Lawrence on a Sunday afternoon and find her on her bench on the Common, waiting for him. She kept the day free and would wait till three and not charge him if he failed to show up, as occasionally happened. Her price was four dollars and Allen paid it out of his allowance and knew his mother would approve.

Addie Grace still watched him.

"I wonder you don't kiss me good night," she said.

"I'm a gentleman."

"I wonder you don't try, even so."

"If I did you might slap me."

"I might. I might not."

"I don't want to risk it."

He was lying on his side facing her. He closed his eyes but knew she still watched him.

"I bet you've kissed a smart of girls," she said.

"I thought you were tired," he said.

"Well," she said, "if you're not interested . . ."

He opened his eyes and rose on his elbow. "You've been kissed plenty, I take it," he said.

"No," she said, "I've not."

"They must have wanted to," he said.

"None that I cared to be kissed by. Anyway, where was I to meet them? Chartwell's like a prison, as far as that goes."

"I thought you liked it there."

"I liked being away from Uncle Gordon, and don't change the subject."

"Close your eyes," he said.

She closed them.

"Relax your mouth," he said. "Let the kiss shape it."

He bent to her. Closed his own eyes. She did as he'd said and he only half heard a wagon go by below. The kiss went on awhile, and they broke it finally as by mutual consent and looked at each other in a new and searching way.

"I swan," Addie Grace said.

Allen smiled. "Good night, brat," he said, and turned over and closed his eyes and soon slept.

SEVEN

They went north into Wisconsin, a land of sprawling farms, of valleys and lakes and wooded hills and gorges. It was fertile country, Edenic, between settlements. The towns looked staid and prosperous, neat brick buildings and great shade trees that must have stood there when the land was a wilderness inhabited, if at all, by the Indians.

The noon meal stop was in a town called East Janesville, and as they moved toward the door Allen and Addie Grace passed three men playing cards. They'd reversed a seatback and sat facing each other. They were playing draw poker and they did not look up. Two humorless-looking men of middle age and a younger man, pale and rosy cheeked.

The eating house occupied the floor above the train station, a big, bright room with trestle tables. Allen and Addie Grace bought their tickets and went in and saw, alone at the end of a table, as if people were shunning him or he them, a boy her age or younger. He was thin and pallid and wore an old sack coat that was too large for him, and he looked like some adolescent tramp or vagrant, hunched morosely over his plate. Allen and Addie Grace looked at each other. Addie Grace nodded. They went over and sat down across from the boy.

"Mind if we join you?" Allen said.

The boy looked at him. He looked at Addie Grace. Shrugged.

"Allen Winslow. This is Addie Grace Lord."

"Irwin."

"Irwin what?" Allen said.

The boy studied him. His dark eyes shifted, fell on Addie Grace. He had a sharp, pixie like face, a wing of black hair across his forehead.

"Kohn," he said.

"Nice to meet you," Allen said, and reached across the table and gripped Irwin Kohn's long, bony, fragile-feeling hand.

The waiters came, setting platters down in the hurried way of these eating houses. Beefsteak, boiled potatoes, thin dry slabs of apple pie. Irwin took up his fork and began eating.

"Where are you going, Irwin?" Allen said.

Again Irwin eyed him a moment before answering. "Helena, Montana," he said. "I got an uncle's going to meet me in Bismarck. Take me up there on a boat. Through Indian country."

"Why, we're going to Bismarck," Addie Grace said.

Irwin stopped chewing. He nodded, as if he'd suspected it.

"We can keep each other company," Allen said. He was feeling an unaccountable urge to befriend the boy and saw that Addie Grace was too.

Irwin nodded.

"If you want to," Allen said.

"Sure."

"Allen's going out with General Custer in a few days," Addie Grace said.

Irwin paused again in his eating and studied him. "I wish I was," he said.

Allen smiled. "No you don't."

"Sure I do. See the country. Kill some Indians."

Again Allen smiled. "What's in Helena?"

His uncle owned a dry goods store there, and Irwin was going to work for him and live above the store. His parents had come to America from Heidelberg, Germany, when Irwin was a baby. His father owned a meat market in lower Manhattan, and life there was regimented by synagogue and family and was, apparently, inimical to Irwin's temperament and ambition. His parents had had no objection to his going West.

"I'll have my own store one day," he said. "My own house. What would I do in New York City?"

"Have your own meat market," Allen said.

"I don't like the smell of them. All that blood."

"I think you've very brave to travel all this way alone," Addie Grace said.

"I know how to look out for myself," Irwin said.

"How old are you?" Allen said.

"Old enough."

"Fourteen, I'd say."

"Fourteen going on twenty," Irwin said.

Irwin Kohn found trouble right away. He'd been sitting in the next coach forward, and he came looking for Allen and Addie Grace twenty minutes after the train pulled out. He was hauling a bulging carpetbag. He heaved it onto the rack and stood braced against the swaying of the train.

"There's a card game up there," he said.

"I know there is," Allen said. "So what?"

"I want to get in."

"Are you crazy?" Allen said.

"I never lose at poker. I have a mathematical brain."

"Irwin, those are grown men. Professional gamblers, likely."

"So am I," he said. "They won't let me in, is the thing."

"Good."

"They might if you talk to them."

"And say what?"

Irwin only turned and went forward, toward the game.

"What on earth?" Addie Grace said.

"God Almighty," Allen said, and got up.

The poker players had laid their cards on their laps and were looking up at Irwin. The young one wore a ratcatcher jacket and checked trousers. His straw-yellow hair was oiled, and he had a mustache to match. The older two were bearded in the Grant fashion and their faces closed and inscrutable. They were of similar builds and looked like twins. One wore a linen duster, the other had stripped to his vest. Some paper dollars and change lay tossed on the seat beside the younger man. He jerked his head at Irwin.

"He with you?"

"Yes he is," Allen said.

"I'm Mr. Wilson. This here's Mr. Jenkins and Mr. Caldwell. And you might be . . . ?"

"Allen Winslow. My friend Irwin."

"Irwin what?" said Jenkins, the man in the linen duster, studying his cards.

"Kohn," Irwin said.

"Jew," said Jenkins. "Short for Cohen."

"Deal me a hand," Irwin said, "we'll see who's the dumb Jew."

"I never said dumb."

"No such thing as a dumb Jew," said Caldwell.

"Where'd you learn to play poker at?" Wilson said.

"My cousin taught me," Irwin said. "If he was here he'd skin the three of you."

"Let him in the game, Wilson," Jenkins said. "Mr. Winslow here has vouched for him."

"He ain't but a child," Wilson said.

"His money's still good. Let him in."

"How much do I need?" Irwin said.

"Two-dollar limit," Wilson said.

The train swayed, shuddered over a bad piece of roadbed. Allen looked at Wilson. His smile went up sideways, not malicious but smug. The two others looked from Irwin to Allen and back again, biding the outcome patiently and with no strong feeling, either way.

"You'll be square with him?" Allen said.

"What are you, his nanny?" Caldwell said.

"His friend," Allen said.

"We'll lift his money, but we'll be square with him," Wilson said.

"Like he was our own son," Caldwell said.

By the time the conductor announced the evening meal stop Irwin had won fifteen dollars and neither he nor the three men would interrupt the game. The woodstove was going now, and Wilson had taken off his ratcatcher and his tie and collar.

"Bring me something back," Irwin told Allen. "A piece of chicken or something."

"Kosher chicken," Jenkins said.

"Bring him some bacon," Caldwell said.

The train was slowing. People got up and moved to the doors, pushing past Allen.

"Hear you're going on campaign with General Custer," Jenkins said, his eyes on his cards.

"As a noncombatant," Allen said.

"Even so, I admire it. It's about time the Indians were dealt with. Tell the general to kill a few for me."

"For me too," Caldwell said.

Wilson looked up at Allen. "If you see one of them butcher boys came by this afternoon, you might refer him."

Irwin laid two cards down on the seat and Caldwell dealt him two more. Addie Grace had come up. She took Allen's arm. The three men looked up from their cards and took in her face, her figure. Addie Grace did not meet their gazes until Wilson spoke to her.

"Evenin', miss," he said.

"Good evening," she said.

Jenkins and Caldwell eyed her in silence then went back to their cards. The train crept to a stop, throwing Addie Grace gently against Allen's shoulder. The coach doors were opened, and they went on.

"Don't forget my food," Irwin called after them.

The overhead aisle lamps had been lit, casting their dim oily light and sullying the air with wick smoke. It had gotten quiet. The card game continued, and at ten by Allen's watch he went forward and stood over the card players again.

"You still ahead?" he said.

"Ask them," Irwin said.

"About twenty dollars, I should say," said Jenkins. He still wore the linen duster, though it had gotten very warm in the stove's aura.

Irwin dropped two quarters into the pot, which was on the seat between him Caldwell, and Wilson played his hand, fanning four sixes. Irwin showed him four tens and gathered up the money and deposited it in the deep pocket of his coat, which hung over the seat arm.

"Son of a *bitch,*" Wilson said.

The floor around them was strewn with the wrappings of the food they'd bought from a butcher boy. Jenkins drew a half-empty quart bottle of whiskey from the side pocket of his duster and drank. He offered it to Caldwell, who declined with a shake of his head, and to Wilson, who took the bottle distractedly and had a good long pull.

"I don't suppose you'd consider quitting," Allen said.

"The game ain't over," Wilson said. His pale eyes had narrowed and hardened. He was losing.

"Is the young lady your bride-to-be?" Jenkins said.

"She's his pigeon," Irwin said.

"You better keep a close eye on her. Wilson, here, is having untoward thoughts."

"And you ain't?" Wilson said.

"In my heart of hearts, maybe," Jenkins said. "You're a lucky man, son."

"Boy must live right," Caldwell said.

"Can we play cards?" Wilson said.

Addie Grace watched him come back down

the aisle. He pulled the blanket down from overhead and sat down and covered them.

"He's up twenty dollars," he said.

"He isn't either."

"He is, for a fact. Maybe he knew what he was talking about."

Allen lowered the seat, and Addie Grace turned into him and snuggled down under the blanket, and in its privacy her arm went around his waist.

"Everything on this trip is upside down," she said. "I've never been so happy."

Allen wondered if he could say the same. He'd been happy with Katie Doyle on the spring afternoon she woke him with a kiss and told him, perched naked on the edge of the bed, that she'd marry him in one heartbeat if she were a lady, educated and respectable. He'd been happy the first time he saw her naked, slithering out of her chemise with her back to him, turning slowly, as in some measured, brazen dance, and stopping to eye him with a haughty tilt of her head. She was as honest as anyone he'd ever known. There was no meanness in her.

"What are you thinking?" Addie Grace said.

"Nothing."

"Yes you are. You're thinking about being

happy. With another girl."

"All right," he said.

"You'll tell me about her sometime."

"Sometime."

"You certainly have had the start of me, haven't you," she said.

It was rhetorical and he made no answer, and in another minute she was asleep, curled against him, trustful as a child.

Waking from time to time to the rocking of the train or the whistle, Allen knew the card game was continuing by the men's low voices, carrying back indistinct across the sleeping riders. Once, as he lay awake, Addie Grace stirred in her sleep, and he kissed her parted lips and she made a sleepy, sensual groan and slept on. He woke again to rain on the window and a sodden landscape of low green hills and woods. Addie Grace had turned in her sleep and lay facing away from him. Allen got up, careful not to wake her.

The coach was nearly empty and felt lightened, hurtling along with skittish jerks. Irwin and Wilson were asleep sitting up, opposite each other, and Jenkins and Caldwell were gone. Wilson's oiled yellow hair had fallen down lank around his ears. The blush was gone from his pale face. Irwin had

107

covered himself with his sack coat. Allen stood watching them sleep, then sat down beside Irwin. Wilson opened his eyes.

"Morning," Allen said.

Wilson regarded him blearily. "Morning," he said, then came forward, bowed his head and massaged his temples.

"Shit," he said.

"Where are the other two?" Allen said.

"Bastards got off."

"Got off where?" Allen said.

"I don't know. Some damn town or other. Was about two o'clock. Gave us the slip. Sons-a-bitches picked us clean."

"Both of you?"

"What did I just say?"

"Irwin was up twenty dollars," Allen said.

"They let him. Then they raised the limit and won it all back and every other cent he had. I don't know how they done it, but I know that son of a bitch didn't keep that duster on because he was cold."

Irwin was awake now. He yawned, looked at Allen.

"Hidey," he said.

"I thought you never lost at poker," Allen said.

"It ain't his fault," Wilson said. "You can't beat a good cheater."

"Two cheaters," Irwin said.

"Did you accuse them?" Allen said.

"I told you, they pulled foot. First the one, then the other. Said they was goin' to the washroom. After the train stopped and they didn't come back, it come to me what happened."

"Mr. Jenkins kept giving him whiskey," Irwin said. "It slowed his thinking."

"Slowed yours too," Wilson said.

"Irwin was drinking whiskey?" Allen said.

"Bastards give it to him on purpose," Wilson said.

"We both got corned," Irwin said.

"I don't know what the goddamn hell I was thinkin'," Wilson said.

"How'd they cheat you?" Allen said.

"How the hell do I know? Cards in the duster, I guess. They were professionals, I'll tell you that. They were waitin' for a mark to come along, and that was me. Never had to ask me. I invited my own damn self into the game. I thought it would pass the time."

"It did," Irwin said.

"Shut up," Wilson said.

"Maybe they beat you fair," Allen said.

"The hell they did. Cleaned me out of fifty-five dollars. I ain't got but four left."

"Better'n what I got," Irwin said.

"How much did you lose?" Allen said.

"Never you mind," Irwin said.

"He lost a good forty," Wilson said. He ran a hand through his hair. "Where'd them sons-a-bitches get on, I wonder."

"What does it matter?" Allen said.

"I'll tell you what it matters. I intend to find the sons-a-bitches, get my money back. I'll shoot 'em if I have to. Might shoot 'em anyways."

"They could be anywhere," Allen said.

"Chicago," Wilson said. "I bet that's where they work out of. I'll ask the conductor. If that's it, I'll go there and lay for 'em."

"You might as well go looking for a needle in a haystack," Allen said.

The rain lashed the window. They flew past a town, a brick depot, tiny-looking as a toy house, without slowing.

"Loan me some money," Wilson said. "It might take me a day or two."

Allen looked out at the wet, green world. A week ago he'd been at Phillips, waking to the yellow spring dawn. Thinking about breakfast at the Shawshine Club. About astronomy and English lit.

"I'll pay you back," Wilson said, "I swear. I'll send it on, plus the money the boy here lost."

"If you find them."

"I'll pay you back anyways. You think I'd cheat you after what they done to me?'

"Loan him, Allen," Irwin said.

"You don't hear, you come after me. Harvey Wilson, Brainerd, Minnesota. Got a partnership in a liquor business there. Wilson and Doane, wholesalers."

"How much do you need?" Allen said.

"Twenty."

"Loan him thirty," Irwin said.

"Twenty is fine," Wilson said. "I already got my ticket from Duluth through to Brainerd."

"You'll never find them," Allen said.

"I'll lay for 'em in the station. I 'spect they'll happen by."

"You've no idea they're in Chicago."

"They are," Wilson said. "You'll get your money back. Irwin too."

"Go on loan him," Irwin said.

"Hell," Allen said, "why not?"

Duluth, Minnesota. Allen led his two dependents into the station and bought three tickets to Bismarck, twelve dollars apiece. The waiting room was about the size of a hotel lobby, carpeted and furnished with rocking chairs and a steam radiator. Addie Grace stood in her tartan cape looking out across the maze of tracks toward the bay that cut in from Lake Superior. The station-master told Allen that their train departed

111

at eight in the morning and suggested a hotel called the Immigrant House, which was an easy walk uphill of the station.

Allen put the tickets in his pocketbook and led them out into the clearing afternoon, up the street to the hotel, another two-story wood building with a flat roof and gallery around its four sides. The town was built on a hillside that fell steeply to the water, and, looking back over the depot and a grain elevator, they could see marshes with wooden causeways built out across them on stilts, some freight sheds also on stilts and the slate-gray bay, with docks jutting into deeper water, and a couple of berthed schooners.

There was a line of five or six people at the hotel desk, and the three of them sat down to wait on a leather sofa. The room was larger than the lobby of the Palace Hotel in Chicago, and it was less faded and less ill-lit. After a minute or two Irwin got up and went looking for a washroom.

"How much money have we?" Addie Grace said.

"Just enough," Allen said.

"You'll share a room with Irwin," she said.

Allen looked at her. He was sitting forward with his elbows on his knees. She sat straight, as always. "To save money, I mean," she said.

"I believe I'll have my own room," he said.

Addie Grace glanced at him, then away.

"I don't care to have that little pest know everything I do," Allen said.

"I shouldn't either," Addie Grace said, and in that way it was decided.

He went to her as before, tapping on the brown-painted door and hoping Irwin wouldn't appear while he waited. The lock turned, and there she was. She'd bathed and put on her nightgown, and her fine, spare face seemed both grave and luminous in the soft light of the gas lamp. The room was small and rectangular, with a hooked rug on the plank floor, an engraving of Lincoln in a gilt frame on the papered wall. Four-poster bed. Again he removed his coat and tie and shoes, extinguished the lamp, and this time sat on the edge of the bed until she rolled over to face him, dimly visible in the vague starlight from beyond the high four-paned window.

"I'll miss these hotels," she said. "Miss sleeping beside you."

Her hand went to his thigh, caressed it. No girl save Katie had ever touched him there, but it did not seem forward in Addie Grace. It felt natural. Friendly. The radiator hissed, clanked three times, breathed a long sigh, and subsided.

"Allen."

"What."

"What's the most you've done with a girl?"

Her face was upturned, pale and softened in the dusk. Her hand still rested on his leg.

"Well . . ." he said.

"Well, what?"

"It's easier for a boy than for a girl."

"What is?"

"Kissing. Anything. A boy doesn't get faulted, but a proper girl does. You know that."

"It doesn't seem fair, does it."

"It isn't."

"What's the 'anything' you were talking about?"

"The whole range."

"The whole range."

"Sure."

"Including being intimate."

"It could include that," Allen said.

"Did it?"

Her hand was still on his leg, and he dreaded her removing it, as if once withdrawn it would be lost to him forever.

"Do you really want to talk about this now?"

"I want to know, Allen."

Her hand remained where it was. A wagon rattled somewhere off in the night. A muffled thump of hooves. He knew she was going to pursue this wherever it led, if only because she'd begun it.

"All right," he said. "I've been with someone."

"I thought so. Was she proper?"

"Not in the usual sense."

"In what sense, then?"

"You're sure you want to know about her?"

"Yes I am."

"She was a prostitute, actually."

Her hand came away from him. He had thought she might view a commercial transaction as inconsequential and having nothing to do with her or anyone else he might have loved, but it had been a bad guess. They regarded each other in the dark.

"Was she the only one, this prostitute?" Addie Grace said.

"Yes."

"Did you love her?"

"I liked her."

"You liked a prostitute."

"Her name was Katie Doyle, and she never said a hard word to me."

"As I'm doing now."

"I wish you could hear yourself," Allen said.

"I *can* hear myself."

"No you can't, or you wouldn't talk so."

"And how would you like me to talk?"

"Like yourself and not some damn prig at the Chartwell School."

"I'm sorry, but it's a bit of a shock. I wonder what else I don't know about you."

"Jesus Christ," Allen said.

"Do *not* curse me."

If only she would cry. Then he could lie down and hold her, and they would apologize to each other and it would be over. But she lay still and dry-eyed and seemed to have no more to say to him.

"Maybe I ought to sleep alone tonight," Allen said.

"Maybe you ought to," she said.

He gave her a moment to reconsider then rolled off the bed and moved about collecting his coat, tie, shoes. Addie Grace didn't move, didn't look at him. She still lay on her side with her face toward the window, and she remained so, hardly seeming to breathe, when he let himself out.

EIGHT

"Where'd you learn poker?" Allen said.

"I told you. My cousin. He works at the Black and Tan down on Bleecker Street. Picked it up there."

"The Black and *Tan*?" said Addie Grace.

"Sure. Sweeps floors, runs errands. It's all right: he's nineteen."

"I bet he picked up more than poker," Allen said.

"I bet he did too," Irwin said.

They were riding the Northern Pacific Railway, which terminated in Bismarck but would, when the Indians were beaten, hurry on through the vast country to the west and then across the mountains to Puget Sound. The train rocketed along in the bright morning. They'd reversed a seatback and sat together, Allen and Addie Grace side by side facing Irwin, Addie Grace by the window. The two of them hadn't spoken at breakfast or on the walk down the hill to the depot or yet on the train. Irwin hadn't seemed to notice.

"I been in there with him of an evening," he said.

"You haven't," Addie Grace said.

"Sure I have. There's Chinese in there. There's niggers. There's pretty white ladies. There's some carryings-on, let me tell you."

"I can imagine," Addie Grace said.

"I bet you can't," Irwin said. "There's . . ."

"By God," Allen said, pointing.

The Mississippi River. It wasn't wide here, or deep, or rapid: a placid, green-brown stream that Allen might almost have thrown a baseball across, with trees crowded along its sloping banks. The three of them fell silent, all gazing at the river. The train made its cautious way over the bridge, which ran close above the water. The wheel rumble was sluggish, hollow-sounding. Then they were across, on solid roadbed again.

"I won't ever go back across it," Irwin said.

"Don't talk gum," Allen said.

"It ain't gum. The West is the place for me. I'm going to get rich, have horses. Go hunting. Shoot buffalo. Shoot Indians."

Addie Grace looked at him, shook her head and smiled, then turned back to the window. Allen, looking out past her averted face, waited for her to turn and meet his

118

eye, but she did not, all day.

He pulled the folded blanket down from the rack and shook it open and covered her with it. "I guess I'll sleep on Irwin's side," he said.

"No you won't," Irwin said. "I like to lay down crosswise."

"You're quite welcome to share my blanket," Addie Grace said.

"What's up with you two?" Irwin said.

"Nothing," Allen said.

"Sure it is. I got eyes. What did she do, Allen?"

Allen had covered himself. Addie Grace had turned to face to the window.

"She didn't do anything. Go to sleep."

"Lower the seat, Allen," Addie Grace said.

He felt beside him and found the lever, and they sank back halfway to the horizontal. Irwin lay down and pulled his coat over his thin shoulders. He drew his legs up.

"Maybe *you* did something," he said.

"Maybe I'll box your ears, you don't be quiet."

"She was my girl, I'd make it up to her," Irwin said.

"I wish you'd both hush," Addie Grace said to the window.

"You suppose Mr. Wilson found them two

119

card cheats?" Irwin said.

"I doubt it," Allen said.

"I bet he will. I bet he shoots 'em when he does."

"That was talk," Allen said. "He isn't going to shoot anybody."

"Make it up with her," Irwin said. "How would you feel, an Indian got hold of you and you hadn't?"

"Go to sleep," Allen said.

He slept fitfully and knew that she did too. The woodstoves were going and the air was overheated and noxious with lamp smoke, and there was much restless tossing and coughing up and down the car. He came full awake deep into the night, and she was facing him now, and he waited, watching her breathe, the slightly parted lips, the gentle rise and fall of her chest, but she did not wake up. It was the last thing he remembered.

Then the sun was up and they were awake all three, traversing an empty and alien world. Not a tree anywhere, not a hill, not a gulch or ravine. Grass, pale spring-green, running in long, low swells to the faraway end of the earth. It was an emptiness such as they'd never seen, and the blue sky pressed down on it, fleecy clouds strewn low, where it seemed you might touch them if you had a hill to stand on.

"By damn," Irwin said.

"Where are the buffalo?" said Addie Grace.

"Where are the Indians?" said Irwin.

A long-legged animal, white and mouse-brown with black curved swordlike horns, stood on a rise, watching the train go by.

"Deer," Irwin said.

"City boy," Allen said. "That's no deer."

"Antelope?" Addie Grace said.

"We're out West, all right," Irwin said. "I don't know why I waited so long."

The man came through the coach door past the woodstove and paused with his carpet-bag to look around, and his glance caught on Addie Grace. Addie Grace in a yellow dress, blue sash. He wore a black three-piece suit and a bowler hat. Allen watched him. The man ran his gaze over the nearby seats, glanced again at Addie Grace, and threw his bag up onto the rack above Irwin. He removed his coat; there was a pistol strapped to his leg. He stashed the coat and sat down beside Irwin with his hat on.

"Hidey," Irwin said.

The man turned, considered him. "Hello," he said.

Allen nodded. The man returned it. Addie Grace, who had seen the pistol, was looking out the window. The town resembled Fargo, which they'd passed through some hours ago, with its wide dirt streets and clapboard building fronts. The locomotive was taking on water.

"You folks are from the East, I'll wager," said the stranger.

Allen smiled carefully. "How can you tell?" he said.

"The girls are prettier in the East," the man said.

Addie Grace brought her gaze around to him. "Why do you suppose that is?" she said.

The man grinned. His gaze licked at her breasts, her waist, and came up again. "I don't suppose it, actually."

Addie Grace lifted her chin and looked away. Allen looked again at the gun. The grips were white and the gun itself blue-black. It looked heavy.

"Is that thing loaded?" Irwin said.

"What do you think?" the man said.

"I think it wouldn't be much good if it wasn't," Irwin said.

"You can put a pretty good knot on a man's head with the side of a Remington forty-four," the man said.

"Is it loaded or isn't it?" Irwin said.

"It might be."

"I've got to get me one of those," Irwin said.

"Oh? What'll you do with it?"

"What do you do with yours?" Irwin said.

"Irwin," Allen said, "why don't you leave the man alone."

The man smiled. "He doesn't bother me. Does he bother you?"

"Now and again," Allen said.

"I take it you children are going to Bismarck," the man said.

"I'm going to Helena, Montana," Irwin said.

"Helena. I've not been there."

"I haven't either," Irwin said.

"I hear it's full of Jews."

Irwin looked across at Allen. Allen shook his head. *Leave it alone.* Addie Grace sat as still as if she hadn't heard, her face swung to the window.

"Well," Irwin said, "there's going to be one more Jew when I get there."

The man turned, looked at him as if for the first time. "Jew, are you."

"What of it?" Irwin said.

"I'll tell you what of it. You'll need that revolver, you go around sassing people, talking up smart to them. There's men out here'll shoot a Jew for it. Or a white man, when it comes to it."

Addie Grace turned from the window. "Shoot him because he's a Jew," she said.

The man smiled. "You going to Helena too?"

"That's none of your affair," she said, with another lift of her chin, and resumed watching out the window.

"She's going to Bismarck," Irwin said. "To the fort. They both are. Allen's going out with General Custer."

The stranger regarded Allen with mild interest. "A soldier, are you."

"He's going to be General Custer's secretary," Irwin said.

"His secretary, is it. That sounds right. He takes squaw women with him, why not a secretary?"

"What would you know about it?" Allen said.

"Pardon?"

"I said what would you know about it?"

"I might know plenty. Why do you ask?"

"Allen," Addie Grace said.

"Why don't we drop it," Allen said. "We mind our business, you mind yours." The stranger shifted in his seat, and when he looked again at Allen, his stare was flat, lightless. "I'm going to do you a favor, son," he said. "Two favors, matter of fact. First one is, I'm not going to break both your arms for sassing me."

"I didn't sass you," Allen said.

"Do be quiet, Allen," Addie Grace said.

"She's right, Allen," the man said. "I won't give your girl the eye anymore, but I'll not be sassed. Not one more time."

Allen looked at Addie Grace. She held his gaze, and mute appeal softened her eyes. *Please. Please stop.* He looked past her out the window. The conductor strode by on the station platform, looking at his watch. The train was running late.

"The second favor," the man said, "is to give you some advice to pass on to your Colonel Custer and General Terry. You're going to find more Indians than you're expecting. Crook and Gibbon, the lot of you. There's been an exodus from the agencies, and the agents aren't reporting it. There's two, maybe three thousand fighting men waiting for you on the Powder River. Tell that to Colonel Custer."

The train was moving. Allen watched the little wooden station slip away. Some boys sat on a baggage cart with their legs dangling, watching the train.

"How do you know all this?" Allen said.

"I know the Indians. I've dealt with them.

Still do. Tell Colonel Custer you rode the train with Joe Merriwell. Tell him I said hello." The mockery had come back into his eyes, an edgy, mirthless light. "That should please him," he said.

"I'm going to get some air," Allen said.

He could feel her gaze on him as he rose. He went down the aisle to the rear door and pushed it open and stepped out onto the platform between coaches, into the noise and wind. The coach swayed, lurched; he gripped the railing with both hands and looked off across the pale green sea of prairie under the low luminous roof of the sky. Out toward the horizon the clouds seemed to float mere feet above the ground.

After some minutes the door opened and Addie Grace staggered out and he turned to her and she wrapped her arms around him and held on as if for dear life, as if the shifting platform might fling her off the train. Allen held her, braced back against the railing. He put his face to her blowing hair, smelled its summery sweetness.

"He'll *shoot* you, Allen," she shouted into the wind. "He's not to be trifled with, could you not *see* that?"

"I want to talk to you," he said.

"We're not allowed out here," she shouted. "The conductor says to get inside or he'll skin you."

"I shouldn't have left you alone with him," Allen said.

"Come back and stop riling him," she said.

"I need to tell you something," he said.

But then the door opened and the conductor jerked his head, ordering them inside, and Allen took her hand, and they went.

Merriwell smiled at him. "Feeling better?" he said.

"Some," Allen said.

"We apologize for provoking you," Addie Grace said.

Merriwell looked at her, smiling. He looked at Allen. "You were provoked yourself," he said.

"I'm sure it wasn't ill meant," she said.

"Oh yes it was," Merriwell said.

Addie Grace bit her lip and looked to the window. Allen watched Irwin, who was watching Merriwell and faintly smiling, as if this were an amusing interchange among strangers.

"I'm a forbearing man," Merriwell said. "You children are lucky, all three of you."

He tilted his bowler down over his eyes, folded his arms, bowed his head, and was asleep, accustomed, it seemed, to sleeping upright on a jostling train.

NINE

The Northern Pacific depot in Bismarck was surprisingly small and nondescript, a one-story brick building on concrete pilings with mullioned windows, a peaked roof, and a chimney at either end. People were strung out along the platform in the midday sunshine, and among them Irwin sighted a man, gangling and bearded, who wore a frock coat and John Bull straw hat.

"That's him," Irwin said. "Remember our story."

"It's *your* story," Allen said.

"You don't got to lie, you just nod your head."

Joe Merriwell opened his eyes, adjusted the bowler. He looked around at the three of them and smiled his mocking smile and did not speak. The train ground to a stop. Irwin was on his feet, pulling down his bag. Merriwell rose, found his. He got into his coat.

"Mind what I told you about the Indians," he said.

"I'll pass it on," Allen said.

Merriwell took a final look at Addie Grace, his gaze openly appraising as before. "Watch yourself with those soldiers at Lincoln," he said. "I'd especially stay away from Captain Keogh."

He smiled and turned and moved toward the door. Irwin followed him. Allen stood up, reached for his valise.

"Wait," Addie Grace said. "Let's let him go his way. The train isn't going anywhere."

He looked down into her eyes and saw himself there, saw the man he wished to be. He sat down and she took his hand. The coach was emptying. Below them on the platform men shook hands, men and women embraced. Irwin and his uncle had gone into the station. Joe Merriwell had disappeared around the corner.

"I expect he was right about the Indians," she said.

"I doubt it," Allen said.

"I expect he was," she said. "Now I have two people to worry about. You'll be careful?"

"Of course I will."

"And Allen . . ."

"What."

129

"It doesn't matter about the prostitute."

"Addie Grace . . ."

"Hush. It doesn't matter. It happens all the time, men and prostitutes. If I judge you, I have to judge half the world. What would I have cared about a prostitute if Mr. Merriwell had shot you?"

She turned into him and put her hand to his waist and offered herself to be kissed. Allen leaned out, looked up and down the aisle. The coach was empty.

"Move over here away from the window," he said.

Irwin and his uncle were sitting on a bench in front of the depot. Ruben Kohn stood up, smiling. The smile cut lines across his bearded face and aged him.

"Mr. Winslow," he said. "Miss Lord."

Allen set the bags down and shook his hand. Ruben Kohn shook hands with Addie Grace.

"You have been so kind to my nephew." He spoke in a thick German accent. "Please. Sit down. We talk. Irwin, move yourself over."

The street in front of them was very wide, and the plank buildings along it looked temporary, hastily built. They looked belea-guered by weather and the sheer disorienting immensity of air and sky, and they stood close to one another, huddled, as if for mutual comfort. The light was hard, a uniform glare that seemed to come not from the high white ball of the sun but from the sky itself, ubiquitous, scouring the wooden buildings and the wagon-rutted, hoof-pocked street.

"I owe you money, Mr. Winslow," said Ruben Kohn. "How much?"

"I didn't keep a close count," Allen said. "It wasn't much."

"I'd say about thirty dollars," Irwin said.

Allen laughed. "It wasn't anything like thirty dollars," he said.

"The man has stole more than that from Irwin. Them pickpockets, your father should have warned you, Irwin."

"This one was an expert," Allen said.

An ox-drawn wagon went by, canvas-covered, creaking and rattling, driven by a man in a Stetson hat and high boots. Across the street stood a weathered clapboard building with a false front: GOODNOW & IVES, WHOLESALE DEALERS IN BUTTER, CHEESE, AND EGGS. Next to it a cigar and liquor store: ONLY PURE LIQUORS SOLD HERE.

"I know he is not easy, our Irwin," his uncle said.

131

"He livened the trip up for us," Allen said.

"I told them about working at the Black and Tan," Irwin said. "Give him thirty dollars, Uncle Ruben."

"I have not seen Irwin since he is eight years old. Was when I live in New York. Even then he was difficult. He don't listen to his father, to the rabbi, no one. Eight years old. You should be paid for what you done."

"The train ticket was twelve dollars," Allen said. "That would settle it." He looked up and down the wide street, which ran both ways to the horizon, and wondered where the river was, the fort.

"This will settle it." The uncle reached inside his coat and dug a coin out of a vest pocket. It was a double eagle.

"No," Allen said. "Really."

"Come. You earn it. It is my way to thank you. It is Irwin's."

"Take it, Allen," Irwin said.

Allen shrugged and accepted the heavy yellow coin and dropped it into the pocket of his cutaway.

"I'm grateful, Mr. Kohn."

"No, I am grateful. The whole family will be. There is another thing. Irwin has tell me you are going with the soldiers against Chief Sitting Bull. You and Miss Lord's brother. I have something to help. To keep God present when you are in need of Him."

From his coat pocket he produced a leather pouch. He loosened the thong drawstring and removed a piece of lacquered wood the size and shape of a small knife handle. A strange trident-like symbol was scripted in black on one side.

"The Mezuzah," Ruben said. "It is attach beside our door, but I bring it with me for protection, because the river pass through the Indian country. Inside is a prayer from the Torah. It is keeping God present and remind us He is here. I give it to you now. Me and Irwin give it."

"You won't need it going home?" Allen said.

"We are in a boat. It is safe."

"What did you bring it for if it's so safe?" Irwin said.

Mr. Kohn looked at him and shook his head wearily. "Mr. Winslow, you have earn the Mezuzah."

It weighed almost nothing. The smooth, stained wood felt soft. A hole had been bored in one end and sealed with glue and a wooden stopper.

"What's this?" Allen said, pointing to the symbol.

"A Hebrew letter. Stand for God, *Shaddai*. Do you believe in God?"

"I don't know," Allen said.

"It is okay. God don't stay away because you don't believe in Him."

Allen stored the Mezuzah in his inside coat pocket. He stood up. "Where's the river?" he said.

"Is down that way. You take the omnibus. You find it at the livery stable up the street there."

"We'll write to you, Irwin," Allen said.

"Care of Kohn Dry Goods, Helena," Ruben said.

"Oh I hate good-byes," Addie Grace said.

She stood up, and Ruben with her, but Irwin stayed seated, tucked back with his thin legs stretched out, his worn scuffed brogans.

"Shalom aleichem," Ruben said. "Peace be to you." He gave Allen his hand.

"Good-bye, sir," Allen said.

"Good-bye, Mr. Kohn," Addie Grace said.

Irwin peeled himself from the bench, looked off down the street and offered a lifeless hand to Addie Grace, who stepped in past the hand and embraced him. Irwin stood passive a moment and then hugged her back, hard.

"Good-bye, Irwin," Allen said. Irwin's hand felt frail in his grip. Loose little bones.

"I wish I could go with you," Irwin said.

"The Indians would never recover," Allen said.

"Bring me back something. A headdress. A scalp."

"Be quiet, Irwin," said his uncle.

"I'll keep this by me," Allen said, patting the coat pocket where he'd stored the Mezuzah.

"God will be there," Ruben Kohn said.

They saw their first Indians outside the livery stable. Rees, they would learn, also called Arikaras, one of the tribes that scouted for Custer. They stood with their arms folded, one speaking, the other gravely listening. They were more bronze than red, Allen thought. A warm color. Rich. One wore a red-dyed flannel shirt, denim trousers, and a black felt hat with two feathers in its band, the other a white buckskin tunic decorated down the front with two ladders of black quills. Their hair fell to their shoulders. Both wore moccasins.

The one stopped talking, and they eyed Allen and Addie Grace with dour but unhostile curiosity. They looked at the valises and the Gladstone. Allen nodded in a friendly way. The Indians returned the nod, unsmiling. Allen followed Addie Grace into the livery office.

It was a small room, aromatic of sawdust. Behind the counter a man sat sideways to a rolltop desk with his feet up on an open drawer, reading a newspaper. He tossed the newspaper down and stood up.

"Miss Lord?" he said.

"Why, yes," she said.

"Ed Sample. Dr. Lord set me to watching for you. I met the Duluth train, but didn't see you on it."

"I'm afraid we lingered," Addie Grace said.

"You must of. Third day I met that train. I like to give up. They're going out in two or three days, you know."

"We'd like to get to Fort Lincoln soon as we can," Allen said.

"The next ferry don't leave till three. I'm to drive you to the landing. You might want to eat a bite first."

They said they would, and he recommended the Do Drop Inn down the street, where a steak and eggs dinner sold for twenty-five cents.

"You're going out with the army, ain't you," Ed Sample said.

"Yes sir," Allen said.

"It's a whole crowd going along. General Custer's got some relatives on board, I hear. Mark Kellogg's going. Telegraph operator, writes for the *Bismarck Tribune*. He's going to write it up for some big paper in New York City."

"Which one?" Allen said.

"One of 'em, I don't know. They say it'll make him rich. It's going to be some party when old Custer catches up with them devils. Like to see it myself."

"The Do Drop Inn, you say."

"Two blocks down, on your right," Ed Sample said.

The omnibus was an open-sided wagon with a pair of benches under a roof or awning, drawn by a single horse. Allen and Addie Grace were the only riders. They sat behind Ed Sample, holding hands, silent. The sun had moved down from the meridian, but the light, if anything, was harsher, whiter, more blinding. They rolled west on Main Avenue, past the little depot and switching yard with its several idle locomotives and strings of day coaches and freight cars, past a saloon and feed store and the whitewashed Capitol Hotel, where two men sat on rockers on a little gallery and silently watched them pass. There were a few women about, shopping baskets on their arms, and they saw two cavalrymen come out of a shoe and boot maker's, their

137

uniforms looking faded, sun-bleached. There were no trees. They passed another saloon, and another, and heard noise within, men's voices and the tinny notes of a piano. A drugstore, liquor dealer, barbershop stood shoulder to shoulder along a boardwalk.

Allen leaned forward and spoke to Sample. "It seems quiet. I heard it was rambunctious here."

"You come over at night, you'll see some doings," Sample said over his shoulder. "Was a man kilt only a few nights back over to the Exchange Saloon. Another got kilt a couple weeks ago at the Champion. Was a fight over a billiard game. Shot him with a double-barrel gun."

Addie Grace looked at Allen and he smiled, shrugged. *It's a bad business, but it won't touch us.*

"There's been a right smart of soldiers from the fort kilt over here," Sample said. "They get liquored up, you know. One gets shot, next night his friends come over looking to even it up. All got government Colts, so it ain't no shortage of weapons when they go at it."

"Is there no law?" Addie Grace said.

"The constable. But the fights are usually what you'd call two-sided. Both parties own the blame, or don't own it, depends how

138

you look at it. A fellow'll usually get off on self-defense."

The town petered out to freight sheds and shanties and, farther on, isolated houses, anomalies, domestic and built to last, with shade porches and shake roofs, barn and privy out back, perhaps a clothesline where bed sheets and red union suits danced in the prairie wind.

"It's some big grumbling at the fort," Ed Sample said over his shoulder, "because didn't nobody get paid come payday. Old Custer's holding on to the money till they're clear of here. Don't want to lose half the regiment in bar fights before he takes out after Sitting Bull."

The land now rolled suddenly downhill, and before them, on the other side of a fringe of bottomland trees, was the Missouri River, a mile wide, steel blue, sparkling in the fierce Dakota sun. The far bank was also wooded, with rolling pale green grassland rising beyond to meet the blue sky. There was no sign of the fort, or of any human presence. They rattled in a downhill zigzag course over humps and declivities, descending to a riverside clearing, worn to hard, bare dirt, where various weathered sheds stood in random placement, and where the side-wheeler *Denver* lay berthed.

"The fort's over yonder," Ed Sample said, pointing south. "It's about forty-five minutes to get there, what with the current and all. These steamers ain't the US Navy."

The *Denver* was a diminutive one-wheeler with twin stacks just forward of the pilothouse. She had an open forward deck where a canvas-covered wagon stood, and its horse. Several wagons stood uncovered and empty on the landing. Sample turned the horse, swung the omnibus around, and stopped. It was a quarter to three. A second wagon was inching over the broad ramp onto the steamer, the horse reluctant, hooves tapping a nervous dance, as if the animal were blind and feeling its way. A man came off the steamer and took the bridle and drew it aboard, talking to it.

"When you get across," Ed Sample said, "tell the soldiers who you and are, and one of 'em'll run get you a buggy. You don't want to hoof it with them bags."

"What do we owe you?" Allen said.

"Nothing, sir, Dr. Lord has took care of it. Your ferry too."

They had been holding hands all this time, and now Addie Grace released his, and Allen climbed down and lifted out the bags. Addie Grace got down with the rum-

140

pled blanket, which was begrimed now and stained.

"Tell Mr. Dolan who you are, and you won't need no ferry ticket," Sample said.

"You've been most kind," Addie Grace said.

"Tell Sitting Bull hello for me," Sample said.

"I'll do that," Allen said.

"Miss Lord, you stay on the Lincoln side of this river while he's gone."

"I intend to," she said.

"Good luck to both of you," Ed Sample said.

The old river steamer shook to the vibration of her engine as if the ague were on her. They moved easily enough at first, but near mid-river the current grabbed the *Denver* and took her downstream, driving her sideways. They beat their way across it by slow degrees and were better than halfway when the current took them south past Fort Lincoln, a sprawl of buildings on a long, gentle slope, all in formal arrangement, like a diffuse but well-ordered settlement or town.

"I thought there'd be walls," Allen said. "A stockade."

He and Addie Grace stood at the railing,

he with his arm around her waist. It was chilly on the river, and she pressed herself against him.

"George says the Indians will slip in of a night and steal horses, but there's no fighting. It's actually quite jolly. There are picnics. Sleigh rides."

"You'll have a grand time while I'm gone."

"I'll be miserable," she said.

Out of sight of the fort the steamer finally lunged clear of the current into slack water and immediately swung upriver, moving easily again. It was almost four o'clock, and the sun hung above the bare rolling country to their left. Below them the wagoneers came out and began backing their horses into their traces, talking to them.

"Allen."

He leaned back and looked at her. Her eyes were squinted, her face pale in this hard, flat light, her hair aflame. He pulled her in again.

"I'll wait for you," she said. "You and George. I shan't go back East until you come in."

"It could be a while," he said. "Past when school starts."

"I shan't leave until you're back."

"Aren't you in enough trouble already?"

"It isn't trouble," she said. "It's my new

life."

Her brother was on the wharf, his hands thrust down in his pockets, smoking a cigar as the steamer swung in parallel to the landing. Addie Grace stretched up on her tiptoes, waving.

"George," she cried. *"George Lord."*

Lord located her, plucked the cigar from his mouth, and grinned. He wore spectacles with smallish oblong lenses and had the longest handlebar mustache Allen had ever seen. It was waxed and as curvilinear as a great pair of horns.

"George!"

He waved to her. The *Denver* slid to a stop some ten yards from the bulkhead. Two soldiers had come down to the landing, and the deckhands threw the lines to them. They made her fast, and the *Denver* pivoted in on the aft line. Lord was directly below them now. His face behind the handlebar was sculpted in the neat, straightforward way of his sister's. He wore a dark blue flannel officer's coat unbuttoned over a blue fireman's shirt, cavalry trousers and boots, a trooper's campaign hat shading his face. He took a final pull on his cigar then dropped it and ground it out with his heel.

"It's the second damn boat I've met

today," he called up to her.

"George *Lord,*" she said.

"You'd better get used to some cussing, Gracie. It's rough out here."

"Your mustache, George."

"You like it?"

"I do not."

"I didn't think you would. Come on down, will you?"

She took Allen's hand, and they went in through the saloon, empty already, and down the stairwell to the freight deck. The engine had gone silent, and the hands were running the ramp out from the gangway on the forward deck. Some twenty passengers were waiting to get off, two officers among them, and the two enlisted men they'd seen coming out of the shoemaker's in Bismarck. They moved with the little assemblage — soldiers and frock-coated civilians and several women — up the ramp to where George Lord waited, smiling, eyes on his pretty sister.

"I didn't think you'd make it," he said.

Addie Grace put her bag down and fell into his arms. "We lost a day or two with late trains and so on," she said. "When do you leave?"

"Day after tomorrow."

"So soon?"

"We're late as it is. General Gibbon's been in the field a month now."

Allen had set the bags down. The passengers moved past them, drifting off in twos and threes. A fleet of conveyances — buggies, buckboards, a carryall — were waiting, most of them driven by soldiers. The first freight wagon was laboring up the steep ramp. A deck hand was pulling the horse as before, the horse balking at the incline, stamping and snorting.

"Mr. Winslow," Lord said. He had bright blue eyes like Custer's, but where Custer's blazed like blue suns, George Lord's danced, twinkled.

"Yes sir," Allen said and gave Dr. Lord his hand.

"Don't call him sir," Addie Grace said.

Lord fingered the upcurled end of his mustache, appraising his sister. The hard light glanced off his spectacles. "You look damn pretty," he said. "I'm going to have to beat the boys off with a stick."

"Can I pay you for my passage across the river?" Allen said.

"You've paid it," Lord said. "Anybody travels a week with Gracie ought to get passage to Europe, never mind across the Missouri River."

He picked up Addie Grace's two bags, and

Allen hoisted his own, and they followed Lord toward the buggies and wagons, many of which had headed up the worn trace past the long, low buildings near the river. Lord lifted the bags onto the rear of a double buggy, where a trooper sat on the box holding the reins, hunched with his wrists on his knees. Allen deposited his valise, and the three of them climbed up behind the soldier, Lord and Addie Grace on the front bench. Addie Grace slid close to her brother and took his arm. The driver roused the horses and swung the buggy around, and Addie Grace turned and smiled happily at Allen.

"Georgie," she said, "your mustache is ridiculous."

"Wait'll you see Godfrey's. It's twice as long as mine."

They passed what Allen now saw were six immense stables, arranged in a great rectangle. On the other side of the road crouched a white clapboard barracks with clothes drying on lines, uniform parts and undergarments. Outside one of the entries two lean, sun-browned women stood talking, watching the wagons and buggies go by. They wore plain cotton dresses and aprons, no hoops or bustles. Again Addie Grace dropped Allen a look, a smile, over her shoulder.

"What are you smiling about?" Lord said

"Who are those women?" Addie Grace said.

"Laundresses. Wives of enlisted men. Laundresses Row, they call this. What's all this smiling about?"

"I'm happy to be here. Can I not smile?"

In front of them now were the enlisted men's barracks, three buildings at least as long as the stables set along one side of a huge quadrangle. They swung to the left of the southernmost of the barracks and entered the quadrangle, a trampled, nearly grassless field, hoof-churned and dusty, with myriad clumps of dung baking in the sun. A flagpole stood near its center. Ahead of them two buggies and a buckboard were fanning out in different directions.

"The Parade Ground," Lord said. "That swell-looking house in the middle up ahead is the Custers'. You'll be their guest, Mr. Winslow."

"I will?" Allen said.

"Allen, how distinguished you are," Addie Grace said.

"I guess the general took a shine to him," Lord said.

"And why wouldn't he?" Addie Grace said.

Lord glanced at her, said nothing.

A white picket fence, like something transposed from another time and place, ran along this residential side of the field, which was opposite the barracks. Behind the fence stood a row of commodious off-white clapboard residences with front verandas, dormers, gable ends, a shade tree here and there. It might have been the back street in some somnolent New England town: Fall River, Salem, even Andover. The Custer house was more ample than its companions, taller and more rambling. The veranda was elevated, up a wide flight of steps, and there was a bay window to the south.

"Officers Row," Lord said. "Gracie, we're down to the right, last house."

The driver wheeled the buggy alongside the fence and stopped in front of the Custer house, where there was a turnstile gate. They got down and retrieved the bags. The soldier saluted and gave the reins a shake, and the buggy rattled lightly away.

"Are the Custers at home?" Allen said.

"Wait a moment," Lord said. "I'd like a word."

The Parade Ground looked to be a quarter of a mile across. On its north and south sides stood several large, plain, functional buildings painted the same off-white. There was no one about. The sun was still high, the air cool but with the caress of spring in it.

"What's up with you two?" Lord said.

"Whatever do you mean?" said Addie Grace.

"Holding hands. Secret smiles. Sweethearts already?"

"It's not your business, George," Addie Grace said.

"It sure as hell is my business."

"Do not curse."

"I love her," Allen said.

Addie Grace looked at him, head cocked, as if she didn't quite take his meaning. He met her gaze and nodded.

"Is that a fact," Lord said.

"Yes it is," Allen said.

"Gracie?" Lord said.

"And I love *him*," she said.

"Well," Lord said. "Well, well, well."

"George, you're embarrassing me," Addie Grace said. "I did not come thousands of miles to be bullied."

Then Custer stepped out onto the veranda. "What is this, a war council?" he said.

He wore a white buckskin jacket and fringed buckskin leggings and a broad-brimmed white hat. He folded his arms and struck a pose, a knee canted, and even here, from outside the picket fence, you could see or maybe only feel the blue incandescence of those deep-set eyes.

"Your protégé here has been making love to my sister," Lord said.

"Successfully, I hope," Custer said.

"Looks like it," Lord said.

"Well done, Allen," Custer said.

He unfolded his arms, came down the veranda steps. Lord drew a steel pin, unlocking the turnstile, and they went through in turn, lifting the bags clear, Addie Grace still with the gray blanket. Lord relocked the turnstile. There was a plank walkway between the fence and houses. They crossed it. Custer waited for them at the foot of the steps. His face was sunburned, and the sun seemed to have hardened him, turned him more compact and muscular than the willowy athlete Allen remembered from the Willard Hotel.

"Miss Lord," he said, and removed his hat and inclined in a brief bow. "Welcome to Fort Abraham Lincoln."

Addie Grace passed the blanket to her brother and curtsied. "Thank you," she said.

Custer shook hands with Allen, and his grip too seemed to have hardened. "Appears you had a good trip," he said.

"Yes sir," Allen said.

"A sweetheart wasn't what I had in mind,

Armstrong," Lord said.

"Well, you got a throw-in," Custer said. "Escort and sweetheart."

The door creaked and bumped shut, and Elizabeth Custer stood in the shade of the veranda, smiling down on them. *Yes, of course,* Allen thought. She was pretty rather than beautiful, but it was a prettiness that was beauty's equal, more intricate in its components, more delicate, more perishable. She wore a ruffled collar, lavender silk dress over a crinolette or bustle. Eyes black and bright and vivacious, auburn hair in a chignon, curls embroidering her temples and forehead.

"Miss Lord," she said. "Mr. Winslow. How splendid you've come. George, you and your sister must dine with us. Tom and Miss Wadsworth are coming. The Calhouns. I've no idea what Bos and Autie are doing."

"They're going to the play," Custer said.

"Perhaps Miss Lord and Mr. Winslow would like to see the play instead," Mrs. Custer said.

"It's foolishness," Lord said. "Tripe. *Michael Somebody, the Demon Lover.*"

"It's *Michael Erle,*" Custer said, "*the Maniac Lover.* You're a snob, George."

"I'd love to dine with you, ma'am," Addie Grace said.

151

"Yes ma'am, I would too," Allen said.

"Eight o'clock then," Mrs. Custer said, and a smile lit her quick, dark eyes.

Lord thanked her, passed the blanket back to Addie Grace, and picked up the two bags. "Front and center, Gracie," he said.

Again hugging the blanket, she looked at Allen and he at her, and with a smile of regret and longing she turned and followed her brother down the gray plank walkway.

"Handsome girl," Custer said, watching her.

"Yes sir," Allen said.

"Propose to her, did you?"

"Tell him it's not his business, Mr. Winslow," Mrs. Custer said.

"It *is* my business," Custer said. "I engineered the whole thing."

He picked up the valise, and Allen followed him up the wide painted steps.

"I'm afraid we're rather primitive here, but I can offer you a bath," Mrs. Custer said, and opened the door.

"Thank you, ma'am."

"George never mentioned the girl was handsome," Custer said.

"I think it sneaked up on him," Allen said.

"Time he knew it," Custer said.

TEN

In the coming weeks he would think with an almost disbelief of the house and its felicities, its comforts, its large hospitable rooms with their Brussels carpets and lace curtains and potted plants and high windows paned with spring sunlight. Books. Musical instruments: piano, harp. The doors and trim were of varnished oak, the walls of plaster as white and smooth as cream. Custer was a hunter and taxidermist, and even his trophies — head of a buffalo, a deer, several antelope, stuffed crane, eagle, fox — seemed to have adapted themselves to the gentility and refinement of the place, acquiescent in their new incarnation as decorations, conversation pieces.

Allen's room was on the second floor looking out on the Parade Ground. The bed had a carved oak headboard, and he imagined it in a room, say, in the Medici Palace. Marble-topped vanity, rocker, and table on which lay *Oliver Twist* and *The Mill on the Floss*. He would think of this room, this house, and wonder how George Custer could have so eagerly left it to hunt Indians in wild, forbidding country hundreds of miles away, and how he could so easily imagine returning and resuming a life of leisurely dinners, musical evenings, parlor games. As if the earth stopped turning while you were gone, and only began again when you were back at Fort Lincoln in the house with its piano and harp and velvet sofas. But the earth did not stop turning. It turned and it turned, and no journey ended where it began.

The regiment circled the Parade Ground counterclockwise in a column of four, slow, sitting erect and stone-faced while the band, mounted on white horses on the near side of the flagpole, regaled them with "The Girl I Left Behind Me." Swallowtail American flags stirred lazily in the breezeless air above the vanguard of each company — like medieval banners, Allen thought — these guidons stretching back at long regular intervals to the opposite side of the quadrangle, where the regiment emerged from behind the barracks in an endless-seeming procession. The men wore their dress uniforms: visored helmets sprouting golden horsetail plumes, dark blue sack coats with yellow collars and golden tassels.

"I see this and I always feel fortified," Libbie Custer said.

Allen turned, looked at her, standing next to him on the veranda behind Custer, who had no thoughts for them now, nor could hear them for the music and thud of hooves and jangle of accouterments. Her bright dark eyes were constantly darting, seeking, as if nothing were too small or banal to interest or delight her. She had long eyelashes and a cupid's bow mouth, and Allen thought suddenly of his mother and Custer at the Willard and wondered why Custer would take such a risk and why he would want to.

"Aren't they magnificent, Mr. Winslow?"

"Would you call me Allen?" he said.

She smiled, touched his arm. "Allen," she said.

"Yes," he said, "they're a sight, all right."

"I'm sorry you missed drill. That's when you really see something. The speed, the discipline. I'll think back on it when you're gone and take comfort."

Company C, which was in the command of Custer's younger brother Tom, had led the regiment, every man on a light sorrel horse, and Allen had seen then that each company had its identifying mounts: sorrels, bays, blood bays, blacks, the striking milky grays of Company E. As each new company approached for review, the commanding officer would shout an order and the sergeants would take it up: *Present arms, Pree-sent arms!* Then a great scrape of steel as sabers were drawn, the men holding them vertical before them, myriad gleaming arcs in perfect alignment up and down the column. *Eyes right,* came the order, and all heads would turn in unison to look at Custer on the edge of the veranda, saluting now, every man returning it as he passed.

The band kept it up. Horns, fifes, drums, the horses seeming to step in time. "The Girl I Left Behind Me" was measured, supple, wistful. Allen knew it from the Rebellion, and now he heard the sadness in it.

"The general *would* adopt this for the Seventh," Mrs. Custer said. She smiled. "To vex me, I sometimes think. He's a terrible tease, Allen. You'll see."

"I already have."

"The other regimental song is much jollier. 'Garryowen.' A drinking song, of all things. The general doesn't drink, as you may know."

"I heard that," Allen said.

Eyes right.

Present arms!

"That's Lieutenant Calhoun," she said. "The handsome one. He commands Company L. He's married to the general's sister. You'll see them tonight."

Calhoun grinned as he saluted Custer. They watched his company move on by. There were troopers here hardly older than Allen, beardless and smooth-skinned and boyishly slender, but the majority had a veteran, weathered look, and the hard gazes of fighters.

"That pink-faced man is Captain Benteen," Mrs. Custer said. "Company H. He hates the general and says the vilest things. Be on your guard against him." She bit her bottom lip, watching Benteen's company pass on their blood bays. "Lies," she said, "that don't bear repeating."

The band, with hardly a pause, struck up a new song, a brisk, buoyant, rollicking melody that lit Mrs. Custer's eyes.

"There!" she said, and again touched Allen's arm. " 'Garryowen.' Isn't it just right, Allen? They play it coming in. Nothing ever sounded so good."

"We've got to shake loose from Terry,"

157

Custer said.

"And the infantry," said Tom Custer.

"Why from the infantry?" said their sister, Margaret Calhoun.

"Because if we don't we'll never *find* Indians, let alone engage them," Tom said. He had little resemblance to his brother. His pale eyes were narrow and looked almost Asian. There was nothing of George Custer's warmth and ebullience in those eyes; Tom's burned coolly, fixedly, with cat-like patience. You could imagine him holding a grudge, nursing it. On his right cheek he wore a straight horizontal scar.

"What is this called?" said Emma Wadsworth, who was visiting from Monroe, Michigan.

"Game pie," Mrs. Custer said. "It's one of Mary's specialties."

The dining room windows ran from floor to ceiling and were twilit now in a satiny violet-gray. Candles burned on the table and lamps in wall sconces. There was wine, to Allen's surprise, though not in front of the general or Mrs. Custer. A trooper in dress uniform and white gloves waited table.

"What's in it?" said Miss Wadsworth.

"Everything," Custer said. "Venison, rabbit, pheasant. One of the hounds, I wouldn't be surprised."

"You'd wake snakes if it was," said his sister. "He treats the dogs better than he does his men, Miss Winslow."

Mrs. Custer laughed into her hand. "Miss *Lord,* Maggie. She's George's sister."

"Well, I knew that," said Maggie Calhoun. She had the pale blue Custer eyes and an attractive pout. Miss Wadsworth's face was a perfect oval. This, Allen decided, as the white wine deepened him, was a collection of very pretty women.

"Mr. Winslow is over there," George Lord said. "He's been pursuing my sister."

"What else is there to do on a long train journey?" said Lieutenant Calhoun. He was very fair, with white-blond hair. Handsome, as Libbie Custer had said, but fleshy.

"Question is, was the pursuit successful?" said Margaret Custer Calhoun.

"She won't tell me," Lord said. "Says it's none of my affair, which it is."

Everyone looked at Addie Grace, seated on Custer's right. They looked at Allen at the other end of the table, on the right of Mrs. Custer. He wore his dirty cutaway, a clean shirt and tie, the only man not in uniform. Custer wore his sailor's shirt with the wide collar, his red cravat.

"Cat's got their tongue," Lord said.

"Cat does *not,*" Addie Grace said, "and

159

I'll thank you to keep your trap shut, George Lord."

"That's the girl," Custer said. "Stand right up to the sawbones."

"You'll be glad enough to have me when you find Sitting Bull," Lord said.

"If I *do* find him," Custer said.

"We'll find him," said Jimmy Calhoun.

"Let's please not speak of Sitting Bull," said Mrs. Custer.

"Oh, why not?" Custer said.

"We're going to settle him, Libbie," Tom said. "For good and all."

"I'm sure you will," she said, "but I don't like to hear you talk so."

The trooper had come in with the wine bottle. Tom Custer crooked a finger and the soldier refilled his glass. Custer's gaze shifted over to watch this, and there was a loud silence, as if some unpleasantness were expected, but Tom lifted his glass and drank without looking at his brother, and Custer returned his attention to his wife.

"Let's have no more of this gloom," he said.

"Well," said Maggie Calhoun, "I still don't see why you don't want the infantry. It's more men, isn't it?"

"I'm wondering the same thing," Miss Wadsworth said.

160

"God almighty, I *did* explain it," Tom said. "Infantry slows you down, obviously, and Indians don't sit still. They run. Scatter. The whole problem is to get hold of them."

"*Do* let's change the subject," Mrs. Custer said.

"You're right, Libbie," Tom said. He glanced at her, then down. "I should learn to keep quiet."

"You should learn nothing of the sort," Mrs. Custer said.

"Gracie, tell them about the gunfighter on the train," Lord said.

"I didn't say *gun* fighter," Addie Grace said. "Only that he *had* a gun. You tell it, Allen."

Attention swung to Allen.

"Go on," Addie Grace said.

"He got on in Jamestown," Allen said. "He said he knew you, General. Joe Merriwell."

Custer's fork stopped halfway up. "Merriwell, was it."

"Yes sir."

Allen looked down at Addie Grace. She wore a borrowed green dress, and her hair was luminous in the candle and lamplight.

"What happened?" Custer said.

"He took a fancy to Addie Grace," Lord said.

"Allen stood right up to him," Addie

Grace said.

"I didn't," Allen said.

Custer was watching him, and Allen felt the hard glint of his eyes, a new appraisal going on. "Well done, Allen," he said. "The man's no good. Runs a brothel in Bismarck. I believe he sells guns to the Indians on the side. He was post trader for a while at Fort Robinson and got to know some of the troublemakers."

"I had to tell Allen to be quiet, or there'd have been a row, sure," said Addie Grace.

"How wonderful," Mrs. Custer said.

Her hand was on Allen's wrist. A fragrance of perfume. Her dark eyes seemed to catch and distill the candlelight.

"I'm glad you're riding with us, Allen," Custer said.

"Hear, hear," Calhoun said, and raised his wineglass.

"I wonder you didn't kiss her," she said. "I wonder you didn't get down on your knee and *propose* to her."

"What did you want me to do, slap her hand away?"

"You enjoyed it, Allen Winslow. Don't tell me you didn't."

"Well, sure," he said.

A chilly spring night under the blue-black,

star-whirled sky; a low sky, like the daytime blue, not so much above them as circumambient, engulfing. A slice of moon overhanging the river. They had left the Custer house with Lord and walked to his quarters at the end of the row, and Lord had said good night and gone in, and now Allen and Addie Grace sat on the bottom porch step. Lord shared the house with the two other surgeons and their wives, and they had gone to bed, apparently, for the first floor windows were dark.

"Did you get a bath?" Allen said.

"Don't change the subject."

"She *is* quite pretty," he said.

"I'm sure you think so."

"Don't you?"

"Yes, but you needn't make a fool of yourself."

"Did I?"

"You couldn't take your eyes off her."

A sentry came by, beyond the picket fence, strolling with his rifle on his shoulder. He looked at them, nodded cordially, went on.

"I had what they call a hip bath," Allen said. "You sit in a wooden tub with your legs hanging out. They fill it with cistern water."

"I am not interested in your bath," she said.

"When the cisterns run dry they fill them with water from the river. They bring it up in wagons lined with tin."

"It was improper for her to touch you like that."

"Like what?"

"You didn't notice, I suppose. What with all your wide experience with prostitutes and such."

Allen smiled. He turned, drew her to him.

"She *is* beautiful, Allen."

"So are you."

He pulled her in tight and kissed her, so neither of them saw Boston Custer and Autie Reed come up, nor heard them till Reed spoke.

"Evening," he said.

Allen quickly released her.

"Don't let us interrupt you," Reed said. He was grinning.

"We beg your pardon," Boston said.

He was fair like his older brother, clean-shaven, with the high Custer cheekbones and deep-set eyes, but with this difference: some vague melancholy or moodiness clouded his face. Reed was a trim handsome schoolboy. They both wore sack coats and matching trousers, string ties.

Addie Grace had straightened and looked away.

"You must be the general's new hire," Boston said.

"The question is, who is *this*?" Reed said.

"Addie Grace Lord," Allen said. "I'm Allen Winslow. Mr. Custer and Mr. Reed, I guess."

"Mr. Autie Reed," Reed said.

Addie Grace took Allen's arm. Autie Reed put his hands in his coat pockets and cocked his head over in an attitude of boyish swagger, and Allen saw a dull light in his eyes and knew he'd been drinking.

"What was your name again?" Autie said.

"Winslow."

"Hers, I mean."

"Miss Lord," Allen said.

"Can't she talk?"

"She's Dr. Lord's sister," Boston said. "You knew that. We been expecting you."

"What's her *name,* is what I'm after. Her first name."

"I told you her name," Allen said. "How was the play?"

"Right comical," Boston said. "Autie, let's go home."

"I'm about to go home myself," Allen said.

"To the general's house," Autie said. "Why is he in the general's house and we're in

165

Tom's, is what I'd like to know."

"You were in the general's house, you couldn't get corned," Boston said.

"Who's corned?"

"You are. Let's go home."

A second sentry passed. Allen gave him a wave, and he waved back. Reed glanced at him, then turned a drunken smile on Addie Grace.

"You want to go riding tomorrow?" he said.

"What's wrong with you?" Boston said. "She's taken."

"I don't ride," Addie Grace said.

"You're in Dakota Territory and you don't *ride*?"

"Not with you," Allen said.

"Hey," Autie said.

"It's his girl, Autie," Boston said. "Stop it now, and go on home 'fore the general sees you." He took his nephew's arm and turned him, and Autie moved wobblingly down the plank walkway.

"I'm sorry about this," Boston said. "A soldier sold him a bottle. He gets ornery when he drinks. There's a lot of drinking now we're about to leave."

"You might want to sneak him in," Allen said. "Your brother'll be home by now."

"I imagine Tom's too busy with Miss

Wadsworth to take any notice," Boston said. "Anyway, Tom isn't opposed to drinking. The general gets after him for it. Drinking. Cussing. He can be right hard on Tom."

"But not on Autie."

"Got a soft spot for him. His mother's the general's half-sister and a good deal older. She's been like a mother to the general, and the general'd do anything for her."

"Take her son into Indian country, for instance."

"Autie's dead set to go. Then he finds out about you and gets a little put out, thinks the general moved you up ahead of him. He's down as a herder, but it doesn't mean anything."

"Neither does secretary," Allen said.

"I know that, but Autie doesn't like the sound of it. Thinks it might say what it means."

"What's your job?" Addie Grace said.

Boston was standing over them with his hands in his coat pockets. Now he looked away and smiled a bleak half-smile.

"Guide," he said. "And I've never been south of the Yellowstone River."

"Then what will you do?" Addie Grace said.

"Not much I don't want to. We're going to have a grand time, all three of us. You

167

wouldn't tell the general Autie was corned up, would you?"

"Not on any account," Allen said.

"Well. Good night to you. Nice to meet you, Miss Lord. You *are* pretty, if you don't mind me saying it."

"I don't mind," she said.

"Good night, Boston," Allen said.

"Everyone calls me Bos."

"Good night, Bos," he said.

They watched him recede into the starlit night, hunched, with his hands pocketed. Slow. Thoughtful. Solitary. The moon had climbed higher above the river. From the bald hills behind them to the west came an occasional bawl from the scattered cattle herd. One of the guardhouse sentries stepped out into the pale moonlight and called out, "Eleven o'clock and all's well," and the two walking the perimeter repeated it in turn, and then a sentry at the infantry post up the hill to the north, and another, down near the stables, a final, distant iteration of the shuttling echo.

"A grand time," Addie Grace said. "A regular frolic. Do you give *no* credence to Mr. Merriwell?"

"He's a scoundrel," Allen said.

"Scoundrels can be right," she said, "and why did you not tell me you love me?"

"I thought it was obvious."

"I'd have enjoyed hearing it all the same," she said, and turned her face up in the soft whitish light before he could answer, and their kiss this time went uninterrupted.

Custer's study was to the right of the hallway as you entered the house, and the general was at work there, writing an article for *Galaxy* while Mrs. Custer sat opposite him, at a table against the wall. An oil lamp burned between them. A log fire danced on the hearth under the oak mantel.

"Come in, Allen," Custer said, writing.

Mrs. Custer closed her book. "We were about to send out a search party," she said.

Above the general in a gilt frame hung an engraving from a photograph of his younger self, the jaw set, gaze fixed and implacable: profile of a warrior. There was an engraving, too, of General Sheridan, and the immense stuffed head of a grizzly bear, not acclimated to domesticity as the parlor specimens seemed to be but with its mouth wide open in a silent roar of injury, outrage.

"I guess it took a while to say good night," Custer said.

"I wish it had taken longer."

Custer put down his pen. "He said he didn't want to be saddled with her, Libbie.

Didn't want to be a nanny. Destiny, Allen. Didn't I tell you?"

"Always listen to the general, Allen."

Mrs. Custer rose, taking up her book. "Good night, Allen." She extended her hand, wrist bent gracefully, and he wondered if he was meant to kiss it. He stepped forward, took it in his. He didn't kiss it.

"Good night, Mrs. Custer. I thank you for your hospitality."

"And I thank *you* for lending me a sympathetic ear."

Their bedroom was the room beyond. At the door Mrs. Custer paused. "Don't be long, Armstrong. You've a busy day tomorrow."

The door closed with a solid thump.

"Sit down, Allen," Custer said.

Allen did, in Mrs. Custer's chair. "What was that about?" Custer said. "Lending an ear."

"Nothing, really."

"It wasn't about nothing."

"No sir. It was about that pink-faced officer. With the white hair."

"Benteen."

"Yes sir."

"Benteen's all right, just bitter. He's had four children die before they were a year old. Spinal meningitis. It's made him spiteful. Jealous. He's a good soldier, all the same. All my officers are. It's the best regiment on the plains."

"So I understand."

"Tomorrow you join it. I'll write you a requisition, and my striker, Burkman, will take you over to the stables and pick you out a horse. The quartermaster will put you on the payroll. You're going to need clothes. Have you money?"

"About thirty dollars."

"The post trader'll outfit you for about that much. See how much he wants for a rifle, and I'll advance you money if you need it. You'll want a repeater. A Henry or Winchester."

"If it's all right, I'll skip the rifle," Allen said.

Custer eyed him. Smiled. "Are you a Quaker, Allen? A utopian?"

"I'm a secretary," he said.

Custer smiled. *Touché,* he said.

"I told you how I felt about the Indians. I'll come with you, but I won't help you kill them."

"They'll kill you as soon as look at you."

"I'll stay out of their way."

Custer was watching him closely. Assessing him with open and amicable curiosity. "A compromise, then: a government Colt.

The quartermaster'll issue it, and it won't cost you a cent."

"I don't think so," Allen said.

"You'd look ridiculous without a weapon. The civilian packers are armed. The surgeons. You run into a rattlesnake, you might be sorry."

Allen shrugged. "All right."

"I'll write the order, and an order for an A tent. Draw a mess kit. Haversack. Saddle, saddlebags, nosebag, and so on."

"One more thing, sir. Mr. Merriwell seems to think there are more Indians than you realize. He says they've been leaving the reservations."

"The Seventh can handle them."

"He was pretty emphatic about it."

"The Seventh can handle anything it runs into." Custer took up his pen. He dipped it. "How was your mother when you left her?" he said.

Allen looked at him. His eyes were clear, bright, empty of any double meaning or irony.

"I haven't seen her since Washington," Allen said. "I believe you've seen her since I have."

"Yes I have," Custer said. Again he dipped his pen, tapped it, shedding an excess of ink. "There are extra blankets in the cedar chest if you're cold," he said. "Sleep well, Allen."

"And you, sir."

ELEVEN

He wished he could march out at the head
of the Seventh and the Seventh alone, but it
was to be instead a ponderous host of
infantry, civilian packers, teamsters, herds-
men, farriers, mules, cattle, wagons, Gatling
guns, and platoons to operate them. This
lumbering column, half of it afoot, would
move at a snail's pace, and any Indian with
half a brain would outrun and outwit it, and
he would have despaired of any distinction
for himself and his regiment but for the near
certainty that sooner or later Terry must cut
him loose with the Seventh to pursue the
slippery hostiles, bring them to bay, strike
them.

All day the three superannuated river
steamers shuttled back and forth from
Bismarck, bringing laden wagons, horses,
mules, cattle, men. The wagons and mules
were assembled on the flat table of land
behind the commissary and quartermaster's

174

storehouse, a white canvas city with the mules picketed out beyond and the packers and teamsters traipsing unendingly back and forth loading tents, weaponry, tools, feed, and boxes of hardtack, salt pork, and coffee. The post was a beehive.

The enlisted men were exempt from their usual duties and spent the day reshoeing their horses, conditioning their saddles, writing letters, trying to dicker the post trader down for the hat, shirt, corduroy trousers, quart cup, or skillet they had so far been unable to afford. There was drinking in all three barracks, as Custer well knew, but today hc made no inquiries, ordered no inspections.

Mid-afternoon Burkman brought Custer's sorrel, Vic, to the house, saddled, then went and fetched the interpreter Fred Gerard, and Custer and Gerard rode across the bustling post to the Ree tipis above the river, just north of the stables. The Rees declined to live in the log cabins that had been built for them and had erected tipis north of the empty cabins. Oddly — it had amused Custer — they'd fashioned them from canvas, issued by the government, and these Ree tipis were a dingy rain-grayed white, quite unlike the sheer white hide ti-pis of the wild tribes. It was something to chaff Bloody Knife about.

Children were playing in the dusty out-skirts of this small tent village. A boy of perhaps ten or eleven had gotten hold of a hammerless Navy revolver and was using it to command his younger playmates, lifting it in his two hands and gesturing them first one way then the other, like a dance master. A squaw on her knees, scraping a hide, eyed the two officers curiously.

Bloody Knife's tipi was on the river end of the village, and Custer and Gerard dismounted at a respectful distance from it. They ground-tied their horses and went a little nearer. Gerard called out in Ree.

"I hope he's sober," Custer said.

"There's always the chance," Gerard said.

The tent flap was thrown back, and Bloody Knife stepped out, ducking his head. He wore a faded cotton shirt and denim trousers. His long hair was thick and had begun to gray. It was parted in the middle. He smiled in the laconic, knowing way he had when he saw his old friend Custer unexpectedly and said hello, *nawah cira,* in his own tongue.

"Nawah cira," Custer said, then told Gerard to tell him that he wished to talk for a few minutes and thought they might walk down by the river.

176

Bloody Knife answered in Ree and disappeared inside.

"He's coming," Gerard said.

He reemerged wearing a black wool vest. As they passed the horses, Custer spoke to Vic, and he looked at him and nodded and went back to cropping the sparse grass. Gerard's horse never looked up. The three men strolled toward the river, where cottonwoods grew, casting their cool, dappled shade. In the distance across the river was the flat bluff where the ramshackle saloons and brothels known collectively as Whiskey Point had been until the river flooded a year ago, sweeping them all away as in some Biblical retribution. The Heart River came in from the left, separated from the Missouri by a low, wooded promontory. They stood by the Heart, watching it swirl along in the sunlight to join the Missouri.

"We're getting old, you and I," Custer said, and Gerard translated.

"Then we're lucky," Bloody Knife said. His father had been an Uncpapa Sioux, and there was a Siouan secretiveness and obduracy in his lightless eyes and firm-set mouth and jaw.

"I have a pleasant surprise for you," Custer said.

"Because I'm old?" Bloody Knife said

through Gerard.

"Partly. Mr. Gerard is going to take you to the quartermaster, and you'll make your mark and become a guide, which will put you above the other Rees."

"I already am above the other Rees," Bloody Knife said.

"You will be paid more," Custer said.

"How much more?"

"Double."

"Good."

Custer smiled. He looked at Bloody Knife. The scout was studying the river. Patient. He leaned forward and spat.

"You don't sound grateful," Custer said.

"Why should I be grateful?"

Again Custer smiled. "For so much money, I'll expect you to be brave."

"Tell your soldiers that. Tell them there's big fighting ahead. They think it will be like going into the Black Hills, but it will not."

"They don't think that," Custer said.

"The Rees," Bloody Knife said, "are worried. She Wolf weeps and says let them go without you. All of our women are acting in a like way. It doesn't look right to them."

"It never does."

"Are your women easy in their minds?"

"About as usual."

"Let us lead the parade tomorrow,"

Bloody Knife said. "Let us ride ahead of the soldiers. We'll make a brave show and lift the spirits of the women. Your women and ours."

Custer and Gerard looked at each other. "Are you getting this right, Fred?" Custer said.

"I think so, sir," Gerard said.

"Tell him it's General Terry's decision, and that I'll speak to him. Tell him I think it can be done."

Gerard translated.

Bloody Knife nodded.

"Tell him it's my last campaign," Custer said. "Can you say lecture tour?"

"I can find a way."

"Tell him I'm going to leave the army and go East and become rich giving lectures. I want him to come and appear with me. Tell him —"

"Wait a minute," Gerard said, and spoke to Bloody Knife at some length. Bloody Knife watched the river.

"Tell him we can become rich together," Custer said.

Gerard did, and Bloody Knife looked at Custer and smiled. "You talk, and that makes you rich in the East?"

"If the talk is good."

"I didn't hear that it made Red Cloud rich."

"Red Cloud only talked once. And he met the Great White Father. You could do that."

Bloody Knife grinned. "I want you to be the Great White Father," he said.

Gerard smiled, translating this. Custer smiled. "No chance of that," he said.

"Why not?" Bloody Knife said.

"I have enemies," Custer said. "As you do. What about coming East with me?"

"We've a long road ahead of us," Bloody Knife said. "Let's talk about it later."

It annoyed Custer to be put off in this way, but he knew he'd get nowhere by pushing it. No one could understand his fondness for Bloody Knife, and very often he did not understand it himself.

"Go with Gerard and make your mark," Custer said. "And remember who it was who did this for you."

"You'll remember your promise about the parade?"

"I only promised to speak to General Terry about it."

"Speak to him with an eloquent tongue."

"I always do," Custer said.

TWELVE

They rode up over the hills to the west and out onto the trackless gently contoured prairie, among the scattered hundred or so cattle that would feed the column and on past them toward the rolling horizon. Allen's mare's name was Ginger, and her intuition and responsiveness were a new experience after the summers riding his uncle's farm horse, an obedient but listless mare named Princess. Ginger had belonged to a trooper in Tom Custer's Company C and had seen hostile Indians and seen fighting. She was a light sorrel with white socks and a white blaze on her forehead, for which cavalrymen had a superstitious dislike but which Allen thought smart, distinctive. She was seven or eight years old, according to the trooper who had chosen her for him, and she had a deeper chest than Princess, and more musculature in her legs. She was solid, compact: a warhorse. The *US* brand on her left shoulder, *7C* on her left rump.

"You'll be sore tomorrow," Lord said. "Your legs."

"Not very," Allen said.

Lord looked at him, handlebars flaring out, waxed. "Cocky bastard, aren't you."

"No sir."

"Don't call me sir."

"I've been playing baseball this spring. It keeps your legs strong."

"Baseball," Lord said.

"Yes sir."

"What did I just tell you?"

"How should I call you, then?"

"My name is George, or hadn't you heard?"

They were trotting the horses, still moving west, the sun directly above them. A trio of antelope watched them pass from a knoll. Allen was wearing the blue wool fireman's shirt and white corduroy trousers and hat he'd purchased at the post trader's. The hat was a broad-brim white Stetson, like Custer's and Tom Custer's. The quartermaster had given him cavalry boots and an overcoat. He'd given him a Colt and holster and cartridge belt and a handful of cartridges.

"You can ride, I'll say that," Lord said.

"I wouldn't be here if I couldn't."

"Don't flatter yourself. There are new

recruits back there who never rode till a few weeks ago."

Lord sat relaxed with the reins in his left hand. Allen had always posted when trotting, but this was the cavalry way, and he stayed in the saddle as Lord did, absorbing the horse's gentle, rhythmic bounce up through his back. He had declined spurs at the quartermaster's and already knew he didn't need them with Ginger. Lord didn't wear spurs.

"How do you get in the cavalry if you can't ride?" Allen said.

"The cavalry isn't particular," Lord said. "They took you, didn't they?"

"I'm not in the cavalry, George."

"You could be. They'll take thieves. Riffraff. Foreigners. There are men in the regiment can barely speak English."

"I thought it was the best regiment on the plains."

"It is."

They came to a ridge and slowed the horses to a walk and climbed it diagonally. On the grassy summit they reined up and sat looking out over the endless pale green hills.

"The noncoms are first rate," George said. "Tough. Brave as hell."

He dismounted and let the reins fall to

183

the ground and sat down. Allen got down.

"Drop the reins," Lord said.

"She won't run off?" Allen said.

"If there are no Sioux around she won't."

Allen ground-tied her and sat down beside Lord with his knees drawn up, flattening the long, sharp grasses beneath him. Gazing out from under his hat brim, his Stetson, which made him feel savvy and self-assured, as if to put one on made you a veteran of the plains. Lord removed his eyeglasses and cleaned them on his shirt. He squinted and looked blind without them. He put them on again and pushed them into place with his index finger.

"I suppose you think I've been hard on you," he said.

"Addie Grace said you were insouciant. She said you were fun. I'm waiting."

Lord tore a blade of jade-green grass and tasted it. He spat it out, felt in his coat pocket, and brought out a half-smoked cigar. He found matches in another pocket and lit it.

"She told me how you looked out for her," he said. "Kept the men off her. The rowdies. How you slick-talked the police in Buffalo."

"I told you: I love her."

Lord removed the cigar from his mouth, blew smoke. "She's got it pretty bad for you,

I'm afraid."

"Why are you afraid?"

"Because it happened so damn fast."

"So what?"

Lord made no answer, but only removed the cigar again and studied it, smoking, between his thumb and forefinger.

"It's going to go hard on her, this running away. Our aunt and uncle treat her like a scullery maid as it is. They could turn her out. It wouldn't surprise me."

Allen watched a hawk circle, coasting down lower to scrutinize them and then, satisfied, winging on.

"Suppose I stop a bullet when we're out in Sioux country," Lord said. "She'd be alone. Penniless."

"No she won't," Allen said.

"You don't have to marry her. Better you don't, at least for a while. But I want you to see she gets back East. See she gets situated. Those damn Ruggles won't care I'm dead. They'll turn her out anyway. She'll be in a hell of a jackpot."

George Lord ground the stub of his cigar down into the bent grass, the white dust that grew it.

"I'll look out for her," Allen said.

He turned, meaning to give Lord his hand on it, but Lord had risen and was slapping the chaff from his army trousers. "That's all I ask," he said.

THIRTEEN

Autie Reed and Boston Custer caught the last ferry, walking all the way from the brothel on Seventh Street and arriving at the wharf as the shore hands were coiling the lines to cast them off and the deck hands unfastening the ramp to the gangway. Boston had been reluctant to go, fearful that the general would find out, but Autie had begged and badgered him until a clandestine foray across the river seemed preferable to listening to him talk. It was why his nephew was here: the general, back in Monroe, had finally said yes, he could come, so Autie would leave off hectoring him.

In the saloon of the *Josephine* they found Captain Keogh, who had been at Little Casino's also and had passed them on the road coming back on his big bay gelding, Comanche. Keogh wore his white buckskin jacket and Boston and Autie wore theirs for the first time — breaking them in, Autie had said. Keogh, sitting at one of the round mahogany tables with a bottle and glass before him, gestured them over. Autie sat down with Keogh happily. Myles Keogh, with his red-brown vandyke: Mephistopheles, daredevil, soldier of fortune. He'd fought in the Rebellion and before that wars, and the Pope had given him a medal, which he wore on a thong around his neck. Women were crazy for him; tonight he'd been with Little Casino herself, and a few nights ago Miss Wadsworth, slightly drunk, had dropped a remark about Keogh and Libbie, and Tom had spoken sharply to her. Bos said he caned his men and cursed them prolifically, and that too raised him in the eyes of Autie Reed.

"You boys enjoy yourselves over there?" Keogh said. He spoke with a brogue that shaped his voice in pleasing rises, drops, and elongations, made rough music of it.

"Yes sir," they both said.

It had been Autie's first time, and Little Casino had figured that out and given him her youngest girl, name of Betsy. She was shy with him and not very helpful, and he was thinking about the rather desultory hour he'd spent with her and wishing he'd been less shy himself, more explicit as to his expectations. Clearly you had to do this a few times to get it right.

"You won't tell the general where we've been, will you," Boston said.

"Christ no," Keogh said. "Get yourselves glasses."

"No thank you," Bos said.

"I wouldn't mind," Autie said.

"Johnny," Keogh called to the barman, "give this lad a glass."

Autie got up and went to the bar. The steamer was nearly empty; enlisted men had been confined to barracks on this last night. A couple of civilians, teamsters maybe, stood drinking at the bar. They eyed Autie, considered his buckskins, as he accepted the tumbler. He sat down again, and Keogh poured him a couple of inches of bourbon.

"Our last fuck for a good long while," he said.

Boston and Autie looked at each other. Autie smiled. He took a burning sip of whiskey.

"It's a wandering life," Keogh said. "We're sailors, boys. We go to sea and live the spartan life and come home to our rewards. The ladies love a sailor. Especially us ones that ride horses."

Keogh had been drinking heavily. He'd ridden Comanche down the hill to the river drunk, but you would not have known it, he sat the horse so easily.

"Sir?" Boston said.

"What, lad."

"How come you to go with Little Casino tonight?"

"Now, what did I just tell you?" Keogh said. "The ladies love a sailor."

"I never saw her go with anybody," Boston said.

Keogh drained his glass with a flip of his big wrist. He set the tumbler down, uncapped the bottle, poured. He wrapped a hand around the tumbler but did not lift it and instead sat staring past it, at nothing. Withdrawn, until they thought he'd forgotten them or no longer cared for their company. The engine droned, rumbled, below them.

"The women are drinking of some poison," Keogh said. "They're all in a sweat, like it's Balaclava we'll be riding to. It got across the river, this poison. Did your girls not give you the special treatment?"

"Not that I noticed," Boston said.

"Yours, son?"

"He wouldn't know," Bos said. "It was his first time."

Keogh grinned. He picked up his glass and drank. "Congratulations," he said.

"When we come back, won't we have fun," Autie said. He drank.

"You look up that same girl and see what happens," Keogh said. "She'll fuck you till you can't walk, no extra charge."

"That'd be fine with me," Autie said.

"It's a soldier's reward," Keogh said.

Pretty Maggie Calhoun played the piano, song after song without pause, as if the music held time at a standstill and there could be no leaving this safe comfortable room, with its twilit bay window and snapping hearth fire, so long as she played. As if she could stave off midnight, sunrise, reveille, the departure. She played "Beautiful Dreamer," "Little Annie Rooney," "Jeanie with the Light Brown Hair," "Aura Lea," "The Golden Vanity," and, smiling, "When You and I Were Young, Maggie." She played "The Battle Hymn of the Republic" and "Rock of Ages." The general sang along in a flat but robust baritone that rather drowned out the other voices: Tom's, which was surprisingly soft and silken, Emma Wadsworth's, Calhoun's, Annie Yates's, George Lord's droning baritone, Addie Grace Lord's sweet, airy soprano.

Libbie Custer did not sing, nor did Allen nor Lieutenant Yates nor Lonesome Charley

Reynolds, the famous scout, who stood apart, back from the lamplight and the warmth of the fire, thoughtful, downcast. Libbie sat with her head cocked down, listening intently, as if there were some answer for her in the music, some clue to what was to come. Finally Maggie did pause, turning to glance about the room, looking quickly from face to face, searching each for — what? — affirmation, perhaps, a mutual belief in the music's power to hold them here now and always, to bind them together down the years, to preserve them into their distant old age. She swept them all with her anxious gaze, her wan, comely smile, and set her hands to the keys and began again.

"I'm going to sit awhile with Allen," Addie Grace said.

Her brother looked at her in the yellow light spilling through the Custers' front doorway, where Libbie and the general stood, she with her arm in his. George Lord looked from his sister to Allen, not liking it.

"Don't keep him up long, Gracie," he said.

"Love, George," Custer said from the doorway. "It's better than sleep."

"I'll take sleep," George said.

"I think both are in order," Libbie said.

"Don't be terribly long, Allen."

"Be as long as you want," Custer said. "Good night, everybody," and he and Libbie turned, and the door closed on them.

Tom Custer and Miss Wadsworth were walking arm in arm, south toward Tom's quarters a couple of doors down. In the distance across the Parade Ground they could see the dim figure of Charley Reynolds moving slowly toward the barracks. The lamps in the Custer parlor went out, and it was dark now under the porch roof.

"Good night, Georgie," said Addie Grace, and kissed George's cheek.

"Reveille's at five," he said.

"We're quite aware of that," she said.

George glanced at Allen and nodded, then turned and went down the steps half sideways, moving slow and woodenly, as if with reluctance. Allen and Addie Grace sat down on the top step and watched him go down the plank walkway past the darkened houses, the random isolate cottonwoods on either side. Addie Grace pulled her cape tighter around her.

"He's behaving dreadfully," she said.

"You're all the family he has. He'll come around."

"I wish he had a girl," she said. "I know he wants one. He only pretends he doesn't."

One of the sentries passed. He seemed not to notice them up here. Addie Grace took Allen's arm. She rested her head on his shoulder.

"Allen, listen to me."

"Sure."

"You don't have to go. They can't make you."

Allen leaned away and looked at her. "What's all this?"

"The songs tonight. The wives all so sad. They're frightened, Allen. I am too."

"I have to go. I've signed on."

"You aren't in the army. You haven't sworn any oath."

"I've no place to go. Mother fixed that."

"Stay here. With me."

"How would that look? Me sitting here, afraid to march out."

"You're not afraid, and I don't care how it looks."

"You would, in time."

"No," she said. "No I wouldn't."

A cow or steer lowed over toward the western hills, a querulous, dismal sound. Far to the north a coyote barked in falsetto, yammered.

"I'm in it now, Addie Grace. There's no going back."

"And you'll not change your mind."

"I can't."

She leaned forward and put her face to her palms, as if she needed privacy to think. She uncovered her face and met his gaze.

"Then here's something we must do," she said.

They climbed the stairs in stocking feet, Allen behind her, lighting their way with an upraised candle. The stairs were nailed solidly and did not creak. He closed the bedroom door very quietly, set the candle on the bedside table, and took her in his arms. They spoke in whispers.

"I have to undress, don't I."

It made him smile. "It'd help."

"I'd rather you didn't watch."

She moved away from him, outside the pocket of candlelight, and sat down on the rocker and bent to unlace her boots. Allen peeled off his coat, his tie. He sat down on the bed and removed his shoes, his socks He unbuttoned his shirt. Addie Grace had risen. She'd stepped out of her dress. She laid the dress across the rocker. She turned her back to him and looked down and unlaced her corset. She dropped the corset at her feet and stepped out of her petticoat, out of her pantalettes. Allen had finished undressing and gotten into bed. Addie

Grace stood with her back to him and her head bowed. Then she turned.

She was in shadow, but he could see her. Pale. Milky. Long-legged, small breasted. Lissome. He threw the covers back and she got in and lay facing him, eyes wide open, waiting for whatever came next. He put his hand on her smooth, warm shoulder and ran it around and down her back. The arch of her hip surprised him, and the firmness of her long back, and the softness of her inner thigh. Her breasts were the only girlish thing about her.

"You did watch, didn't you."

"You're beautiful," he whispered.

She smiled. "Am I?"

"What if you get pregnant?"

"I don't think I will."

"But if you did."

"You'd have to marry me."

"I'm going to anyway."

"Then it doesn't matter."

He moved to her, and she shifted onto her back, and he came over her and kissed her.

"Slow," he said.

"It'll hurt, won't it."

"I don't know."

"They say it does the first time."

"I'll be gentle."

"I know you will."

"If I do anything you don't like, just tell me."

"You never would," she said.

He could not tell if it hurt her. She cocked her knees and threw her head back and closed her eyes, much as Katie Doyle had often done, and he could not tell what she was feeling. Then he rolled back and she slid over into his arms. Her smell was wildflower-sweet, and he wondered how she kept herself so in this place of privies and hip baths and river water for washing and drinking. She slid her arm around his waist.

"I love your smell," he said.

"I should hope so."

"Did it hurt?"

"No. A little."

"Must you leave?"

"Not yet."

"George won't come looking for you?"

"He's asleep. He wouldn't anyway."

In a little while he was ready for her again, and this surprised her. It took longer this time, and Addie Grace moved with him, relaxing into it, letting it take her where it would. Allen groaned at the end, and she knew this was a compliment and hugged him for it.

They lay awhile, quiet. Then the sentries called two o'clock, and Addie Grace kissed him and swung out of bed as if she'd been doing this for years and went looking for her clothes.

He walked her home, both silent until they reached the surgeons' house at the end of the row. A tree grew near the plank walk, and they embraced in its shadow, where the sentries couldn't see them. No cattle bawled, no mules brayed at the wagon park. The stillness seemed empty, unpeopled.

"Are you all right?" Allen said.

"Fine."

"You won't regret it?"

"Not if you don't."

"I'm not likely to."

"Perhaps you'll think less of me now," she said.

"Perhaps I won't," he said.

"No?"

"God no."

"Allen?" she said.

"What."

"You enjoyed it, didn't you?"

"Of course I did. Did you?"

"Yes. Of course."

"It takes longer for a girl."

"What does?"

"The enjoyment. It's easier for the man. You'll see."

"It needs practice, doesn't it," she said.

"It needs not worrying about," he said.

"I did enjoy it, all the same." She smiled up at him, her face close to his in the darkness. "My love," she said.

"My love," he answered her. "My Gracie."

FOURTEEN

A haze overhung the post, suspended like a ceiling of gauze or gossamer with the air clear, transparent beneath. Reveille was sounded at five, and an hour later the Seventh Cavalry and the four companies of infantry that would go with it were assembled on the Parade Ground, the Seventh in a long double rank with the infantry arrayed behind it. On the cavalry's right flank were the fifty or so Ree scouts on their ponies, also in a double row. The Ree ponies were so much smaller than the big-chested army horses that they looked like dwarf animals. The Rees wore buckskins or white men's shirts and vests. They'd tied their hair back with rawhide or red ribbon.

Sitting their horses facing this silent somber army were General Terry, Colonel Custer, Custer's adjutant, Lieutenant Cooke, Custer's trumpeter, and his personal and regimental color bearers. Behind them, more loosely arranged, were the surgeons, the newspaper correspondent Kellogg, Boston Custer, Autie Reed, and Allen Winslow. Beside Allen, on a mare named Lulu, sat Mrs. Custer, sidesaddle, in a wool cloak and becoming man's black Stetson. Custer wore his fringed white buckskin jacket and leggings, as did Boston, Autie, and Kellogg. Tom Custer wore them, and so did Myles Keogh, and Lieutenants Cooke and Smith, and Captain Yates. Major Reno and Captain Benteen would not. Not if George Custer did.

Silence. Horses snorted, nickered, blew. General Terry dug his watch out from under his sack coat, opened it, looked at it, put it away. The morning was chilly with the haze interceding against the rising sun. Terry rose in his saddle, seemed to sigh, and lowered himself again. Custer turned, found Libbie and shot her a wink. She smiled, said something to Allen, who had been looking back over his shoulder at Addie Grace Lord, standing with Maggie Calhoun behind the picket fence, where the officers' wives had gathered. Emma Wadsworth was there also and the Custers' cook, Mary. Every woman clutching a balled handkerchief.

"Colonel Custer?" Terry said.

George Armstrong Custer smiled. "Yes

sir," he said. "Lieutenant Cooke?"

Lieutenant Cooke gave the order and the band, in the front rank, struck up "Garryowen." The parade began, the Rees peeling off to lead it, counterclockwise around the post. Allen rode beside George Lord, with Drs. DeWolf and Porter on George's other side. The surgeons wore linen dusters. Allen wore his fireman's shirt and the gun belt and holster, the heavy Colt, which was empty of cartridges. Libbie was well ahead of them, with her husband. The band came behind them, blaring "Garryowen," all brass and fifes. The tune frisky, saucy, a drinking song, an Irish jig, piping them gaily to war.

The Rees now were beating drums and wailing a tuneless dirge-like song, a counterpoint to "Garryowen" that drifted like woe itself across the chill and lightless morning. They passed the big granaries and the one-story clapboard hospital, where three inmates watched them from the gallery, wrapped in blankets. They passed the log guardhouse. Standing at attention with his carbine, the sentinel saluted.

The Ree women and children, the old men, stood along the trace in front of the empty cabins raising a plaintive din of moans, singing, and spoken adjuration. The women wore dresses of deerskin or cotton and some were young and pretty. Some stood, some knelt with their heads bowed in tragic resignation or prayer. Allen saw a child struggling with his mother to get away and run after the column. He looked at Lord and George managed a smile and shrugged. He had shortened his handlebar last night.

They turned right, behind the stables, the river now to their left, the landing, where the *Denver* was tied. The two sentries smiled, waved, cheerful; thankful, perhaps, for being left to garrison duty. The band kept it up and the Rees wailed their dirge and hit their small drums.

They swung around the stables and passed Laundresses Row, where the women had come out for a last look at their husbands. They were young and plainly dressed, and worry cramped their faces. Two or three wept into handkerchiefs.

"Maybe a parade wasn't such a good idea," Allen said.

"The damn Rees were supposed to lift our spirits, for Christ sake," George said.

They were now following the route the double buggy had taken two days ago bringing Allen and Addie Grace up from the steamer. They passed the barracks and skirted the Parade Ground toward the women waiting behind the picket fence. They passed the quartermaster's storehouse, the commissary with its round overhanging roof like a coolie's hat.

They came to the end of the picket fence and General Terry raised a hand and the column halted just south of the last house on Officers Row. The band ceased playing. The Rees had fallen quiet, and again the post was enshrouded in silence. Officers were dismounting up and down the column: Smith, Yates, Calhoun, Benteen, Tom Custer. The surgeons, Porter and DeWolf, got down. They all went quickly toward the gathered women, watched stonily by the enlisted men and noncoms, who had no such privilege.

"Are you coming?" Allen said.

"We've said our good-byes," George said.

Allen swung himself off of Ginger. The insides of his thighs burned from the ride yesterday, worse than he'd thought they would. Addie Grace watched him come stiffly toward her with tears in her eyes. He removed his hat as he approached her. She wore another borrowed dress — from one of the surgeons' wives — sky blue, and the straw sailor's hat he'd first seen her in. Some of the officers were pushing through the turnstile while others came along the inside of the fence. They moved apart with their wives. Fair Jimmy Calhoun hooked an arm around Maggie's waist and led her away. Tom Custer placed his hands on Miss Wadsworth's hips, a bold thing to do in public, and smiled into her tear-stained face before he kissed her.

"I know I look a mess," Addie Grace said. Her cheeks were wet, and she looked sorrowing and radiant and beautiful.

"You're the prettiest girl here," he said.

"I'm so frightened, Allen."

"We'll be back," he said. "Me. George. We'll come back the best of friends. He can walk you down the aisle."

He took her in his arms.

"You'll write," he said.

"Pages and pages. Have you the Mezuzah?"

"It's right here."

"Have you *Great Expectations*?"

"In my saddle bags."

"You'll look out for George."

"Promise."

"And yourself."

"Both of us."

He kissed her and held it. The officers had begun to break away, percolating out through the turnstile and along the fence. Maggie Calhoun sobbed, pressing her handkerchief to her mouth, as she watched Jimmy go out. Miss Wadsworth wiped her eyes with the sleeve of her dress. Allen leaned back, holding Addie Grace.

"See that you behave yourself," he said. "I don't want you kissing anybody while I'm gone."

Her eyes filled again, and the tears spilled down. She smiled. "Oh, I just might meet some charmer and can't help myself," she said.

"I'll come back and bust his nose," Allen said.

He kissed her once more, briefly, and they separated. Allen put his hand gently to her cheek, let it linger a moment, then smiled and redonned the Stetson and walked away from her.

He did not look at her again until they were riding toward the long low rise to the west. The band had jumped into "The Girl I Left Behind Me." He'd heard it sung often during the Rebellion, but the words now spoke themselves in the sprightly melody with such clarity and force it was as if they'd been written for him alone, his valediction, his heart song,

The hours sad I left a maid
A lingering farewell taking
Whose sighs and tears my steps delayed

I thought my heart was breaking . . .

Addie Grace waved, stretched up on her tiptoes, and Allen returned it, then went past the last house on Officers Row and lost her.

In hurried words her name I blest
I breathed the vows that bind me
And to my heart in anguish pressed
The girl I left behind me.

They rode up the treeless hillside toward a shallow declivity carved against the pale sky — their gateway to a future none could have imagined — and at this moment nature played the trick or stunt that to most would seem portentous but which, to the men, seemed only marvelous, a good omen if anything, as if they marched unearthbound, like gods.

The sun had begun to brighten the haze and in it, overhead, rode the mirrored column, not reversed but in duplicate, stretching out over the ridge, over the declivity, and vanishing into the sky beyond. A mirage, Libbie Custer called it. Addie Grace Lord saw it, lifting her skirt to run between officers' houses and watch Allen and her brother ride out of sight, and the vision stopped her dead, made her knees go weak. She stood hugging herself, trembling. Ghosts, she thought. A ghost army, which the sun will burn away as if it had never been. And as she watched, so it happened.

■ ■ ■ ■

PART TWO:
SCAFFOLDS

■ ■ ■ ■

Their first camp was in a loop of the Heart River thirteen miles from Fort Lincoln, and it was here, on the early morning of May the eighteenth, that Custer told Libbie good-bye. The men had been paid and she would go back to Lincoln with the paymaster's wagon, which waited now some twenty feet away, mules slumped and patient in their traces, the paymaster rolling himself a cigarette. All about them, the camp was being dismantled. Tents were collapsing, men were rolling their blankets and packing their saddlebags. Teamsters were reloading their wagons. There was the nerve-grating braying of mules. A bitterness of smoking fires on the cool air.

They had shared his narrow cot and coupled upon retiring and again when he woke her some hours later, and both times when he was done she'd wept, wetting his hard thin chest with her tears. What there had been of equanimity and her customary belief in him and the regiment had now given way entirely to the presentiments that had alternated with them, coming and going like dark scudding clouds in the weather of her moods. This damn apprehensiveness: it was infectious, and he did not know how it had begun, who had introduced it into their midst. He had never seen Charley Reynolds so glum.

Now she wept anew, throwing her arms around him, abandoning herself for all to see. He let her cry on him awhile, then peeled back her arms and held her facing him.

"You're a soldier's wife, Libbie," he said.

"I know," she said and sniffed.

"Be brave, then."

"I will when I have to be."

"You have to be now."

"No, Armstrong. No I don't."

Burkman stood by, holding Lulu's reins. A slow, strapping man, illiterate, dour, quarrelsome, alcoholic, and devoted to the Custers in the unquestioning selfless way a dog is devoted.

"Give me a kiss," Custer said, and he could not help thinking of Benteen and his plain, charmless wife and wondering if he was watching this.

She tasted of coffee.

"We'll all be back soon," he said, "and there'll be good times again."

"We'll go back to Monroe," she said, brightening. "And New York. We'll leave this place, Armstrong."

"Sure we will."

"Do you promise?"

"Of course," he said and turned. "John?"

Burkman brought Lulu forward and Custer helped Libbie mount her. Burkman handed up the reins. She sat sidesaddle with her pleated skirt spread around her, looking down at them through her tears.

"Say, Mrs. Custer, how old are you?" Burkman said, the voice thick, slow, gruff.

It brought new tears but also a smile; this was an old joke between them, the closest Burkman ever got to teasing anybody. Custer was a little tired of hearing it.

"Why, John," she said, "you know . . ." She sniffed, wiped her nose with her wrist, fought back more tears. "You know the general doesn't want me telling other gentlemen my age."

"Yes ma'am," Burkman said, "I done forgot."

"And John," she said and leaned down and placed a hand on his powerful shoulder. "You'll look after the general, won't you?"

"Yes ma'am."

"Thank you, John."

"Good-bye, Libbie," Custer said.

"Be careful, Armstrong."

"I will be," he said.

Fort Abraham Lincoln
May 17, 1876
My Darling Allen,
You never heard such weeping, such sobs. I had left them, had run like the girl that I am to watch you ride away over that depression or draw and saw your image in the sky, men and horses reflected in soft rainbow colors, the blue of the uniforms rather like stained glass. All of you riding away into the sky. What a fright it gave me!

And gave the wives, who, when I returned, had gathered in a sort of huddle and were weeping and sobbing as I have said, clinging to each other and dampening each other's shoulders with their copious tears. Well, I saw that *somebody* needed to be steady and dried my own tears and went among them in a quiet, reassuring way, telling them it was only — which I scarce believed myself — a marvel of nature and that a herd of cattle or a Sunday school picnic going the same way would have produced the identical effect, and would they have found *that* frightening? My words, I think, were wasted, but my manner and countenance seemed to give comfort, and I found myself — who initiated it I cannot say — embracing Mrs. Calhoun, whose grief seemed beyond consoling. We stood like that, entwined, for the longest time. Finally she let me go and held me with a hand on each shoulder and looked at me through her tears and smiled in the bright sad way she did last night, pausing in her playing. "Do you know what, Miss Lord?" she said. "They will never know how hard it is on us. They will never understand." The women at last began to disperse, moving disconsolately toward their different houses on Officers Row. It was over. You were gone. The day seemed to stretch ahead so long and empty I thought I should go mad.

How quiet it is. A horse thumps slowly by on the Parade Ground. A steamer whistles in the distance. The general's hounds know he's gone and raise a ruckus at any strange sound, thinking I suppose that they must be extra vigilant in his absence. How I will pass the time I do not know. There are books in this house, and at the Custers', as you know, and all up and down Officers Row. I shall be quite sagacious by the time you come in. I intend to finish *Eight Cousins,* just to spite

you. "Junk," indeed. You don't know everything, Mr. Winslow.

I do not relish the idea of spending the
summer as a housemate of Mrs. Porter and
Mrs. DeWolf. They are both nice enough
and have been kind, but there is an absence
of spark in them, of life. I would not have
said this ten days ago, but out here one
notices any blandness of character. It stands
out in this dramatic place and seems unfit-
ted to it. The West is no place for mice.

A circuit-riding chaplain, a Capt. Drummond, has arrived and taken up residence
in Tom Custer's house. He will be here
some weeks, it is believed, to provide succor
to the unhappy wives. Services will be held
in the Commissary Building, but I shan't
attend, for I have had my fill of religion both
in the suffocating Protestantism at
Chartwell and my aunt and uncle's joyless
Unitarianism. If there is a loving God He
will watch over you without my asking Him
to.

Your impious
Addie Grace

May 19
My Dearest Addie Grace,
Custer brought dogs! You may have no-
ticed that two were gone from the backyard

menagerie at the Custers'. One of them, name of Blucher, had been left behind at Lincoln but came after us, sniffing our trail, and caught us halfway to the Heart River, where we made our first camp. He was wild to be with Custer. These staghounds adore him. They lope along beside him as we march and sleep in his tent, draped over him on his cot, George says, like so many garments.

It is slow going so far and I'm beginning to let myself hope that General Gibbon or Crook, one, will have found and fought the Indians by the time we get out there. This morning we set out at five, and almost right away struck a stream so swollen from the rains that we could not cross and must detour far to the south, losing hours of time. The ground is sodden and the heavy wagons sink into it to the axles and must be dragged out by double teams of mules. The teamsters curse a blue streak, and I think of you and smile. We made about ten miles and quit at noon, and a savage thunderstorm hit us as we were making camp and many of the wagons not arrived yet. The enlisted men, before they can do anything else, erect the officers' tents and stoves and arrange their furniture, and they had scarcely done with General Terry's when the storm let go in all its fury, catching the rest of us unsheltered.

The sky was as dark as night. Lightning forked, the wind roared, and the raindrops quickly turned to hailstones the size of hickory nuts. The horses were terrified, and we all had to rush to hold them except the officers, whose strikers do everything for them. Poor Ginger whinnied and rolled her eyes and flung herself this way and that as I held her reins and spoke to her while the hailstones battered us. The mules bucked and kicked in their harnesses, and the crack of bullwhips cut across the din of wind and thunder and clattering hail. The cattle bawled in fright.

The storm abated by and by, leaving the ground a quagmire that sucked you down to your ankles. What misery! Everyone except General Terry and the senior officers — and Custer's staghounds — who had sought refuge in Terry's tent, was wet to the skin. Teams went back to the tardy wagons to help drag them through the mud.

Our camp today is on flat, open ground with no tree or stream in sight, a mile or so from a long, shapely hill or butte, formed of sandstone, I am told, and quite striking against the empty sky. There is no wood for fires. The alternative is "buffalo chips," but any that could be found were wet, so there are no fires except for the officers, for whom firewood is brought in their respective wagons.

When the sky was clear again the scout Charley Reynolds — he was at the Custers' on that last evening, you will remember — rode off alone and returned an hour later with an antelope slung across his horse's haunches. The antelope was cut into steaks for the officers, and I partook with George in his comfortable wall tent with Drs. Porter and DeWolf. The three surgeons share a striker, an amiable private named McAllister. He calls George "Doc," and George slips him food from his table. I am seeing the "insouciant" George at last. He is in high spirits and jokes that at the rate we are moving Sitting Bull will have died of old age before we find him. "Roughing it" clearly suits your brother, and I can detect a slight thaw in his treatment of me.

Despite George's sanguine view of the Indians, which I am beginning to share myself, the camp is laid out as though Indians might strike us at any time. The wagons are huddled at the center, animals about them, well-guarded, and then our tents, arranged by company, with pickets at close intervals and mounted pickets beyond them. No Indians could surprise us and I can't imagine any would want to. We are a host, over 1,000 fighting men, but I believe too that Custer was right that first night at dinner: we are too slow to come to grips with an elusive and wily foe, and that would suit me.

The candle is guttering down — I am lying on my cavalry blanket in my snug A tent — and reveille will be blown at four-thirty, so I will end. A courier, one of the Rees, will go back with mail tomorrow or the next day. I have scarcely spoken with Custer and in fact have hardly seen him. I make a fine secretary, don't you think? I think of you every minute, sweet girl I left behind me.

With all my love,
Allen

Fort Abraham Lincoln
May 20, 1876
My Dearest,

You'll never guess. Mrs. Custer has invited me to move in with her! I shall sleep in the very room you and I . . . how does one say it? I will not be vulgar. It is inappropriate to my feelings that night and ever since. Oh how can an act so *devotional* and that harms *no one* be thought sinful or wrong? I cannot ever go back to the Chartwell School with its sanctimonious teachers and mistresses who probably never once lay with a man!

"Miss Lord," said Mrs. C, "I have a favor to ask. I'm never without company in the evening if I choose not to be, but I must always return to an empty house, and I hate that. To return with you, or to find you there, would be *such* a comfort." Then she smiled in that dimpling way she has, brightening her eyes and adorning them with pretty crow's feet, and who could refuse her, man or woman? Not that I wanted to. I am not sure I *like* Mrs. Custer — I have not forgiven her for being so forward with you — but her prettiness and vivacity, rather than casting me down as they first did, now seem infectious or elevating. I feel pretty myself in her presence and very much older.

Miss Wadsworth left today. A soldier drove her to the river landing in a buckboard. Mrs. C and I saw her off. She was weeping, dabbing at her eyes with a handkerchief. "Don't be blue, Emma, you'll be back in the fall," says Mrs. C. "Oh but do you think Tom will have me?" says Miss Wadsworth. "Of course he will," replies Mrs. C. "My dear, he *adores* you."

Ha. The buckboard rolled away across the Parade Ground and Mrs. C said, "Our Tom will never settle down with any woman. He is married to the General and always will be." I looked at her, wondering if she thought this a good or bad thing, but she only gazed out at the diminishing wagon, squinting her eyes and biting her lip, thoughtful, as if she'd heard my question and could not find an answer to it.

Oh Allen, do not marry the General, for you are pledged to *Someone Else* of a gentler nature who will not lead you into the wilderness to fight red Indians with whom you have no quarrel and who will, to the contrary, keep you *safe*.

How quiet it is. The Parade Ground seems haunted by the ghosts of men and horses. We have dined several times with the visiting chaplain, who likes wine very much and becomes extremely amiable under its influence. Mrs. C attends his Sunday service more, I think, to humor him than to keep any covenant with God. I have told Mrs. C that I am a runaway from Chartwell, and what did she do but tell Capt. Drummond at table! The chaplain was drinking wine as usual and seemed not at all put out. He is a graduate of Yale Divinity and has little use for Unitarians, by the way.

I have read *Oliver Twist* and *Silas Marner*. I shall be *most* sagacious.

Your
Gracie

■ ■ ■ ■

May 21

My Dearest,

At noon this day the weather cleared gloriously, and moods improved accordingly. This damn rain — excuse me — with its soggy ground and muck and penetrating chill were making everybody grum and irritable save Custer, who rides far ahead of the column — miles — with Reynolds and the Ree Bloody Knife and the two dogs, scouting our route and I think merely enjoying himself. He will disappear for hours, even the better part of a day, and come in dust-begrimed, his fair face sun-blistered, his eyes alight with the joy he takes in being in motion on horseback and in this wild, barren, empty country he so loves. No weather depresses him, and I doubt he misses Libbie or any woman, his heart is so full.

The land changed too when the weather did, monotonous prairie giving way to great wide valleys with jade-colored hills in the distance and the grass thicker and more healthy. A fragrant west wind blew. And so we moved along, cavalry in two wings, right and left, wagons and infantry in between, cattle lagging along behind. I ride with

George ordinarily — he has become quite tolerant of me — but today, in the heartening weather, I fell in with Autie Reed and Boston.

Bos is quite adrift. He lacked even the mettle to attend college or university — George tells me the General was much fussed about this — and the only real job he has ever held was with his brother-in-law's freight office in Monroe, Michigan. He did not work there long. He has been at Fort Lincoln for nearly a year, employed as a "forager" and now as a "guide," both positions being fictions, excepting the salary, as you know. Poor Bos. With his buckskins he wears a high-crowned narrow-brim hat that you might see on the streets of Boston and beaded moccasins rather than boots. The ensemble is ridiculous — he looks as if he'd been dressed by a committee.

"Tell him," Autie Reed said to him as we rode along, "about the trick we played you with that Springfield." Bos smiled faintly — his smile always seems resigned, regretful — and did not take his eye off the way ahead. "You tell it," he said. It is an old gag, apparently, and I wonder Bos fell for it. They get you on the range for target shooting with a Springfield rifle, and after you shoot once or twice they give you a cartridge meant for an infantry Springfield, a bigger, longer gun. The two cartridges look the same but the infantry cartridge contains more powder. Tom Custer handed one to Bos while Autie and the General looked on, no doubt stifling great laughter. Bos put the cartridge in and the gun to his shoulder and pulled the trigger.

"It like to have tore my shoulder off," he said, "and the noise made me jump, I'll tell you."

"Uncle Armstrong near broke his gut laughing," Autie said.

"Fine set of brothers I got," Bos said.

"You wait," Autie told me, "they'll joke you too one of these days."

"No," said Bos, "they don't know Allen good enough to joke him. They know me too good, that's the trouble."

"Well," says Autie, "why don't they joke me? They know me pretty well, I'd say."

And here Bos gave a dry little smile and says, "That's why they don't joke you." Autie snorted and shook his head. He is usually quicker than Bos, but not always. He is meaner, for sure.

For instance: first thing, before every new camp is made, the men wade into the brush slashing with their sabers, cleaning out the rattlesnakes. They bring them out limp and decapitated. Autie borrows a saber and pitches in happily, slashing away with gusto and thinking it great fun.

It is nighttime, Gracie, and the band is playing. Custer sits in his camp chair with his arms folded and his head tilted back and eyes closed, letting the music wash over him. He smiles. Everything delights this man; he inhales the elixir of life with every breath.

A courier is expected tomorrow and I will look for mail from you. George says hello and promises to write soon. We still have seen no buffalo, only their leavings. We see elk and antelope and today passed a prairie dog town. They emerge from their holes and study us like curious busybodies as we pass.

All my love,
Allen

May 23
Gracie Dearest,
Indians! Three of them, silhouetted against the blue sky on a ridge some miles away, moving slowly, regal in their progress, as if haste were beneath them. Their tribe could not be ascertained, even by the Rees, but the prevailing theory is that they were Sioux who had left one of the reservations and were on their way to join Sitting Bull. I

thought, of course, of Mr. Merriwell and his warning.

Autie Reed said he was happy to see some Indians and hopes to see a good deal more. He and Boston carry rifles that hang from their saddles in leather scabbards and that they say they will use on the Sioux. Bos jokes about sending a buffalo robe and scalps home to his mother in Monroe, which I find obnoxious but forgivable in poor Bos. Even George smiles at his naïveté, and the hat, and the moccasins, and by the looks and smiles of the men, I judge they consider Bos a simpleton. Autie is no simpleton and says he will kill Indians and return home in the fall and "have something to tell the fellows."

Yesterday we passed two low conical rises that the white men call "Twin Buttes" and the Indians the more descriptive "Maiden's Breasts." These, as you can imagine, occasioned quite of bit of ribald humor up and down the column. Autie said they reminded him of his girl back home and asked me if they did mine, and I told him it was none of his business. His girl's name is Polly and she is younger than he, Bos says, and her father a blacksmith in Monroe. He says he knows for a fact that Autie never saw her breasts in the flesh.

Bos and Reed eat with Custer, who takes his meals in the hospital tent, which so far has been used for only that purpose, a source, I think, of some resentment in the ranks. Among the regular party at table are Lt. Cooke, Capt. Yates, and Lt. Smith and of course Calhoun. George would be welcome and I think I would, but George feels his place is with Porter and DeWolf, and I feel mine is with your brother. It is no deprivation; McAllister prepared roasted rib of antelope tonight, and a delicious soup.

The wind comes from the south now and is very dry and warm. It has become as hot as summer, and the mosquitoes have hatched in their myriads, and I am eager to stop swatting them and cover myself in the veil I brought. They slaughtered several cattle this evening, and the iron-like smell of blood hung on the wind. Good night, my love. The "Maiden's Breasts" reminded me of you, all right. Or should I say *yours*.

Your vulgar and devoted
Allen

May 27
My Own Gracie,
There is, I am compelled to tell you, an unpleasant side to Custer, which stems, perhaps, from the same driving impatience

that makes him fearless. We have come to the famous "Badlands," a forbidding landscape of hills, buttes, and escarpments of stone and clay, almost bare of vegetation. It is as if the land had suddenly turned angry, warning men not to trespass here. The massive formations come in many shapes — rounded, conical, flat-topped — like weird sculptings, all scarred and runneled by eons of weather. Some are flat-sided and evoke the Pyramids. They may be white, ash gray, or a clayey red. To get across the Alps would seem as easy, but we must get through somehow, and there is a valley, some miles in, through which a stream runs. Custer knows this country, having passed through during the Yellowstone expedition three years ago, and as usual he ranged far ahead to find the stream, and here arose the trouble that ignited his ferocious temper.

The column arrived at a place where the trace diverged. Custer was still miles ahead. General Terry summoned the Negro interpreter Isaiah Dorman, who sometimes rides out with Custer, and asked him which way he thought Custer had gone. Dorman guessed wrong. We rode 6 miles out of our way — the infantry are walking, remember — before Custer came back and found us. And did he light into Dorman! He did not curse but called him "nigger" and "stupid" and twice swatted him across the face with his hat till poor Dorman was on his knees in contrition. A good number of the men witnessed it and I knew by their faces that they found this unfair and excessive. Nor was it over: today Dorman must walk. You will say, "Well, the infantry walk," but their brogans are made for it while our cavalry boots are not, and poor Dorman by the end was limping painfully from blisters.

George says these rages pass like storms and that Custer does not hold a grudge, as Captain Benteen and Major Reno do. How George loves Custer and takes delight in Custer's affection for him! I do not say this in disparagement, for I have felt Custer's spell and will admit to a tug of pique at having been ignored by him thus far, a feeling not so unlike being passed over by a girl one fancies.

Gracie, the sun has roasted my face red as an Indian's. The mosquitoes are an awful nuisance. I am getting on in *Great Expectations,* though it is difficult by candlelight and with reveille looming at 3 or 4 o'clock.

We have finally seen some buffalo, ponderous shaggy things, but not many.

Your own
Allen

Fort Abraham Lincoln
  May 28, 1876
  My Darling Mr. Winslow,
  A steamer called the *Far West* arrived
today and the post reacted with such delight
you'd have thought Santa Claus had surprised us with a steamboat full of gifts, so
humdrum is life here these days. The
steamer was laden, to be sure, but not with
toys, bringing, rather, supplies for the fort
and for you, my dear, who will be met by
this same steamer on the Yellowstone River.
Word came up from the landing that it was
the *Far West* and all the officers' wives
hastened to greet her, all rattling down in
their various conveyances. Mrs. C took me,
of course. I am her constant companion
now, and she has begun confiding in me.
  The captain of the steamer is Grant
Marsh, a thin, straight, elegant man with
beautiful manners whose pleasure in Mrs.
Custer's company was conspicuous. They
were unloading, hauling boxes and trun-
dling barrels up the ramp where soldiers
grappled them into wagons, and Captain
Marsh invited all of us ladies on board. He
led us up some stairs to the saloon and

231

there, to our surprise — mine at least — ordered the steward to prepare us luncheon. The room, though small, is quite fancy: linen tablecloth, ceiling lamps and candelabra, velvet curtains. Capt. Marsh made to excuse himself, explaining that he must oversee the work below, whereupon Mrs. C rose from her chair and cocked her head in that way she has, and entreated him to stay. "We should be *so* pleased if you would," she said sweetly. Capt. Marsh hesitated — duty called, you could see that — then, with a shrug and a smile, replied that he would be "honored."

Mrs. C had something up her sleeve. She and Mrs. Smith were seated at the end of the table closest the door, and Capt. Marsh sat down between them, as they knew he would. I was next to Mrs. C, and how charming and attentive she was to the captain! You will perhaps think less of yourself when I tell you that she *touched* Capt. Marsh's arm twice or thrice just as she touched yours, a trick of hers that works *wonders* on men, it seems. The meal concluded — canned peaches for dessert, how wonderful they taste out here — the ladies began to rise and move toward the door, all except Mrs. C and Mrs. Smith. "Captain Marsh," said Libbie, "may we have a word?"

The Captain nodded and settled back down. I made to go, but Mrs. C said, "You may hear this, Addie Grace. It concerns you too." I pulled my chair back in. "Captain Marsh," says Mrs. C, "we should like to go with you to the Yellowstone." The Captain stared at her. Absently, he found his napkin and wiped at his mustache with it. "Mrs. Smith and I," said Mrs. C, "and Miss Lord. The General said we might. Didn't he tell you?"

Capt. Marsh put down his napkin. "No ma'am," he said.

"Well, he told *us,*" says Libbie. "It only depends on your being willing."

"Mrs. Custer," he said, "have you seen the staterooms on this little boat?"

"Capt. Marsh, I have slept in tents on the Kansas plains. I have spent nights in buildings where snow blew in through cracks in the walls."

The Captain saw that he must change his tack. "I have no space for you," he said, "but if you wait a week or two the *Josephine* will be heading upriver and you can come in her. She's bigger than the *Far West.*"

Her bright black eyes fixed on Capt. Marsh, who could not meet them. A moment passed. She smiled and touched his arm. "You're quite right," she said, "and it

233

was wrong of us to press it." ("Us?" Mrs. Smith never spoke a word.)

And so we debarked, and Captain Marsh received a lingering handshake for his trouble. They were loading on supplies now, for *you,* forage and medical supplies and ammunition, etc. A soldier drove us up the hill in a two-seater and let us down by the picket fence. The sun was down toward the hills, and the shadows creeping out. Mrs. Smith and Mrs. C exchanged pecks on the cheek and separated. "Mrs. Custer," I said, as we strolled toward the house, "did the General really say you could go to him?"

She looked on me mildly. "He did not," she said, "but he'd have been glad to see me."

"Will we go on the *Josephine*?" I asked.

"No, child. If Captain Marsh won't take us, Captain Simmons won't."

We had climbed the steps and gone inside and closed the door, and here she turned to me and gathered me in her arms. She smelled like roses. "Oh Addie Grace," she said. She was weeping.

You must be careful, Allen. You must, you must.

Ever your sweetheart,
Addison Grace Lord

Camp on the Little Missouri River, Dakota
Territory
May 29
Darling Gracie,
Still no Indians. General Terry expected
to find them in these Badlands where Davis
Creek meets the Little Missouri, but there
are none, nor signs of any. We have been
here two days. The camp is splendid, plenty
of water, and the grass rich for grazing. I
have had a bath in the river and wrung out
my clothes, and it was comical to see the
men frolic in the water, wrestling and
splashing each other like boys. They are
weary, especially the infantry, who are sent
ahead with alternating companies of cavalry
to build bridges at every river crossing, often
three and four times a day. Mean work, and
the men grumble.

I am suffering from sunburn and mosquito
bites (poor Ginger's fetlocks become constantly entangled with cockleburs) but must
confess that there is exhilaration in this hard
life, a sense of achievement. Could my
mother have been right in sending me? Per-
ish the thought.

The striker Burkman would see to Ginger

if I wished, but I curry and groom her myself. I feed her, waiting in line with the enlisted men to draw corn and grain from the quartermaster. George laughs at me, tells me I am a plebian at heart, as perhaps I am.

Yesterday Custer went out with four companies, including Tom's Company C and a gaggle of Rees, looking for the Indians Terry is so anxious to find. He took his nephew, who begged to go, ever eager for the opportunity to shoot an Indian. He was disappointed, as was Terry. At six this evening the detail returned, Custer and Autie and the Rees leading them in. You should have seen them! Coated head to foot with red mud, and the horses lathered and muddy. The General came cantering in ahead of everybody and popped down off Dandy as light and agile as when he'd begun the ride 13 hours ago. Burkman hustled over and took Dandy's reins. Terry came out of his tent. Custer smiled and swatted some red dust out of his buckskin. His face burns very pink and never seems to brown.

"Well, Colonel?" said Terry.

"It's bosh," Custer said, meaning Terry's notion that there are Sioux hereabout. "No Indians have been here for months, not even a hunting party." Terry's face fell. You've seen him: a thoughtful, sad-faced, languid man, and a wallflower alongside of Custer. Men had gathered in to hear, and they nodded as if they'd suspected as much.

Then in comes Autie, grinning, and reins up sharp and swings down off his horse and looks for someone to give the reins to. It was Bos who took them, Burkman being occupied with Dandy. Custer was following Terry to his tent. "By God we had a jolly time," says Autie. "You fellows should have come. We crossed that damn river over 30 times. The bottom was like quicksand and the horses kept slipping down and throwing us. By God it was funny. The General says we put in 50 miles, and you'd know it if you'd been along." I rather wish I had.

Dearest, you must write as often as you can, for the mail gets through as reliably as the post back East, carried by the intrepid Ree couriers, who come and go almost daily. They seem utterly at ease in the assignment, impervious to any thoughts of danger on their journey, which becomes longer by the day. They know the land as we never will, were born into its mysteries and hazards and move through them freely. They are said to be afraid of the Sioux, but I have seen no evidence of this.

237

Yours devotedly,
Allen

June 2
Dearest One,
Snow! We made about 10 miles on the
31st, working the wagons through a gorge
so narrow that they must squeeze through
one at a time with much hacking away at
the embankments and pushing them up
inclines, the men throwing their shoulders
into it, with much cursing.

The day was gray, raw, windy. We made
camp at 2 p.m. and that evening an icy rain
commenced to fall. The enlisted men were
huddled around fires with their coats over
their heads, dispirited and silent, while the
senior officers luxuriated in the warmth of
their Sibley stoves. Somewhat guiltily I accepted an invitation, with George, to take
supper with Custer. Tom was there, as
always, and Autie and Bos, and Calhoun
and Cooke, with his long, forking Dun-
dreary whiskers.

We dined on a Rocky Mountain sheep,
which Reynolds had brought in. The rain
beat along the tent walls. There was much
joviality, for they had played Bos another
joke. The three Custer brothers had ridden
ahead of the column when Bos felt a call of

nature and stopped. Tom and the General rode on and then circled back around a hill, dismounted, and spied down on Bos as he was completing his business. Bos cleaned himself up and mounted and looked around in some confusion as to where they'd gone — a "guide" receiving 100 dollars per month! — and the General fired a shot over his head, and then another. Bos thought the Sioux were upon him sure and spurred away in a panic and would still be riding, I think, if his laughing brothers had not overtaken him.

George and I crept back to our tents in the rain, and I slept warm with blanket and clothes piled on and woke to the blizzard. It was the 1st of June! Reveille at 3 but we went nowhere, not even Custer, except to see to our poor horses. Ginger, standing with her back to the wind and driven snow, seemed glad to see me, nickered and nuzzled my hand with a cold nose. The horses and mules are miserable and the men not much better. I built a fire in front of my tent, which did help, though some smoke blew in, and lay close to it and read *Great Expectations.* The snow fell all day. The pickets stood on the surrounding hills frosted from head to foot. The men went about cursing the weather.

In the afternoon the newspaperman Kellogg popped into my tent uninvited, with pencil and notebook. He is in his 40s, I should say, bespectacled, with rather protuberant eyes. He wears white buckskins, like Custer, a faux Indian fighter, and is correspondent for the *Bismarck Tribune* and the *New York Herald Tribune.* I told him my life story in four or five sentences while he scribbled in his notebook. I told him I'd solicited Custer for my position and did not mention Mother. "I've noticed you don't carry a weapon," he said.

"Sure I do, a Colt," I said.

"But no rifle," said he.

"No sir."

"Why not?" he said, his pencil poised.

"I'm a noncombatant," I said. He smiled as he wrote it down. "I've got me a Spencer carbine," he said, "and I hope to use it."

He closed his notebook, pocketed his pencil. "They're vermin, Mr. Winslow, don't you agree?" I said I didn't think we understood them any better than they understand us, at which he smiled an ugly and condescending smile and took his leave, stepping around my campfire.

Vermin? This from an educated man. How the two races, white and red, will ever live by side I cannot think.

Good night, sweetest,
A.

"You're feeling poorly, General," Custer said.

"Heat stroke," Terry said.

"Only on the plains," Custer said. "Was it two days ago it snowed?"

"Three," Terry said. "I'm all right now."

He was sitting slouched in his camp chair. His coat was unbuttoned. Boots muddied. Custer had sat down on Terry's cot. The stove had just been lit, and the air in the spacious tent was still cool, thin-feeling. Heat stroke. Custer could not imagine it. He could not imagine being laid low by any weather. He didn't know what heat stroke was, exactly.

"Your man Reynolds," Terry said.

"He made a mistake, Alfred," Custer said. "He's the best white guide out here."

"What did he do, lose his head?"

Custer smiled. It stretched his sun-baked skin. He imagined it cracking. "Charley Reynolds doesn't lose his head," he said.

"We marched eighteen miles for nothing. The men are wearing out. Think of the infantry."

"They rebound," Custer said. "They do what's asked of them."

Terry lowered his head, rubbed his forehead. He was becoming discouraged, Custer knew. He'd thought they'd find Indians on the Little Missouri and could not have been more wrong. Now he wondered whether they'd find them, at all.

"How in hell am I going to get a wagon train to the Powder River?" he said.

"I'll find a way, Alfred. Tom and I. We'll take Weir's company and the Rees."

"It's the worst of the Badlands. You won't find a road through."

"Yes we will."

"I've no choice but to trust you," Terry said.

"If that's a compliment, it comes out pretty lukewarm," Custer said.

"You worry me, George," Terry said.

"I worry a lot of people, and they're always wrong."

"Find a wagon road to the Powder," Terry said.

Fort Abraham Lincoln, June 3, 1876

My Darling, Darling Allen,

I have had such a fright, and I intend never to *see* my Uncle Gordon again, whose spite and willfulness know no bounds. Aunt Ruth, at the very least, is his silent accomplice and has likewise seen the last of me.

I have taken to walking as a way of filling the tedium. Yesterday morning at about 10 o'clock, I set out from home with *The Pickwick Papers* and went east across the Parade, which is going to weeds from disuse, intending to walk by the river, as is my wont. Mrs. C has given me a parasol and it is a welcome aid against the fierce light and sun. I was passing Laundresses Row when it dawned on me that there was a man following some distance behind, on his way, presumably, to the landing. A laundress was hanging clothes to dry, and she paused to study the man as he came on, and I briefly turned, following her gaze. I gave it no more thought and went on and turned right at the landing, where the *Denver* was tied. There is a cottonwood tree close to the bank, below the stables, where it is pleasant to sit and read and watch the river go by. I sat down with my back to the trunk and opened my book. A moment later I became aware of the man I'd seen minutes ago now advancing toward me. He wore a derby hat, sack coat and vest and bow tie, and an inexplicable pang of fear shot through me at sight of this well-dressed stranger. *Something was wrong.* He came on rather casually, looking about him at the river and the stables, and I averted my gaze and pretended to be absorbed in my book.

"Miss Addison Grace Lord." He stood over me, and now a second man, bearded and uncouth, materialized some distance back, watching with his hands to his hips, in case — I saw in an instant — he should be needed. "I am not that person," I said, for I saw it all.

"I wasn't asking, I was telling," the man said. "You have a look at this" — producing a visiting card from inside his coat — "then get up and we'll get a move on." I took the card. "Pinkerton's National Detective Agency," it read. The detective's name was William Cadwalader and he was "licensed," though it did not say by whom. "Your uncle sent me," he said, taking back the card. "You're going home." His assistant had moved closer. He was dressed in slovenly Western attire, a tough from Bismarck, I had no doubt.

"I must go fetch my things," I said.

"There'll be none of that," said Mr. Cadwalader. "I have a change of clothes for you. I have what you'd call your female necessaries. You get on up, now. You don't want to try my patience."

My darling Allen, I was *not* your brave girl, terror turned my insides to jelly. I envisioned a week on trains with this horrid man or perhaps the two of them, and, strange to say, thought of how dirty I should become, how slovenly and unwashed. Mr. Cadwalader would have hauled me to my feet had I not complied — he is a large man — and I rose on weak knees, leaving my parasol but still clutching *The Pickwick Papers.* Mr. Cadwalader took my arm with a steely grip, and I knew flight was out of the question.

He had crossed the river in a large skiff rowed by his thuggish hireling. Why he chose not to come on the steamer I cannot say, unless he feared some interference — a valid fear, as you'll see. The skiff looked small to me, you know how the river whirls and swarms along, but I remembered that soldiers cross in the dark of night in canoes to enjoy the delights of Bismarck and did not worry so much about drowning. We climbed down, the skiff rocked, Mr. Cadwalader sat me beside him in the stern and kept my arm until we'd shoved off. The *Denver* was some 30 rods away and I saw a deck hand pause in his work to watch us debark and felt a spark of hope. The sun beat down and the light glancing off the river hurt my eyes. "This here is Mr. Brown," said Mr. Cadwalader. I made no answer, nor looked at either of them. "He'll not be traveling with us," Mr. Cadwalader said. Still I said nothing. The river slid us sideways, but Mr. Brown was a powerful oarsman and pulled us across slantwise, angling north toward Bismarck. "Come, come," says Mr. Cadwalader. "Your brother's gone out, there's nothing for you here now." At that I began to weep. I was growing less afraid of Mr. Cadwalader, and it did seem to me that you, and George, would surely come to me in Cambridge as soon as ever you could, but a feeling of *loss* sat heavy in me. Something was being taken from me that I would never have again.

I believe it took us an hour to labor upriver to Bismarck, and I wept and did not speak once. "There, there," said my captor. And: "Won't anybody hurt you, Miss Lord. I'm a professional man and not in the hurting business."

Mr. Brown drove us straight to the railroad depot in a buckboard and left us, and I hope never to see him again. Inside the depot were two carpetbags. One of them, I believe, contained the change of clothes and female "necessaries" Mr. Cadwalader had mentioned. The train was not to leave for another hour. We sat down side by side in the platform shade. "It'll do you no good to

cry help," said my abductor. "Your uncle's
your guardian and has a lawful right to fetch
you home." He smoked a cigarette. He
looked at his watch from time to time but
did not seem impatient or restless.

It was nearly the end of the hour when
Mrs. Custer arrived, accompanied by two
soldiers. She swept around the corner like a
whirlwind, and were her eyes spitting black
fire! "What," she said, addressing Mr. Cadwalader, "do you think you are doing?" She
wore white gloves and carried a parasol and
looked lovely in a new way, resolute and
fiery. The soldiers stood in back of her,
unarmed but for their pistols. One of them
was a sergeant. Mr. Cadwalader stood up,
smiling easily, and presented his card.

"You must be Mrs. Custer," said he.

"I am," she said, "and I demand an answer
to my question."

Mr. Cadwalader shifted his weight, still
easy. "Her guardian requires she go home,"
he said. "She's run away illegal, as I'm sure
you don't know, or you'd not have abetted
it."

Mrs. C looked at me. "Why Addie Grace,"
says she, "did you not tell him you were
married?" I am so slow, Allen. I did not see
what she was about and only stared at her.
"She was married at Fort Lincoln," says

Mrs. C, "before her husband went out on campaign. Addie Grace, why didn't you say so?" Now I understood, fantastical as it was. Readily, I joined the game.

"I didn't think it would do any good," I said.

"She has no guardian but her husband," said Mrs. C. "I'm sure you know the law of that."

Mr. Cadwalader looked off across the tracks, thinking. "I'll want proof," he said.

Mrs. C turned. "Sergeant Riley," she said, and he reached under his coat and came out with a parchment document, which Mrs. C handed to Mr. Cadwalader. Our *wedding certificate,* dearest, dated May 14. We were married by the visiting chaplain, Capt. Drummond, who signed it, though he was not even *at* Lincoln on the 14th. Mrs. C signed it as a witness, and Mrs. Calhoun, and "George Armstrong Custer."

"Had your guardians' permission, did you," said the detective, perusing the certificate.

"No sir," said I, "I only met Allen on the train."

"Pretty quick work," said the detective.

"Quick or not, it's done," said Mrs. C.

Mr. Cadwalader looked at her. He looked at me. "Consummated, is it," he said. I blushed red and thought to tell him it wasn't his business, but Mrs. C jumped in.

"Yes," she said firmly, not knowing how *true* she spoke.

"Well then," says Cadwalader, handing back the certificate, "I guess I'll go home. Tell me, who is this lucky Mr. Winslow?"

I looked at Mrs. C. She gave a short nod. "He's from Salem, Massachusetts," said I. "His father died a hero in the Rebellion."

"Employed by General Custer, is he," said Mr. Cadwalader.

"Yes sir," I said, "but you may tell my uncle he is *not* a soldier and has no intention of shedding any blood."

"Very good," says the detective.

"You should be recompensed at least partially," said Mrs. C, reverting to her kittenish manner and *touching him on the arm.*

"I intend to be fully recompensed," he said, and I saw that he meant it, which will be bad news for Uncle Gordon.

It was the laundress who had alerted Mrs. C. Mr. Cadwalader had not looked right to her and she had gone to the river and found my parasol and seen the skiff in the distance, making for Bismarck. She had dashed to find Mrs. C. The *Denver* had brought her specially, an hour before its time.

Thus are we married, Allen, and we have proof of it. I am an *honest woman*. Captain Drummond, whose ethics seem somewhat elastic, did indeed sign the certificate, after, I am sure, some cajoling and arm touching by Mrs. C. Mrs. C signed for her husband in excellent imitation of his hand. We returned to Fort Lincoln on the *Denver*.

I must stop, it is very late, but I must tell you that Mrs. C looked in on me last night as I lay in bed awake, bringing a candle to light her through the dark empty house. She put the candle down and sat on the bed in its soft light, as my mother did long ago, and stroked my hair and told me I was a brave girl. I do love her, Allen. She has told me to call her Libbie.

Your own
Addie Grace Winslow

Camp on Powder River, Montana
June 8
Gracie My Love,

I have met Custer's enemy, Benteen, and a gentler and more genial officer, Lt. Harrington, who is second-in-command of Company C under Tom Custer. My encounter with Harrington was providential, but Benteen apparently was waiting his chance and saw it when we arrived here yesterday

250

after one of the worst marches so far, toiling over stony ridges and down deep ravines, a struggle especially for the teamsters and their wagons, with even more than the usual cursing of the mules. The day was hot and the men and animals parched, and when we came at last to the green valley of the Powder there was a stampede of men and beasts, and the officers let them go.

It was about 7, the sun descendant in the yellowing sky. The Powder twists along in its basin in great loops, and like most "rivers" I have seen out here would be called a stream in the East. Evergreens grow along its banks, and I left Ginger to drink and sought some privacy amidst some trees — there is not much privacy to be had, as you might imagine, and I will not go into camp plumbing arrangements, which would horrify you — and as I emerged on the side away from the river, I stood face to face with Benteen. His company had been one of the first to the river. I believe he had followed me.

"Sir," he said, "we've not met. I'm Fred Benteen." He has a round face and thick white hair and is likened by some to a beardless Santa Claus, but there is no benevolence in his gaze, which seems to be appraising you closely and not much liking what it sees. I shook his hand. More and more men and animals were arriving at the river — the teamsters had let the mules out of their traces — and there was considerable hollering and splashing, and we two were apart from it, near the trees.

"You're Mary Deschenes' son," Benteen said. I confessed to it. "Beautiful woman," he said. He is from Virginia, though he fought for our side in the Rebellion, and a gentlemanly drawl softens his voice. "I hear she and Old Hard Ass are good friends." (Gracie, I must write this as it happened.)

"Sir?" I said.

"Old Hard Ass. The Marat of the 7th Cavalry. Author of *My Lie on the Plains.*" I began looking around for a rescuer. (*My Life on the Plains,* he meant, Custer's celebrated memoir.) Even Autie Reed would have been a welcome sight. "I was wondering," Benteen said, "what your mother calls him."

"Sir," I said, "was there something you wanted to say to me?"

He smiled, and it is a mordant smile, sour. Smiling, he turned toward the trees and unbuttoned and commenced to relieve himself. "I just don't want to see you get in any trouble over this."

"Over what?" I said, after a moment.

Benteen finished his business. "Custer's

got his baby brother along; he's got his silly fool of a nephew. A retinue. Did you know that those worthless boys are receiving 100 dollars a month from the government?"

"It's what I'm receiving," I said.

"Just so," said Benteen. He dug a pipe out of his coat pocket, a meerschaum, and lit it, patiently drawing the flame into it while I waited. I looked around for George, Bos, Autie, *anybody*. Benteen shook out the lucifer and took a long pull on the pipe. "There may be trouble about it," he said. "Another Custer scandal. He was court-martialed in Kansas, you know. Left his regiment in the field and ran home to see his wife. Feeling horny, I imagine."

"Sir," I said, but he kept talking.

"If he hired you as a favor to your mother and the press were to get hold of it . . ." He eyed me now in a sly sidelong way, sucking on his pipe, and I knew he'd like nothing better than for "the press to get hold of it."

"Captain Benteen," I said, "these rumors about the General and my mother are lies, and with all due respect I don't think my job is your business. You want to court-martial me for that, go ahead." I was re-minded of Mr. Merriwell in the calm, faintly smiling way he looked at me.

"You've more gumption than the other

two," he said. "It may save you." He walked away, trailing pipe smoke, the smell of which reminded me of home. Save me from what? I wondered.

It was then that Lt. Harrington came by, too late to interrupt Benteen's attempt to cow me — partially successful, I will confess — but in time to observe Benteen's acidity and my unease. The two officers nodded to one another in a chill and distant way, and Harrington turned and watched Benteen move off to see to his men. Harrington is in his late 20s, I should think. His face is open and agreeable. "I imagine that was about the General," he said.

"Yes sir, it was," said I.

"Henry Harrington," he said, and gave me his hand.

"Allen Winslow," I replied.

"I'll tell you a story, Allen Winslow," he said, "if you'll allow me a minute."

I moved away to afford him some privacy — he is a more modest man than Benteen — and afterward we walked the short distance through the trees to the river where I had left Ginger, who watched us come, wondering where I'd been all this while. There was much bustle and activity on the campsite behind us, but the stock had been watered and canteens filled, and it was pretty quiet now by the river. Harrington sat down in the grass, crossed his ankles, and leaned back, and, while I unsaddled and groomed Ginger, told me that Benteen had disliked Custer in some unaccountable way from the very first, and that it came to a boil after the fight on the Washita River, where Major Elliot got himself killed.

Elliot was a great friend of Benteen's. They had served together in the Rebellion. After the village had been captured and the terrible work of burning it and rounding up prisoners was going on, Elliot led 20 men down the river, unauthorized, looking for more Indians to kill. "Here's to a brevet or a coffin," he famously cried out as he rode away. As you may know, he found more Indians than were congenial to his purpose, and he and his detail were found two weeks later, shot full of arrows and their throats cut, frozen solid in the Kansas snow. It is Benteen's contention that Custer callously abandoned Elliot to his fate, but according to Lt. Harrington, Custer didn't know where Elliot had gone, or why, and the Indians were massing downriver and he must withdraw or risk being overwhelmed himself. It was a good bet, anyway, that Elliot had fought his way back to the supply train. Benteen was *enraged.* He has not

255

stopped talking about it to this day.

"We're a divided regiment," Harrington said, "Benteen and Reno on the one side, Custer on the other."

"Who has the preponderance?" I asked.

"Why, Custer," said Harrington. "He is opposed by a handful of drunkards and misfits. A willful minority." He fell silent. I curried Ginger's back and flank.

"Why are you telling me this?" I said.

He was gazing across the narrow, coiling, dark blue river. "I didn't want Benteen to poison your thinking," he said.

"I shouldn't worry about that, sir," I said. Harrington, smiled, nodded, picked himself up, and went away whistling, leaving me, I will confess, feeling like a pawn in a dark and spiteful game.

I miss you sorely,

Allen

PS — I am forgetting an important piece of news. A few days ago three scouts from General Gibbon's command came seeking us. Gibbon is waiting for us on the Yellowstone and sends word that the Indians are south of the river and quite numerous. Three of his men made the old mistake — will people never learn? — of wandering off to hunt and the Sioux got them. The band no longer plays of an evening, and the night pickets have been doubled.

PPS — Today the Rees killed a buffalo and the surgeons obtained some. It is hardly different from beefsteak and very good.

Camp on the Powder River
  June 9
  My Lovely Girl,
  We are still here. General Terry has gone north to the Yellowstone, where the steamer *Far West* now lies. Your friend Captain Marsh is there, and General Gibbon.
  I have just spoken about this business concerning my mother to Custer in his tent, alone with him finally but for the staghounds, which lay about exhausted from running game. Custer for once was in residence in the daytime. He was working on another article for *Galaxy,* making use of this lull on the Powder. His orderly — it was not the slow-thinking Burkman who usually guards him — recognized me and admitted me with a nod. Custer was at his little field desk; he smiled and waved me in. He wore the gray-blue flannel shirt he wears under his buckskin, open down his chest. It was warm in the tent. I sat down in a camp chair. He put down his pen. His mustache has gotten bushy, but his hair was scissored off close to the skull before we set out, as

you may remember.

"I've missed you," he said.

"I've missed you, sir," I returned.

"You're having fun, aren't you," he said.

"Yes sir, I am."

"I want to see more of you," he said.

"I'd like that," I said.

"Come to our mess whenever you like. Let me know and I'll tell the cook." I said I would. "Have you any complaints?" he asked. "Are the men treating you well?"

"Fine," I said.

"No aspersions," he said, "on your position or salary?"

"One," I said. "By Captain Benteen. It's why I'm here."

Custer smiled. The incandescence in his eyes had softened to a twinkle. "The dyspeptic Benteen," he said.

I recounted our meeting. Custer's gaze rested on me the while, attentive, patient. "Captain Benteen," I finished, "must have heard some rumor. About my mother, I mean."

"It isn't a rumor, is it," Custer said.

I looked down in embarrassment. "No sir."

"I've never worried about your discretion," he said. "I took your measure at the Willard and haven't been disappointed."

"Thank you, sir," I said.

"Benteen," he said, "has said worse things about me. He's got a plain spiritless wife, and I told you about his four children. He's an unlucky man. Bad luck makes men snappish. It makes them spiteful. But he's a good soldier, as I also told you, and he'll do his duty. We can't worry about him, Allen. He'll say what he'll say."

I took up my hat, rose from my chair. A sudden boldness swept me up. "Do you love my mother?" I said.

Custer had remained sitting, looking up at me from the little collapsible desk. "I'm fond of her, yes," he said.

"But not as you love Mrs. Custer," I said.

"You know the answer to that," he said.

"Yes I do," I said.

Yours *entirely,*
Allen

Camp on the Powder River
June 10
My Own,
Here we are still! General Terry returned from the Yellowstone today bringing with him a most remarkable man, a scout and interpreter, whose addition to the command vastly increases my confidence in our collective good sense and my own safety. Mitch

259

Boyer is his name, and he rode in his youth with the famed mountain man Jim Bridger. He was attached to General Gibbon's column and has been snatched away to serve us. He is half-French, half-Sioux and as red-brown as any Indian, though he dresses as a white man, in shirt and leather vest and boots. He is thickset, not tall, his dark face broad and strong-boned, with bright expressive eyes. He speaks an English all his own, French-accented and strewn with oddities of usage and phrasing. Custer was so overjoyed he threw his arms around him, much to Boyer's amusement. I had drifted out behind Custer to watch their arrival, and Custer, in his elation, took me by the arm and thrust me at Boyer, introducing me as his "good friend and secretary." Boyer's hand was as rough and hard as sandstone and his grip like a vise, but he was smiling. "Secretary," he said, "what's that mean?" Custer laughed and clapped me on the shoulder. "Anything you want it to," he said jovially.

This happened mid-morning. At day's end, around 5 o'clock, Major Reno and the 6 companies comprising the 7th's Right Wing departed on what is expected to be a weeklong scout of the country to our west, with Mitch Boyer to guide him. Reno took no wagons — he will be moving too fast — only mules, which were selected from the wagon teams and proved not accustomed to serving as pack animals, or at any rate not inclined to. They are fitted with pack saddles called *aparejos* on which whole barrels and boxes can be piled and lashed down. The teamsters blindfolded the mules while they loaded them, and the mules seemed not to mind, but the moment the blindfolds came off they commenced to buck, kick, and bray, their burdens loosening, slipping down, and soon dropping off altogether and sometimes breaking. One irate mule took off galloping and raising such a ruckus it was feared he'd stampede the cattle herd. The cursing of the teamsters, and soldiers too, was beyond anything I'd ever heard. Some of us laughed pretty hard, but Custer said it won't be so funny when we are in the thick of things.

The Powder River is yellow in color and dyes our clothes when we wash them. This is our drinking water! We leave it tomorrow for the Yellowstone.

Ever your
Allen

"I only wanted to tell you that when the regiment marches, you'll lead it," Terry said.

Custer had stood up when he'd come in.

The hounds had woken and lifted their heads and eyed Terry briefly and gone back to sleep. Terry had never entered Custer's tent, and Custer could not think why. Maybe it was pure happenstance. Terry, of course, was a private and solitary man.

"You gave the scout to Reno to humble me," Custer said. "To show me you're in command."

"I gave it to Reno because I didn't want the men and the horses worn down before we fight. You don't know when to ease up. You go and you go and you go."

They'd remained standing. Casting vague soft shadows on the tent wall. Custer now dropped onto his cot beside the hound called Tuck. Tuck raised his head, glanced at him. Terry stood looking down with his hands clasped behind him. His long coat was open.

"Reno won't find any Indians," Custer said. "Or if he does find them, he won't fight them."

"The idea is to locate them," Terry said.

"He locates them, he'll alert them," Custer said. "They'll go up north of the Yellowstone or into the Big Horn Mountains, and we'll be all summer trying to get hold of them."

Terry smiled. "There's another reason I

sent Reno. I hate to say this, but I don't know how we're going to get the wagons to the Yellowstone."

"You've just been up there," Custer said.

"It's bad country. I couldn't have taken wagons."

"You want me to scout a way, as usual."

"As usual."

"Sometimes I think it's why you brought me. Like those guide dogs for blind people."

"Be careful, George."

"I'm sorry, Alfred. I'm all-overish. I just want to get to it. Find the hostiles. Hit them."

"We all do," Terry said.

Fort Abraham Lincoln
June 11, 1876
Dear One,

I have put Mr. Cadwalader and his henchman behind me, an unpleasant memory that ended well, but I no longer walk alone to the river. For exercise I circuit the Parade, going round and round it, which is monotonous, but *safe* from abductors and Bismarck thugs. The different soldiers on duty outside the Guardhouse chaff me good-naturedly, as do loiterers in front of the Commissary or the Quartermaster's storehouse. Aunt Ruth and Uncle Gordon (*I have not forgiven*

263

them nor ever will) say that it is *evil* to sup-
press the Indians and perhaps it is, but it is
evil work done by mortal men with some
good in them, and I cannot wish them ill.
Libbie says the General does *not* believe in
Extermination, as some "civilized" Ameri-
cans advocate, and that he much admires
the spirit and prowess of the Sioux and
Cheyenne, just as he admired the courage
of his adversaries in the Rebellion.

Have you heard the name "Monahseetah"? She is a Cheyenne maiden who was
living in the village on the Washita River
when the General attacked it. There is, I
think, a *secret* concerning Monahseetah
and the General, and I think Libbie knows
it. There were a great many captives taken
after the fight, and Monahseetah consented
to act as go-between and "interpreter,"
though she does not speak English. The
General brought the captives back to the
fort in Kansas where the regiment was then
posted, and Libbie could not but note Monahseetah's "dazzling beauty" and a certain
"affinity" between her and the General.
"But of course," says Libbie, "the General
is ever drawn to beautiful women and they
to him — it is a price I pay for having such
a perfect husband." According to Libbie,
"that vile Benteen" has whispered it about

that Monahseetah slept nights in the General's tent, as did other Cheyenne women with other officers such as Smith, Yates, Calhoun, and Tom. (It all sounds rather lecherous, but as a *Fallen Woman* myself, who am I to judge?) Libbie recounted all of this in an insistent and almost urgent way, as if to convince me that the tales are untrue. Really, I think it was *herself* she was trying to convince. Her claim that the General harbors no malice toward the Indians may be true, but I don't suppose it will do the Indians any good when he finds them. It did not, at the Washita.

Oh Allen, try to stay out of it. At bottom Libbie has little regard for the Indians — perhaps she has seen too much, the remains of men burned alive and dismembered, etc., and there is evil on both sides, it seems to me. It has become, as you can plainly see, a *confusion* to me. So *just stay out of it.* Then come back and we will go home and make sense of it together, if we can.

Do be good, no Cheyenne maidens in your tent, and I will be ever your

Gracie

Camp on the Yellowstone River
June 11
Dearest AG,

We broke camp at 5 this morning and made a hard march of more than 20 miles, up and down ridges and through creeks and gullies, bedeviled the while by cactus and biting insects, and some 12 hours later reached the Yellowstone River, where the *FarWest* awaited us. A sutler had come up and erected his tent, and inside it a makeshift bar of planks laid across barrels, and he has done a brisk business selling whiskey. The steamer brought mail, three letters from you. Custer and Terry were indulgent as to the liquor, and it is a drunken camp tonight with much raucous singing about the campfires, and the Rees beating drums and arguing drunkenly among themselves.

After supper Bos and Autie showed up in my tent, each with a canteen with whiskey sloshing about in it. They offered me a pull — several, actually — and I accepted. Bos said Tom stole his gloves today and that he is getting "damn tired" of being joked by his brothers. "Joke them back," Autie said. "Put a rattlesnake in Tom's tent."

"By God, I will," says Bos.

"I don't think that's such a good idea," I said. Autie took a pull at the canteen and laughed.

"I'll steal his hat," Bos said.

"Steal his boots," Autie said.

"By God, I will," Bos said, but I believe it was the whiskey talking, or so I hope.

The canteen went around and quiet set in, and I knew Autie had come in to tell me something. Pretty soon he says, "The General means to leave you and me behind when he cuts loose with the regiment."

"Cuts loose where?" I said.

"South," says Autie, "haven't you heard? He's to go after the Indians with just the 7th. Terry stays with Gibbon. The infantry stays. They'll come on slow while the 7th chases Sitting Bull in good earnest. Uncle Armstrong means to leave you and me on the *Far West.* I want you to talk to him. Tell him you want to go. If he takes you, he'll have to take me."

This was news, indeed. I felt a strange mixture of relief and dismay. I shall miss the travel and the camping, and George and Custer and Bos. "He won't listen to me," I said.

"He might," Autie said. "Anyway, you've got to try."

"You talk to him, Bos," I said.

"He won't listen to Bos," Autie said.

"No he won't," Bos agreed sadly.

I reached out my hand, asking for the canteen. Autie surrendered it and I had myself a long drink. "I'll talk to him," I said, "but don't get too hopeful."

"Keep at it," Autie said. "That's how I do. After a while he wears out and says yes." And so they left, unsteady on their feet, but Custer was aboard the steamer with Terry and was none the wiser.

Gracie, darling, you can relax. When Custer goes hunting his Sioux I will be on the Yellowstone, safe aboard the steamer. I will finally have time to finish *Great Expectations* and write endless, passionate letters to my sweetheart.

Always your
Allen

Fort Abraham Lincoln
June 13, 1876
My Own,

You'll never guess! Yesterday when the steamer brought the mail across came an envelope addressed to you from Mr. Harvey Wilson, Brainerd, Minn., which Libbie saw fit to entrust to me. I could not constrain my curiosity and made bold to open it — you will forgive me, I hope — and discovered within a money order for $30 (!) and a letter from Mr. Wilson, whose hunch regarding Chicago proved wonderfully prescient. He explained that he hung about the two stations, Wells St. and LaSalle, dividing his time about equally, sleeping on the public benches and obtaining food from vendors, all the while observing the passing humanity with an "eagle eye" — laying siege, so to speak. On the third day his patience was rewarded, for who should come through the concourse at LaSalle, fresh off a Westbound train, but Mr. Caldwell! I could not improve on Mr. Wilson's account of what happened next, and here it is:

The son of a bitch never seen me & I follered him out. He didn't carry no luggage & I guess he had just got done playing his tricks on some other fool such as me & Erwin for he had $$$$ on him all rite. I follered him on to that bridge near by to the station & wasn't no one about it was near about dark & I layed him out with a stick he still never seen me. Wilst he was flopping around tryeing to get his barings, he must of thought a strong box had fell on his head, I hit him another crack wich put him out cold & then lifted his pocket book & emptyed it for him of $90. Allen I am sending you $30 not $20 becuse you was good to me & trusted me & I told you by god I wuld pay you back. I am sending money as well to Erwin in Helena Mont. I am sorry I did not get the other feller Jenkins but when he sees what I done to his frend he myte think 2x before he goes to cheeting at cards agin.

It was lucky for him I didn't shoot the son of a bitch.

Darling, I shall keep the money safe for you, and Mr. Wilson's remarkable letter, which we will mightily enjoy in our old age. You might want to write him when you return.

Two days ago Libbie received a shipment of fresh strawberries by express from St. Paul, and invited the surgeons' wives to dine with us. (Capt. Drummond has left the post.) Mrs. DeWolf worries greatly, though her husband writes cheerful letters and seems to be enjoying the strenuous outdoor life. He tells her the Indians are nowhere to be seen and says it is pretty clear to him you will not see one all summer. I am much encouraged.

I have read *Wuthering Heights* and *Villette.* My legs have grown quite muscular with the walking. I think you will approve. Libbie has taught me piquet and cribbage. Cards! How raffish I feel! Libbie has her raffish side, do not doubt it. I wonder if the General quite sees it.

The days have grown long, not just with waiting but in literal fact, the sun burning round and white from 4 in the morning till long past supper, and the light as you know washing everything as though it had been

270

painted on with a brush. One so feels the lack of *shade* out here.

We should take Boston Custer East with us. He needs to get out from under his brothers' shadows. I will speak to George about it when you come in. We shall have so much to talk about!

Your raffish
Gracie

Camp on the Yellowstone River
June 14
My Dear Mrs. Winslow,

It is settled: Autie Reed and I will *not* march with Custer when Terry turns him loose — he will move south, as Autie said, up a creek called the Rosebud — on the trail of the Sioux. I waited a day and spoke to Custer after "Taps," when the camp was asleep and the only lamplight came from the *Far West,* standing alongside us like a low distended palace, and here and there, very soft, against the canvas of an officer's tent. Custer, always the last to retire and the first to rise, was at his desk, as usual. Burkman gestured me in, in his surly way. Custer seemed pleased to see me. His tent sits very close to the steamer.

When all else fails, tell the truth. I recounted my conversation with Autie Reed,

271

leaving out the whiskey. I said I was here only to keep the peace between myself and Autie, and that, while I was sorry in a way, I thought the decision to leave the two of us behind was both wise and sensible. I said I hoped he would allow Autie to believe I'd spoken otherwise.

Custer has a way of watching me as I talk, his gaze steady on me, and a little smile creeping out under his mustache. He never interrupts me and takes his time answering. "You seldom regret what you do, Allen," he says, "but you almost always regret what you don't do."

"Sir?" I said, not getting his drift.

"You'll always regret not coming with me," he said.

"I thought," I said, "you'd decided against it."

"And I have," he said.

"Then," I said, "you ought not to charge me" — I looked around at the amber-lit walls; a mosquito whined — "with coward-ice."

"You know I'm not saying that," Custer said.

"Timidity, then," I said.

"Not that, either," Custer said. "You've courage enough. I wouldn't have taken to you if you didn't. I don't like a poltroon,

Allen." I smiled. I do not think of myself as particularly courageous, only *sensible.*

"It's going to be more dangerous than you allowed it to be at the Willard that night," I said.

"I never said it wasn't dangerous. That was your mother's idea."

"You let her think it," I said.

"I let her think you'll come to no harm, and you will not. I'd see to that even if you rode with me."

"But it's settled," I said.

"I hope so," he said, rather cryptically, whereupon I said good night and took my leave.

Today the men relinquished their sabers, which were packed in crates and will remain here when we march tomorrow. I am told they aren't much use in fighting Indians, and they do make a deal of noise, clinking and jingling as the men trot along. How we will clear the brush of rattlesnakes remains to be seen. Bos says large sticks "work just as good." We will soon leave the band behind, as well, and the wagons. It is beginning to feel serious.

I Love You,
Allen

Camp on the Tongue River

June 16

Gracie Love,

Today occurred events that trouble me deeply and make me glad I won't be present when the command meets the Indians. We marched all day yesterday and today made camp on the Tongue River, some 2 miles below the Yellowstone, on bottomland where some Sioux had spent part of the recent winter. All about, in random scatter, stood naked tipi poles, lean-tos made of sticks and bark and sagebrush, and "wicki-ups," which are oval-shaped huts of hide and bark or brush built on arched poles. The main attraction, though, were burial scaffolds, which stood on posts somewhat higher than a man's head, upon which the bodies of men, women, and even children reposed, wrapped in colored blankets and provided, as if to assist them in another world, with bows, arrows, utensils, bone whistles, and all manner of trinkets. We made camp, and before stable call, as if a signal had been given, the men — I should say *some* of the men — went at the wickiups and graves like Vandals let loose on a museum.

Custer and Tom rode around to inspect the remains of the village that they might learn something of the enemy, and they did nothing to stop the pillage. Tipi poles were pulled down, wickiups smashed flat to the ground. The scaffolds were pulled down, spilling their contents every which way, and the men tore the blankets from the desiccating corpses and helped themselves to their possessions, to carry away as souvenirs. Men cavorted about the camp on horseback displaying arrows, horn spoons, necklaces, as if they'd won them at the county fair. The interpreter Dorman toppled a scaffold and dragged the half-mummified body of a young man to the river and slung it in because, they say, it smelled so foul.

Autie and Bos found me at the river watering Ginger as the mischief was raging. "Hurry up or you'll miss out," Autie said. He knows I have failed to move Custer so far as to our accompanying him up the Rosebud but believes I will prevail.

"Why don't you leave it alone?" I said.

Smiling, Autie showered me with more or less good-natured curses. "Namby-pamby," he said. "Nancy boy." I only shook my head. "Come on," Bos urged me, "find you something to send Miss Lord." Again I shook my head, how little he knows Miss Lord, and they shook theirs in bemusement and spurred off to desecrate some graves.

Autie appropriated a bow, six arrows, and

a pair of beaded moccasins, which he proudly displayed to me, visiting in my tent after supper. These arrows are fearsome things, as long as my arm, with flat, triangular, razor-sharp heads of iron a good finger's length in size. Autie says he will carry them home to present to his sweetheart, Polly. He said he will "surprise her" with them, and I have no doubt he will. Bos has a feather headdress but I didn't see it. Gracie, I don't like it. It puts us in the wrong, somehow, if we were not there already. Autie chaffed me, called me a "little old lady." "All I need now is a scalp," he said, and Bos said he would lift one too and send it home to his mother. There is a kind of lunacy taking hold as we come nearer the enemy, which I would almost call blood lust.

The mules gave more trouble today, throwing their packs off and sometimes refusing to move, but no one is laughing anymore. The band played "Garryowen" as we rode away, the last music we will hear, save bugles, for many a day.

Ever your
Allen

Fort Abraham Lincoln
June 17, 1876
Sweetheart,

Came a letter today from my Uncle Gordon *disowning me.* Ha. He does not know it, but I disowned *him* before he did me; I was *first.* Mr. Cadwalader, still in Uncle Gordon's hire, went nosing around and found out your age, and the identity of your mother, whose reputation, I must say, is a deal less than stellar.

Far from being Addison Grace Lord, you are Addison DISGRACED Lord, wrote my uncle, *and, caring so little for Ruth's and my patronage, you shall not have it. You have placed yourself in the hands of your stripling of a husband and his trollop mother and must abide the end. We shall bundle up your books and clothes and send them to you at that misnamed fort. Your ingratitude astounds us as likewise your cowardly flight, under cover of darkness, from the Chartwell School.* There was more in this vein, but you have the idea.

I ran immediately to Libbie, and we sat together on the top step of the piazza while she perused the letter. I watched her closely as she did and, once, her face darkened — her eyes narrow and the prettiest little wrinkles knit her brow — and she looked out across the Parade, thinking. I said nothing, and she went back to the letter and finished reading it. Then she refolded it and returned it to me. "You'll stay here," she

277

said, "until you and Allen decide what you wish to do. You'll be married here, and the General will give you away." She turned, trained her pert, infectious smile on me. "Your Uncle Ruggles sounds dreadful, child. You're well rid of him." She took me in her arms then, as a mother would, an aunt, a sister, all rolled into one, and I clung to her for dear life.

We separated, and again she contemplated the now-verdant Parade, her face drawn up quite serious, and said, "Is Allen's mother so bad as a trollop? I hear she's very beautiful."

"Beauty is skin deep," said I.

Libbie chucked her head forward and laughed a little melody. "So it is," she said, "and no less lethal for that."

I chose my next words with care. "She's a widow," I said, "and keeps company with one man, then another, which is her right. Uncle Gordon's a dried-up old prude."

"Lawrence Barrett introduced her to the General," Libbie said. "I rather thought she and Lawrence were lovers."

"They were," I said quickly, though I knew no such thing.

"Has Allen spoken of his mother's acquaintance with the General?" Libbie asked.

"His mother sought the General out," I

said, "to solicit him about Allen. It was only a practical thing." I am a poor liar as you have seen, but here, I believe, I quite rose to the occasion.

"A practical thing," says Libbie, as if testing the phrase for its weight or lack of it. "Well!" she said, brightening. "You'll be my daughter till Allen comes to claim you."

So I will, and how overjoyed I am that you will not march *into the jaws of death,* and I shall delight in picturing you on the deck of the *Far West,* reading Mr. Dickens and penning love letters to:
Your very own
Addie Grace

Camp on the Tongue River
June 19
My Sweetheart,
Reno is still out. Two Rees came in at sunset, sent by him, with the news that he found a trail and followed it to Rosebud Creek, in violation of General Terry's orders. Apparently he pursued the Indians no further — much, I have heard, to Custer's disgust.

George is disappointed that I won't be going with the regiment. "I was counting on you," he said, "to assist me."

"I've never seen much blood," I said.

"It's time you did," George said, rather unkindly. He has come down with a sore throat and cold in his chest.

When you write him next you might tell him you approve of my staying behind and in fact have been encouraging such sentiments right along. I would not want your brother to think me a shirker or worse. This is not the Rebellion. We are not fighting to emancipate any slaves, or I would "hold my manhood cheap" were I to keep out of it. I would say this to him, but I fear it would sound as though I "do protest too much." You might say it for me, Gracie.

It is very late, and I must close.

As ever,
Allen

He had never heard Reno laugh, had never seen him smile broadly. His young wife — Custer had to admit she was handsome — had died two years ago, and Reno had transferred his affection to the bottle, to which it had been no stranger in the first place. He drank, brooded, fantasized winning some prestige for himself. Without the girl, whose family was of the aristocracy back East in Harrisburg, Pennsylvania, Reno was nothing. A drunkard. A peeping Tom, it was alleged.

Now he'd botched the scout as Custer had foretold and disobeyed Terry's orders to boot, and Custer wanted to get to him before Terry did and ask him what in God's name he thought he was doing. With Benteen's left wing Custer had raced the steamer, moving parallel to, but out of sight of, the Yellowstone. They could see the twin threads of smoke from her stacks when they came up out of a defile or canyon, the smoke vanishing when they descended again into the hot shade of these narrow and unpredictable passes.

The race was won by the *Far West*. She was snugged to a hastily rigged pontoon bridge next to Reno's bivouac when Custer brought the left wing in, and Reno was already aboard. Custer threw himself off of Dandy and left her for Burkman. He strode aboard across the bridge and found Reno and Terry in the saloon, with Terry's aide-de-camp, Captain Hughes. They were seated at the end of the linen-covered table, Reno across from Terry and Hughes.

"You made good time, General," Terry said, looking up.

Custer was dusted red-gold all over and his face filmed in sweat. Only now did he think of this. He took his hat off.

"With permission, sir," he said.

"Sit down," Terry said.

He did, at the head of the table, and tossed his dusty hat onto a chair. Hughes nodded to him, smiled cordially. Reno watched him with dark beadlike eyes. The Man with the Dark Face, the Rees called him.

"Well, Major Reno," Custer said.

Reno eyed him venomously. It was true that Reno hated him. He and Benteen. He did not like to think about it, but it was plain as day.

"Your orders," Custer said, "were to stop —"

"We've been through that," Terry said. "The major has been reprimanded."

"Reprimanded?" Custer said. "He ought to be court-martialed."

"He found a trail," Terry said. "The hostiles were recently in the valley of the Rosebud."

"Oh?" Custer said. "And how many are there?"

"A lot," Reno said.

"You didn't follow them," Custer said.

"The scouts thought they were too many for me," Reno said.

"He wasn't supposed to go as far as he did," Terry said.

"So we don't know how many Indians

we're after, or where they're headed."

Reno and Terry looked at each other. Two dull, joyless men. Reno with his black moods. Captain Hughes looked on in the quiet noncommittal way of a good subaltern.

"We're going to find them," Terry said. "It's a matter of time."

"If they get into the Big Horn Mountains, we won't find them," Custer said. "Major, if you're going to disobey orders, you ought to do some good with it."

Reno smiled faintly. Sardonic. "You know all about that, don't you, sir?"

"Gentlemen," Terry said, "you two are going to need each other."

"It's just . . ." Custer said.

"Never mind, George," Terry said.

"Such an opportunity. God."

"Never *mind.*"

"We know they aren't on the lower Rosebud," Reno said. "That's something."

"It's more than something," Terry said.

"All right, say it is," Custer said. "Then what's the plan, General?"

"Captain Hughes," Terry said, "reach over there and get that map."

June 21, 1876
My Dearest Addie Grace,

283

I am going with Custer after all. We leave
tomorrow, south up the Rosebud. Don't fret
or worry. I have promised you all along to
behave with the utmost caution, and this
way — look on the bright side — I can keep
an eye on George, who is still uncomfortable with a sore throat and cold.

Someday I will look back on this and
understand my decision better, but for now
I must attribute it to a compulsion so
similar to *fear* in the way it began to nag
and haunt me that perhaps it *was* fear. You
will say, *Fear of what?* and my answer, if I
have one, is fear of a life spent regretting
the moment I said *No, I will stay here.
Whatever happens, I am safe aboard the
steamer, comfortable, idle. Go without me.*
Mighty events are impending, I can feel it,
and I am part of them now, willy-nilly, and
some inner voice commands me to see them
through to the end. You regret what you
don't do, Custer said, and I suspect he is
right. I did not want to come out here in
the first place but come I did, and it seems
to me it could be the mistake of a lifetime
to abandon the journey so near to its
conclusion, whatever that conclusion might
be. I am coming to believe in Destiny. There
is one for all of us. You and I are but one
example. Custer reads his destiny like a

summons in the affairs of men and entrusts himself to it, and he is destiny's darling. Gracie, I have to go. I have come this far.

Autie is going. He succeeded in persuading his uncle where (he thinks) I failed. It happened last evening. We were camped about two miles east of the Rosebud at the place Reno had landed after his ill-done scout. I had blown out my candle and was nearly asleep inside my mosquito veil when Autie inserted himself into the pitch darkness of my tent. "Allen," he said, "you'll never guess what." In his excitement he'd never sounded more the schoolboy, had never sounded more innocent. He might have been announcing he'd just won the Latin Competition or made the starting 9 in baseball. I pulled the veil from my face. I knew.

"I caught him at just the right moment," he said. "He thinks Reno might have queered the whole thing and he's in a hellacious mood. The regiment's going to follow that trail Reno found, but the General's afraid Reno's spooked them and they'll be all to hell and gone. I started in on him and he hardly heard me, he was so boiling. I said, 'Please, Uncle Armstrong. Oh God please. I'll be a laughingstock at home. All the fellows will want to know what I was doing sitting on a boat while you fought the Indians. I'll be called every kind of name.' He'd sat down when I came in, but his mind was somewhere else. Now he looks at me. You know how he does, those eagle eyes. He looks at me a long time. 'All right,' he says, 'but you're going to listen to me, and there isn't going to be any funny business with you and Bos. Just shut up about killing Sioux and lifting scalps and so on, and *do what I tell you.*' I said I would. I came straight over, Allen, to let you know. If you want to come — and I bet you do — go see him right away. The time is *ripe.*"

Just like that, the die was cast. Perhaps I felt some concern for Autie, with the thought I might save him from his own recklessness and miscalculation. I think I did. There isn't an ounce of fear in him — he seems blind to the menace in this stark land of jagged buttes and crags, of barren prairies. For a day or two I had felt the gnawing of that imagined lifelong regret, and now it seized hold of me and shook me — Autie Reed go, and not I? — and not many minutes after he left me I was on my way to Custer's tent.

He smiled when Burkman ushered me in, as if he'd been expecting me. He was at his desk, writing. "I was about to send John to get you," he said. "I was going to ask you if you'd changed your mind. I see that you have."

"May I ask why you changed yours?" I said.

"I didn't change it," Custer said, "I gave in."

"You changed it," I said.

He looked away, gazing into some private distance with a pensiveness and sobriety I'd not seen before. The dogs were strewn around like sacks as usual. "It's beginning to feel funny to me," he said.

I waited. Nothing. "How?" I said.

He shook his head, shook the thought away. "Anyway," he said, "I'd as soon have him where I can keep an eye on him. If I leave him on the Yellowstone, some sutler'll sell him whiskey, cheat him of his money, and then won't I hear it from Lydia." He studied me, unsmiling. I was still wondering what felt "funny." "You'll be doing me a favor by coming," he said. "You'll keep Autie from doing anything stupid. Bos has no influence over him." He then told me, in a businesslike way, that we would move in "light marching order," meaning no tents except the officers', and only A tents for them. He said he could not make an exception for me. "You will be sleeping in your clothes, on the ground," he said. "You will be living on hardtack and salt pork." Rather than dismayed I felt an odd exhilaration, imagining the warm ground under me and the starry sky as my roof.

"Thank you, sir," I said.

He looked at me with a quizzical glint in his eye. "For what?" he said. "I don't know," I said and laughed, and he did too.

The plan, as I understand it, is to trap the Indians between our command and General Gibbon's. Gibbon has all the infantry and cannot move as fast as we. General Crook with upwards of 1,000 men is somewhere to the south, but no one knows where or what he is doing, and we are not counting on his help except to block the Indians if they flee that way. Everyone is afraid they will get clean away, and I won't mind if they do. If Custer gets hold of the Indians he'll make mincemeat of them, I've no doubt, and I can only hope it will be less barbarous than the affair on the Washita, where women and children were shot down and the village was burned and horses slaughtered.

We have picked up six Crow Indian scouts, relinquished to us, as Mitch Boyer was, by General Gibbon. The Crows are quite different from the Rees in appearance, being larger and paler-skinned and, according to

George, more cleanly. They wear their raven hair swept back in a pompadour or else gathered in a tuft, like an exotic bird's, atop their heads. The Sioux are their ancestral enemy — they positively *hate* them and are eager to help Custer whip them. They know this area as the Rees do not, and Custer is delighted to have them. Boyer speaks Crow and will deal with them.

Gracie, this will perhaps be my last letter for a while. The Rees will carry Custer's reports and Mr. Kellogg's newspaper dispatches to the Yellowstone, but no mail. If the Sioux do not escape into the mountains it should all be over in a week or two, and then we will all come home, and you and I will get on with our lives. Wait for me.

Always your
Allen

After their final conference aboard the steamer, Terry and Gibbon walked with him to his tent, and the three men stood talking. It was mid-afternoon and the white sun shone down blindingly. Men were going back and forth across the pontoon bridge, unloading forage, lugging the heavy sacks on their shoulders, which bent them like old men.

"I've been in the field since February,"

General Gibbon said.

Terry and Custer looked at him.

"I've waited a long time," Gibbon said. "I've a right to be in on it."

"What right?" Custer said.

"You know damn well what I mean," Gibbon said.

"For God's sake," Terry said. "You sound like two children arguing about the last piece of cake."

"I haven't said anything," Custer said.

"Don't be greedy, George," Gibbon said. "That's all I'm saying. Leave some Indians for us."

Custer smiled. "I won't," he said.

"Won't *what?*" Gibbon said.

"That's enough," Terry said. *"Enough."*

That seemed to end it for now. Terry smiled, shook his head, indulgent of this bickering. "Get some rest tonight, George," he said, and he and Gibbon looked at each other and headed back without speaking.

The stove and all but one camp chair had been left at the depot on the Powder River, and the twelve company commanders crowded into the tent, kneeling or squatting. Custer received them sitting on his cot. He had stripped off his buckskin jacket. The smell of their bodies and unlaundered uniforms thickened the warm stale tent air, and Custer wished he'd held the meeting outside. Tom knelt a few feet away, hatless, watching him with patient intensity, as he might the face of an oracle. Benteen crouched off to his right, his wide, clean-shaven face, which was burned candy pink, bobbing stubbornly at the edge of Custer's vision. He was smoking his meerschaum and it was adding its sweetish stink to the malodorous air.

"Gentlemen," Custer said, "we move out tomorrow noontime. I guess you all know that."

They did.

He told them the mules would carry fifteen days' rations of hardtack, coffee, sugar, and salt pork and fifty extra rounds of ammunition per man. He said that each trooper would carry twelve pounds of oats and suggested that the company command-ers pack additional forage on their mules.

"General Terry," Custer said, "offered me four companies of cavalry from Gibbon's command, and I said no."

At this, looks were exchanged.

"Why?" Benteen said.

"If we aren't enough to whip the Sioux, four more companies won't make a differ-ence," Custer said.

"How many hostiles are there?" said Benteen.

Custer glanced reprovingly at Reno. "Nobody knows. Could be up to a thousand."

"A thousand," Benteen said.

"Possibly," Custer said.

Lieutenant Godfrey interposed. Godfrey had trimmed his handlebar mustache, but it still stuck out almost horizontal on either side.

"The mules that went with Major Reno are pretty worn out," he said. "What if they break down?"

"I don't know," Custer said, "but I do know this: we're going to follow the trail as long as it takes. We'll follow them to Nebraska if we have to. Keep that in mind, and bring what you want to. We may be living on horse meat before this is over."

"And when we find them . . ." Benteen again. He'd taken the pipe out of his mouth and was examining it curiously, as if it had suddenly tasted wrong to him.

"You had a question, Captain?" Custer said.

Benteen looked up and smiled a quick, tight, malicious smile. "Sir," he said, "if it comes to a fight, I hope you intend to support your officers better than you did on the Washita."

Silence. Benteen's smile looked as if it had been waxed onto his face. Custer saw Tom glance darkly at him. Jimmy Calhoun looked down into his lap.

"I'll support anyone who obeys orders," Custer said.

"That's not what I asked you," Benteen said.

"You want to talk about the Washita?" Tom said. "Talk about that boy you shot."

It jarred the smile from Benteen's face. "That goddamn boy, as you call him, was aiming a pistol at me."

"How old was he?" Custer said. "Six? Seven?"

"He was old enough to shoot me," Benteen said.

"Was he."

"He had a goddamn army Colt," Benteen said.

"Dismissed," Custer said. "All of you."

"He had it full cocked," Benteen said.

"Dismissed," Custer said and turned his back on him.

Fort Abraham Lincoln
June 22, 1876
Oh, Allen,
News has come of General Crook's fight on the Rosebud Creek and, far worse, new

293

reports of Indians deserting the agencies to take the field against you, at least 1,000 more than General Sheridan knew of, or General Terry, *or* Custer. I have taken to saying a prayer at night, the 23d Psalm, which I have always loved, and thanking God, in whom I scarcely believe, for keeping you *safe* on the very steamboat where I dined on sweet canned peaches not so long ago. Can you feel my recent presence? The telegram about the Indians came today from General Sheridan in Chicago, and Captain McCaskey sent the *Josephine* steaming upriver with it. Pray God it reaches General Terry in time.

Libbie noticed the commotion, Captain McCaskey and others in agitated discussion on the Commissary gallery, and went straight over. Captain McCaskey did not want to give her the awful truth, but she wormed it out of him and I wish she had not. They are leaving the agencies in *droves* and all going to join Sitting Bull. I was making my daily circuit of the Parade with sun hat and parasol and saw her hurry away from the Commissary in a distracted state, head lowered, cutting across the Parade and skipping up the porch steps, holding her skirts. I went to her, of course.

I found her in their bedroom, in her

wicker rocker, weeping silent tears that rolled like pearls down her cheeks. Perhaps it is a terrible thing to say, or to have thought, but to me she'd never looked so lovely. Hers now was a *tragic* beauty, never to be brightened except by her General, never to be approached or won by any other man. It was as if he'd *died,* Allen, and she a widow, and I had to stop and collect myself, as when you wake from a nightmare and realize none of it is true. In a moment she smiled at me, thanking me for coming, and it was a smile of perfect desolation.

"Why Libbie, what is it?" I said.

"He'll be killed," she said. "He, Tom, Jimmy, probably more. I can feel it like a cold fist around my heart."

"Stop it," I said and knelt before her and took her hand, which was cool as marble. "Stop it, stop it, stop it," I said.

"Oh, child," she said, and told me about the telegram. They are guessing *at least* 2,000 warriors and perhaps as many as 3,000. *Oh, thank God,* I selfishly thought, picturing you, as I so often do, on the deck of the *Far West.* "But then," Libbie said — the tears still fell freely but her voice never quavered — "I think I've known it all along. It has never felt right. There was always some wrong note in it, a mistake being

295

made, only nobody knew it. And then the mirage. Those ghosts in the sky."

"But Libbie," I said, "no one's been killed yet. General Crook lost but 10 men."

"General Crook had 1,000," she replied, "and he was beaten and has withdrawn from the field. Do you not see, Addie Grace? The Indians didn't run. They fought Crook all day, *and Armstrong and General Terry don't know it.*"

"But they will," I said, "just as soon as the steamer catches them."

She did not immediately answer, but sat rocking slowly. I still knelt and held her hand, but she seemed oblivious of me, her tearful gaze fixed somewhere far away. "No," she said, "they've left already. Armstrong has gotten his wish. He and Tom. They're hunting Sitting Bull as fast as ever they can. They will find him. They will come upon 3,000 warriors."

"But you can't know they've left," I said.

"I can know it, and I do," she said. "Do get up, child," she said, but I remained as I was, looking up at her. Her face was wet and her eyes very full, but for now, at least, the tears had ceased to roll down. The air was hot and still and humid. I heard voices go by the house and fade away.

"Do you remember when I asked you

296

about the General and Allen's mother?" Libbie said.

"Sort of," said I evasively.

She regarded me mildly through her tears. "You are not," she said, "a very good liar, Addie Grace."

"Why, what do you mean?" I said.

"Stop," she said. "I know it was done out of kindness, and I love you for it, but the truth was in your eyes, and is in them right now." I could not think what to say. "He lay with Monahseetah too," she said.

"How do you know?" I said.

"The General is like you," she said, "he's a poor liar, though he thinks otherwise." She was weeping again, or perhaps had never stopped, but the tears now came in a gradual, intermittent way, a slow leakage.

"Why do you allow it?" I said boldly.

She sniffled and wiped beneath her nose with the back of her pretty hand. "Because he always comes back to me," she said, "and when I have him I have *all* of him, as the others do not." She thought a moment. "And then," she said, "one always thinks they'll change, or that they might."

"Does Mrs. Calhoun know?" I said, after a tactful interval. "Mrs. Smith?"

"I imagine they do," said Libbie, "but I could never speak to them as I'm speaking to you. They'd be uncomfortable knowing that I know. Perhaps they'd feel sorry for me. It's their secret and the General's, and everybody's happy."

"I don't feel sorry for you," I said.

"I know that," she said, "and it's why I tell you."

"I might be a little angry at the General," I said.

"You mustn't be," she said, and reached down and stroked my hair back from my face. Then she ducked down and kissed my cheek — it was like the touch of a butterfly. "I once thought to even the score," she said, "with — can you guess? — Captain Keogh."

"Captain Keogh!" I exclaimed. But he *is* handsome, Allen, with his Vandyke and those bold, devilish eyes.

"I'd had a dream or two of him," Libbie said, "of a quite *provocative* sort. He looks on me favorably, I know."

"All men do," I said.

She smiled. "He's often danced with me at the officers' balls, and it would not, I think, have taken much to provoke him to some recklessness."

"Then why didn't you?" I said, rather wishing she had, surprising myself with how *depraved* I have become.

"It would be a kind of death for me,"

Libbie answered. "I couldn't do it any more than I could hurl myself off a cliff."

We remained as we were for what seemed like a long time. More voices passed the house. A wagon rattled by. Libbie regarded the floor, as if she read something there. She had ceased to weep but I did not know when. "It will be up to me," she said finally, "to comfort Maggie and the other wives, but I shan't be able to comfort myself."

"This is all for nothing," I said, no longer believing it. She was weeping again. Again she smoothed the hair from my face and gave me another soft kiss. I thought of you, and her fear took hold of me, cold in my breast, and I remembered my dream of George in the burning building, and the wailing of the Rees when you left, and the mirage. If General Sheridan is right, there are more Indians gathered than ever before in history, and George and all the regiment are riding straight at them as fast as the General can lead them. Oh, Allen, it has never felt right, as Libbie says. There is a flaw in it somewhere. The entire enterprise is built on some great mistake or falsity. We must go East as soon as we can and never come back here.

Now we wait. I shall walk, read, and give comfort where I can. Time creeps along in weary inches. The sun stands still in the sky. Destiny is a dream, a fantasy, a deception. Seize good luck when it comes your way — a girl on a train, for instance — but do not delude yourself that it is all part of a *Plan*. God, if He does preside over us, has better things to do than make valentines and war heroes. I love you, Allen.

Ever Your Valentine,
Gracie

Charley Reynolds had cut his left hand and now it was infected, and pain and sleeplessness haunted his face, which was dolorous in the best of times. Grant Marsh had looked at the swollen hand and given Lonesome Charley a stateroom and advised him to forgo the advance up the Rosebud. Charley, in Custer's presence, had asked Terry to release him. Custer had held his tongue but Terry had looked at the hand and laughed and asked the scout if he was the same Charley Reynolds who had ridden alone with news of gold out of the Black Hills, or if another, less intrepid Charley Reynolds had swapped places with him. Charley had shrugged, said it was only Captain Marsh's idea, and that he would go if General Terry thought he could be of use.

It had come back to Custer that Marsh

300

had also tried to talk Bos and Autie out of going, telling Bos he would give him turns at the wheel when the steamer moved upriver carrying Terry and Gibbon. The child in Bos had brightened at the prospect and he'd wavered, but then Autie had asked him about the buffalo robe he was going to send home to his mother and the Sioux scalp he was going to take, and Bos had changed his malleable mind again. It was all right, but Marsh's concern for Charley and the boys was yet another annoyance, another jarring note.

Now Custer moved the lamp closer and took up his pen and dipped it. *My Darling,* he wrote, *I have but a few moments to write, as we start at twelve tomorrow and the hour is late. Do not be anxious for me. You would be surprised how closely I obey your instructions about keeping with the column . . .*

The trader had come up today, again, and done a robust business in whiskey and straw hats. You couldn't stop it; it was an enlisted man's right to buy whiskey with his own money and officers could drink all they wanted, and he could feel the insobriety, like garish music in the night beyond his tent walls. If only liquor didn't make men stupid. *If only . . .* he thought. If only what? He didn't know.

The night is very dark, he wrote, *the sky clouded over and moonless. I hope to have a good report to send you by the next mail. A success will start us all back toward Lincoln . . .*

A sudden wind blew, stirring the trees by the river. Rain pattered briefly on the tent roof. The superstitious Rees began to sing in the distance, wailing, warbling, keening. Their obligatory death song. A lugubrious, arrhythmic slapping of drums. Bloody Knife drunk, no doubt. In the steamer saloon Tom and Keogh and several others — Custer didn't know who; Jimmy Calhoun, maybe — were at poker. They'd be drinking too. Just about everyone was. Autie, probably. Bos.

He wondered where Allen Winslow was.

I send you an extract from Genl. Terry's official order, knowing how keenly you appreciate words of commendation and confidence in your husband: "It is of course impossible to give you any definite instructions in regard to this movement, and, were it not impossible to do so, the Department Commander places too much confidence in your zeal, energy and ability to impose on you precise orders which might hamper your action when nearly in contact with the enemy." So you see, Dearest, I am relied upon to get this done and in my own way.

The wind had died. The Rees sang on but it sounded listless now, perfunctory. Then, on the deck of the steamer, men broke out in song: "Silver Threads Among the Gold." Custer put his pen down to listen. Reno was up there, drunk and in good voice. Custer stood up, stepped out into the darkness where Burkman was walking guard. The singers were Reno, Godfrey, Cooke, young Jack Sturgis, fresh from the Point and eager for his first fight. They stood at the rail with their arms about each other's shoulders. They were singing "Lorena" now. Custer turned, reentered the tent and sat down at his tiny desk.

I had an unpleasant set-to with Benteen at officers' call today, he wrote, *and I came down harder on him than is my wont. The man has begun to depress me. His dislike for me has been ever constant, but it seems to have become cancerous of late . . .*

They were singing "Aura Lea," a lovely song from the Rebellion, like "Lorena," which he'd last heard in the parlor at Lincoln the night before they marched. The men on the deck sang it well and sadly, as it should be sung. Again Custer put down his pen. The Rees had stopped their noise, and he wondered if they were listening to this

impromptu concert. He thought about joining the singers and knew he could not,
because Reno was there, and because they
were drinking.

"With permission, sir."

It was Mitch Boyer. Burkman had waved
him in without challenging him. A smile
played across his flat, seamed, canny face.
He brought an odor with him of leather,
sweat, tobacco, which Custer found pleasant. A smell like new-turned black earth.

"Good evening, Mitch."

"And to you, sir." Boyer removed his hat.
His English had a French flavor, odd lifts
and elisions creeping in here and there,
grammatical oddities. Custer wondered how
he felt about joining this war against his
father's people. "They sing good, don't
they," he said.

They were going on with "Aura Lea."

"Reason I come in," Boyer said, "the
Crows have call you a name already, and I
thought you would like to hear. They like
you, General. They hear you follow a trail
till it end, and when your food give out you
eat mule. That's the kind of man they want
to fight under. They say they eat mule too."

Custer smiled. "What is it they call me,
Mitch?"

"Son of the Morning Star," Boyer said.

It sounded mythic. Immortal. He must tell Libbie. *Tell Benteen,* he wanted to say. "Thank them for me," he said. "Tell them if they find the Sioux for me, I'll whip them."

Boyer looked down into his hat. He raised his gaze to the ceiling. The smile had fallen away. "It's a lot of Sioux up the valley," he said. "Sioux, Cheyenne. Arapaho. Lot of 'em."

"Then they'll be easy to find," Custer said.

"It won't be no trouble finding 'em, General."

"Good night, Mitch."

"Yes sir," Boyer said.

Custer watched him go, deliberate and dignified in his shabby white man's clothes. The men on the deck were singing "Shenandoah," and Custer wished again he could go up there and stand with them in the warm damp river darkness and join his voice to theirs. A moth tapped at the lamp glass, bounced off, tapped again. He found his pen and dipped it. Again he wondered where Allen Winslow was. He would tell Allen he was Son of the Morning Star, and maybe Allen would tell Mary Deschenes. He wondered what she was doing at this moment and reckoned, with the hour's difference in time, she was finishing another performance of *The Lady of Lyons,* perhaps even now curtseying to the tumultuous applause, radiant in the stage lights, some décolletage as she lowered herself, the perfect smile.

Cheyenne, Boyer said. But Custer knew that. Knew they were allied for this last great stand with the Sioux. He wondered where Monahseetah was. Fort Robinson? He doubted it. Suppose she was among the hostiles he was hunting now. Suppose she was. The women, he thought. Oh, such women. He was tired, he realized. He'd been sleeping three or four hours a night for a very long time, and fatigue now took him like a drug or potion and he set the pen down and fell back in his chair and dropped his chin to his chest, thinking to doze briefly, and so Burkman found him at daybreak.

■ ■ ■ ■

Part Three:
Garryowen

■ ■ ■ ■

ONE

The valley of the Rosebud was wide and flat and the hills on either side a dry, bled-looking green, like faded velvet. Some were faced with gray stone, which was seamed and scored by the eons of weather. Willow trees and cottonwoods, thickets of cherry and wild roses grew along the creek, which soon shrank to a shallow trough hardly bigger than a ditch. Teal-gray sagebrush littered the valley floor, and the grass was knee-high and jade green in some places, golden in others. Shreds of cloud raced across the sky, running their shadows across the valley.

"By God," said Autie Reed, "this is the life."

"Yes sir it is," Bos said, "and you've stood it damn good."

Autie looked at him. "Why wouldn't I?"

They were riding with headquarters, at the front of the long column. A steady murmur of hoofbeats, rattle and clink of accoutrements. The white dust rose around them and hung in the air. They'd left the Yellowstone at noon, as planned, passing in review before Terry and Gibbon while the assembled trumpeters blew an all-brass "Garryowen."

"You never were out here," Bos said. "It takes some getting used to. Allen, you've stood it good too."

"We'll stand anything you can," Autie said. "You're the one's always getting sick."

"Not anymore," Bos said. "It sets you up out here."

Autie smiled. "Won't we have some stories to tell," he said.

"I bet you'll tell Polly all about how you whipped Sitting Bull," Bos said.

"I bet so too," Autie said.

"Tell her you done it single-handed."

"I won't tell her anything isn't true."

"Tell her about that girl at Little Casino's," Bos said.

"What girl?" Allen said.

"Little whore over to the brothel on Seventh Street," Bos said. "We went over there on the last night while you all were singing songs in the parlor. The general would of whipped our asses if he found out."

"I guess I'll leave that part out," Autie said.

"I would if I were you," Allen said.

"Do you mean to see her again?" Bos said.

"Soon's we get in," Autie said.

"I don't wonder," Bos said. "Captain Keogh told Autie after we whip the Sioux, the girl'll fuck him till he can't walk."

"You'd better go see her," Allen said.

"You ever been fucked till you couldn't walk, Allen?" Autie said.

"I don't think it's possible," Bos said.

"Do you have a girl, Bos?" Allen said.

"He's too shy," Autie said. "He only goes with whores."

"I wouldn't if I had a girl," Bos said.

"Why not?"

"What would Polly think, she knew about such carryings on?"

"She'd pitch a fit."

"Well, then."

"It's a whole separate thing, a whore and a sweetheart," Autie said. "A separate compartment."

"Don't count on it," Allen said.

"When I do have me a sweetheart," Bos said, "you won't see me running around with whores."

"You'll find somebody," Allen said. "She'll be a lucky girl too."

"You'll still go with a whore, you get a chance," Autie said.

"Will not," Bos said.

The Rees were scouting the distant hills on either side, their little ponies stepping daintily along the faraway summits, moving tiny and deliberate in single file, disappearing sometimes among clumps of fir trees or down the far sides, then visible again against the sky, threading their way.

Bos said the Rees were afraid of the Sioux.

"Hard to believe," Allen said.

"I bet Bloody Knife isn't afraid of them," Autie said.

"I don't know about afraid, but he doesn't *like* them," Bos said.

"He's half Sioux for Jesus sake," Autie said.

"Well, the Ree half doesn't like them. He was brung up by the Rees, which were his mother's people, and one time when he was young, he took it into his head to go visit his father. Soon's he showed up —"

"How young?" Autie said.

"I don't know how young. *Young.* You want to hear this or not?"

"Go on tell it."

"All right, then. Soon's he showed up, what did the village do? They went at him with sticks, beat him black and blue. After they beat him, they stripped him down naked, took everything he had, and turned him out on his horse. Everybody laughing, jeering him. Women too. Girls. That's the Sioux for you."

They rode awhile not speaking. The day had warmed, and deer flies rose and hovered and bit, and the men slapped the backs of their necks and cursed. Allen didn't doubt the story. It was a pitiless land, and it made men pitiless.

"Red bastards," Autie said.

Later that first morning Mitch Boyer dropped back and rode with them awhile. His mount was a large deep-chested buckskin with white socks, and everything about the man struck Allen as authoritative and genuine in the quiet steady way that honor is genuine, and true courage.

"Where's your rifle, Mr. Secretary?" he said.

"He doesn't carry one," Autie said. "He's a Quaker."

"A Quaker," Boyer said.

"Means he doesn't believe in killing people."

"I never said that," Allen said.

"He won't load his Colt," Autie said.

"What you come out here for?" Boyer said.

"His mother sent him," Autie said. "She

313

thought to harden him up. Make a man out of him."

Boyer seemed not to have heard. "Someone shoot at you, you don't shoot back?" he said.

"I told you. He's a Quaker, Mr. Boyer."

"I don't ask you, I ask him," Boyer said.

"I can't say what I'll do," Allen said.

Boyer eyed him, smiled, not unkindly. He felt inside his leather vest and found his pipe, keeping the reins in his left hand. He put the pipe in his mouth, dug out a match, leaned down, and struck it on his boot. He lit the pipe, drew on it, removed it, and blew a sheet of smoke.

"It's a lot of Indians up ahead of us," he said. "I don't think nobody know how many."

"The general knows," Bos said.

"No," Boyer said, "the general don't."

"He'll whip however many he finds," Autie said.

Boyer smiled. "You boys be careful," he said.

They made only twelve miles on the twenty-second, slowed by the ungovernable, infuriating mules. The mules shook their packs off. They left the column on any whim, packers and soldiers cursing them, lashing them, dragging them back into line.

The campsite was level and grassy, with willows and cottonwoods thick along the creek. After they'd settled in Allen led Ginger down among the trees, where the strikers were grooming their officers' horses and putting them to drink.

"Whyn't you stay up on the Yellowstone, where you be safe?" said a private named Klein. He spoke with a German accent. *Vare you be safe.* He was stripping the saddle off Captain Yates's bay gelding. On the other side of the creek, where the ground rose toward the hills, the sentries were walking their beats.

"I considered it," Allen said.

He lifted the McClellan saddle and set it on the ground. Ginger looked back at him.

"You're my good girl," he said.

"Maybe they don't pay you, you stay back," Klein said, "is that it?"

"Could be," Allen said. He did not know if the enlisted men knew of his hundred-dollar salary. He hoped not.

"I don't think that's it," said Private Galvin. "I think Allen wants to find him a squaw."

"You ever fuck a squaw, Allen?" said Private Kelly.

"Not yet," Allen said.

315

He felt under the saddle blanket. She was dry, and he pulled the blanket off. He found the brush and comb and sponge in his saddlebag and began brushing her down, talking to her as he worked, thanking her for being so good and obedient and smart. The mud and dust on her was more red than brown. He took up the comb and pulled it through her tangled, pale-brown mane. He told her he'd take her to Cape Cod when this was over, give her a life of leisure on a farm.

"You watch out," Klein said. "A squaw, she cut your balls off she don't like how you do her."

"Allen's got him a girl back at Lincoln," Kelly said. "He don't need to risk it with a squaw."

"Is a pretty girl," Klein said.

Allen had opened the hook from the comb, and he put his shoulder to Ginger's and ran his hand down her leg and lifted her hoof, speaking softly to her. She did not object. He cupped the fetlock joint in his hand and used the hook to dig out the mud and debris from the hoof bottom.

"Mr. Boyer says there are a lot of Indians where we're going," he said.

"That ain't what I'd call news," Kelly said.

"He says there are more than Colonel

Custer realizes."

"Custer don't care. He'll pitch into whatever's there."

"They won't stand and fight," Galvin said, "I don't care how many they are. I don't say they're afraid, but they don't fight like white men."

Allen was cleaning Ginger's hind hooves now. There was a sharp pebble in the frog of her left hoof, and she twisted back as he hooked it out but did not try to bite him.

"That there's a kind-hearted horse," Galvin said.

"She's my good girl," Allen said.

Hardtack, salt pork: the staple of both armies in the Rebellion. You fried the hardtack in pork grease and it had no taste of its own. It was the first time the boys had cooked for themselves. They'd built a fire of sagebrush and sticks.

"We're soldiers now, by God," Autie said.

"The hard bread isn't so bad as they say," Bos said.

"Hard bread. Sowbelly. Sleep under the stars. Tomorrow we make our own coffee. Won't we have some things to tell," Autie said.

A half moon dangled above the eastern hills. Campfires burned along the trampled camp street in front of the row of officers' tents. The picketed horses and mules stood quiet with night coming on. Beyond them, across the square of the camp, the enlisted men's fires could be glimpsed, and you could hear the murmur of their voices, an occasional languid chorus of laughter. Somewhere over there a harmonica trilled and quavered.

"Would you of fought in the Rebellion, Allen?" Bos said.

"Yes I would. Slavery's an evil."

"You'd shoot a white man and not an Indian?" Autie said.

"I didn't say I wouldn't shoot an Indian," Allen said.

"Then load your Colt," Autie said. "A man without a gun isn't anything out here."

"Leave off, Autie," Bos said.

An orderly came riding bareback down the row of officers' tents and stopped halfway and called an order the boys couldn't make out. Lieutenants Cooke and Smith emerged from their tents in their undershirts. Captain Keogh came out.

"Officers call," Bos said.

"How come they don't bugle it?" Autie said.

"Indians," Bos said. "We're getting close."

"What does a Sioux look like, I wonder,"

Autie said.

"About like the Rees," Bos said, "except they're all painted up. Got more feathers too."

"How would you know?"

"They've been Sioux at Lincoln. They come in to talk to the general. They squat around in a circle and use sign."

"What do they talk about?" Autie said.

"I don't know," Bos said. "This and that."

"Wish I'd seen it," Autie said.

"You stay out here long enough, you'll see everything," Bos said. "I wouldn't trade it for anything."

"Don't you ever want to go back, Bos?" Allen said.

"I might do, someday," Bos said.

"If it wasn't for Polly, I wouldn't go back," Autie said.

"Good reason not to have a girl," Bos said.

Burkman shook him awake with a rough hand. Allen rolled over under his blanket and pulled off the mosquito veil. Burkman was leaning over him with his hands on his knees, like an outfielder at the ready. Allen could smell horse on him, and mansweat.

"Bub," he said, "the general wants to see you."

Allen threw back his blanket. Bos and

Reed were asleep under their veils, Bos with his head on his saddle. They'd lain down well out from the trees. The stars swarmed over the curve of the valley sky. Allen pulled on his boots and stood up.

All but a few of the officers' tents were dark. The mules and horses were quiet. Along the far perimeter a few fires still glowed red. Allen did not know what time it was, it was too dark to read a watch without a light, but the slim moon had moved halfway over to the western hills.

"You were asleep," Custer said.

"It's all right," Allen said.

Burkman had set the cot up outside his tent and Custer was sitting on it in his gray-blue flannel shirt. He was slumped forward, one leg partially extended, the knee bent, his hands to his thighs. White buckskin britches with fringe, Wellington boots. Graceful, even in contemplation, in repose. The candle on the camp table had burned out. The dogs lay asleep near his feet. Burkman took up his rifle and crossed the camp street. He turned, shouldered it, and stood watching Custer.

"Sit down," Custer said.

"Here, sir?"

"Go on."

Allen sat down beside him on the taut

320

canvas. Somewhere a mule brayed.

"They'll be the ruin of us, those animals," Custer said.

"I've learned some new curse words since I've been out here," Allen said.

Custer smiled. "The teamsters know them all."

"They invent new ones," Allen said.

They sat. The mosquitoes were at them, and they waved them off, slapped at them. There was a faintness of sweat in Custer's shirt, but he himself, his breath and body, had a clove-like fragrance. Burkman brought him water daily, or he bathed in the rivers and creeks. He brushed his teeth religiously, George said.

"Your father was an abolitionist," Custer said.

"Funny you should say so. Bos was after me about it tonight. Whether I'd have fought in the Rebellion. I said I would."

"To free the slaves."

"Of course."

"I never saw any harm in slavery. The Negroes are simple people. It was a way for them to live. Be provided for."

"You fought," Allen said. "Fought hard."

"To preserve the Union. Most of us did. We didn't care a lick about slavery."

Beyond the trees on the other side of the

creek a sentry called out. Eleven o'clock and all was well. Allen wondered how he knew the hour. A sentry to the north repeated the cry. A coyote yapped, trailing off into a tremulous sorrowing howl. Another answered it.

"Did you ever read a book by Frederick Douglass?" Allen said.

"I was never tempted."

"He wrote three of them. Mr. Douglass is a brilliant man."

"He's the exception."

"You're wrong, sir. There are Negro doctors in Boston. Lawyers. Teachers. They're as smart as white people."

Custer smiled a thin smile. Weary. Allen thought the blue glimmer in his eyes was muted tonight. A thinner luminosity.

"Could a Sioux Indian write a book like Mr. Douglass's?" he said.

"I imagine so."

"A Cheyenne? Could that rascal Bloody Knife write one?"

"Suppose Frederick Douglass had never learned to read," Allen said. "Suppose he'd never escaped slavery, been kept down, whipped, worked to death. We'd never know what he could do, would we?"

Custer shifted beside him. He drew in his right leg and extended the other. He folded his arms.

"The Sioux don't have the wheel," he said. "They don't have pottery. They're living in their own stone age."

"Does that make us right?"

"What do you think?"

"You know what I think," Allen said.

Again Custer shifted his weight. He refolded his arms. "It doesn't matter," he said. "There's no stopping it. There never was."

"There might have been," Allen said.

"When?"

"I don't know."

"How?"

"I don't know that either."

Silence. Each of them stared at the ground before him, the dry, flattened grass.

"Charley Reynolds made out a will last night," Custer said.

"You're tired, sir. You should sleep."

"Cooke made one out."

"I'd say that's reasonable before a fight."

Custer turned, eyed him almost sadly. He shook his head, but Allen could not take meaning in it and wondered if Custer even knew himself.

"I thank you for your company, Allen."

"I enjoyed it," Allen said.

"Good night, then."

"Good night, General."

He heard George cough and he crouched and let himself in through the tent flap. The air felt unnaturally warm. There was a worrisome sweetish smell of bodily neglect.

"It's me," Allen said. "What are you doing awake?"

"Don't sit on my specs," George said.

"They're right here. Are you all right?"

"Damn throat's killing me. I feel like hell."

"Since when?"

"Today. It walloped me. I'm going to ride with the mules tomorrow. The general's changed things around. The mules'll all be in the rear, one big pack train. I ride back with them, I won't have to push so hard."

"I'll ride with you," Allen said.

"The general won't let you, and I don't need you anyway." He coughed, and the cough pitched him forward in the darkness.

"Do you need anything?" Allen said. "Water?"

"McAllister's looking after me. He's a good fellow. I hope nothing happens to him."

"The other surgeons can't do anything for you?"

"There's nothing for a cold but to wait it out."

"It's more than a cold."

"No it isn't."

"I'll come back at reveille," Allen said.

"I can't sleep, Allen. If I had some whiskey I could."

"You've plenty of whiskey."

"It's for the wounded. DeWolf and Porter wouldn't approve."

"The hell with them."

"Find me some, will you?"

"It's past midnight, George."

"Tomorrow," he said.

"I'll try."

"There's plenty of it around. Take some money out of my saddlebag."

"Yell out if you need anything."

"I need whiskey," George said.

Two

The scouts found the trail midmorning of the twenty-third. The six Crows, with Boyer, Bloody Knife, the interpreter Gerard, and Lieutenant Varnum, had dismounted and were walking around inspecting the ground, which was trampled and hoof-pocked and scored by the dragged poles of tipis. The Indians had come from the west and turned south beside the Rosebud. Custer saw the scouts and galloped ahead alone, the two dogs sprinting behind.

"How many?" he said, swinging down off Vic.

"It's a pretty good number," Varnum said.

"Pretty good isn't a number, Lieutenant," Custer said.

Gerard spoke to Bloody Knife. Bloody Knife answered him. He'd tied a red bandanna about his head. He wore a red plaid shirt, buckskin trousers like Custer's.

"He says we'll know better when we come

on their campsite," Gerard said.

"Let's get after them," Custer said.

They found the campsite five miles on. It spread across hundreds of yards, from the creek to where the hills began their rise to the west. There were the wide circles of worn dead ground where tipis had stood, too many to count. The bent poles of wickiups. The ashes of large fires. Animal bones, gnawed and broken. Old buffalo robes, blankets. Horn spoons. A couple of brass kettles. A child's doll fashioned out of clay, a clay pony. The boys sat their horses, taking it all in.

"By God, think what was here," said Autie Reed.

"Sitting Bull hisself," Bos said.

"By God," Autie said again.

They sat watching Custer, standing with his hands to his hips, listening to Boyer and Gerard, who was translating for Bloody Knife. The Crows were wandering about and squatting and digging around in the ashes. The Crows wore buckskin jackets and leather vests, and there was something secretive and guarded about them, a disinclination to meet a white man's gaze. They picked up bones, examined them and tossed them away. They traded looks but did not

327

speak. Kellogg was strolling around, making notes. The staghounds had each found the leg bone of an elk or buffalo and settled down to gnaw on it.

"I hear Major Reno brought some whiskey along," Allen said.

"He brought a whole keg," Bos said.

"Bullshit," Autie said.

"It's loaded on a mule," Bos said. "I saw 'em do it."

The conference was breaking up, everyone mounting up. Charley Reynolds removed the arm with the infected hand from its sling and used it to mount his horse, grimacing as he pulled himself up. Varnum rode on ahead with the Crows. Custer popped onto Vic smoothly and weightless-seeming and waved headquarters forward. Calhoun's Company L was only now arriving, and Custer sent Cooke back to tell Jimmy to keep moving, then spurred out ahead of headquarters with Reynolds beside him and the dogs in pursuit.

"Does Reno share his whiskey around?" Allen said.

"That'll be the day," Bos said.

They were moving again and presently crossed the corral of the Indian village, acres of ruined ground dotted with droppings, the grass eaten down, the sagebrush torn, tattered.

"It's a lot of them," Bos said.

"How many do you think?" Autie said.

"Lord, I don't know," Bos said. "Ask Mr. Boyer."

"Who else has whiskey besides Reno?" Allen said.

"What are you after?" Autie said.

"Dr. Lord's sick. He needs some sleep medicine."

"Hell, he can have all the damn whiskey he wants."

"He won't take it. It's for the wounded."

The trail resumed, the beaten grass and trampled sage, the hundreds of pole-cut incisions. The day was the hottest yet, and gnats hovered around them in busy clouds. Gnats, deer flies. The fly bites burned and itched, both.

"Charley Reynolds might have a bottle," Bos said. "I saw him buy one from that trader on the Yellowstone. I bet Mr. Kellogg has got one."

"I need it tonight," Allen said.

"We'll think on it," Bos said.

They struck a second campsite, a second village, not two miles from the first, and a third, some five miles from the second. They halted at the third and Custer dismounted and again walked around with Boyer, Gerard, and Bloody Knife, putting questions to them.

"How many damn villages *are* there?" Autie said.

"The more the better," Bos said.

Allen looked at him and shook his head, thinking *Jesus.*

Mark Kellogg had gotten down from the mule he rode and was strolling about making notes. Now he picked up a fire-blackened hatchet and turned it over, studying one side and then the other.

"That's a white man's hatchet," Autie said.

"There's blood on it," Kellogg said, perhaps to himself.

"Jesus Christ," Autie said.

Kellogg tossed the hatchet aside and unpocketed his notebook and wrote in it.

"Where do they get hatchets?" Allen said.

"They give 'em out at the agencies," Bos said.

"What the hell for?" Autie said.

"To live by. Hatchets. Knives. Winchester rifles."

"Why don't they give them cannons while they're at it," Autie said. "Give them dynamite, why not?"

Bos smiled. "An Indian wouldn't know what to do with dynamite," he said. "A cannon, either."

"They know what do with a hatchet," Autie said.

They made camp on the east side of the Rosebud, the side opposite the chewed, droppings-littered Indian trail. Out west of the trail ran a line of gray barren hills with fir trees clotted along its summit. Above the hills, very low, floated wisps of cloud, like broken drifts of white smoke.

Allen groomed and watered Ginger. He drew his oats and led her to the officers' corral inside the camp perimeter and picketed her where Galvin and Kelly were feeding their officers' horses. Allen looked for Burkman, saw him some distance off, crouched in front of Vic and Dandy, watching them eat.

"That son of a bitch down yonder is dumb as a stump," Kelly said.

"I wonder can he fight," Galvin said.

"I imagine so," Kelly said. "No brain, no pain."

Allen had fastened Ginger's nosebag and she was eating. "When would you expect the pack train to get here?" he said.

"Midnight," Galvin said.

"It's Benteen's detail today," Kelly said. "Old Benteen's cussin' a blue streak, I bet.

He'll come in mad as hell."

"Dr. Lord's back there with them," Allen said. "He's sick."

"I heard he was," Galvin said.

"I don't think he can ride till midnight," Allen said.

"Don't listen to him," Kelly said. "Another hour they'll be here."

"If he don't mind dust and cussin', doc'll be fine," Galvin said.

"Another hour?" Allen said.

"I imagine so," Galvin said.

The two boys and Bos built a fire and took turns frying their salt pork, their hardtack, then sat in the dry grass with the fry pans cooling in their laps and ate. It had been two hours, and the pack train hadn't come in.

"I should have ridden with him," Allen said.

"Leave off," Autie said. "You aren't his nanny."

"Someone's in a bad mood," Bos said.

"I'll be in a worse one, you don't shut up."

They ate, cutting the colorless grease-sodden meat and bread with their tin forks.

"Could something have happened to the pack train?" Allen said.

"The Sioux ambushed them," Autie said.

"The Sioux are ahead of us, not behind," Bos said.

"It was a joke," Autie said.

"It wasn't funny," Bos said.

Allen finished eating and set his pan down. He reached around and found his coat. He dug out his pocket watch. It was twenty minutes past eight. He swore to himself and shut the watch. He scrambled up.

"I'll be back in a while," he said. "Bos, wash my fry pan, will you?"

"Where you going?"

"Where I should have been all day," Allen said.

"Christ sake, take your Colt," Autie said.

"He's right, Allen," Bos said.

Allen waved the idea away and imagined his father looking on, approving.

He bridled Ginger and cantered her bareback past the staring sentinels and north down the valley, the way they'd come. He'd made no more than a mile when the pack train appeared, moving toward him in its roil of dust. He slowed Ginger to a walk.

Benteen had deployed a company in front of the mules, another beside them, and a third behind. The mass of men and animals came on until the first dust-gilded soldiers could be made out, riding four abreast, a sergeant carrying the fluttering guidon. Allen did not see Benteen. He did not see George. The men eyed him as they passed with sullen curiosity and did not speak, and Allen knew they'd had a hard day of it with the mules. He was in their dust now, and he backed Ginger and checked her and sat watching for George or Benteen. Company B rode alongside the mules, the men as trail-worn and out of sorts as the company in front. Allen leaned forward, patted Ginger's hard smooth neck and told her he was sorry to keep her up so late.

Benteen was at the rear, with his own company, H. A trumpeter rode with him, and a guidon bearer.

"What the *hell* are you doing?" he said.

Allen saw that Benteen wasn't going to stop, and he turned Ginger and walked her abreast of him. "Sir," he said, "where's Dr. Lord?"

"Back of us."

"Back where, sir?"

"I couldn't tell you. He stopped to rest a while ago."

The trumpeter and flag-bearer glanced at Allen, at Benteen, both expressionless.

"He's sick, sir," Allen said.

"I'm aware of that," Benteen said.

"Where's your weapon?"

"Did his horse give out?" Allen said.

"You think I'd leave a white man in this country without a horse?" Benteen said.

"I hope not, sir."

"Where's your weapon? Your saddle?"

"Where I left them," Allen said.

"Get the hell out of my sight," Benteen said.

"Yes sir," Allen said and turned Ginger and nudged her to a trot.

He had not been out of speaking distance of humans since they'd left Fort Lincoln, and now, alone in this emptiness of prairie and naked hills, he understood how truly isolated they were. How far away from everything they knew, understood. Custer loved it for its high drama, its extremes, but it wasn't his country and never would be. You might as well try to claim the moon.

Allen didn't suppose it was dangerous where he rode now. The regiment had swept through not many hours ago; the Rees had scouted the hills. The Sioux were ahead of them, moving south, a destination in mind. Still, he watched the darkening trees along the creek, the gaps between hills, and those wooded ravines. He watched the flat, empty valley stretching before him for a stir of dust, not ruling out a solitary rider, a renegade traveling alone, a misfit, an exile, who would be no less likely to kill him on sight. He thought of his pistol, holstered and empty with his gear near the campfire, and was even now content to have left it, as if doing so were a victory of sorts.

He found George a couple of miles on, walking his horse near the tree-marked creek. George in his linen duster. Ginger knew him, or knew he was a friend, and she pricked her ears and veered toward him of her own accord. George stopped walking and watched them come. Ginger slowed, halted without being told, and Allen slid down her smooth, slippery flank and dropped the reins.

"Are you trying to get yourself scalped?" he said.

"I was afraid I'd fall off," George said.

"What the hell'd Benteen leave you for?"

"He had to. Where's your gun?"

"Don't start," Allen said. "Can you mount?"

"I think so," George said.

"Look at your damn glasses."

"They're all right," George said.

"Like hell they are," Allen said, and took them off his nose and wiped the sweat, the dust, on his shirt. Oblong lenses, thick.

Allen fitted them back in place.

"I got tired," George said. "I'm all right now."

"Get on your horse."

"Give me a boost."

Allen locked his hands together and George stepped up into them. He grasped the pommel with both hands.

"All right?" Allen said.

"All right."

Allen lifted, slung him up onto the horse. He handed the reins up. He mounted Ginger, and they set out at a walk, side by side. It was getting dark.

"Where's your saddle?" George said.

"Where the hell do you think?"

"No saddle, no gun. Did you find me some whiskey?"

"I'm working on it."

"I want it tonight."

"I'll find some," Allen said.

The fires were burning down, but the officers still sat by them. Talking, smoking. Benteen and Keogh, on camp chairs, stopped talking and watched him pass.

"Glad you made it in," Benteen said.

"Thank you, sir."

"I wonder Custer let you go wandering the country alone. He'd catch hell from your mother, something happened to you."

Allen kept walking, toward the north side of the perimeter, where the native scouts made their bivouac. He had turned George over to McAllister and had groomed and fed his horse and picketed her and Ginger. It was full dark, the slim moon on the move. He had not been back to his own campsite.

Mitch Boyer was crouched by a fire, smoking his pipe, with Bloody Knife and one of the Crows. They were conversing in sign language with Bloody Knife, cutting runes in the air with their fingers and the flat of their hands. Etching, slicing, tracing circles. The Crow was smoking a cigarette. They looked up at Allen.

"Mr. Boyer," he said.

"You call me Mitch," Boyer said.

"Mitch, I have a favor to ask."

"Sure," Boyer said.

They were looking past him: someone coming. Allen turned around. Lieutenant Godfrey, strolling with his hands clasped behind him, hatless. He'd lopped off his bushy handlebar and without it looked like a young university professor.

"Good evening," he said.

"Evening, Lieutenant," Boyer said, removing his pipe.

"Am I interrupting something?" Godfrey said.

"Just some talk," Boyer said.

"What do you think, Mr. Boyer?"

"About what, sir?"

"All of it," Godfrey said. "I hear you're apprehensive. That you don't like the look of things."

Boyer returned the pipe to his mouth and drew on it, looking out toward the horses. Godfrey waited, hands in back of him as before. The Crow smoked, looking away. Bloody Knife watched Godfrey. Boyer again removed his pipe. He exhaled a ribbon of smoke.

"Lieutenant," he said, "did you ever fight these Sioux?"

"I fought them on the Yellowstone," Godfrey said.

"How many you think there is?"

"Colonel Custer says fifteen hundred."

"You think we can whip that many?"

"I guess we can," Godfrey said.

"What if it's more?" Boyer said. "Two thousand. Three thousand. You think we can whip that many?"

Godfrey smiled a thin smile. He looked at Allen, nodded a belated greeting. Bloody Knife had taken it all in in his quiet, sage way, as if he'd understood every word but was withholding comment for now.

"I think if we all do our duty God will look out for us," Godfrey said.

"You ask Him to, okay, Lieutenant?"

"I'll be glad to," Godfrey said. "Good evening to you."

They watched him walk away, slow, hands still clasped behind him. The Crow spoke and Boyer answered him. The Crow smiled in a dry and mordant way and shook his head. Boyer spoke to Bloody Knife with his hands and Bloody Knife answered briefly, then looked off into the night.

"Bloody Knife thinks he going to get killed," Boyer said. "Is a voice speak to him. Tell him what is ahead. Sit down, Allen."

It was the first time Boyer had used his name. Allen dropped down beside him. Bloody Knife eyed him with solemn cordiality. Allen remembered Bos's story of Bloody Knife's humiliation at the hands of the Sioux. How they'd beaten him and turned him away naked. The Crow finished his cigarette and tossed it backhand into the fire.

"We be on 'em soon," Boyer said. "Tomorrow or the next day."

"Why don't you tell General Custer what you told Lieutenant Godfrey?" Allen said.

"I did tell him. He goddamn tired of hearing it."

"What's going to happen?" Allen said.

"Lot of men going to die," Boyer said. "You boys be careful. Tell that nephew."

The Crow asked Boyer what was being said and Boyer told him. The Crow repeated it to Bloody Knife with his hands. Bloody Knife nodded, then looked at Allen and nodded again. Allen returned the nod, an understanding passing between them.

"What you come over here for?" Boyer said.

Allen looked at him. The broad, seamed face patient, knowing; elderly yet not elderly, a gleam in the eye, latent humor, laughter waiting to break out as the world amused him.

"I need some whiskey," Allen said.

Boyer smiled. "I bet you do."

"It's for Dr. Lord," Allen said. "He's sick. He doesn't want to drink any of the surgical supply."

"They be needin' that supply," Boyer said.

"He knows that."

"Okay," Boyer said.

"Okay what?"

"How much you need?" Boyer said.

"What time is it?" George said.

341

"I don't know. Eleven o'clock. You want a cup?"

"No."

Allen uncorked the bottle and George took it in the coal-gray darkness. You could smell the whiskey, sweetly astringent. George took a drink. It started him coughing.

"You all right?" Allen said.

"Fine." George drank again, coughed. "What did you tell Boyer?"

"The truth. He liked it that you won't drink the surgical whiskey. Said he'd finally met an honest sawbones."

"How much do I owe you?"

"Nothing. He said I can pay him when it's over, if he's still alive."

George took in a deep breath. He drank and did not cough this time.

"Listen, George. Boyer says there might be three thousand fighters where we're going."

"So what."

"So *what*? We don't have a thousand."

George drank again. "I took a bath in the creek," he said. "I think it brought my fever down."

"I don't think Custer's listening to Boyer."

"Of course he's listening to him."

"Bloody Knife told Boyer he's going to be killed."

"He's afraid of the Sioux. All the Rees are. The Crows too." He took another swig.

"Don't make yourself sick," Allen said.

"I *am* sick," George said. "I just want to be drunk." He took one more long swallow. "Give me the stopper," he said.

Allen put it in his hand and George corked the bottle. He smacked the cork in with the flat of his hand.

"I'm going to ride with you tomorrow," Allen said. "Can you keep up with headquarters?"

"I think so," George said. He lay back, settled himself on his side. He closed his eyes.

"George."

"What."

"We can't beat three thousand Indians. We can't beat *two* thousand."

"Good night," George said.

"Did you hear me?" Allen said.

"I heard you," George said and took in a long breath and was asleep.

He was awake, as Allen knew he would be, sitting outside at his camp table, writing a letter by candlelight. The two dogs slept at his feet. Allen did not see Burkman.

"Hadn't you ought to be asleep?" Custer said, writing.

"If I could have a word," Allen said.

Custer wrote to the end of a sentence, marked it with a period and laid the pen down. "Sit down," he said.

Allen sat down on the cot. Custer turned in his little chair, rested an arm on the table.

"We're getting close to them," he said.

"Yes sir, I can feel it."

"The scouts think they'll turn west, into the valley of the Little Bighorn River. It's the next one over."

"I ran into Mr. Boyer tonight," Allen said.

"Ran into him."

"Yes sir."

"Put some scare into you, did he."

"He says we could be up against two or three thousand warriors."

"He doesn't know that," Custer said.

"What if he's right?"

"What if he is?"

"Do you want to take on that many Indians?"

"I want to see this thing through. Finish what I began."

"You don't want to wait for General Terry and General Gibbon?"

"Wait how long? Suppose I sat here and the Indians scattered into the Big Horn

Mountains. Went up into Canada. I'd look like a fool. A poltroon."

"No one would say that about you."

"They'd have reason to."

"No one knew there'd be so many Sioux," Allen said.

"It doesn't matter, Allen. There's no turning back."

"You keep saying that."

"Who would want to?"

"I guess I would."

Custer smiled. "Do you know Gray's *Elegy*?"

"Yes sir. I had it by heart middle year at Phillips."

" 'Far from the madding crowd's ignoble strife,' " Custer said.

And Allen: " 'Their sober wishes never learned to stray.' "

They looked at each other in the soft light of the candle. Custer hadn't shaved today. His stubble was a fine corn-silk yellow.

"Gray is wrong," Custer said. "It wasn't penury that consigned those people to that country churchyard. To that obscurity."

"*Chill* penury," Allen said.

Custer smiled. "Chill penury. They had choices, Allen. Wider destinies open to them, penury or no."

"Not all of them."

"The lucky ones," Custer said.

One of the hounds lurched up onto its front legs, leaned sideways, and scratched behind his ear.

"What about the enlisted men?" Allen said. "What choice do they have?"

"I said the lucky ones."

"The Indian women. The children."

"You aren't listening to me."

The candle was nearly gone. Custer turned, looked at it. He leaned and blew it out.

"Benteen killed a boy at the Washita," he said. "A child. He said the boy put a gun on him and maybe he did, but he was a child, and he was shot through the head. Afterwards we killed their ponies. Cut their throats. More than eight hundred of them. They were wild with terror and it was hard to get at them, and it took a while. They screamed like humans. I finally sent a second detail and told them to shoot what were left."

"And you'll do it again," Allen said.

"If I have to."

"Why?"

"If I don't, someone else will. And I can do it more efficiently. More humanely, if it's possible."

He looked away into the night. Somber.

Pensive. He looked again at Allen.

"I have to see this through," he said.

"Have to or want to?"

"They're the same thing," Custer said.

"Destiny," Allen said.

"Yes. And you have to trust it, Allen."

"Even when it doesn't feel right."

"Especially then," Custer said. "Good night, Allen."

"Good night," Allen said and rose from the cot and left him.

Autie Reed had gotten drunk. So had Bos. Autie was sitting in a stupor, legs folded tailor-fashion, staring dully and unhappily into the embers of their fire. An uncorked bottle stuck up between his legs. He looked up at Allen.

"Where you been?" he said.

"With Dr. Lord," Allen said.

Bos lay on his side under his blanket and mosquito veil. "We found you a bottle, but we drunk it," he said.

"I found one," Allen said. "What's going on here?"

"Nothing," Autie said.

Allen dropped to the ground. "What's the matter, Bos?" he said.

"He can't hold his liquor," Autie said.

"I didn't ask you," Allen said. He was pull-

347

ing off his boots.

Bos put his mosquito veil aside and sat up. "You get damn mean when you're drunk, Autie Reed," he said. His pale eyes shone unfocussed and glassy.

"What happened?" Allen said.

Autie lifted the bottle, took a slug. It was more than half empty. "He got after me about that hatchet in the Indian camp. Said I was letting it spook me."

"I never said such," Bos said.

"I didn't like it, so I reminded him of something," Autie said.

Allen turned, looked for his blanket, his veil. The night was cooling. The encampment was silent. The thin air held a smell of sage and woodsmoke. A bird or tree frog piped up down near the creek.

"Go on, Autie," Bos said, "tell the whole world I'm a coward."

"Shut up," Autie said.

"Where'd you get the bottle?" Allen said.

"We bought it off of Kellogg," Autie said. "Bastard jewed us out of four dollars."

"It was supposed to be for you to give to Dr. Lord," Bos said, "but you never showed up. You can have what's left."

"I don't need it."

"Hell, we waited a damn hour," Autie said.

Bos now lay on his back, eyeing the vivid

stars, sadly drunk. Wistful.

"What did he say to you, Bos?"

"I don't doubt he'll tell you," Bos said.

Autie looked into the fire. Sullen. Brooding. "Bos backed down from a fight in Monroe one time," he said.

"That's *it*?" Allen said. "That's what all this fuss is about?"

He shook out his blanket. In four hours they'd be packing up, riding.

"Fellow bloodied his nose and he took it," Autie said. "And him a Custer."

"Let's go to sleep," Allen said.

"I agree," Autie said.

"I bet you do," Allen said.

"What's that mean?" Autie said.

"Fellow thought I bumped him on the sidewalk and wanted to fight me," Bos said, watching the stars. "Popped me one on the nose. Autie was just a little thing. He saw the whole thing and didn't forget it, either."

"This is a mountain out of a mole hill," Allen said, "but you're a son of a bitch to bring it up."

Autie's gaze came up quick, eyes bleared and flaring. "Who is?" he said.

"You are."

"Go fuck yourself."

Allen was on him before he could get up. The bottle went over, spilling whiskey into the flattened grass. He took Autie by his shirt collar and put him down and pinned him hard, thinking he'd desist. Far from desisting Autie struck at him, catching him near his Adam's apple, swung again, and grazed his jaw. Allen drew back to hit him but Autie twisted sideways and Allen's punch only caught him on the ear. Autie rolled clear and both boys scrambled up but Bos was between them now, shoving them apart, and they let him break it up.

"You stupid bastards," he said.

Allen and Autie eyed each other, breathing hard. Autie had sobered up. His eyes were narrowed, and Allen knew he'd be a handful to whip but thought he could do it.

"Fightin' with each other and us in Sioux country," Bos said.

"We're done," Allen said, and turned away. He realized only then he was in his stocking feet.

"Autie?" Bos said.

"Sure," Autie said. "The hell with it."

"Lord, what foolishness," Bos said, the last words spoken among them that night.

THREE

They found the scalp midmorning of the twenty-fourth.

It was hotter still, and the flies and gnats were a torment. The scouts were moving more and more slowly, and Custer held the column back, pausing often, the men sitting their horses, waving and slapping at insects, talking very little. More trails converged, the valley now so churned and scored it looked like plowed ground. The buttes to the west were red and the hills khaki green, with the usual fir trees bunched along their summits and spilling down the draws and ravines.

They came to yet another campsite, this one spread over slow-rising ground to the west of the creek, ascending all of a sudden to a giant vertical outcrop of palomino sandstone, towering like four snaggled molars, the land beyond banking steeply up to a range of red and white buttes. Below the rocks, where the ground began to level down toward the creek, was a tall mast-like pole planted solidly in the ground. Bound to the pole with a rawhide thong was the desiccated scalp.

The Rees and Crows were exploring the area around the pole, with Varnum looking on, when Custer and Boyer arrived. Their horses picked their way through the campsite, the wickiup frames and debris of utensils and blankets and garbage. Custer and Boyer dismounted. Charley Reynolds came up, and Gerard, and Kellogg, hurrying on his mule. Kellogg got down and walked over to the scalp, which hung at eye level, and pulled out his notebook. A Crow named Half Yellow Face approached Boyer, leading his horse. He spoke to Boyer, and Boyer put some questions to him.

"That there's a sundance pole," Boyer said. "Somebody make medicine here, General."

"I know what a sundance is, Mitch," Custer said.

"Half Yellow Face say they find pictures show dead soldiers. They find other signs. Painted stones, which means they got good medicine. They know we're coming, General."

"Someone take that scalp down," Custer said.

Bloody Knife was nearby, and he said something to the other Rees and strode to the pole and tore the scalp from its rawhide bind.

"Poor bastard," Boyer said.

The rest of headquarters had arrived. They gathered round the sundance pole, mounted, in a half circle. Sergeant Vickory got down and stuck Custer's battle flag with its crossed sabers in the soft, dry ground.

"Who wants this scalp?" Custer said.

"Sergeant Finley collects them," said Henry Voss, the trumpeter. "Company C, sir."

"All right," Custer said, "see that he gets it."

Gerard spoke to Bloody Knife and Bloody Knife said something back, sharp. Gerard spoke again, and Bloody Knife smiled and handed him the scalp.

"You hear me about the pictures, General?" Boyer said.

"I heard you, Mitch."

"They know we're coming, sir."

"You said that."

Now Godfrey's Company K came in, four abreast with a sergeant out on the flank. Godfrey halted them and came forward.

The scouts had pretty much finished inspecting the campsite, and they stood in their two groups, Rees and Crows, talking quietly and casting grave glances at Custer.

"We'll rest here half an hour," Custer said. "Private Voss, go on back and let the company commanders know."

A sudden hot wind had sprung up from the west, and as Voss turned his horse the swallowtail that Vickory had planted fell over. Godfrey, who was closest, swung down off his horse and wrestled it back into the ground.

"Thank you, Lieutenant," Custer said.

The swallowtail fell again. Godfrey heard it and turned back. He lifted it in front of him and stabbed the ground, hard, then stood watching to see if the flag would hold. It didn't. It nodded, nodded some more, went down. No one moved to help Godfrey. No one spoke. Horses snorted, stamped, but that was all. Godfrey took the flag up again and probed with it, looking for soft ground, and found some. He dug the staff into the ground, leaning his full weight on it. It held.

"Thank you, Lieutenant," Custer said again.

"Sir," Godfrey answered, and still there was silence, weighted and moody, broken only when they were moving again and could no longer hear the warm, dry, malevolent-seeming summer wind.

"You ever see the ocean, Bos?" Allen said.

He'd been thinking about Buzzards Bay, steel blue and stirred by the southwest wind, which blew hazy and golden in the summertime. Remembering the feel of rising out of the water into the warm salt-scented air, a breeze-borne sweetness of rugosa roses.

"I've seen lakes," Bos said.

Autie glanced irritably past Bos at Allen, then went back to observing the countryside. The three of them had built their fire, made coffee, and packed up without speaking to one another. They'd ridden all morning in silence.

"You ought to see an ocean at least once before you die," Allen said.

"Well, I'd like to see it."

George was riding just ahead of them, at the rear of headquarters. His fever had come up again and Allen was keeping an eye on him.

"Tell me about the ocean," Bos said. "What's it look like?"

"It's blue, dumbass," Autie said.

"It is sometimes," Allen said. "Sometimes

it's green. Sometimes gray. It's got more moods than a lake."

They rode awhile. The valley floor all dug and scored. Hundreds of Indians had passed by here. Thousands.

"Go on with the ocean," Bos said. "The ships that go on it. What's in it. Whales and such."

"You'll have to come see it for yourself," Allen said.

"When we come to your wedding," Bos said. "We'll have us a sea bath, Autie."

"Just what I've always wanted," Autie said.

"It isn't any need to be cranky," Bos said.

"Shut up," Autie said.

"All right, I will," Bos said.

They halted again at one o'clock. Godfrey brought his company up, and the men dismounted and sought the shade along the creek. Godfrey found Custer with Tom Custer, Cooke, and Boyer under a willow tree. They were eating hardtack. Gnawing at it. Custer had made Tom his aide-de-camp when they left the Yellowstone, and by that appointment would keep him at his side at all times. Godfrey saluted and told Custer he'd seen a trail branch off to the east some ten miles back.

"That isn't possible," Custer said.

"I saw it," Godfrey said.

"General," Boyer said, "look here. If it's some Indians take a different road, let 'em go. We got plenty still in front of us."

"Get Varnum up here," Custer said.

Boyer nodded slowly. He got up, shoved the cracker into his vest pocket, and went looking for his horse. He came back with Varnum twenty minutes later. Varnum's face was stubbled and wore a film of sweat and red dust. He had slept little and had not been out of his clothes since the Yellowstone. He left his horse and followed Boyer over and saluted.

"Godfrey saw a trail branch off about ten miles back," Custer said. "I want you to scout it out. Take some of the Rees."

"Sir, the scouts have been all over this trail. Reynolds has been studying every inch of it. They wouldn't let anything go by."

"You want to take Gerard?" Custer said.

Varnum took off his black slouch hat and passed his sleeve over his forehead, smearing sweat and dust. He put the hat back on, adjusted it.

"I imagine it's a detour, Colonel. A small party, getting around some hills or something."

"Go find out," Custer said.

Three of the Crows came in a little before four o'clock. Boyer led them to Custer. Along the creek the men were seeing to their horses, building fires for coffee. The antic wind had quit, and the smoke twisted lazily up in the heavy air.

"These boys find another big campsite," Boyer said. "It's about twelve miles from here. The ashes still warm."

The three Crows hung back of him, watching Custer. The youngest of them — he could not have been twenty — said something, and Boyer turned around and answered him. The young man spoke again.

"What is it?" Custer said.

"He want to know what the Crows supposed to do when you catch the Sioux."

"Tell him the Rees are going to steal horses while the soldiers do the fighting. Tell him he can do that if he wants to be a man."

Boyer translated it. The young Crow listened with his eyes downcast. Half Yellow Face smiled. It was he who answered Boyer. Boyer answered back, sharp.

"What?" Custer said.

"Nothing, sir."

"Tell me," Custer said.

"He say the Crows are men, but he don't know about the soldiers."

"Don't take it, Armstrong," Tom said.

But Custer only removed his Stetson and wiped his forehead with his sleeve, as Varnum had done. He put the Stetson back on.

"Tell him the soldiers will follow me, and I'll show them how to be men," he said. "Tell him I can show the Crows."

Boyer translated it.

Half Yellow Face spoke.

"He say Son of the Morning Star is plenty man and he don't worry about it," Boyer said.

"Thank him for me," Custer said.

Varnum returned with his Rees and announced that the diverging trail had been no more than a detour, as he'd thought, which rejoined the main trail a few miles on. All that hard riding for nothing, but if Varnum was annoyed with Custer, he showed no trace of it. Custer put the column in motion again.

They stopped at about eight o'clock on the east side of the Rosebud, where the grass had not been grazed by Indian ponies. Cottonwoods and willows grew thick along the creek, and wild roses bloomed. The order went around to keep fires small and extinguish them early. Keogh, whose turn it was today, arrived with the mules an hour later in a foul mood, and the men smiled at his cursing. The men groomed and fed their horses and picketed them by company. They spread their blankets. The thin moon rose on a gun-blue sky. To the west, beyond a steep clay-gray bluff, coyotes bayed, yipped.

The Crows came in again, and Boyer brought all six of them to Custer, who was sitting on a camp chair in front of his tent with the staghounds at his feet. Tom sat on the ground beside him, smoking. Cooke sat with his long legs stretched out, ankles crossed. Cooke had been saving some raisins and condensed milk and was sharing them now with Tom and the general. They had punched a hole in the can and were passing it back and forth.

"The trail turn west along a little creek," Boyer said. "Go across the divide toward the Little Bighorn. They ain't but a day ahead of us, General."

"Tommy," Custer said, "go get Varnum."

Tom took a last drag on his cigarette, rubbed it out on his boot heel, and scrambled up.

Reno's little choir, which had sung on the

deck of the *Far West* on the eve of their departure up the Rosebud, had gathered again. Custer, looking down the belt of trees along the creek, could see them standing shoulder to shoulder in the dimming twilight. Dr. Porter and Dr. DeWolf had joined them. They were singing "Annie Laurie."

"Pretty, ain't it," Boyer said.

The Crows stared at the singers thoughtfully, as if they would reserve judgment.

Varnum, following Tom, had brought his supper with him, his salt pork and grease-fried hardtack, in the fry pan he'd cooked them in. "Permission, sir?" he said.

"Sit down, Lieutenant," Custer said.

Varnum dropped onto the grass and cradled the fry pan in his lap and began eating. Tom remained standing. Arms folded, a knee canted. The mosquitoes had come out.

"Tell him what you've learned, Mitch," Custer said.

"There's a place near the divide," Boyer said, "a big hill that the Crows know. You get up there, you can see all the way down the valley of the Little Horn. Fifteen mile. If Sitting Bull down there, you see him from that hill."

The singers had concluded "Annie Laurie" and moved into "Little Footsteps."

"We'll need a white man to go take a

look," Custer said.

"I guess that means me," Varnum said, eating.

"You and Mitch. Take the Crows and a Ree or two. Take Reynolds if he can do it."

Varnum, still holding the fry pan, heaved himself to his feet. Boyer turned and told the Crows what was happening.

"Send someone back when you've gotten a look," Custer said.

"Yes sir," Varnum said, and he and Boyer moved away, slow, Varnum still with the panful of supper, the Crows following silently.

"What time are we moving?" Tom said.

Cooke raised a hand to quiet him. "Listen," he said.

They were singing "Nearer My God to Thee." One voice rose above the others, a choirboy's tenor that carried sweetly out in the bluish half-light, Reno and the rest of them singing under it, adding their deeper voices in deferent harmony.

"Jimmy Sturgis," Tom said.

There let the way appear, steps unto Heaven;

All that Thou sendest me, in mercy given . . .

"Lugubrious damn thing," Custer said.

Nearer, my God, to Thee, nearer to Thee;

Though like the wanderer, the sun gone down,

Darkness be over me, my rest a stone . . .

"We'll move at eleven, eleven-thirty," Custer said.

"The moon's going to set," Cooke said. "It'll be dark, Armstrong."

"Boyer says there's a creek we can follow," Custer said.

Yet in my dreams I'd be nearer, my God to Thee . . .

The hymn was over. Some officers had gathered to listen, and their applause rose thinly in the quiet of the camp. It was getting dark. Cooke excused himself and went off toward the creekside trees for some privacy. Tom folded himself down beside Custer's chair and sat with his knees drawn up, his arms wrapping them.

"It's our last fight, isn't it," he said.

"It's mine," Custer said.

"I wonder what I'll do."

"Come back to Monroe, marry Miss Wadsworth."

"I wish I felt like it," Tom said.

"You owe her," Custer said. "Make an honest woman of her."

Tom looked up. The twitch of a smile. "You ought to talk," he said. "What are you going to do, you go East with Libbie and

363

your actress friend starts coming around?"

"Keep them apart," Custer said.

"I hope so, for Libbie's sake," Tom said.

Custer looked at him in the near dark. Unbearded, nut-brown face, the white scar, memento of Sayler's Creek, a Rebel ball. Tommy had jumped a breastwork on his horse and shot their color bearer and scooped up the flag. There was no braver man.

"You're sweet on Libbie, aren't you," he said.

Tom shrugged, looking out toward the shadowy trees. "A little."

"More than a little."

"I'm happy, Armstrong. I have everything I want."

Custer smiled, thinking how young Tommy still was, how innocent of life's ambiguities and distractions. "Nobody has everything they want," he said. And then: "Go collect the officers."

The three of them lay under their blankets by George's little A tent listening to the coyotes and the chirr of insects in the grass near the creek. The striker McAllister had cooked George some salt pork and left him bedded down with the whiskey bottle.

"He's welcome to it," Autie said. "I had

enough last night to last me till we get home."

"There'll be a smart of drinking then," Bos said.

"Hard to believe it's finally on us," Autie said.

"There's no hard feelings amongst us, is there?" Bos said.

The question hung there. A mosquito whined and lit; Allen slapped it. There was a fragrance of wild roses in the air, and he would remember it long afterward. He would remember Lieutenant Sturgis singing "Nearer My God to Thee."

"I was hasty," Allen said, "and I'm sorry for it."

"Autie?" Bos said.

"I'm over it," Autie said.

"Well, that's good," Bos said, "because —"

Major Reno was standing over them, thickset in his dark-blue coat, hatless, eyes coal black, coal bright in the gloom. They sat up. Reno had come up from the creek, out of the shadows. He carried a canteen. He stood very still, regarding them closely, looking from face to face as though one of them, he did not know which, held an answer he needed. The three of them looked at each other. Reno had never spoken to any of them.

"The three pups of the Seventh," he said.

Reno did not sound drunk, but from his ponderous gravity and deliberation Allen thought he must be.

"We break camp in an hour, did you boys know that?" Reno said.

Again they looked at each other.

"No sir," Bos said, "didn't anybody tell us."

"I'm surprised Colonel Custer didn't tell you. Doesn't he tell you boys everything?"

"Not everything," Bos said.

"Sir, did you have something you wanted to say?" Allen said.

Reno uncapped his canteen. He tilted it up and drank. Whiskey, sure.

"I wanted to tell you about the guardhouse at Fort Hayes," he said, capping the canteen. "You know about that?"

"How would we?" Autie said.

"I didn't think so. It wasn't like the one at Lincoln. It was a hole in the ground. A pit, you might say. Twenty feet deep, thirty, I don't know. Deep as hell, anyway. Covered it with logs, cut a hole in the logs and a ladder going down. Nights Colonel Custer put the prisoners down there."

"He never did such," Bos said.

Reno smiled. "In the wintertime, no less. There'd be so many of them they couldn't lie down. Just imagine the sanitary conditions."

"Sir, we'd like to get some sleep if we could," Allen said.

"Ask him about the time General Sheridan wrote to him, told him to stop flogging his men. Ask him about those fellows who deserted in Kansas. The kind of justice they got."

"Are you about finished?" Autie said.

"He's going to march us all night," Reno said. "He's going to wear us out, men and horses, then let the Sioux have at us. He'll get half of us killed. Good evening, gentlemen."

They watched him move off down the tent street, slow and slightly shambling, carrying his canteen.

"What the hell was that?" Autie said.

"He hates Armstrong," Bos said. "You know that."

"He's piss-ass drunk," Autie said.

"Let's get some sleep," Allen said.

"I never saw anyone flogged," Bos said. "I saw 'em bucked and gagged, but not flogged."

"So what if he did?" Autie said. "It's rough out here."

Allen lay down and pulled his blanket up.

"Armstrong never put prisoners in any

pit," Bos said.

"So what if he did," Autie said. "Thieves. Deserters. What the hell?"

Allen closed his eyes and smelled the wild roses. Tomorrow or the next day it would be over, and he would take Addie Grace away from here forever. He saw her in the saffron-yellow dress she'd worn the day they arrived at Lincoln, in the cool spring afternoon on the deck of the *Denver*. He tried to remember her naked and could see only the lovely contour of waist and hip and lower leg, and the milky radiance that seemed to course under her skin. Then Bos was shaking him awake in the dark, and the regiment was moving out.

The trail lay over rolling terrain slanting up from the creek, and in the moonless dark horses slipped and stumbled, the men cursing not the horses but this blind midnight march, which seemed too groping and slow to gain them any advantage on an enemy they had not yet laid eyes on. You could see nothing of where you were going, only the pale billowing dust of the company ahead of you. The men at the rear of some companies kept up a tapping of cups on fry pans or carbine slings to guide the men behind them, a tinny clangor ringing out dull and monotonous in the dust-choked air. The dust stung in the eyes and invaded throat and nostrils.

Custer rode out ahead with Bloody Knife and Gerard and the two dogs trotting beside him. Half Yellow Face wasn't far forward of them; they could hear the footfalls of his horse, could hear it snort and blow, and were following the sounds. After a while, on the brow of a ridge, they overtook Isaiah Dorman.

"Are they watching to the left?" Custer said.

"As good as they can," Dorman said.

"I want them to scout any trail they see. I don't care if it's three lodges. I want all camps driven down to the Little Bighorn. *All* of them, Isaiah."

Bloody Knife wanted to know what that was about and Gerard told him. Bloody Knife spoke sullenly.

"He says you oughtn't to be so particular," Gerard said. "That you'll find enough to suit you in the main camp."

"Tell him if he wants to go home and be with the women he can," Custer said.

"He's just nervous," Gerard said. "He'll be all right."

Bloody Knife spoke again. Perhaps he'd understood the crack about the women.

"Now what?" Custer said.

"He says there's a big fight coming and beyond it he won't see another sun."

Custer shook his head. "I'm getting a bit tired of this," he said.

Ginger staggered up the rises and felt her way down through the blind draws, unhesitating, dutiful to this necessity, senseless as it seemed, and Allen had never loved her so much. He spoke to her, leaning forward over her ear; thanked her, promised her he'd make it up to her.

The boys and Bos rode behind headquarters and George with them, breathing its bitter dust. George kept closing his eyes and drawing deep breaths, as if there were some sustenance in the foul air. From time to time he uncapped his canteen and drank, and Allen knew his throat was hurting him.

"We can drop out," he said. "Rest awhile."

"I wouldn't do that, Allen," Bos said.

"I'm all right," George said.

His mare, whose name was Cassandra, tackled the broken terrain as willingly as Ginger. George worked with her, sitting loose and deep in the saddle, leaning when she climbed, but his breathing was labored, and Allen rode close enough, when he could, to grab his arm or catch him if he should fall.

"What do you suppose is the point of this?" Allen said.

"Sneak up on 'em," Bos said.

"Sneak up on them," Allen said. "Maybe if they were deaf."

"I guess Uncle Armstrong knows what he's doing," Autie said.

"At least the deer flies aren't out," Bos said.

They halted sometime before dawn, still some miles short of the divide between the Rosebud and the Little Bighorn, beside a twisting trickle of water called Davis Creek on the map, where there was room to spread out and some grass for the horses and mules. On either side, north and south, the dark hills swept skyward, providing good concealment. The men slid stiffly down from their saddles and put their horses to drink, but the water was alkaline and the horses drew back from it, stamping and nodding vehemently, as if outraged. The men relieved themselves in the darkness across the creek, then slept by their horses, some with the reins wrapping their wrists. Some removed saddles, some only slipped the bits out. An unlucky few from each company had been sent up to the hilltops to stand sentry, and how they stayed awake, if they did, no one knew.

Custer gave Dandy to Burkman and crawled under a chokecherry with a dog snuggled against him on either side and slept. In his dream Libbie was waltzing with Myles Keogh at an officers ball in the commissary storehouse at Lincoln. Keogh was in his buckskins, she in a pale green dress and white satin gloves to her elbows, arching back in the crook of his wrist, smiling brilliantly up at him. Keogh's eyes were on her, bold, aglint, lascivious.

I'd better cut in on this, but Libbie glanced at him over her shoulder and said, *Not now, Armstrong. Go away.* He stood there, sensible of the looks, the stares. Vinatieri's band was playing "Garryowen," and Custer wondered why, considering they were waltzing, then remembered that it was Keogh who had introduced him to the song, a relic from his service in the Irish Papal Guard. They were playing it for Keogh, evidently. *I have to put a stop to this,* and he went after them, chasing them across the dance floor. *Go away, Armstrong.* Keogh was ignoring him, eyeing Libbie in a way you couldn't mistake, and again Custer stopped, rooted to the spot, paralyzed. *Go away, go away,* and he did not know what to do.

Allen unsaddled Ginger, peeled off the sweated saddle blanket and rubbed her back with a damp cool fistful of grass from the creek bank. There was a handful of oats left in his forage sack and he gave them to her in her nosebag, then lay down with Autie and Bos and George, whose horses were picketed a few feet away. Men had lain down on the ground all about them, and the sour smell of horses was strong in the motionless air between the hills.

"It's really happening, isn't it," Autie said.

"We'll hit 'em today," Bos said. "Tomorrow at the latest."

"You need anything, George?" Allen said.

"Just this bottle," George said.

The bivouac had grown quiet. Somebody broke into a snore. Allen hadn't bothered with the mosquito veil. None of them had. George, up on his elbow, took a swallow of the whiskey. A horse snorted, and another, as if in reply. A coyote yapped from beyond the south hill. George corked the bottle. He lay down and covered himself. A soldier had got up and was threading his way among the loungers and sleepers toward the creek. The coyote had ceased its barking. George's breathing leveled down. He was asleep.

"We come a long way together, haven't we," Bos said.

Autie had snuggled down under his blanket. "Go to sleep," he said.

"The Three Musketeers," Bos said. "All for one, one for all."

"Go to sleep."

"It's good you two made it up," Bos said. "We're friends for life now, you realize that?"

"Damn right," Allen said.

"Autie?" Bos said.

"I never said we weren't," Autie said.

"Good night, then," Bos said.

"Night," Allen said.

He dreamed he was bathing with Addie Grace in Buzzards Bay on a windy summer's day with the waves rolling in lace-white, tossing them gently about. He was treading water, being lifted and lowered by the marching waves, and she was swimming toward him, breaststroke, coming on slowly, smiling at him across the water. He treaded water, waited. She drew up close. Her wet face was a foot from his, still smiling, and he realized she was naked. *Why, Addie Grace!* he said. *What of it?* she said. *I'm of age, am I not?* He tried to think if she *was* of age and could not remember what the age was, and she put her hands on his shoulders and he held her and was naked too, and then they were ashore on the wet, soft sand at the water's edge, and he was looking down into her lovely worried face. *Don't leave me,* she said. *If you leave me, I'll have no one. Of course you will,* he said, but she said she would not, not ever, and so he promised her, told her he loved her and did not *want* to leave her in any case. *Well then,* she said and smiled and raised her arms above him. He took her on the wet flat brown-sugar sand, and it was lovely.

FOUR

Burkman woke him, leaning over him with a cup of coffee and a hard cracker. The dogs raised their heads, slapped the ground with their tails. The colorless dawn had crept up the eastern sky, and in the thinning darkness men were moving about or crouched by sagebrush fires trying to boil coffee. The coffee Burkman brought him was lukewarm and alkali-bitter, but Custer drank it off and handed back the tin cup and thanked him.

"What time is it, John?" he said.

"About four o'clock, I make it."

"I'll tell Mrs. Custer what good care you're taking of me," Custer said.

"You eat your cracker, General," Burkman said.

"I will by and by," Custer said, and lay down on his back and put his Stetson over his face and fell into a dreamless doze.

They built a small fire at dawn and fried

hard crackers, saving their last slabs of salt pork for later. None of them wanted to make coffee with water horses wouldn't drink. George ate half a piece of salt pork and said it was all he could do. He said his throat hurt too much to force hardtack down it, even grease-fried. Dr. Porter came by and knelt and felt his forehead and said his fever had come back pretty high and that he ought to stay back with the pack train. He said they were going to cross the divide today, then hide somewhere and attack the Indians at dawn tomorrow.

"Tomorrow," Autie said. "What did we ride half the night for?"

"So as to rest today, I imagine," the surgeon said.

"We can use it," Bos said. "Horses too. They're about wore out."

"Get some sleep, George," Dr. Porter said and moved on.

Allen, Bos, and Autie shaved in the creek then sat down by the dying fire. Day broke, dyeing the world in its summer colors. Queen Anne's lace and purple coneflowers nodded in the grass along the creek. Soap-weed yucca, clumped white bells above the pale quills of their leaves, stood here and there, random. The bluff to the north was chalk white. The air was soft and not badly tainted by the smells of horses and dung and the human waste across the creek. The mosquitoes had quit biting and the gnats and flies weren't out yet.

"It's awful pretty here," Bos said.

"Good day for a picnic," Autie said. "Some bread. Some cheese. Wouldn't some buttermilk taste good out here?"

Allen was thinking about his dream, Addie Grace naked and wet in the wet sand. Her brother had been sleeping not three feet away, and Allen wondered if dreams can pass from sleeper to sleeper at that distance and hoped not.

"How far is it to the divide?" Autie said.

"A short ride," Bos said, "then a fine long rest."

But then a Ree named Red Star rode in with a note from Varnum, galloping zigzag as he approached, in this way announcing that he'd seen the enemy, which changed everything.

It was Dorman who carried Varnum's note from Red Star to Custer, who was sitting on the ground with Tom and Cooke, talking idly and watching the quiet stir of the encampment. Men were grooming their horses or leading them to what was left of the creekside grass. Some talked quietly by the smoking fires, some had gone back to sleep.

Custer read the note and scrambled up and called to Burkman and told him to bring Dandy, unsaddled. He sent Cooke to find Gerard and then threw himself onto the mare and rode her at a brisk trot to the scouts' bivouac, which lay along the creek a couple of hundred yards down. Kellogg saw him and jumped up in his long underwear and followed along. Tom had found his horse and reached the bivouac moments later.

The Rees were gathered in a half circle, sitting or squatting, listening to Red Star. Bloody Knife sat a little apart, smoking a cigarette. He eyed Custer sourly and went back to listening to Red Star. Someone brought Red Star a cup of coffee. Custer dropped to one knee, and Red Star glanced at him and stopped talking. Cooke came up on foot, bringing Gerard. The two of them stood with Tom, in back of Custer. Kellogg stood behind all of them, scribbling in his notebook.

"Ask him what he saw," Custer said.

Gerard put the question to Red Star.

"He says the Indians are very many," Gerard said.

Red Star spoke again.

"He's a bit upset about our fires," Gerard said. "He says do we think the Sioux have eyes like white men."

Custer looked down, thought about this. The fires might have been a mistake, and he wondered why he'd authorized them. He looked Red Star in the eye and saw a wary and reticent opacity. He sent him a smile then glanced back at Tom.

"You see my brother, standing here? His heart is dancing. A captain of soldiers, and he's afraid. Only after we've whipped the Sioux will he be a man."

Gerard translated it. The Rees looked at each other. There were a few dry smiles, not many, and Custer saw that the joke had failed to erase the doubt, the sullenness.

"When we get to the Sioux camp," he said, "it'll be your job to run off their horses. Steal or run them off, whichever."

Gerard told them and they nodded, grunted assent.

Bloody Knife spoke.

"What is it?" Custer said, expecting nothing good. He was getting tired of his favorite scout.

"He says we'll find enough Sioux to keep us fighting for three days."

"Tell him one day will be plenty," Custer

said and rose and walked away from them.

The lookout, which Varnum called the Crow's Nest, was a northern promontory of the Wolf Mountains some four miles from their campsite on Davis Creek. Red Star led the way, backtracking, up and down the endless hills, in and out of the draws, the sun now well clear of the rolling horizon, the air warming, thickening. Custer had brought Gerard, Bloody Knife, and a Ree named Stabbed, an older man who was the Rees' leader after Bloody Knife. They rode in silence, at an urgent canter, Custer pressing, pushing Red Star and his weary mount while the others followed.

The land began its final ascent, studded now with low pines and wind-gnarled junipers. Dandy pulled out in front of Red Star and Custer urged her on, for the way was clear now, the summit dead ahead. The ascent grew steeper and the mare danced, staggered forward, trampling feathery blue lupin, kicking through clustered pink roses, Custer leaning into the climb. The air thinned and now held the sweet scent of pine and sage.

Dandy, struggling now, stiffened and pricked her ears, and in a moment Custer saw why: the horses of Varnum's detail, picketed in a kind of hollow just where the hillside steepened suddenly to nearly forty-five degrees. Custer stopped Dandy and was off her almost simultaneously. He left her untied and went on up the steep slope. His boots felt heavy, his thighs burned. The pine smell grew sweeter. Up he went, sweating, breathing hard.

Varnum met him below the summit, scrabbling down, slipping. He was even more darkly stubbled than before, more filthy.

"I think they've seen us," he said and turned and led the way uphill. "We saw two of them, looked like an old man and a boy, about a mile away. Reynolds and Boyer and a couple of the Crows went after them, but they didn't have any luck."

"How do you know you were seen?" Custer said.

"That old man and that boy were running, sir."

Custer glanced back. The others had left their horses and were clambering up behind him, strung out among the little trees.

"It's a big village, anyway," Varnum said.

They stepped up onto the summit. It was broad and more or less flat, strewn with more wind-stunted pines and junipers. A cool insistent breeze blew, herb fragrant, making a doleful rustle in the trees. They crossed to the north side and found Boyer and Reynolds and their scouts sitting on wind-smoothed outcrops of golden sandstone, looking north over the miles of hills. Custer stopped, looked out. The land, high and low, was a sun-faded green, giving way finally to a diaphanous bluish haze out near the horizon. Immediately below them the grassy hillside fell away nearly sheer. In the near distance trees marked the straggling course of Davis Creek. Far away to the west rose the smoky-blue Big Horn Mountains, capped, still, with snow.

Reynolds stood up wearily, then Boyer. Reynolds had pocketed his bandanna sling, but his hand was wrapped in a dirty bandage. Field glasses hung from his neck. The Crows were smoking. They rubbed their cigarettes out on the stone and got up.

"Good morning, gentlemen," Custer said.

"The village is right where I told you," Boyer said.

"I'd like to see it," Custer said.

Gerard arrived, with Red Star and Stabbed not many paces behind him, both of them breathing hard.

"I guess this old man is stronger than Bloody Knife," Custer said, meaning Stabbed.

"He's coming," Gerard said.

Reynolds stood beside Custer and stretched out his right arm, pointing. "That's the valley, sir. It's about fifteen miles from here. You can see the pony herd."

Custer sighted along Reynolds's rigid arm. "I don't see a thing," he said.

"You see the valley?"

"Where?"

"Beyond those far hills. Where the haze is."

Bloody Knife had come up, sweating in his flannel shirt, glancing about him irritably. He said something, but Custer didn't ask Gerard what.

"Look for worms," Boyer said.

Custer looked at him. "Do what?"

"Look for worms, sir. That's the pony herd. They look like worms crawling on the ground."

"I don't see them," Custer said.

"General," Boyer said, "if you don't find more Indians in that valley than you ever saw before, you can hang me."

"Hang you," Custer said. "A lot of damn good that'd do."

Reynolds had unlooped his field glasses. "Look for dust," he said. "That's the pony herd."

Custer peered through the field glasses

and the sere green hills and dark pines jumped closer, and after a while, in the still-distant wide, shallow bowl of the valley far beyond he did see something vapor-like and distinct from the haze. He returned the glasses to Reynolds.

"All right," he said. "There's a village down there. I don't know how big it is."

"I do," Boyer said.

The Crows had stood by silent and indifferent-seeming, gazing out toward the valley, glancing with not much interest at the white men as they spoke. Now Half Yellow Face stepped toward Custer and spoke to him directly, as if Custer knew the language. Custer let him finish then looked at Boyer.

"He is telling you to attack today," Boyer said. "He say you have been seen, you don't got no choice."

"We don't know we've been seen."

"We have been," Varnum said.

"What do you think, Mitch?" Custer said.

Boyer shrugged. "I'm damn sure they seen us," he said.

"Charley?"

Reynolds's gaze was far away, down the valley of the Little Bighorn, and he'd never looked so lonesome. A Mexican beauty had broken his heart, people said, and he had never loved again. He had attended college in Illinois and read Latin, read Greek. Now he shook his head, as if to dislodge some troubling thought or memory, and looked once more at Custer.

"They know we're here," he said.

"Then it's time," Custer said.

The regiment had come nearly three miles in their absence, still following the creek, and Reno had hidden them in a wide valley-like ravine. Custer swung down off of Dandy and handed Burkman the reins and told Voss to blow officers call, the first bugle music since "Garryowen" on the Yellow-stone. The officers came flocking around; some, from a distance down the ravine, weaving among the resting men and mounts on horseback. Hughes and Vickory had jammed the two flags into the ground. The officers sat down, and Custer stood to address them in his buckskin jacket and red cravat, folding his arms and canting a knee forward; theatrical, assertive, a stance elegant even to his enemies and perhaps especially to them. Allen, Bos, and Autie worked in behind the officers to listen. Boyer and Reynolds had come in and dismounted. Mark Kellogg, who had sent his last dispatch by courier on the morning of the twenty-fourth, opened his notebook and jotted the date at the top of the page. *June 25.*

Seize the initiative, hold on to it straight through to the end. It was the simplest of formulas, and yet the Rebellion had nearly been lost because men shrank from it. He told his gathered officers that there was a big village fifteen miles away on the river called the Little Bighorn. He said he had not seen it but the Indian scouts had, and so had Boyer and Charley Reynolds, so it must surely exist. He told them that the Indians had discovered them, and that the regiment would therefore move immediately to the attack. He ordered the company commanders to assign five men and one non-commissioned officer to help guard the pack train, and he said companies would march as they became ready, the quickest in the advance, the slowest to come behind with the mules, back from the fight when it began and likely to miss it altogether.

"We're ready now," Benteen said.

Custer looked at him. Pale eyes, colorless, coldly bright. It was unlikely that his company, or any company, was ready, and everyone knew it.

"You checked with your first sergeant, did you?" Custer said.

"I don't need to check with him. Company H is ready, Colonel."

Custer nodded slowly, trying to think what to do. He did not want Tom jumping into this.

"All right, Colonel Benteen," he said, "the advance is yours."

"Sir?" Reynolds said.

"Mr. Reynolds," Custer said.

Reynolds was standing beside Boyer in back of the seated officers. "I should have said it sooner but I'll say it now," he said. "This is the biggest bunch of Indians I've ever seen."

"It's more Indians in that valley than we can handle," Boyer said.

It brought a pall of silence down on them and Custer thought if he could do it again he would not have brought Mitch Boyer. He was even beginning to wonder why'd he'd brought Reynolds. Boston Custer plucked a blade of grass and studied as if he had not heard Reynolds or Boyer. Autie Reed glanced at Allen and quickly away. Allen looked down into his lap and thought of Addie Grace Lord and what she might be doing and saw her reading a Dickens novel in the shade by the river, where a breeze cooled her and kept the insects away from her pretty neck and face. He tried again to remember what she'd looked like in the starlit darkness of the Custers' guest bedroom, breasts and hips and legs.

"You don't have to go in with us, Mitch," Custer said. "You either, Charley."

"That ain't the point," Boyer said. "I'll go anywhere you will."

"I'm going to that valley."

"I go with you."

"Charley?" Custer said.

"Of course I'm coming," Reynolds said.

Allen was sitting on the dry spiny grass with Ginger's reins dropped beside him. Bos and Autie sat facing him with their horses in back of them. It was hot in the ravine, which was sunk below whatever breeze might be blowing. Allen got up and dug in a saddle-bag and found the Mezuzah. He pushed it down into the right pocket of his corduroy trousers.

"What in hell is that?" Autie said.

"A good luck piece. A fellow gave it to me in Bismarck. Old Jewish fellow. It's got Hebrew writing on it. Calls on God to keep an eye on me."

Autie smiled. "Think it'll work?"

"Worth the try," Allen said.

"We stay close to Allen," Bos said, "maybe He'll watch over you and me as well."

"We *will* stay close," Autie said. "It's the plan, isn't it?"

Allen sat down again. He unbuttoned his holster and drew out the blue-black revolver, which had been riding his hip, unloaded, all these weeks.

"What are you going to do with that?" Autie said.

Allen didn't look at him or answer. He broke open the gate. He slid a cartridge from its loop on his gun belt and pushed it into the cylinder.

"Well, goddamn," Autie said.

"You're doin' right, Allen," Bos said.

"Maybe," Allen said.

"No maybe about it," Bos said.

Allen inserted another cartridge, and another, lifting the hammer and turning the cylinder and pressing the cartridge in with his thumb. The cylinder clicked softly as it revolved. He added a fifth cartridge and snapped the gate shut.

"You got God, you got a gun," Autie said. "You're in it now, Allen. You're in all the way."

"Maybe," Allen said and pushed the gun into its holster and buttoned it.

George was sitting on the ground in his soiled duster with DeWolf on one side of him and Porter on the other. Custer squatted in front of him and put a gauntleted hand on George's leg above his boot.

"How you feeling, my friend?" he said.

"I'm all right," George said.

"He isn't all right," Dr. Porter said.

"I want you to stay back with the pack train," Custer said.

"Not a chance," George said.

"We've been telling him, General," Dr. Porter said. "It's like talking to a post."

"Listen to me," Custer said. "There'll be plenty for you to do, time you get there."

"I'm not staying back, Armstrong," George said.

"Be sensible," Porter said.

"I *can't* stay back," George said.

Custer smiled and let his hand go to George's leg again. He slapped it gently. And again.

"I didn't think so," he said.

He found Bos, Autie, and Allen Winslow with their horses, checking girths, retying blankets. All down the ravine the men were getting ready to ride. Corporals and sergeants were going among them checking rifle shells for verdigris one final time, trying the extractors of Colts while the men stood by waiting to be rebuked or com-

391

mended.

"You boys ready to ride?" Custer said.

"Damn right," Autie said.

"I want the three of you near me at all times," Custer said. "When the fighting starts, you do what I tell you. You do it fast, and you don't argue with me."

"We don't want to miss anything," Autie said.

"That sounds like arguing, Autie."

"When the fighting started, you said," Autie said.

"No arguing, period," Custer said. "You start, I'll send you back to the pack train."

"We're just glad to be here," Bos said.

"And we appreciate it, Uncle Armstrong," Autie said.

"Be sure you do," Custer said.

Stabbed was anointing the bare chests of the younger Rees with red clay he'd brought in a pouch all the way from Fort Lincoln. He'd poured water on the clay, made a paste of it. The young Rees had opened their shirts, their buckskin jackets, and were stepping forward in turn, closing their eyes as Stabbed smeared on the clay, using two fingers. Bloody Knife stood watching, holding his rifle tilted back carelessly on his shoulder. Uphill a short way stood a Ree named Young Hawk, singing the flat tuneless dirge the Rees had sung on that last parade around Lincoln.

"Medicine against arrows and bullets," Gerard said.

"I want to speak to them," Custer said.

Gerard told Stabbed and Stabbed said give him another minute, he was nearly done. He had a broad mournful face and wore his hair long and parted in the middle, like Bloody Knife. Young Hawk still sang, a slow, tremulous wail.

Bloody Knife said something in Custer's direction, and Gerard translated.

"Their horses are tired."

"Tell him ours are too."

The last young Ree opened his cotton shirt and Stabbed painted his chest, daubing the clay in a circular motion. The boy stepped back, unsmiling. The Rees closed around Custer and Gerard and squatted.

"I want you to ride fast today," Custer said. "Make up your minds to go straight to their camp and get their horses. Take as many as you can."

Gerard translated it.

"You're going to have a hard day," Custer said. "I want you to keep your courage up. The younger of you will get some good experience."

They listened to this somberly. Then Bloody Knife spoke again. He was squatting to the side, apart, positioned like a first sergeant. Gerard glanced uncertainly at Custer, and Custer told him to go on and say it.

"He says he's remembering the day you were going to shoot him in the Black Hills."

Custer closed his eyes and massaged them with thumb and forefinger. The older Rees knew the story and were smiling. The boys looked from Bloody Knife to Custer in mute surprise.

"I was joking," Custer said. "I asked you to come back, and I apologized."

"A wagon got stuck and you thought it was my fault, and you aimed your carbine at me."

"I apologized."

"It wasn't a good thing, even so. If I'd been crazy too we might both be dead."

Bloody Knife had not adverted to this embarrassing incident in the two years since it happened, and Custer wondered what perverse caprice was at work here, today of all days. The younger Rees had begun to smile.

"Tell him Bloody Knife is my brother," Custer said. "Remind him what I said before: when this is over I'm going to take him east with me. Tell him he'll be honored wherever he goes. I'll introduce him to the Great White Father."

Bloody Knife listened to Gerard with his brow furrowed, his eyes squinted thoughtfully. Custer had never known his age but guessed now he was in his mid-forties.

"Bloody Knife thanks Son of the Morning Star," he said through Gerard, "but I'm going home today. I'm going home to my people."

Young Hawk had stopped singing. Custer looked at Bloody Knife's stubborn pensive face and tried to think what to say. He'd known men in the Rebellion who'd foretold their deaths, and it struck him that what they'd felt, what Bloody Knife was feeling now, was abandonment. God, destiny, luck — whatever you called it — had deserted them. It would be an unbearable loneliness, and his heart went out to the obstinate and cheeky Ree.

"Tell him," Custer said, "that I don't want him to drink all our whiskey tonight after we've whipped the Sioux."

Gerard translated it and a chorus of laughter went up, and even Bloody Knife smiled.

The men waited for the order to move out,

sitting four abreast, the companies stretching back at fifty-yard intervals, noncoms out
beside them, a trumpeter front and rear.
Custer had pushed Dandy hard already and
would ride Vic into battle. Burkman had
saddled and brought him with the dogs,
Tuck and Blucher, pacing beside him with
wide-eyed expectant faces. Autie Reed was
mounted beside Tom and in front of Bos
and Allen.

"Well, John," Custer said.

"I ought to be going with you," Burkman
said, sullen, eyes to the ground.

"You've stood guard three nights," Custer
said.

"*He* oughtn't to be going," Burkman said,
with an irked nod at Autie. "Him neither,"
meaning Allen.

"Don't take it out on us because you can't
go," Autie said.

"It ain't right," Burkman said.

Custer took Vic's reins from him. He
tossed the reins over, hooked his foot in the
stirrup, stepped up and swung the other leg
over. "If we send for more ammunition, you
can come up then," he told Burkman.
"You'll be in on the home stretch, John."

"I don't like it, General. I pure don't like
it."

"Take hold of the dogs," Custer said.

Burkman did, leaning over with a fist on each leather collar. Tuck and Blucher knew what it meant and lunged to get free of Burkman's iron grip, rearing on their hind legs and emitting a string of wild dolorous cries, yips, howls.

"I'll see you two old friends tonight," Custer told them, and touched his spurs to Vic and set the column, the day, in motion.

FIVE

They rode up over the long, gradual rise of
the divide, still following the Indian trail,
the beaten ground and pole scorings, the
droppings of ponies. The Wolf Mountains
rose off to their left, gray cliff faces and dark
pines scattered over the pale green hills and
inclines. The hooves of the big army horses
beat a low, steady-rolling thunder. Tin cups
rattled, carbine slings jingled their merry
music. The talk he could hear was cheerful,
confident, ribald. There was talk of squaws,
the usual puerile speculation and fantasy,
and of scalps to be brought home as me-
mentos.

They descended to another narrow creek,
which threaded west toward the Little
Bighorn. They followed the creek. A little
after twelve noon Custer halted them and
rode out of earshot with Cooke. Cooke took
out his notebook and pencil. Custer told
him that he was dividing the regiment into

three battalions, which would be commanded by himself, Reno, and Benteen. There would be five companies in his battalion, three each in Reno's and Benteen's, and he named them as Cooke wrote.

Cooke trotted back to inform Reno and Benteen. Custer dismounted. He took off his gauntlets and stuffed them in the pockets of his jacket. He peeled off the jacket, rolled it up, and tied it behind his saddle. His blue-gray fireman's shirt was sweated to his back. He did not remove his red cravat. He remounted and walked Vic back.

Benteen, who had the advance, had already come forward on his blood bay. He saluted in an offhand way, looking past Custer's shoulder to where the creek meandered away into the distance.

"Hadn't we better stay together?" he said.

"You'll have Weir's company and Godfrey's, beside your own," Custer said.

"That's not what I'm asking you," Benteen said.

Custer turned in his saddle, pointed southwest, where, a mile away in the gin-clear distance, a ridge swept up, gray-green, to meet the bright sky.

"I want you to scout the other side of that bluff," he said. "Keep going until you're sure there are no Indians out that way. Pitch into anything you see."

"Can I take a surgeon?"

"You won't be gone that long. As soon as you see the valley you turn right and get back to me, fast."

Cooke had brought Reno up. Reno had a three-day beard filling in around his black mustache. His dark gaze shifted, slid here and there, as if it couldn't fasten on anything, and Custer wondered if he was already drunk.

"Lieutenant Cooke told you what we're doing," he said.

"Yes sir," Reno said. He would not look at Custer, would not meet his gaze.

"Go on, Colonel Benteen," Custer said.

Benteen turned his horse back.

"Get back to me quick as you can," Custer called after him.

Boyer was approaching with Half Yellow Face behind him.

"He want me to tell you don't divide your men," Boyer said.

"I'm getting tired of this," Custer said.

"He want me to tell you, so I do."

"Tell him to do the scouting, and I'll take care of the fighting," Custer said.

Allen had often felt their isolation, but never as intensely, as oppressively, as this. Benteen had led his three companies off to the left at an angle of forty-five degrees and vanished into the repetitious hills and ridges, where they could ride for miles, days, and the country would be as empty, as reiterative, as changeless. Custer's battalion now was moving along the right side of the creek, Reno's on the other. Reno had a hundred twenty men, and as the battalion wended along above the creekside trees in a column of fours, it looked paltry and fatally finite against the south climbing hills and nearby Wolf Mountains. As if Allen, looking across the creek to the slope where they rode, were viewing them through the wrong end of a telescope.

Bos and Reed had gotten quiet, gazing about as they rode. George was lagging but Allen didn't dare drop back where Custer couldn't see him. The two other doctors, DeWolf and Porter, were riding with Reno, Allen did not know why. Reynolds, too, had gone with Reno, and so had the Negro Dorman. They rode at a rapid walk and the red-brown dust rose around them, powdering men and horses. There was little conversation anywhere and Allen felt the weight of the midday heat and the cobalt sky, hard and flat and low above their heads.

Kellogg was having trouble with his mule.

He pushed it forward, kicking it repeatedly and savagely, the mule responding with a willful-seeming sluggishness, as if under protest. He passed the boys, still flailing the mule with his heels, and Bos and Autie looked at each other and smirked.

Then Bos said, "Shit," and turned his horse aside and walked her, limping badly, out of the way. It was her left foreleg. Allen and Autie turned their horses and followed Bos to the right, away from the creek. Bos jumped down and picked up the left front hoof and peered at it, hoping to find a pebble, but there was none. He dropped the hoof. The mare stood disconsolate, with her head bowed and her black tail drawn in between her legs.

"She's gone lame," Bos said.

Custer had come back at a near gallop. Vic danced, chucked his head, impatient to keep moving, and Custer reined him in, throwing his weight back.

"She's dead lame," Bos said. "I don't know what happened."

"Wait with the pack train and stay with it," Custer said.

Tom Custer had doubled back to join them. Headquarters had gone on and the Gray Horse troop was passing. Yates looked over and Custer shouted to him to keep moving.

"What'll I do with Angel?" Bos said.

"Leave her or shoot her."

"I can't *shoot* her," Bos said.

"Let's go, Armstrong," Tom said.

"Find Burkman," Custer said. "Get your-self a mount and come up when he does, you hear me?"

"I hear you," Bos said.

"Be damn sure you do," Custer said, and wheeled Vic and was off, Tom chasing him in the reddish cloud of his dust.

"Well, *damn,* Bos," Autie said.

"Let's go, Autie," Allen said.

"I wonder could I borrow somebody's horse," Bos said.

"Whose?"

"I don't know."

"All the spares are back of us," Allen said.

"Shit," Bos said.

"We'll kill a couple of Sioux for you," Autie said, snapping Bos a grin, turning his horse.

"See you tonight," Allen said, and reined Ginger around and kicked her to a gallop.

There was a campsite around a bend in the creek where two tipis still stood, one of them half down, sagging over sideways. Allen had seen the Rees' canvas tipis at Lincoln and these seemed pristine by comparison, a dusky but strangely lambent white. The site stretched a half mile along the creek. Fires smoldered. Bone utensils, cook pots, and scraps of food lay about in hasty abandonment. The Rees had dismounted and a dozen of them were busy attacking the tipis with their knives, slashing furiously and to no apparent purpose. Bloody Knife was no part of this, having ridden ahead with Varnum.

"What the *hell* is going on?" Custer said and swung himself down off of Vic.

Several Rees spoke and Gerard translated.

"Look inside," he said.

Custer drew back the tatters of the standing tipi. Inside was a burial scaffold and on it a dead man wrapped like a mummy. Arrows, a bow, a revolver, a pipe, were arrayed beside him. Allen, twenty feet away, could smell the rotting corpse's sweetish stink, like the smell of a dead rat in the wall, a dead animal under the house.

"I told them to ride fast," Custer said. "To go straight to the camp and steal horses."

Gerard translated it, and the Rees traded glances and looked at the ground or off to the north, where a chalk-white bluff shrugged on the sky.

"We go when you go," one of them said

through Gerard.

Custer turned, looked at Tom. Tom shook his head and spat past his leg.

Custer's orderly today was an Italian named Giovanni Martini from Benteen's Company H whom Henry Voss, for some obscure reason, had taken out of turn in the daily rotation. This was Voss's prerogative as chief trumpeter, but Custer wondered why he'd chosen a foreigner today, of all days.

"Burn the tipis," he told Martini.

Martini looked at Voss. "Get your ass down and set fire to 'em," Voss said.

"Where *fiammifero*?" Martini said, and mimed striking a match on his leg.

"Matches, you dumb bastard," Voss said.

"Where is matches?"

Custer was striding toward the creek. Reno, over on his side, had fallen behind and was just now drawing even. Custer took off his hat and waved it, summoning him. Reno turned his command down toward the creek, which had widened here to about thirty feet and was nearly dry. There were trees on either side and the column broke apart and crossed it as they could, in no formation.

Martini had dismounted and Tom Custer had tossed him his box of lucifers. Martini found some sagebrush and ignited it against the tipi wall. Allen wondered why Custer had ordered it and could think of no decent reason. It seemed an affront to propriety, like the desecrations on the Tongue River. An action you took at your peril.

"I feel bad for Bos," Autie said.

"Bos'll get over it," Allen said.

The first tipi had caught easily and the flame raced up to the crossed lodgepoles. The fire snapped viciously, sent up a slow billow of black smoke.

"It won't feel right without him," Autie said.

"I wish they hadn't done that," Allen said, watching the fire.

Gerard had ridden up onto a hill to the west of the white bluff and was looking toward the valley, standing up in his stirrups. He turned and began to yell and wave his hat in long arcs, and everyone turned to look up at him, headquarters and the Gray Horse Troop waiting fifty yards back.

"There they go, boys," he said. "They're running! They're running like hell!"

Reno's men had come up out of the creek some distance upstream. He'd gotten them back into formation and now they came forward, past the Gray Horse Troop, and halted. Reno walked his horse to Custer, threading among the debris and smoking ashes. Custer remounted Vic. Gerard was returning, the horse picking its way carefully, slantwise, down the hill. The Rees gathered in, leaving their horses. Kellogg leaned forward with his notebook on his mule's neck, writing.

"They're on the jump, Major Reno," Custer said.

"Yes sir, I heard."

Reno cast his black gaze upstream toward the Little Bighorn, brooding, as if he did not fear going there but resented having to.

"I want you to go after them," Custer said. "Try to bring them to battle. I'll support you."

Gerard arrived, grinning.

"Tell your friends here that the Sioux are running and to get after them," Custer said.

Gerard spoke, and several of the Rees answered, talking over each other, vehement.

"They don't want to go until we do," Gerard said.

Custer looked away toward the creek with squinted eyes.

"Then tell them this," he said. "If any man of them isn't brave I'll take his gun away and make a woman of him."

Gerard looked at him. "Are you sure?"

"Say it," Custer said.

Gerard spoke. The older Ree Stabbed answered and it tore a burst of laughter from the others.

"What?" Custer said.

"He says if you do the same with the soldiers, it will take you all day and all night."

More laughter, as if it were equally funny in English.

Custer closed his eyes. Opened them. Smiled. "Take these circus clowns with you, Major Reno," he said.

But the Sioux weren't running.

Reno was leading his battalion forward at a brisk trot — Cooke and Keogh had gone with him, to report back — when Varnum and Bloody Knife came back from their scout. The two tipis continued to burn, embittering the air with the smell of smoke and burning hide and, perhaps, flesh and bone.

"The valley's full of Indians," Varnum said.

"Fred Gerard saw them running," Custer said.

"Not the main village," Varnum said. "It's on the west side of the river. We couldn't see much of it because of the hills."

"*Ota Sioux,*" Bloody Knife said. "*Ota Sioux,*

ota Sioux."

"Reno's going to attack them," Custer said. "He's got Gerard and the Rees and a couple of the Crows with him."

"Then I better go along," Varnum said.

"Take Bloody Knife with you."

Bloody Knife understood this and he looked thoughtfully at Custer. "Good-bye," he said in English. "My friend. Good-bye."

Custer turned Vic, swung him so he could put a hand on Bloody Knife's arm. "Tonight we drink whiskey," he said. "Tonight we laugh together."

"No whiskey," Bloody Knife said and kicked his horse forward, kicked him again to a canter.

"I'll see you in a while, sir," Varnum said.

"Good luck, Charles," Custer said.

Varnum saluted and was off after Bloody Knife, hunched down over the withers, riding hell-bent for the valley.

They were moving again, walking their horses, scanning the hills and bluffs to their right. Boyer had come back with four of the Crows and said that he'd seen the village but did not know how big it was.

"It doesn't matter now, does it," Custer said.

"Well, I guess it don't," Boyer said and

reined his horse around and called to the Crows to follow him.

Cooke and Keogh came back from accompanying Reno, their white buckskins powdered reddish brown, horses lathered. They reined up and turned their horses and walked them with Custer. They'd ridden with Reno all the way to the Little Bighorn. They said it was about three miles away. Reno had crossed it and would proceed up the valley toward the village. They said the river was about fifty feet wide and belly-high to the horses. They said there'd be no trouble crossing it.

"We ought to send for Benteen," Tom said.

"He'll be along," Custer said. "Let's water the horses."

The order went back and the men dismounted and led their horses to the creek. Reno's dust still hovered in paling drifts in the distance out ahead. Behind them, some miles back now, the dust of the pack train rose like smoke from a distant wildfire. Allen and Autie Reed led their horses to the creek and filled their canteens with the cool silty water while the horses drank. Autie still wore his buckskin jacket. It was frayed and cracked and had gone from milk white to dingy buttermilk.

"Allen," he said, "I want you to do me a favor."

"Sure."

"I want you to tell Bos you don't think badly of him on account of what I told you. About backing down from that fight."

"I did tell him."

"Tell him again. He respects you, you see. He'll be all right about it if you buck him up."

"I think he's all right now," Allen said.

"Things bother Bos that he doesn't let on."

"I'll talk to him," Allen said.

"I oughtn't to have said what I did," Autie said. "I get mean sometimes."

"Maybe you oughtn't to drink," Allen said.

"I can be mean sober. Nobody stands up to me. Ma. Uncle Armstrong. You're the first one."

"It almost got me a whipping."

Autie smiled. "Friends?"

"Friends," Allen said.

He found George sitting in the shade with his spectacles off, laving his face and neck with a yellow cavalry bandanna. His horse had watered and was waiting for him with her reins dangling. She looked at Allen with wide despondent eyes, as if imploring him to do something for her ailing master. Behind them and extending along the trail upstream the men were mounting and forming up.

"We have to go, George. Reno's across the river. He'll be fighting any time now."

"Wet this for me, will you," George said, offering up the bandanna.

Allen took it and submerged it in the ankle-deep creek. George took it and again soaked his face. He passed it over his neck, front and back.

"I'm burning up," he said.

"Wait for the pack train," Allen said.

"I can't. Porter and DeWolf both went with Reno."

"Can you mount?" Allen said.

"Sure," George said.

He retied the wet bandanna, then slid a hand under the placket of his fireman's shirt and brought out his glasses. He held them up to the light then fitted them on his nose.

"Where's your duster?" Allen said.

"I tossed it. It was too damn hot."

Allen helped him rise, lifting him under an arm. He stood a moment, as if uncertain of his balance, then turned to his horse. Allen picked up the reins.

"Jesus, George," he said.

George took hold of the pommel and

412

lifted his left foot into the stirrup. He hauled himself up and over. Allen handed him the reins.

"You ever been to New York City?" George said.

"Of course I have. My mother lives there."

"She does?" George said.

"Are you all right?" Allen said.

George smiled. "We're all going to go there," he said. "You and me and Gracie. Eat at Delmonico's and go ice skating in the park."

"Wait for the pack train, George."

"Delmonico's," George said and nudged his horse forward.

They were almost to the river when they finally saw Indians. Fifty of them, maybe sixty, on a hilltop, sitting their horses motionless against the flat sky. Watching the soldiers come on as calmly as if they were content to see them come and had rather expected it. Custer raised his hand, halting the column. "By God," Autie whispered.

Most of them were naked in breechclouts or leggings, their faces and bodies painted in lurid shades of vermillion, yellow, black, white, and to Allen they looked other-worldly, avatars of some bygone age of spectacle and sorcery. Their bodies were

413

lithe but muscled, and it struck Allen that they were healthier, stronger, better-fed than the soldiers. Some few wore shirts. They wore feathers in their loose raven-black hair. Rifles rested across their horses' withers. Many carried bows slung on their shoulders and wore quivers packed with white-feathered arrows. The horses, too, were painted, red and yellow lightning bolts and zigzags. Yellow feathers hung plaited in their manes like gaudy appendages. Devil animals.

They looked at the soldiers and the soldiers at them, and the only sound was the snort and nicker of the cavalry horses, wary-sounding, as if the animals didn't at all like what they saw.

"Armstrong?" Tom said.

Custer sat thinking. The Indians sat still and silent. Patient. Custer turned, found Cooke over his right shoulder.

"We'll go after them," he said. "Column of twos, in line. At the trot."

Cooke wheeled his horse to spread the order.

"Are we coming?" Autie said.

"Stay with me and keep quiet," Custer said.

He looked again to the hilltop and the Indians were gone, as if they'd dematerialized into the blue air. The battalion was reforming, the five companies lining up parallel, in twos. It took only a few moments. Custer turned Vic all the way around to watch, Tom was up with him, and Cooke and Voss and George Lord and Mark Kellogg and the Italian Martini and the two guidon bearers and the two boys. He turned Vic back around and kicked him, and he crouched back and sprang forward and a yell went up among the men, and they urged their horses up the long gentle slope, chasing the vanished Sioux.

Six

He led them down the other side of the hill, galloping now, and up a second long incline, Vic taking it in strong, sure lunges. They halted across the broad high summit, breathing hard, horses and men, and looked down, across the green river, at the village. It lay west along the narrow, looping, tree-hemmed Little Bighorn, acres of tipis stretching north out of sight behind the bluffs shrugging up on their side, and he knew it was the biggest he'd ever seen. The sun had fallen halfway down and in its deepening light the tipis were a lambent off-white. Out beyond them, visible only by its dust, was the pony herd. The Indians they'd chased off the hill were nowhere to be seen. Custer raised the field glasses he'd borrowed this morning from DeRudio, DeRudio protesting in his stilted English.

I buy them in Vienna. I pay dear for them.

You'll get them back, Lieutenant, he'd said.

He scanned the village, south to north and back south. There was a stir toward the south end, dust rising, dogs in an uproar, men gesticulating, women in their hide and calico dresses running this way and that. He saw a squaw come up out of a tipi clasping a child to her breast. Some of the women were making for the pony herd. Some were leading children by the hand, moving north. He thought of Monahseetah and wondered if she was down there somewhere. He wondered if she'd married again and if her husband would be fighting today. He lowered the glasses.

"The squaws are running," he said. "I don't see many braves."

"Maybe they're on a hunt," Tom said.

"Either way we've caught them napping," Custer said.

Then, far down across the river, Reno's battalion appeared from behind some woods, charging up the vast theater of the valley in two lines, tiny in the distance. Reno was out in front, identifiable by his white straw hat, with the guidon bearers right behind him. Braves were coming out of the village to intercept them, racing their ponies up and down, raising the dust. The sight of the galloping troopers brought a cheer from the men on the hill; Custer looked back and smiled.

"Steady, boys," he said. "There are plenty down there for all of us."

He looked again at the village, at Reno's two lines moving up the broad valley, and felt a familiar heart swell of renewal and vindication. Vic felt it and pranced sideways and chucked his head.

"Get Kanipe up here."

Cooke turned, stood up in his stirrups, and hollered for the sergeant. Kanipe came up, his horse skittish, dancing.

"Go back to the pack train," Custer said. "Tell McDougall to bring them up fast. Any packs get loose, tell him to cut them and keep going."

Kanipe saluted and turned his horse.

"If you see Benteen, tell him to get up here quick."

"Yes sir," Kanipe called over his shoulder, and the soft thud of his horse's hoofbeats receded down the long slope of the hill.

The fight had begun, gunfire, down in the valley. The savage, lovely, redemptive sound of battle. The valley was his, the hills, the river, all of it. They went on at a trot, over the dusty sage-strewn hills high above the river and parallel to it. Again he halted them, this time in the shade of a hill out of sight of the river, and left them there and climbed the hill with Tom and Cooke, the horses flinging upward in effortful lunges. From this new elevation they could see more of the village. It was huge, no doubt about it, and he knew that he could not yield the offensive, could not stop pressing.

In the valley now Reno's men had dismounted and formed a skirmish line, every fourth man behind it holding four horses. They were some two hundred yards from the edge of the village and Custer cursed Reno silently for not getting in closer. The gunfire was steady, sharp, a sound like strings of firecrackers, and the blue-gray smoke hung lazily in the air. The Indians were in constant motion, darting, feinting, galloping up and down, and he did not know where all of them had come from.

He took his white hat off, stood up facing the valley, and waved the hat in a slow arc against the sky, urging them to stand strong. He put the hat back on and turned in his saddle and looked at his own men, huddled in the shade at the foot of the hill.

"We've got them, boys," he said. "We'll finish them off and go home."

It brought another cheer.

"Where do you suppose Benteen is?" Tom said.

"He'll be along," Custer said.

He wished Reno had gotten closer.

Boyer and his four Crows came up the hill from the south. They'd been scouting along the river.

"Big village ain't it, General," Boyer said.

"You didn't see Benteen, did you?" Custer said.

"Saw his dust two, three mile back. He's coming, I guess."

"Tell the Crows they've done their job and can go home," Custer said.

Boyer spoke to them. They nodded and looked away, and he knew they weren't going to stick, which was too bad, because he needed every man.

"What are you going to do, Mitch?" he said.

"I told you what I gonna do," Boyer said.

"You're free to go."

"I know I am," Boyer said.

They proceeded down a narrow ravine, which took them away from the river. The ravine was dotted with scrub cedars, which the horses wove among, walking now. It was terrifically hot down here. The men were quiet. There was the clink and jingle of carbine slings, the dull thump of hooves.

Behind Custer, Henry Voss was joshing Autie and Allen.

"You boys ready to see the elephant?"

"Sure we are," Autie said.

"Going to use that rifle, are you?"

"I brought it, didn't I?" Autie said.

"Where's your rifle, son?"

"Nowhere," Allen said.

"He forgot it back at Lincoln," Autie said.

"Ain't that a inconvenience," Voss said.

The ravine emptied into a broad shallow coulee that slanted gradually down in the direction of the river. They spilled out into the coulee, still out of sight of the river, and Custer halted them. The men, sweating, got down and tightened their girths. They drank from their canteens. Custer called for Giovanni Martini.

"I want you to find Captain Benteen," he said. "Go as fast you can. Do you understand me?"

"Yes sir."

"He don't understand half what he hears," Voss said.

"Find Captain Benteen," Custer said.

"Yes sir," Martini said.

"Go back the way we came. Same trail." Custer pointed to the south. "Tell him to come quick. You understand? Big village. Come quick."

"Yes sir."

"Tell him to bring the ammunition packs," Custer said.

"He ain't going to remember it," Voss said.

"Wait a minute, orderly," Cooke said, and drew out his notebook, his pencil, and bent over with the notebook on the withers of his white horse. He scrawled the note to Benteen and signed it, *W. W. Cooke.* He tore the page, folded it twice, and handed it to Martini. Martini pushed it down into the inside pocket of his sack coat, saluted, and turned his horse back up the cedar-strewn ravine.

Allen turned Ginger and walked her back to George. George sat his horse, slumped and perspiring and feverishly pink. The light glinted off his little spectacles.

"How you feeling?" Allen said.

"Fine," George said.

"You don't look it."

"I'm warm, is all. It's a damn big village, isn't it."

"George, listen to me. If you go back I'll ride with you."

"I can't leave Armstrong without a surgeon."

"It's your last chance," Allen said.

"Yours too," George said.

Allen looked south, to where the sere,

browning, sage-strewn hill touched the sky and thought of the safety that lay in that direction, the land running empty and now threatless all the way to the Yellowstone. He thought of turning Ginger and riding away, farther and farther from all of this, and wanted to, and could not. He shrugged, smiled wanly at George.

"I'm not going to leave you," he said.

"I never thought you would," George said.

He came cantering down the ravine, through the low cedars, the men eyeing him with amusement or disdain or both as he brought the horse down from canter to trot to walk and went on past them toward headquarters. He reined up, sweating, breathing hard.

"Hey, Bos," Autie said, smiling.

"What the *hell* are you doing here?" Custer said.

"What I intended right along," Bos said.

"You idiot," Tom said.

"Idiot yourself," Bos said.

Tom swore under his breath and looked away.

"Did you see Benteen?" Custer said.

"I passed him right back yonder, about a half hour ago," Bos said. "I saw your messenger. He'll fetch him up in no time."

"That looks like McDougall's horse," Custer said.

"It's his extra," Bos said. "Name's Sally. Said he was glad at least his horse'll see some action."

"We'll talk about this later," Custer said and wheeled his horse away from Bos.

"Well, I knew he'd take a fit," Bos said.

"Never mind," Autie said. "Me and Allen are damn glad to see you."

"I thought you would be," Bos said.

Then Boyer rode down over the hill on the south side of the coulee and the men all watched him come and were silent.

"Reno been whipped," he said. "He been run out of the valley back across the river. Sioux rode 'em down like buffalo. Chase 'em up into the hills."

Custer sat thinking. It seemed to be true: the firing had moved across the river, it was coming over the hills from the south. Reno. *I should have known.*

It happened so fast Reno was never able to take control of the situation. Might as well try to direct a hurricane. The skirmish line had swung counterclockwise under deadly pressure and then had melted back into the timber, and now Reno did not know what to do. The firing was deafening. Balls sang in the air, sheared off twigs and leaves. Arrows hissed, stuck in tree trunks. The Indians shrieked as they fought, blew eagle bone whistles. They were infiltrating the timber. They were everywhere.

Some of the men fighting in the woods never heard Reno's order to mount and ride. He was at the edge of the trees on the south side, where a short skirmish line still held the Indians back to the west. Bloody Knife was with him. Reno had mounted, dismounted, mounted again. Bloody Knife thought he was going crazy. The second time he had trouble locating the right stirrup, kept kicking it as he tried to get his foot in, and Bloody Knife watched this sadly, understanding that Reno was drunk.

Reno got his foot in the stirrup. Evidently he still could not decide, for he only held his horse in and looked wildly about at his skirmishers, who had begun to pull back toward the woods, and at the mounted Indians swirling half-visible in the smoke. He began to sign to Bloody Knife, asking him what the Indians would do if the soldiers left. The answer was easy, but before he could give it Bloody Knife went home to his people, as foretold, shot from behind through the head, spraying reddened bits of brain and bone against Reno's jacket and shattering what was left of his composure.

Custer led them uphill, away from the river, in fours. Boyer's news had spread back through the command and there was no sound but the muted drumming of hooves, the creak of leather, the clink of carbine slings. Bos came up beside him.

"Did I not tell you to stay back with Burkman?" Custer said.

"There's some brothers in this world would be glad to see me," Bos said.

"We're in for a big fight. Reno's retreat complicates things."

"I had to come, Armstrong."

"From now on you listen to me," Custer said.

"Course I will," Bos said.

Charley Reynolds's infected hand was grotesquely swollen. It felt on fire. He was crouched in the timber with the balls humming beelike overhead and twigs and leaf shreds sifting down when Gerard and Varnum ducked down, crouching, on either side of him. The horses were being held in a glade over toward the river.

"Do you have any whiskey?" Charley said.

"A little bit," Gerard said and slid his flask from his coat pocket. "We'll take a last drink together, why not?"

He uncapped the flask and passed it to Lonesome Charley, who took it with his good hand and drank.

Now there was yelling, men were running, crashing through the underbrush, toward the horses.

"What the hell is this?" Gerard said.

"Getting out of here," Charley said and scrambled up, grabbing his Winchester.

He had trouble mounting because of the hand, and Varnum and Gerard took off out of the timber ahead of him. He hauled himself up finally and burst out into the open and joined the dash to the river. The Indians were galloping alongside the soldiers with their rifles laid across their pommels, shooting them out of their saddles. Charley spurred his horse down through a dry bed where the river once had run and up again onto the flat plain, and as he kicked her to a gallop, his horse was hit. She went down, somersaulting, as Charley leaped clear of her.

He scrambled to her on all fours and unsheathed his rifle. He knew he had no chance but felt cool and unafraid, as if this had happened long ago and he were merely revisiting it in his memory. His hand had ceased hurting and whatever pain there was in dying was also long past. The Indians had seen him now, and four or five of them were circling him on their horses, yelling, firing at him with their repeaters. He was killed from behind. There was blood in his mouth, a not unpleasant salty, familiar taste.

There was no plan anymore; he would have to construct the battle according to circumstance. There were two fords, Boyer told him, one at the bottom of the broad coulee and the other downriver about a mile. Custer sent Companies E and F down the coulee to hold the ford until Benteen arrived. Because if the Indians got across the river, warriors in the thousands, these hills and ravines would be crawling with them, and there'd be no way to fight them.

He took the remaining three companies up onto a hill a good mile from the river, and from here they watched events at the ford. It was not going well. Braves were materializing out of the city of tipis directly across. Dozens of them. Hundreds. Yelling, shooting. Yates and Smith dismounted their companies and put them in two lines. The compacted bangs of rifle fire caromed up the ravines and coulees. Arrows flew. More

Indians were swimming their ponies across the river above the ford, and there was nothing to do but call the men back before they all died down there. Keogh's Company I fired a volley into the air, and the men down below jumped up and ran for their horses.

They escaped in a column of twos up a ravine, shooting as they went. Indians now were streaming across the river at the ford, nothing to check them, mounted and on foot, some following the soldiers up the ravine, others circling to the south, working their way around the hill where Custer was. And now there were Indians on a ridge to the north about a quarter of a mile away, sitting their horses, watching him, and he wondered where *they'd* come from.

He took the three companies forward in fours, at a trot, toward the braves blocking their way. Immediately the rearmost company, Calhoun's L, came under fire from behind, the Indians swarming up out of the coulee to harass them. The soldiers turned and fired as they rode. Custer couldn't tell if anyone was hit. He didn't think so.

He led the column down another declivity. The land went up and down, was never level. They climbed another hill in time to see the Indians in front of them dispersing down the cuts and ravines that ran toward the river, scampering their ponies in a way that seemed impish or playful. Scattering, as Indians did, and this reassured him. He must stay on the offensive, must keep them running.

The ravine that was E and F's avenue up from the river was just ahead. Company E, the Gray Horse Troop, emerged first, with Company F close behind. They rode up onto a long high ridge that ran parallel to the river, which was still a mile down. Yates spread them out on the ridge facing downhill, but the Indians had melted into the cuts and swales and did not seem inclined to show themselves. Custer brought C, I, and L up, and the battalion was intact again and, for the moment, things were quiet.

"Sturgis is killed," Yates said. "I had to leave him."

Custer looked away, down toward the river, the village. It was a mile and a half, maybe two miles long. Yates was one of his oldest friends. They'd served together in the Rebellion and had been neighbors afterward in Monroe.

"I lost three others," Yates said. "I had to leave all of them."

"Where the hell is Benteen?" Tom said.

"He can't be far," Custer said, but it was beginning to worry him.

The Indians were on the move, visible intermittently among the rises and the maze of draws and gullies, garish in their war paint. The land was alive with them. More were working their way around to the east. There was still shooting off to the south where Reno was, but it had turned sporadic.

He was running out of options. He needed Benteen's two companies. Eighty men. He needed them. Voss blew officers call and the company commanders came promptly, and Custer moved apart with them, taking Boyer. Mark Kellogg nudged his mule and followed uninvited, and Custer let him.

"We're in a fix, gentlemen," he said.

There was a commotion at the rear of the column where the ridge fell away to the south, shouted curses, men and horses startling, plunging out of line. Arrows. There were answering rifle shots, more shouts. George Lord wheeled his horse and cantered back down the column.

"I should be with my men," Calhoun said.

Cooke stood up in his saddle and looked back. "It's stopping," he said.

"Fuckin' arrows," Keogh said. "Give me a rifle ball any day."

"Everyone shut up and listen to the general," Tom said.

■ ■ ■ ■

Allen, Autie, and Bos were back with Henry
Voss. Vickory and Hughes were a little
ahead. The guidons hung rag-like in the
warm, breathless air.

"The general's been in a lot of scrapes,"
Bos said. "He always does come out of them
in fine shape."

"He better think of something good this
time," Voss said and leaned and spat.

"You can bet he will," Bos said.

"Why'd he send Captain Benteen away?"
Autie said. "It makes no sense."

"Listen to him," Voss said. "General Reed,
here. Knows all about Indian fightin'."

"Well, why did he?"

"Damn if I know," Voss said.

"What do you think he'll do?" Allen said.

"Benteen? Get his ass over here, he knows
what's good for him."

"Custer," Allen said.

"Attack the sons-a-bitches," Voss said.
"It's the only thing he knows."

"Attack the village."

"Sure."

"I'd like to know how," Allen said.

"I would too," Autie said, eyeing the
myriad tipis.

"Hell, Autie," Bos said, "think about that girl at Little Casino's. Settin' there waitin' for you."

"You boys do business at Little Casino's?" Voss said.

"Now and again," Autie said.

"A little young, ain't you?"

"We're in a scrape, but we'll get out of it," Bos said.

Benteen had gone up and down ridge after ridge and decided, finally, that there were no Indians out this way. Later he would call his mission a wild goose chase and wonder aloud whether Custer sent him on it so that he would miss the fight and a share of the renown that supposedly would follow. He turned his command and rode north, toward Custer's trail, at a walk.

Five miles on they struck the creek and crossed it and followed Custer. The pack train, moving even more slowly, was a mile in back of them now, discernible by its dust. They went on another mile, leisurely, and stopped to water the horses and fill their canteens. It was here that Boston Custer passed them, pounding by on Captain McDougall's mare. They lingered for twenty minutes.

When they'd gone another mile, Sergeant

Kanipe came bearing down on them, waving his hat. Benteen halted the column, and Kanipe pulled up.

"The general says for you to get up there quick," he said. "They've struck a big camp."

"All right," Benteen said.

"Where's the pack train at, Captain?"

Benteen gestured with a toss of his head and Kanipe saluted and galloped on. "We've got them, boys," he told the men as he flew by. "We're going to whip the hell out of them."

After another mile Giovanni Martini appeared. Benteen halted the column, and Martini pulled up on his sweating horse, saluted, and dug out the note that Lieutenant Cooke had scribbled. Benteen took the note and read it slowly. He turned to Lieutenant Gibson.

"I'm supposed to come quick and bring the packs," he said. "Now, how can I do both?"

"Maybe he means the ammunition packs," Gibson said.

"It doesn't say that."

"Look at your horse, orderly," Gibson said.

Martini's horse had been shot above the left front leg and a sheet of blood ran down.

"I ain't see that," Martini said.

"Did you see any Indians?"

"Indians in tents, sleeping."

Benteen looked at Gibson. "What the hell is he talking about?"

Captain Weir and Lieutenant Godfrey arrived. Benteen handed Cooke's note to Weir. Weir scanned it and passed it Godfrey.

"Where's General Custer?" Benteen said.

"I think he attack the village, with all them men sleeping."

"What's he talking about?" Godfrey said.

"He's a half-wit," Benteen said. "Orderly, go back to Captain McDougall and get a fresh mount. Understand?"

"Yes sir. Understand."

"Tell Captain McDougall to come on with the packs fast as he can. Understand?"

"Yes sir. Understand."

The battalion went on at a trot. Now they could hear firing, off among the hills to the north, on the near side of the river, and they rode toward it at a gallop, in fours, away from the creek, up into the hills.

The last of Reno's beaten men were climbing the long, steep hill from the river when they arrived, leading their slipping, struggling horses or clambering up on foot. Reno had dismounted. He'd lost his straw hat and had tied a red bandanna around his head. His coat was spattered with Bloody Knife's blood and brains. Officers were yelling commands, trying to get the men to deploy and defend themselves. Benteen halted his column and looked calmly around.

"For God's sake, Fred," Reno said, "stop and help me. I've lost half my men. We're whipped."

Benteen smiled. "I don't think so," he said.

Lieutenant Godfrey was dismounting his men. He ordered them into line along the western edge of the hill, above the river, and they went. Weir deployed his company to the south and east. There was firing, not much. Snipers. Benteen got down off his horse.

"Where's Custer?" he said.

"How the hell do I know?" Reno said.

He would take captives. Women, children. You only needed fifty or so. It had worked at the Washita and could work here, and anyway it was the one solution left to him with Reno out of the fight and Benteen late to it. He left Keogh with Companies C, I, and L on the south end of the ridge and took E and F north, trotting. They could see that end of the village now, and streaming out of it in a disorganized scramble, children, old people, women. Ponies dragged travois, stirring the white dust. Custer pointed: his quarry.

At the north end of the ridge they veered left toward the river and picked up the pace. The descent was gradual, an easy canter. Tom, Cooke, and Voss rode with him just ahead of the boys and Boyer, Cooke's dundrearies blowing back past his face like pennants. Kellogg was keeping up on his lumbering mule.

The descent steepened above the ford, with trees and brush thick on the other side. They could not see much because of the trees, and when it seemed they would gallop unopposed to the river and across it, the thickets on the village side exploded in muzzle flashes and smoke, the air whispered arrows, and Mark Kellogg said, "Oh my God," and slumped forward on his mule and seemed to be hugging it. The mule turned as if it understood what was happening and headed back up the hill, and Kellogg slid over into the tall grass and lay still.

Custer ordered the three boys back, yelling and gesturing, then deployed the men in a line and ordered them to fire at will. The air grew crazed with noise and smoke. A trooper dropped his rifle and cursed and gripped the arrow embedded in his thigh. George Lord, back with the boys, dismounted and came running, bending low, bringing his pocket surgical kit.

The firing from over the river slackened. The soldiers reloaded, held their fire. George had helped the arrowshot trooper off his horse and was using a wire loop to pull the arrow while three men held the trooper down.

"What do we do, Armstrong?" Tom said, checking his horse. Tom's pale eyes darted, the fever was on him, the fight was in his blood now.

"We can't cross," Custer said.

"We've got to. There's a thousand hostages right close by."

"We can't."

They waited for George to extract the arrow and help the man onto his horse, then Voss blew retreat and the line broke up and in moments was a column of fours, going back the way they'd come, briskly and in good order, past the slumped body of Mark Kellogg. There was a broad flat place, a kind of shelf, a few hundred yards below the crest of the ridge, and here Custer halted them. There was firing to the south, where Keogh was.

Custer turned his horse, found Autie and

Allen and Bos. He looked at his nephew with eyes suddenly gentle. "We're going to wait here till Captain Benteen comes up," he said. "I want both of you to stay behind me." He turned, found his brother. "You too, Bos."

"It'll be all right, won't it," Autie said.

"Sure it will," Custer said.

He raised DeRudio's expensive field glasses and peered south, toward Keogh.

"What's happening?" Tom said.

"I can't tell."

"What are we going to do?"

"Wait here."

"Then what?"

"I don't know," Custer said.

For a while Keogh had things under control. A sort of stasis had set in, the Indians keeping back, hiding, the firing desultory, snappish, a quarrel waged at a distance. Company L held the ridge in a disciplined skirmish line a hundred yards long while Jimmy Calhoun and his junior officer, Crittenden, moved up and down, steadying the men, reminding them to aim low, making sure they didn't bunch up. Keogh was on the ridge where he could see what was happening; his Company I and Harrington's C and Calhoun's horse holders were down in a broad swale to the east, unthreatened for the moment.

But the Indians were getting closer to the ridgetop. They were creeping up all those crooked little draws and gullies leading up from the river. One would raise up and snap a shot at the soldiers, and they'd shoot back as he popped out of sight, too late.

Then it began to heat up. The Indians kept multiplying and creeping closer, and a man was shot in the chest, and another took an arrow in his shoulder. The sergeants dragged them back from the line and looked to them, but there was no surgeon here and little to be done. A third trooper hollered *shit* and stood up and staggered rearward with his wrist shattered and bloody where a rifle ball had gone through it. Keogh had had enough. The worst of the fire was coming from a coulee, which seemed to have filled up with Indians. Keogh waved Lieutenant Harrington up from the swale and told him to mount his company and charge down the coulee and clear the sons of bitches out of there.

The quiet on the flat lasted about twenty minutes. Then they began to notice that the land to the south of them, that rolling, buckling mile between the high ridge and

440

the river, was alive with Indians. They did not know when they'd come across the river, or where; it was as if the land had breathed them. There was a deep ravine a quarter of a mile away which seemed to be a highway up from the river. They were working their way up the ravine and up the gullies and crevices, which drained in random erratic courses downhill to the bottomlands, some leading ponies, some riding, all streaming uphill where they would be between the two wings, Custer's and Keogh's, and gain the high ground on Custer.

Gunfire broke out from another direction, north, and the air whined, sang. The horses stamped, danced sideways, and the men held them in, cursing. The Indians were along the brows of the hills two and three hundred yards away, lying flat to the ground, sniping. They were hitting nothing. It was a long way to shoot and their aim was bad, but their numbers were growing.

And so Custer had lost the offensive and there was no way to regain it. He thought some more and called Lieutenant Smith. Smith came forward calmly, almost smiling. Another old friend, habitué of the parlor at Fort Lincoln, singer of songs around the piano. He'd been wounded in the Rebellion and could not lift his right arm above his head or put a coat on without help. Custer told him to take his company down the hill to the deep ravine and clear it out.

Smith said he would and wheeled his horse. He spoke to his trumpeter, who blew the order, and the men on their gray horses took off down the hill in fours. At the edge of the ravine they spread out and dismounted and formed a skirmish line, every fourth man holding four horses. It had taken less than a minute. The skirmishers knelt and let loose and the ravine emptied, the Indians scrambling up the intersecting draws or back the way they'd come, dragging their dead and wounded.

When this was done Custer took Company F up onto the north end of the ridge, a sandy, sage-cluttered hogback. They gained the hilltop — it rose quite steep at its summit — and Voss blew disperse and the men were off their horses, quick, with their rifles. Voss took Vic and his own mount and moved a short way up the slope. Custer told Bos to take Autie and Allen to the summit and stay there. Yates deployed the men in a wide circle running along the ridgetop and bulging downhill to the west, toward the river.

The Indians opened fire from hills to the

north and east and from either side of the ridge to the south. There was no safe place for the horses and each man held his own mount, kneeling, laboring to work his carbine simultaneously, the horses pulling, the men dropping cartridges and picking them up again and cursing. A horse screamed, fell sideways and lay pawing and kicking the air. Another broke loose and ran toward the river.

Hughes and Vickory had planted the flags on the west slope; Voss took Tom's and Cooke's horses. Custer had unsheathed his rifle. Cooke and Tom had unsheathed theirs. The three of them did not kneel; they would fight standing by the guidon and Custer's battle flag. You could see the village in the still-clear distance, a sea of glowing tipis. Horses shrieked, reared, went down. More broke loose and all of them galloped toward the river.

Sergeant Vickory was hit in the abdomen. He let go of his horse and sat down with his legs splayed out, cradling his stomach in his two hands. Cooke turned and cupped his hands around his mouth.

"Dr. Lord! George Lord!"

George came running, bent low, bringing a saddlebag and his little cloth kit. He knelt beside Vickory and told him to lie down.

He found a rag in the saddlebag and pressed it to the wound. Vickory closed his eyes and died.

The Gray Horse Troop seemed to be holding the edge of the ravine with little trouble, though it was becoming murky down there with smoke and difficult to make out. They were shooting across the ravine and down into it while Smith in his white buckskin jacket paced behind them and the horse holders squatted with their teams. There was the question of whether to call them up onto the ridge, but they were pressing the Indians where they were, and it was Custer's instinct to leave them there. He could call Keogh's wing over any time he wanted, and Benteen would arrive at any minute. F had lost half its horses, but not many men were down and he knew he would find a way to survive this fractured and slow-moving battle and maybe, by some stroke of the Custer Luck, turn it.

At the other end of the ridge Harrington had driven the Indians out of the shallow coulee and dismounted his men, and for a while it looked as though Keogh's plan had worked. But then the Indians regrouped on a rise to the south, with more coming up from the river, and suddenly Company C was on the way to being swallowed up.

For a time the men stood in line and fought. Arrows rained down. Cries, curses. Horses were hit. Some broke loose and ran. At one end of the line Sergeant Finley, scalp collector, fell, and at the other end, Sergeant Finckle. Half the company were down, and now panic swept the staggered line and suddenly — it seemed to have occurred to them all at once, no one man began it — they went for their horses, or for any horse they could find, and flung themselves into the saddles and went pounding back up the coulee. Lieutenant Harrington, who was twenty-seven, mounted his horse and tried to slow the pell-mell retreat, bring some order to it, but the last of his men flew by him deaf to his shouts, and he kicked his horse and followed them.

They came flying up onto the ridgetop with Indians in hot pursuit. Calhoun swung his line to the right, to cover them, and more Indians came boiling up on their left, mounted and on foot. There was no longer time to eject and reload the single-shot carbines and hardly time to draw and fire a pistol. The Indians shot them, drove arrows nearly through them, leapt at them with hatchets. Jimmy Calhoun died here with most of his company and with more men of

Company C, who were mounted but did not know where to go, and in their hesitation were shot or pulled off their horses.

Keogh had gone back down into the great swale to the east where his own company had been waiting with their horses and where Calhoun's horse holders still were. Keogh saw what was happening and tried to get his men into line, but there were Indians swooping in off the hill behind them now, and from the south as well, and there was no time to do anything but die where they stood. Keogh was on Comanche, yelling at his trumpeter to blow boots and saddles, his idea being a retreat to the other end of the ridge to join Custer. Comanche had been shot once and now a rifle ball tunneled through Keogh's knee and on into the horse, and down they both went. His sergeants, Varden and Bustard, came running, and what was left of the company sagged in around them, assailed on all sides, and all were slaughtered in a few minutes. Keogh died fighting on one knee, emptying his revolver, flaying his enemies with his bluest curses. Around his neck, as ever, the Medaglia di Pro Petri Sede, bestowed by Pius IX for service in the Papal Army.

The Gray Horse Troop, still down along the

ravine, was set upon from behind, Indians galloping down on them, shrieking, blowing their whistles, shooting, loosing arrows. The horse holders were overrun, the horses lost. The low hills were breathing warriors, and there was nothing the soldiers could do but get into the ravine and try to drive them back. It was clear they could not last long.

The last of Keogh's wing were coming along the ridge toward Custer, running for their lives. The Indians ran or rode alongside like dim ghosts in the smoke, shooting some, pulling others off their horses to be killed with hatchets or clubs. The soldiers came singly or in frantic gaggles of three or four, some mounted, some on foot. None had rifles. There weren't many: eighteen, maybe twenty, out of all of Keogh's hundred twenty-plus men. They staggered up onto the hill, threw themselves on the ground, and drew their Colts.

And so there would be no turning it, no dazzling reprisal of the Custer Luck. He did, briefly, let himself wonder whose fault this debacle was and what move of his own had been fatal, but no answer revealed itself. No matter: it had come down to saving who was left, and Custer put his mind to it.

"Shoot the horses," he said.

■ ■ ■

Instead of joining the stampede north along the ridge to join Custer, Lieutenant Harrington went the other way. His horse was a powerful gelding named Marc Antony, and it seemed to be his idea, though Harrington wasn't exactly sure. He didn't know how it had happened. The horse took him down the south end of the ridge, straight through an advancing party of Indians, startling and scattering them.

He'd escaped! He turned east, nothing ahead of him but the bare, empty, dull-green hills rolling out to meet the sky, the ground flowing away in a blur beneath him. Then he heard yelling behind him and looked back and saw six or seven braves chasing him on their little ponies. The Indians were a hundred yards away. They fired a few shots at him, wildly inaccurate, and settled into the chase. It made good sport, the stakes being what they were, but Harrington was pretty sure they wouldn't catch him. They chased him for five miles. Six. Seven. The noise of the battle receded, died away. The Indians were falling farther back, they were slowing, giving up. He'd gotten away, all right, and the knowledge, sinking in, froze his heart. *My God,* he thought. *What have I done?*

The Indians told the story afterward with a kind of uneasy incredulity. It worried them a little. They were abandoning the chase — several had reined their ponies — when the white soldier did the oddest thing. He felt for his pistol, drew it, put it to the side of his head, fired, and fell over dead. The astonished Indians galloped over to him and took his weapons. They stripped him, did some cutting, and hurried back to the battle.

Custer shot Vic and swung him sideways to the hill as a breastwork, and the men all did the same with their mounts, those whose horses hadn't bolted. Bos let McDougall's mare go rather than shoot her, and Autie and Allen looked at each other and agreed wordlessly that they would not shoot their horses. They were crouched with Bos near the top of the hill and they held the reins firmly, Ginger and the gelding trying to back away, trying to lift and toss their heads, their eyes rolling. Autie had drawn his Winchester from its scabbard and held it propped against his shoulder. Bos had no weapon. He'd forgotten to bring his rifle back with him.

Around the perimeter the men folded

themselves down behind their dead mounts and laid their rifles across them and looked for a target in the growing smoke and noise and movement. There was a metallic smell of horse blood in the air, and the sulfurous odor of powder.

The fight in the ravine was over. The men had slid down the ravine wall, tried to claw their way back up and been killed from above or behind. Lieutenant Smith alone, shot through his lame shoulder and streaming blood, came staggering up through the smoke and dust, his survival a miracle. He dropped to the ground and fanned himself with his hat. Custer knelt beside him and looked for George Lord and could not see him.

The firing now was a savage rolling thunder that was everywhere, near and far. Arrows came arcing down, launched from gullies and behind hills. They struck deep into the dry ground, lanced dead horses, pierced men from behind. The smoke and dust grew denser, a hellish, cacophonous dusk. A pandemonium.

Autie's gelding was hit. His hindquarters gave and his back end went down. Autie let go of the reins and jumped up. The horse was trying to rise on his front legs.

"Shoot him," Custer yelled, but the boys

were up the hill and couldn't hear him. He cursed himself for saying yes to his nephew, yes to Mary Deschenes, vain thing to do in both instances, as if he were God guaranteeing their safety. Autie stood up holding the reins of the floundering horse and Tom dropped his rifle and drew his revolver and ran up the slope, cursing aloud. He shoved Autie away, hard, and put the gun to the horse's forehead and shot him. He seized Ginger's reins and tore them from Allen's grip and yanked her sideways to him and shot her too. She collapsed like a marionette, her legs folding as if boneless, and fell chest first. Tom yelled at the boys to lie down and went running back, bent low.

Allen looked at the blood-welling crater on Ginger's forehead where her white blaze had been, and at her gentle sightless upturned eye. He wanted to touch her but could not, and he turned with no thought of what he was doing and crawled downhill on all fours toward Custer. Autie and Bos hollered at him, he couldn't make out what, and he glanced back and saw them crawling after him. Now Custer was yelling at the three of them, gesturing furiously. *Get back. Get behind your horses.* But they only stopped halfway down the hillside and lay down on their stomachs. Autie had brought his rifle, crawling with it, and he levered a shell into the chamber, lifted himself on his elbows and took aim at something, or at nothing, and fired.

Yates had been hit, and as George ran to him, coming from the north side of the hill, he was hit himself. He stumbled and fell, catching himself as he went down, and Allen thought he'd tripped, then saw the hole in the small of his back, the dark stain on the blue fireman's shirt.

He was up in the bullet-singing air, running. He fell to his knees and pulled George over onto his back. The ball had gone clear through him. Blood soaked his shirt. His hat was gone, and his spectacles, and he looked past Allen at the sky with curious widened eyes, as if there were something up there he'd lost or forgotten and could almost make out.

"George," Allen said. "George."

The gaze shifted, found Allen. George studied him, thoughtful-seeming, and then his eyes rolled up, went glassy, blind, and George was dead. Allen closed the eyelids and lifted George and pulled him in and held him, bloodying his own shirtfront. He thought of Addie Grace and what her wish would be now, and the only answer that came was *Don't leave him.*

■ ■ ■ ■

It was almost over. The hill was covered with fallen men, many of them alive, writhing, crawling, trying to pull arrows out of their legs or bellies, trying to sit up. A soldier sitting spraddle-legged put his Colt to his head and shot himself. The ground bristled with arrows, men and horses bristled with them. Smith had bled to death. Yates was dead. The Indians were working in closer and closer. Horsemen circled in the middle distance, ghostly in the smoke, screeching, blowing whistles, firing. Voss stood up and put his bugle to his lips and blew rally, and Custer looked at him and wondered if he'd lost his mind.

Then a ball hit Custer below the left shoulder, knocking him down like a hard punch. He sat up. He felt dizzy. The ball was inside him, about halfway through, a solid lump, red-hot. Tom and Cooke were kneeling on either side of him.

"Get Boyer," he said.

"Armstrong," Tom said. He was weeping, but not in fright or collapse or even defeat, which was upon them. The tears were merely sad; it was over, and Tom wept for the loss of all that he had, and ever would.

453

"Get him," Custer said.

Cooke had disappeared, but a kind of twilight was on Custer and he didn't know where the adjutant had gone. He hoped Boyer was alive. His wound hurt, deep, and he closed his eyes. Voss was still insanely blowing rally. The firing was slackening around the hill.

Then Boyer was kneeling over him, huge-seeming, dark. A smell of sweat, leather, tobacco.

"Save the boys, Mitch."

"How?" Boyer said, speaking into his ear.

"Get them down into that ravine." Custer's chest was blood-drenched. He felt chilled. "Save them."

"They kill us down there same as here," Boyer said.

"Go on, Mitch."

Boyer turned, squinted down toward the river. You couldn't see much through the smoke. Custer wore two English Bulldog pistols, and he drew the right one and pain erupted inside his wounded shoulder.

Boyer was gone.

"I'm here, Armstrong," Tom said.

"Go with them, Tommy," Custer said.

"Lie back," Tom said. "I'm right here."

Then he raised his rifle, sighted, fired, levered in another cartridge. The explosion seemed muted, and in fact all sound was growing vague, distant. Voss had stopped blowing his bugle, and Custer supposed he was down. He could not see Cooke, either.

Boyer had brought Bos and the boys. They knelt around him. Their three faces were as vivid and bright above him as moons. Bos looked calm, somber. Autie looked confused, bewildered, as if things had run beyond his comprehension. Allen was looking off toward the distant river and Custer could not read him. The faces began to blur. As if he were seeing them through opaque glass.

"Go with Mitch," Custer said. "Do what he tells you."

"I'm not leaving," Bos said.

"Shut up," Tom said.

He could not see Tom.

"You have to, Bos," Custer said.

"I just as soon stay," Bos said.

"I know that," Custer said.

"We got to go *now,*" Boyer said.

He could not see Boyer.

There was very little shooting on the hill. Some wounded, fighting hopelessly on. The able-bodied were gathering on the guidons, Custer knew it without seeing them. Dimly, he heard their voices. The Indians would rush the hill at any moment and he might live to see it and he might not.

"Stay right with me," Boyer said. He had to yell through the din. "Anybody go down, you leave him. You go down wounded, you better shoot yourself."

"We're coming with you," someone said.

Custer still held the revolver. He tried lifting it, thinking he might cover them when they ran, but he couldn't.

"Tell your mother I'm sorry," he said to Allen, then realized they were gone.

Your mother. He saw the beautiful unfeeling lipsticked face of Mary Deschenes and told Libbie he was sorry.

SEVEN

They ran, keeping together, Boyer and the boys and eight soldiers who had come with them, all who were yet unwounded on the hill. The concealing smoke hung all about, like a Salem fog but bitter to the nose, thick and noxious to breathe. Indians, painted garishly, made way for them, surprised by these bold aggressors appearing suddenly out of the smoke. Boyer shot one through the chest, shot at another and missed. Allen heard a crackle of pistol shots behind him. The Indians let them run and came at them peripherally armed with pistols, hatchets, clubs. Boyer and the soldiers would aim their guns at them and the Indians would hesitate, and the chase would continue. A soldier cried out and fell, and another. Two gone, but the smoke still hid them and they were nearly to the mouth of the ravine, and it seemed to be working.

Boyer ran shamblingly, like a bear, but

fast. Autie had left his rifle. They drifted to the right, the ravine on their left. The ground was uneven and matted with dry grass. Running, stumbling. Bos looked resolute, his old lassitude and melancholy vanquished. Autie's face had gone cold, expressionless, and there was pale fire in his eyes, terror or rage, Allen couldn't tell. They'd attracted a crowd by now, Indians running or riding alongside of them, yelling, yipping, blowing those hellish whistles, making sport of it. An Indian darted in and wrestled a soldier down, and his drawn-out inhuman yell as they cut him followed them as they ran.

Autie, just ahead of Allen, stumbled with an arrow through his calf, leather boot and all, the thin steel arrowhead protruding out the other side on a couple of inches of shaft, painted dark with blood. Autie bent down sideways, hobbling, and gripped the arrow as if to wrench it out, then staggered and fell. He had not made a sound. When Allen turned, looking back through the smoke, Autie was crawling in an aimless-seeming direction, dragging his arrow-pierced leg. An Indian followed him, nocking an arrow, and as he bent the bow a foot from Autie's neck, Allen turned from the sight and ran on.

Bos died a moment later, shot from behind. A red rose bloomed on the buckskin jacket below his heart, and Bos looked oddly down at it, still running, as if wondering what it could be, and pitched forward, losing his hat. Allen glanced about and saw that he and Boyer and three soldiers were all that remained.

They followed Boyer leftward into the ravine, which was shallow here, bowl-like, thick with weeds and scrub and cactus. Boyer ran steadily, indefatigably, kicking through the brush, stumbling and righting himself. One of the soldiers said, "I'm kilt, boys," and wobbled, clutching his stomach, and sat down.

The ravine floor plunged to a deep, narrow, brush-choked gully. Instead of following them down into all that dense scrub the Indians were moving out on the two rims, and they got down on all fours and were hidden. Boyer holstered his pistol and crawled forward, and Allen and the two soldiers followed him. Grasshoppers sprang away from them. Both soldiers had lost their hats. One had reddish-brown hair and a mustache, the other a week's dark beard. Allen knew them by sight but not name. Veteran cavalrymen, squint-eyed and composed. Above them on either side the Indians yelled, whooped. It had become a diversion, a game. They fired some shots, guessing wrong where the white men were, and the balls hummed and tore leaves and split a cactus stalk behind them.

"Watch out for rattlers," Boyer said over his shoulder.

"*You* watch out for 'em," one of the soldiers said.

They stopped crawling and lay down and reloaded their pistols. The drifting smoke was above them, the air here hot but clean. Jubilant yells carried down from the hill and they knew all were dead or soon would be. There was shooting, but it was celebratory, and a pounding of hooves, the Indians galloping about putting balls in dead men, as if killing them once were not enough. It was quiet along the edges of the ravine.

"They don't wait long," Boyer said. "They come down after us pretty soon." He was breathing hard. His leather vest was sweated dark. "We try to find a coulee go up that way, south."

"I vote we head for the river," the redhead said. "There's trees down there. Woods."

"I agree," the dark soldier said.

"Indians come up that way," Boyer said.

"They're already up," the soldier said.

The four of them were lying side by side,

like campers. Mosquitoes were biting them.

"I'm thirsty," Allen said.

"I vote we split up," the dark soldier said.

"Go where you want to," Boyer said.

"I'm thirsty."

"Shut up," the redhead said.

"Shock," Boyer said. "He ain't right in his mind."

Allen heard this, thought, *Am I?*

"You boys go on," Boyer said. "We look for a coulee."

"Eddie?" said the redhead.

"Let's go," Eddie said.

They didn't say good-bye. They crawled forward single-file, holding their pistols, and disappeared.

"At the river we can drink," Allen said. Thought, *George is dead I have to tell her tell her how it happened, how he didn't suffer*

"You listen to me good," Boyer said. He pushed himself to a sitting position, and Allen did the same. "We look for a coulee. We don't see one we'll end up at the river anyways."

He looked at Allen's buttoned holster. "Pull your gun," he said.

Allen's hand was shaking. He fumbled the button, opened the holster. The gun was heavy.

"You got loads in it?"

Allen nodded.

"Okay," Boyer said. "Put it in your mouth they catch you, understand?"

"I'm just so thirsty."

"You hear me?"

"Let's go to the river now," Allen said. He could picture it, gleaming in the sun, cold and clear and clean.

"You listen to me and shut up about the river," Boyer said.

"I will," Allen said and thought *I must I must*

The noise up the hill was subsiding. Boyer listened, thought about what he was hearing.

"They going after Reno," he said. "Maybe the river ain't a bad idea. You come on now."

He was on his hands and knees again, crawling, and Allen followed him. They came on the body of a scalped soldier. One of the Gray Horse men. He was lying on his stomach, and his back sprouted half a dozen arrows, driven in from different angles at close range. His hands had been cut off. Flies lit on the dark knobs of his wrists and the blood-wet strip atop his skull. The Indians had not taken his carbine, perhaps had not seen it in the brush, and Boyer unbuckled the soldier's cartridge belt and pulled it from him and buckled it around his own waist. He took up the rifle and crawled on. Allen passed close to the corpse and smelled its blood. His own shirtfront, he realized, was stiff with George's blood. *George,* he thought. *George George George, I left you and how to tell her*

Then, up ahead, an eruption of gunfire, a fusillade, vehement. Indians had found the two soldiers. They must have been coming up the ravine from the river. It went on longer than you would have thought two men could fight off a crowd, dying out finally in a decrescendo of single shots and the yells of the victors.

Allen and Boyer had stopped to listen. The Indians who had been stalking them along the edge of the ravine were shouting, rushing to where the fight had broken out.

"We got to find a coulee or we dead," Boyer said, and was on his feet, crashing through the chest-high scrub, dodging cacti, and Allen running behind him.

They beat their way past the dead of the Gray Horse Troop, lying thick along the narrow ravine bottom. Some lay on the steep ravine wall, where they'd been trying to clamber up, loosening grass and dirt and sliding backward.

They came to a narrow island, which divided the ravine into two deep brushy notches. Boyer chose the left channel, the south side of the ravine, the only direction they could hope to escape in. And they did find a coulee, meandering down from their left, leading away from the river, overgrown and quite deep, with steep sloping walls.

"By damn," Boyer said.

By damn. Allen had begun to think he might not die when he heard the Indians coming up the ravine fresh from killing the two soldiers. They saw him, and as Allen turned up the coulee on Boyer's heels gunshots tattered the air behind him. Boyer had not gone far, and now, fox-cunning, he clambered up out of the coulee on the river side. Allen scrambled up after him, and they ran toward the river.

It took the Indians a few precious moments to discover where they'd gone. They came boiling up out of the coulee some eighty yards back and saw them right away through the thinning smoke. Shots broke across the slope and the air hummed, whistled, and Boyer was limping, hopping, shot in the leg, He said, "Ah shit goddamn," and lowered himself to the ground and rolled and lay prone facing his enemies, drawing a bead with his rifle.

"Run," he said over his shoulder.

Allen stared down at him. Boyer fired. An

Indian, painted yellow and devil-red, flung both arms out and fell backward. Boyer ejected the shell and inserted another and closed the breech. *I can't leave him I can't.* Something stung his neck, a hornet or wasp, and when he slapped at it his hand came away wet with blood, and he knew a ball had grazed him.

"Run," Boyer said, and Allen, neckshot and wet with blood and unable to think, spun and ran, still carrying his Colt pistol.

Boyer was putting up a strong fight and the Indians got low and spread out to encircle him. More were riding down off the ridge to help them. The noise receded behind him as Allen ran, the Indians concentrating on the brave half-white man who was giving them so much trouble, leaving Allen to a single warrior, maybe the swiftest among them, maybe known for his swiftness, who would run the coward down and kill him. Allen ran toward the ravine, thinking to make a stand there *I have to face him at least not be killed from behind Mitch so brave, and Tom think of Tom* and was almost there when the Indian caught him, grappling him with a wiry arm locking his neck, Allen stumbling, tripping, the Indian holding on, riding him down, landing on him, on his back, surprisingly light.

The Indian snatched a fistful of his hair and pulled his head back to cut his throat but there was a split-second hesitation, the Indian fumbling the grip of his knife, and Allen rolled, rolling the Indian, throwing him, the Indian landing hard, arrows clattering, spilling from the quiver, the Indian on his feet in an instant with the knife, Allen up with the Colt, cocking it at last, leveling it at the Indian's bony, white-painted chest.

He was a boy. Fourteen, maybe. At most. He stood in a half crouch in breechclout and moccasins holding the knife with his arm nearly fully extended, almost as if he were offering or surrendering it. His face was painted half red and half white, encircled with a border of charcoal black. He wore an erect white feather and his hair was plaited in two braids. He looked at Allen, looked at the cocked pistol, and his painted face broke in delicate lines of rue and resignation. He was beaten, and it seemed to disappoint him greatly, but not scare him. Out beyond him the shooting continued, Boyer still holding them off.

The two boys stood there. The Indian's gaze flicked down sideways: his bow lay in the grass, too far away to do him any good. He said something quietly, lowered the knife, and looked once more at Allen, who could not shoot him. He could not. The Indians behind him shouted, yelped, rushing in to carve Boyer up, scalp him. Allen let the hammer down and lowered the pistol. He did not know what would happen, knew only that he could not kill this boy.

The boy looked at the pistol, which Allen held down at his side. He looked at Allen. His young eyes cleared, hardened; he was thinking. Allen smiled. The boy looked past him, still thinking. The others were done with Boyer, and some were coming, singing their keyless war cries.

So it was over. Allen was oddly unafraid and only wanted to get it over with. He moved past the boy to the edge of the ravine, and there was a grunt and the boy grappled him down as before, rolling with him down over the edge, Allen letting go of the pistol, submitting *all dead but me now me it's only fair* the boy pinning him on his back, leaning over him and sealing his mouth with his salt-tasting palm clapped over it, silencing him. Allen braced for the knife thrust, but the boy was looking out over the edge of the ravine, stretching up and keeping Allen's mouth sealed. Allen lay still. The boy smelled of woodsmoke and some oily redolence Allen couldn't name.

The boy lowered himself and spoke to him and brought the knife around, Allen flinching from it, the boy pressing with his left hand to his chest now, *don't move,* speaking soothing words and laying the blade against Allen's bleeding neck as if in benediction, stroking gently, one side and then the other, blooding it to the haft. Once more he laid his palm over Allen's mouth, spoke again, sternly this time, and then he was gone, up out of the ravine, scooping up his bow and running to meet the approaching warriors, emitting a wolf-like manful yammer of triumph.

Allen rolled over, looked out. The Indians were a stone's toss away. The boy was showing them his bloody knife as he ran, waving it like a trophy, hurrying to meet and turn them. Allen slid back out of sight and stared at the paling sky, curious to see if the men believed the boy's lie, and if, believing it, they would come with knives and hatchets anyway, to mutilate and scalp him.

He could hear their voices, the singsong gabble of their alien language. The boy's voice was soft, light, against the voices of the men. Someone laughed, a rich guffaw like a white man's. Maybe we all laugh the same, Allen thought. The Indians were leaving. They were moving away, still talking, toward Boyer's remains, then past them, toward the ridge where all had died.

Later he worked his way down the ravine toward the river, moving incautiously and perhaps — he would often think it later — hoping to be seen, killed. The two soldiers had almost reached the river. Flies lit on them busily. They'd been stripped and gutted and their heads caved in, and you could not tell one from the other. Allen stayed back from them, along the slope. The sun was low; the day had finally relaxed its grip and faded to early evening. He could hear a faint sound of shooting to the south, where Reno and Benteen must be. Benteen, who had never come as ordered. Excited women's voices and the hoarser mutterings of old men carried down from the direction of the ridge, and he knew they were using clubs and* knives on the dead *on Bos on George what will I tell her* and dispatching any who might still be alive.

There was open ground where the ravine emptied to the river, the river looping in, almost doubling back on itself, flowing north. There were thick woods in the embrace of the loop on the other side, concealing the village, and more woods on Allen's side to the north. He crossed the flat, where

469

any Indian coming to the river would have seen him, and went recklessly in among the trees, the shade, moving in a fog of indifference.

The riverbank sloped down about five feet. He took off his gun belt — he had retained the Colt, holstered it again — and slid down it and sat in the cold moving water up to his shoulders and drank and washed the drying blood from his neck. The ball had sheared off a piece of skin. He could not see the wound but pictured it as a deep rope burn. The village seemed quiet — he could not tell how close the nearest tipis were — and he supposed all but the youngest Indians were roaming the battlefield, and the men all upriver, fighting Reno. He wondered if the Indian boy had gone there, wondered if he'd killed anybody or been killed himself. He drank. A dog barked in the village.

When he could drink no more he climbed out of the Little Bighorn and went up onto higher ground north of the ravine and lay down in a clump of sage where he couldn't be seen. He had lost his hat and did not know when. His canteen, as far as he knew, was still slung on Ginger's saddle ring, and the memory of Tom shooting her came back and he thought he might vomit up his stomachful of water. He had never heard of Indians mutilating horses, and there was some comfort in that. *But George oh Jesus, what'll I* He remembered the Mezuzah, which pressed against his leg in his soaked trousers, and thought of flinging it away in repudiation, *I did not ask the boy to spare me, I did not,* but a quieter voice stilled his hand.

They killed twelve more soldiers on Reno Hill and wounded another twenty-one. The shooting went on till dark. The night was overcast, no moon, no starlight. The men scraped rifle pits and set boxes of hardtack along the perimeter. The wounded, gathered in a depression in the middle of the hilltop, stirred and groaned through the night. Some spoke delirious nonsense.

Major Reno drank. His keg had come in with the pack train, which had arrived soon after Benteen. Custer's dogs were gone, and Burkman could not say when they'd disappeared, or where, and no one pressed him. Reno refilled his flask as needed. No one was paying him much attention; the command had passed, unspoken, to Captain Benteen.

Down in the great village bonfires sent their flames high into the darkness, and there was an incessant thumping of drums. There was shouting, singing, and also wails of lamentation. There were celebratory bursts of rifle shots, like fireworks, and all about the hill men asked each other where Custer could have gone, and if he might be besieged on some other hill, as they were. Shadows fell in weird shapes on the hillsides, and in their edginess and exhaustion men mistook them for columns of riders, Custer at last, and some even heard hoofbeats and the snort of horses. A bugle sounded down across the river, a tuneless squawking call no one recognized. Reno ordered his trumpeter to blow rally in answer. The call carried downhill, quavering ribbon-like down the gullies, but there was no answer, and they knew an Indian was in possession of somebody's bugle, and wondered whose.

Reno roamed the hill, drinking. He quarreled with a civilian packer and slapped his face, and when the packer came at him, he pulled his revolver and warned him back. He found Benteen alone sometime after midnight and asked him what he thought they should do.

"What can we do but stay here?" Benteen said.

"I think we ought to ride out tonight while

they're down there celebrating. We could get to the Powder River in a couple of days."

"The wounded can't ride anywhere."

"I know that, for Christ sake," Reno said.

"Well, then."

"We'll have to leave them."

"Leave them," Benteen said. "Leave the wounded."

"Anyone who can't ride," Reno said.

"I must not have heard you right, Major Reno."

"You heard me."

"Well, I won't agree to it," Benteen said.

"Then we're all going to die," Reno said.

"No we're not."

"I suppose you think Custer's going to save us."

"I think Custer's abandoned us, the way he did Elliot," Benteen said.

"The shooting we heard today," Reno said, "must have been Custer."

"I didn't hear any shooting," Benteen said.

Reno looked at him in the dark with those black bright spiteful eyes — liquor never bleared or glazed them, Benteen had noticed — and, after some careful if drunken consideration, he nodded in solemn agreement.

"No," he said, "I didn't either."

It rained briefly, and Allen turned his face

473

up to it and opened his mouth to the sparse drops, which did nothing to slake his renewed thirst. He was growing used to the idea that he was going to live, and in resignation to the fact, a sort of sullen compliance, had turned cautious, and would not risk going to the river again. At twilight old men, squaws, and children had gone streaming back to the village, some down the ravine, some over to the north ford, where Custer had first led them and where Kellogg had died.

He lay hidden in the sweet-smelling sage, slapping mosquitoes and listening to the celebration across the river. His clothes had dried, but the night had turned chilly, and he hugged himself for warmth. He thought of Addie Grace Lord and wondered what she was doing now. He found he could not see her face and wondered if she was lost to him, as he was lost to himself, and he wept tears of despair and self-loathing, and wondered why God had spared him and knew there was no reason, none, and therein lay the curse of it. He trembled, as if with the ague, and clutched himself and wept anew.

He guessed it was half past midnight when the noise died in the village, the quiet settling abruptly over all those sprawling acres of tipis, synchronous, as if they had clocks over there. He did not get up right away but lay listening to the stillness, which was pregnant, laden obscenely, with what the day had brought here. The darkness he saw was steeped in blood.

He didn't know if Indians posted sentries and so did not go again to the river, though he was very thirsty. He stood up out of his hiding place and looked about. Nothing, only the dark hills, the black trees by the river, dying campfires where the village was visible beyond the trees. He walked along the edge of the ravine, toward the fateful hill. He must get beyond it, to the east, then work his way south to the creek that had led them here. He figured it was fifty miles to the Yellowstone River. He wondered if he could walk it and gave himself an even chance. Dying, anyway, would be easy and not unwelcome. Lie down and wait.

He looked for Bos and Autie, hoping not to find them, and never did, or did not recognize them. Some scattered bodies lay below the hill, stripped and marble-white in the heavy gloom of the starless night. Allen thought of Addie Grace and knew he must look for George and went up the abattoir that was the hill, picking his way among

475

dead horses and strewn equipment and the naked remains of men, who lay desecrated and bloody with their arms flung out, their heads oddly tilted. They'd been mutilated in every possible way, and no two seemed done the same. He moved in a stench of blood and guts. He saw a naked headless body and the shakes came on him again. His teeth chattered.

Saddlebags had been ransacked, and he began noticing paper money strewn here and there, like autumn leaves, the remnant of payday on the Little Heart River all those weeks ago. Survival was being thrust upon him, and he gathered paper dollars with trembling hands and pushed them down into his damp trouser pocket. He stuffed his pockets with them, pushed more inside the placket of his shirt.

He found Custer where he'd left him. He was reclining in a half-sitting position, naked, against the two piled bodies of Voss and another man. He'd been shot again above his left eye, but he'd been dead by then and the hole hadn't bled much. They'd sliced open his right thigh and skewered his penis with an arrow, discolored swollen phallus on a stick, and Allen wondered if some evidence or suspicion of concupiscence had inspired this grotesquerie. His

476

glassy stare was mild, even serene. As if he were oblivious or else indifferent to what had been done to him.

Ten feet over was Tom, or what had been Tom, and the sight buckled Allen's knees. He fell to the ground and vomited water and then was crawling away, retching, his brain spinning in the wall of his skull, crawling and crawling past maimed reeking corpses and horses already bloating till he rose and stumbled down off the hill to the north, where the bodies petered out, where there was, finally, only grass and sage. *Why?* he wondered. *What made them do such things to Tom Custer? What could Tom have done?* He had not found George, and there was no help for it, he could not go back there. Better perhaps that he didn't.

East, he must get east, then south. He swung far out from the hill, circling it clockwise, his boots swishing in the dry grass. Once, his legs went weak and dropped him to the ground, and he sat awhile thinking he might die here, after all. Die or live, he didn't care. His head cleared and he stood up and walked on, uphill and down, working ever more east, wider and wider of the river, of the swale where Keogh's dead were, of the hill where Reno and, presumably, Benteen and their men, would be spending the night.

Why had Benteen not come? Allen cursed him as he stumbled along, cursed Reno for retreating. But then he saw Mitch Boyer, wounded, lying down to fight, die, telling him to run. He did, and Mitch died alone, and he could not blame Benteen for that, could not blame Reno, and he cursed himself for running, and cursed the Indian boy for granting him a life he did not deserve.

A horse nickered in the darkness. It was standing in a shallow draw. It had raised its head to watch him come, pricking its ears. Its saddle had slid over nearly sideways, bringing the blanket with it. It was a gelding, one of the light sorrels of Company C, and he seemed unhurt. "You think God sent you, don't you?" Allen said. "Well, He didn't, and I didn't ask Him to." The horse eyed him in the dark and whinnied softly. "Don't expect me to be grateful," Allen said.

He loosened the girth and repositioned the saddle. The lariat and picket pin had been lost, but the canteen hung on its ring and was half full. He uncapped it and drank. There were oats in the forage sack. He unbuckled the saddlebags, which were heavy with rifle cartridges, and found as well three hard crackers wrapped in a yellow bandanna. He found dirty underwear, a small leather-bound Bible, and a roll of paper money. He found a kit containing a razor, toothbrush, comb, needle and thread. "Who'd you belong to?" he said. Someone who didn't run. The horse stood patiently, switching his black tail. Allen threw the underwear away. He threw away the rifle cartridges, flinging them out broadcast. He sailed the Bible backhand into a low clump of cherry bushes and told God to strike him dead if He didn't like it.

He rode south, as best as he could tell with no moon or stars, up and down the dry, sage-fragrant hills, slow, reins slack, the horse feeling his way. He sat slumped and loose in the saddle, rolling forward and back to the slow rhythm of his gait, his rhythmic nodding, and several times caught himself dozing off. Twice he stopped to listen for Reno and Benteen. Silence.

He reached the creek a little before dawn. The horse had smelled it and quickened his step. Allen got down and drank the silty water and filled the canteen. The horse drank. He had no idea anymore how near the Little Bighorn might be, or Reno and Benteen, but a deadening fatigue was on him and he doubted he could stay in the saddle. He crawled under a cottonwood, leaving the horse to do what he would, and slept.

The sun was above the hills when he woke, and he could hear a steady rattle of shooting to the west. The Indians were at them again, and Allen supposed Reno and Benteen were well dug in, and that there would be no second massacre. He supposed too that Terry and Gibbon would show up soon, and then, surely, the Indians would depart.

The horse was close by, cropping grass by the creek. He fed him in his nosebag and ate two of the rock-hard crackers. The shooting went on, stubborn-sounding, stalemated. He could see the trail the regiment had made coming in, the grass flattened, the ground dug and beaten by riders now dead, horses shot to make a breastwork. "We have two choices," he told the horse. "We can stay, wait for the fight to be over, and throw in with Reno and Benteen, or we can go. Those are the choices." He lifted his foot into the stirrup and, with effort, pulled himself up and over. He looked west, toward the fighting, toward Reno and Benteen. He looked east, where the Rosebud was, on the other side of the divide. He'd made the choice already. He'd made it last night. He pulled the horse around and rode east.

A man half blind could have followed the trail. He began seeing discarded coats, utensils. There would be dropped boxes of hardtack, and who knew what else. The creek shrank to a trough and he crossed it and rode on toward the divide. Behind him the noise of battle dwindled, as if the hills were absorbing it. The sun shone hot, but if he followed the Seventh's trail back, there would be water all the way to the Yellowstone.

There would be the pale-green hills, the browning valley of the Rosebud, the pastel-blue lid of the sky, fleecy clouds so close to the hills you might climb them, stretch up out of the saddle and grab one. The hot, dry days, the cool nights. The emptiness. A land without laws, rules, compunction of any sort. Where violent death was commonplace and mercy an aberration. He kicked the horse to a trot and rode away from Reno's fight and all fighting forever, into the silence of the sere and desolate hills.

EPILOGUE:
MOONLIGHT BECOMES YOU

He goes out the side door to the moss-patched brick terrace under the grape arbor and out across the green September lawn. Past the ancient chestnut tree, carefully down the curb, step down, step again, into the short street where white clapboard and yellow stucco houses stand in intimate opposition to one another, the street canopied under the limbs of the black oaks and sycamores whose roots snake out under the asphalt, lifting it gently. A street where children can play, where dogs can poke about. Where neighbors can linger, getting out of their automobiles of an evening, to chat. The weather. Baseball. The War.

A warm, sunless afternoon, high white sky, air clear as gin. Leaves getting rusty, some few shedding, collecting along the gutter. Across the street the Sheffields' Plymouth is parked tight to the curb, Don Sheffield at home listening to the ball game, the staticky obbligato of the crowd drifting from an open downstairs window, the companionable baritone of Chuck Thompson doing play by play. Phillies at home versus Brooklyn. Allen is an Athletics fan. Old Connie Mack in his bow tie, running the team since 1901. *They saw Lefty Grove pitch, saw the great Jimmy Foxx hit the long ball. Saw Babe Ruth a couple of times. Gracie loved the ball games. She loved the excitement, loved the passion and irreverence of the home crowd and would laugh at the insults shouted at umpires and opposing players. They would drive the automobile into the city and park on Lehigh Avenue or Somerset and she would take his arm and they would join the crowd streaming toward the brick ballpark in its holiday mood, spilling into the streets, blocking traffic. A smell in the air of roasting peanuts. Vendors calling their wares. Score card lineup here! She had her favorite players. Al Simmons. Wally Moses. Mule Haas, because of his name.*

The street empties into a busier roadway where he must stop and look both ways. Railroad Avenue, because once the tracks ran here, angling westward. He was told by old Mr. Battey, who lived two doors down from them, that Lincoln's funeral train passed here on its somber journey to Illinois. Mr. Battey had been a grown man at the time and ought to have known, but he'd also told Allen that he'd attended a public reading by Charles Dickens in Baltimore in 1867, and Dickens hadn't traveled south of New York on that second American tour. Allen wonders what Mr. Battey really saw. He tries to think when Mr. Battey died. In the twenties, it must have been, after the Great War. His memory has been off lately. Seizing up on him, cramping, refusing to yield up what it knows. He wonders if he should tell Dr. Lowenthal.

He crosses Railroad Avenue, slow and bent, and now must climb the railroad tie steps to the campus. *Get a cane,* Sadie says, *there's no embarrassment in that; you're how many years old?* Up he goes, one step at a time, no pause to catch his breath, and there's a measure of pride in that. There are black oaks here and some undergrowth, a thin woodland with a packed dirt trail running through it, beaten by walkers and the cross-country team. A path cuts through to a parking lot where four young Negroes in their kitchen whites are playing at basketball. Strange. He does not remember a basketball hoop here. He tries to remember the last time he was on the campus and cannot. In the spring, walking with Sadie? He cannot remember drifted snow, the campus trees bare and black and snow-crusted, so it must have been in the spring.

He stops to watch the Negroes at their game. They move in intricate patterns, circling, cutting, stopping on a dime, the ball zipping from player to player. Cat's cradle, Allen thinks. They have noticed him, quick unfriendly glances, then nothing, as if his presence were a matter of utter indifference. He might as well have disappeared, become invisible. Perhaps he has, old flesh and bones melting like smoke into the clear soft air never to be seen again. The ball floats up, drops with a whisper through the net. Nice, one of them says. *Real* nice. They do not look at him.

Allen shuffles on. The parking lot is boxed on one side by a two-story dormitory and on another by the sprawling fieldstone building called Founders Hall, which comprised most of the college when he arrived, cramped little classrooms and offices, dining hall, bedrooms up under the roof. *Dr. Lord, the boys would address him at first, and every year he would correct them. I don't even have a diploma, he would say after some years, when it had become more of an oddity. Then how . . . ? they would say. You didn't need one in the old days, he said. Just some knowledge. And I'd published, you know.* The explanation was that he'd gotten married at eighteen and gone to Europe and begun writing. It was both true and untrue, the married part especially. At first he taught in a windowless coal-smelling room in the Founders Hall basement. Shakespeare. The Odes and Epodes of Horace. English Literature of the Eighteenth and Nineteenth Centuries. You had to be versatile in those days.

The dormitory windows are open on this warm day, and a radio is playing Glenn Miller, in an upper window. "Tuxedo Junction." The Chesterfield Hour. *They're mild, and yet they satisfy.* Satisfy what? Allen has never smoked, but he likes Glenn Miller, likes the big bands. Benny Goodman. Artie Shaw. He likes the Negro musicians. Fats Waller. Louis Armstrong. The girl who sings "Stormy Weather" and whose name will not come to him, though he knows it as well as he knows the others. Sadie came home one day with a phonograph record of "Let's Pretend There's a Moon," said *There's a world of music out there beyond Bing Crosby and that beanpole Sinatra.* He will sit of an evening listening to the phonograph, record after record, till Sadie stands in the doorway with her hands on her hips. *It's ten o'clock,*

Mr. Lord. I have to get my sleep, and so do you. She is tall and stick-thin and carries herself in a manner deliberate, studied, and regal. A pale-brown African princess. A young queen.

He circles Founders Hall, leaving "Tuxedo Junction" and the hollow *thup* of the basketball behind. A ventilator blows a smell of frying from the Founders kitchen. The Paoli Local rumbles in the distance, slowing for the station stop. A cheer goes up nearby, a festive sound. The football game. He didn't know there was one today. How long has it been since he's seen one? He used to go with Bill Post, the Latin instructor who'd played center for Yale. Gracie came sometimes, chic in her cloche hats, teasing and flirtatious with Bill, who never married. The football game. It's an idea. He goes toward the bright noise.

Past the library, past Chase Hall, where his office was, a corner room upstairs where he wrote his essays and short stories and received students who wished to discuss Chaucer with him, or Spenser, or Thomas Hardy. He knew them all. Dickens, of course. George Eliot. More recently he has essayed the provocative Mr. Hemingway and Mr. Faulkner, but they speak a blunt coarse language he can only half understand. He passes the gloomy little infirmary, the new observatory. Well, not so new. Ten years? Twenty? Cherry trees grow here, glorious in the spring. Dogwoods. *Remember walking here summer nights? We made love one time below the grandstand, half-clothed under a starry sky and I brought up marrying you as I did from time to time and you said We are married, and I have the ring to prove it. The conversation always ran that way. He had bought her a sapphire ring one day on the Ponte Vecchio — he'd been paid for a short story by* The Atlantic *— and put it on her finger, sitting beside her on the carved walnut bed. She could not have children, and that simplified things. They never knew why she could not, never pursued it, nor ever bemoaned it. It made sense, somehow.*

A boy and girl come toward him, leaving the game. The boy wears the college sweater, black with a blocky red H. The girl will be from Bryn Mawr or Rosemont. She is pretty, autumn-brown dress with padded shoulders, black hair tumbling to her shoulders, lipstick.

"Who's winning?" Allen says, suddenly wanting to speak to somebody, to be spoken to.

They stop. Look at him, look at each other and again at Allen. Smile.

"They are, sir," the boy says. "Got us by a couple of touchdowns."

"Who are we playing?" Allen says.

"Franklin and Marshall."

"Pretty good are they?"

"Better than we are, I'd say."

Lena Horne. The girl who sings "Stormy Weather" is named Lena Horne. Another cheer rings out, a hopeful sound.

"I used to teach here," Allen says. "Long time ago. Grover Cleveland was president when I got here, if you can imagine such a thing."

The boy and girl pretend to be interested. Perhaps they are. It is a kindly place, this little college, founded by Quakers and still loosely superintended by them. Allen wishes the boy and girl would ask him his name and thinks they might. He would like to tell them that he is eighty-nine years old and so explain his impulsive garrulity, his bent shrunken body which once . . . He wishes they could have seen him ride a horse. Play baseball. He wishes the girl could have.

"Well, sir," the boy says, and takes the pretty girl's hand and draws her on tentatively, a half step.

"Bryn Mawr girl, are you," Allen says.

"Yes sir." She smiles, and he thinks she's going to curtsy. But of course she doesn't

— what an idea.

"So long, sir," the boy says.

"Good-bye," says the girl.

Her green eyes meet his, and she smiles yet again and his heart twitches sadly and pleasantly, and he turns and watches them walk away, hand in hand, until they disappear beyond the library. Allen wonders if the boy will soon find himself in the War and if this preys on him. The War is turning, though, so maybe not. He turns back toward the game, goes on, stops. He can see the old wooden grandstand, the oval cinder track that encircles the playing field, a piece of the bottle-green field itself with its parallel chalk lines. He tries to think who might be at the game that he would know. Not Bill Post; Bill Post is dead. Allen does not know, cannot remember, if you need a ticket to get in, and he slaps the breast pocket of his tweed jacket and it is as he thought, he has not brought his wallet. He stands there.

They lived, posing as man and wife, in a pensione *in Via Maggio. They had two rooms and their bedroom window looked down into a courtyard. An orange tree grew in its center. Chickens scratched. In the warm months voices out of the open windows carried upward, echoingly, in the shaft-like enclosure,* signoras *scolding their children, scolding their* husbands, a man who sang Puccini and Verdi breaking into song abruptly and as abruptly ceasing. Allen would sit on the wide window ledge looking down and listening to the intermittent voices. He remembers the steamy smells of cooking from below and the sweetish mud-odor coming over from the river, which reminded him of home.

He was getting better and had begun writing an occasional Letter From Abroad for the Boston Advertiser. They'd been in Florence for over a year. Addie Grace had a good job tutoring the three daughters of a wealthy expatriate widower named Henry Wentworth Forbes. She had taught school in Concord for a year and then talked her way into a job as a typist at the Fall River Ironworks and worked there another year. They lived in rooming houses, and she put it out that he was writing a novel and so explained his sleeping by day and his disinclination to venture out. He was getting no better and she took him abroad.

There was a myna bird in the courtyard that summer and its humanlike squawk would rise between the four walls and the opera singer would holler at it, of course to no effect. Allen was sleeping nights now, the terrors of the dark receding, and walking alone by the river and improving his Italian chatting with shopkeepers and vendors. He sat on the ledge

491

listening to the voices and the peevish-sounding cry of the bird and began, in his head, a short story about a boy badly wounded in the Rebellion who meets a girl in the day coach of a train. The girl is running away from home. It was his first one, and many others followed.

He is moving again, and the noise of the game drops away behind him. The light is fading, the clear air turning dingy. The classroom buildings are darkened but the lights are on in the chapel-like stone library. Students move here and there across the big quadrangle carrying books under their arms. Allen passes the long high front porch of Founders Hall on a smooth-worn brick walk. Ahead of him is the oldest and largest of the dormitories, a two-story ivied and many-dormered brownstone looming chateau-like in the fading afternoon. Lights have begun to glow in the high windows, some of which are open to the still-warm air. He goes on, toward the porticoed auditorium building, Roberts Hall, where he meant to come in the first place and seems to have briefly forgotten. The hall is unlighted and appears devoid of activity, which is puzzling. He keeps going, crosses the narrow campus road, and climbs the two steps and sees the sign. Lecture, 4:00

p.m. The Mythology of the Old West. Frederick Van De Water, Author of *Glory Hunter: A Life of General Custer.*

Allen pushes back his sleeve, looks at his watch. It is not quite three-thirty. Strange. He meant to leave the house at three-thirty and thought he had. He lets himself down the portico steps and recrosses the narrow road. The brick walk slants across the lawn toward Founders Hall, and beside it is a park bench. He sits down on the bench. The old dormitory building is across the road to his right, and there is music from a corner window. "Moonlight Becomes You." Bing Crosby, whom Allen likes in spite of Sadie.

He will pretend she'll be here, a rendezvous on this bench. She was teaching school, riding her bicycle back and forth, and sometimes he would leave a note for her: *I am at the baseball game* or *I am at Jack & Ethel's — they got hold of some beer!* He would leave the notes hoping she'd come, and she usually did. He will wait for her on this bench. He had thought the girls at the Baldwin School would snicker at her riding the bicycle, but they thought it spirited of her and said so. *She's full of sand, my wife. Not really my wife, not technically, but everyone thought so. I thought so too.* In all those years, only one woman.

He did not fall apart until he came back to her. Until the moment he was in her arms. Only then.

He found two hardtack boxes that had been lost the day before the fight and broken open by Indians and filled his saddlebags. He found the Rosebud and followed it north, traveling by night, and reached the Yellowstone at dawn of the fifth day. He rode east along the Yellowstone. He'd found more hardtack and a box of salt pork along the Rosebud. The oats were gone but the browse was good along the river and the horse seemed to be getting sufficient nourishment. He had no coat and it was good to be moving in the cool of night. His clothes were threadbare and filthy but he washed himself in the river and shaved with the dead trooper's razor.

After five days on the Yellowstone he was wakened at noon by the approach of a large party of prospectors and hunters. They saw his horse and rode over to where he'd been sleeping under a cottonwood. They were riding west. They were armed to the teeth but he saw only curiosity, no malice, in their shaggy squinted faces. Wondering if the news had gotten out, he asked them if they'd had word of General Custer and they had not. He told them he'd ridden with Custer in a civilian capacity and had gotten separated on the morning of a big fight when his horse had tired. He said he didn't know what had happened but feared the worst. He said it was a big village, and when he'd revived the horse he'd gone north, looking for Generals Terry and Gibbon, and hadn't found them. He said he needed to get to Fort Lincoln and hoped to hail a riverboat and did not know what to do with the horse.

The men looked at each other. Take him on the boat, one of them said. Yes, Allen said, but a small boat couldn't take a horse, and there won't be many chances, large or small. He asked them where they were going and they said Fort Ellis. He asked them if they might take the horse and deliver him there, and they thought about it and said they would.

They dismounted and built a fire and shared their dinner of elk and venison with him. The prospectors were after gold and would go on to Helena if they didn't find any around Bozeman. The hunters would supply the army with game and look for other chances in Bozeman. They queried him repeatedly about Custer and he said he hadn't gotten over the divide between the Rosebud and the Little Bighorn and could not tell them.

They gave him a coat and some matches and filled his saddlebags with meat, biscuits, *and a cloth sack of coffee. Payment for the horse, Allen figured. Figured one of them would hold on to it, even with its brand, and it was only a question of who. Gamble for it, maybe. He shook hands with all fifteen or twenty of them and watched them ride away, then turned and walked east with the saddlebags slung over his shoulder.*

Two days later he saw the Far West *go by, bound for Fort Lincoln with its decks covered with Reno's and Benteen's wounded, who lay on straw under the sun. He did not call out. He met a small wagon train of missionaries, men and women, who fed him and asked him no questions. They'd nailed sheet metal crosses to both sides of their wagon beds thinking this would win them safe passage through Sioux country, and Allen said he doubted it, and they smiled and told him he ought to learn to trust in God. He asked to whom they would preach and they said any who would listen, white or red. They said God had called them to it, and Allen pitied them.*

He had lost track of the days when a river steamer took him on. He had to wade out to her across a sand bar. She was small, one wheel, carrying a motley collection of miners, land speculators, and surveyors for the Northern Pacific. They looked at his filthy clothes and took no further interest in him. He told the captain he'd been trying to get to Bozeman when his horse had broken a leg in a prairie dog hole. He gave him six dollars for food and passage to Bismarck. There was no stateroom for him and he slept in the saloon wrapped in the coat the men had given him. It was July, but he had no idea what day, when they reached Bismarck.

He took a room in the Merchants Hotel under the name of Thomas Jones. The desk clerk sold him paper and an envelope and loaned him a pencil. He wrote a letter and spoke to a loiterer on the gallery and said he'd give him two dollars if he would carry the envelope to Fort Lincoln and deliver it into her hand. See that she's alone when you do, he said. If it means waiting, then wait. He gave him the Mezuzah and told him to hand it to her with the letter. He asked the man what the omnibus and ferry cost and the man quoted both fares high and Allen gave him the money and said nothing. He bought a change of clothes at a dry goods store and some crackers and cheese at a grocery and took them to his room in the Merchants and waited.

She was three hours coming. She knocked on the door and opened it and ran to him, weeping. He swung himself off the bed and rose and was in her arms and his chest seemed to cave in on itself, folding him down

*against her, and he was back in the smoke
and noise and the smell of blood, he was
among men sitting up arrowshot and still alive,
among dead men gutted and scalped, and he
remembered Tom Custer mutilated beyond
recognizing and she helped him back onto
the bed, shaking, and sat beside him and put
her purse down and said she had come as
soon as she could and had told no one, as
he'd asked. He felt cold. He lay on his side
and hugged himself.*

*I knew you weren't dead, she said. I just
knew it.*

I should be.

No one should be. Did anyone else escape?

*They killed everyone, he said. We got cut
off and —*

I know, she said. The Far West *came back
on the sixth.*

*I ran, he said. I was with Mitch Boyer, and
they shot him in the leg and I ran away.*

You escaped, she said.

I ran. I left Mitch to die by himself.

*She stroked his hair down. Her face gentle.
Tears swelling her eyes. Why did you not go
to Reno? she said.*

I couldn't face them.

You will eventually.

No. Not ever.

She stroked his hair.

They'll never let me alone if they know I was there, he said. I'll never be free of it.

You need time, she said.

There isn't enough. There will never be.

She stroked his hair. Allen, she said. You must tell me. Is George dead?

Yes. Everyone.

You saw it.

I held him. He was dead. A ball, not an arrow. He died right away. Not many did.

She found her purse and opened it and brought out a silk handkerchief. And, when she could speak again: I'm glad you were with him.

I only left him when Custer sent us down the hill with Boyer, Allen said. Me and Bos and Autie. He thought to save us. If I'd been thinking clearly, I'd have stayed with George. I wish I had.

Thank God you didn't, she said.

She sat with him. Her hand on his shoulder, his neck, his head, stroking his hair. He closed his eyes and imagined her fortitude and serenity flowing into him from that constant gentle hand, but in the dark he saw more smoke and saw a man being pulled off his horse and flailed with hatchet, and he did not know how he would sleep tonight, or ever again.

I saw them cut a man's head off, Gracie. It

*was just before we ran. He was alive. He was
sitting up in a kind of daze and they —*

Allen. Listen to me.

*He closed his eyes. Opened them. Tears
filled them, burning.*

*I have to go back to Lincoln tonight, she
said, or they'll send the army out after me.
Wait for me, can you do that?*

I think so.

*I'll bring you some clothes. Some necessar-
ies. We'll take the first train we can.*

*He made room for her and she lay down
and took him in her arms. He curled against
her like a child, with his head tucked into her
sweet-smelling gingham dress and told her
about the boy who had spared him and how it
had happened, his own inability to shoot the
boy and the boy's more studied act of mercy.
He told of finding the horse and of his journey
to the Yellowstone, and thence to Bismarck.
He did not mention the ghastly sights on the
hill that night, but she'd read reports and
asked him if George had been mutilated, and
he told her he had not been, he was sleeping
peacefully, like Custer — the only lie he ever
told her. She never asked him again.*

*The sun was far over and the light pale yel-
low in the window when she left him.*

Stay, he said.

Darling, I can't, she said. They'd probably

send Reno. Or Benteen.

What'll you tell Mrs. Custer?

I don't know, she said.

I can't do anything, Gracie. I can't think.

I'll be back tomorrow. As soon as I can.

That night came the nightmares. Visions. Noise. He dreamed his throat was being cut, dreamed of being scalped. He saw Autie Reed, his face blood-smeared, coming at him with a gleaming hatchet. They went on for weeks. Months. Years, abating only by degrees.

"Mr. Lord, why do you want to worry me like this?"

Sadie. She stands with her hands on her hips, frowning down at him like some out-of-patience schoolteacher. Allen wonders if he's been asleep.

"I left you a note," he says.

Sadie's face softens and she sits down beside him. She takes his gnarled hand in hers. Smooth, young, honey-brown hand, long, gentle fingers. "No, sir, you didn't," she says.

"I thought I did. I meant to."

His memory is off.

"It was Gracie," he says. "Mrs. Lord. I left one for her. I thought she might attend the lecture with me."

Sadie pulls his hand over into her lap and

enfolds it between both of hers. She lives on his third floor and attends Bryn Mawr part-time, working patiently — she is twenty-four — toward her degree.

"Mrs. Lord can't meet you," she says. "You know that, Mr. Lord."

Allen looks over at Roberts Hall, where people have begun to arrive for Van De Water's lecture. A sedan stops in front of the portico, idling, and a man and woman get out. They slam their doors, and the automobile goes on. There is music again from the open window of the brownstone dormitory. "As Time Goes By."

The fundamental things apply . . .

"How long has it been, Sadie?" Allen says.

"A little less than two years," Sadie says. "She passed right before Thanksgiving."

"I knew that," he says.

"I know you did. It's this lecture, has you all upset."

Their first hotel stop going back East was in Duluth, where they'd had the big fight about Katie Doyle. This time Addie Grace was handling the money, paying at eating houses and dickering with the news butchers, but they were going to declare themselves husband and wife at the Immigrant House and she took his arm and drew him forward to the desk to sign the register. The clerk greeted them and

502

turned the book around. He dipped a pen and proffered it to Allen. Allen took it and thought a moment.

Mr. and Mrs. Allen Lord, he wrote.

"Let's go home, Mr. Lord," Sadie says. "It's almost time for your highball."

"I know what this fellow Van De Water's going to say," Allen says.

"Then why listen?"

"He'll say Custer was a reckless egotist. A glory hunter. Got us all killed."

The music has stopped in the dorm room. People are arriving steadily for the lecture. It is getting darker. Sadie still has his hand in both of hers.

"There was no glory in it, Sadie. Not for anybody. It was human beings at their worst. White. Red. Killers, every one of them."

"Except you, Mr. Lord. And that boy."

"Except us. I wonder what happened to him. Wonder if he got a taste of blood later, and liked it. I expect he did. It's what we're best at: killing."

"You don't want to hear that lecture, Mr. Lord. Let's go home."

He did not speak these heresies to Libbie Custer. He and Addie Grace came home to America in '92, and Addie Grace went to New York to call on her every year, riding the train

503

up and staying an hour or two and returning home by nightfall. Allen went only once, in 1932, a year before the old woman's death.

It was summertime. He remembers the open windows and how hot it was and the languid mutter of automobile traffic down on Park Avenue. A view of the sun-silvered East River. On the sitting room wall was the large framed engraving of Custer that had hung in the study at Fort Lincoln. There was the deer head with its yellowing antlers. The floors were carpeted and there were stuffed chairs and a sofa in shades of damask and burgundy that darkened the room, even with the sunlight falling through the tall windows.

Allen, she said. I'm so glad.

She was sitting in a stuffed chair and did not get up. She held a fan on her lap. There was a cane propped against her chair. She smiled up at them. Addie Grace had said she'd grown stout, and so she had. She wore a dark silk dress that seemed funereal, as if she were in mourning after — what? — fifty-some years, as in fact she was.

Addie Grace leaned down and kissed her cheek. Mrs. Custer extended her hand, and Allen took it. It was weightless and cool.

I should have come sooner, he said.

Yes you should have, Mrs. Custer said.

He dragged two chairs closer and he and

Addie Grace sat down. Mrs. Custer's delicate, chiseled face had broadened and puckered, and he wondered if her long abstemious widowhood had coarsened it and made her plain.

I enjoyed your books, Allen said. It was a lie. She had sent all three, inscribed, but he hadn't read them. Had read no biography of Custer, no history of the fight.

I've enjoyed your articles, Mrs. Custer said. Your stories.

Thank you, he said.

A housekeeper or maid came in with three sweating glasses of lemonade on a silver tray. She doled out the cold glasses, straightened, glanced at Mrs. Custer, and went out.

Thank you, Betsy, Mrs. Custer said.

They sipped their lemonade. The traffic ground along below. A horn beeped.

I want to thank you for keeping my secret, Allen said.

I did it for Addie Grace.

You never resented her for it? Allen said.

Never.

Only me.

You could have done so much for the general's legacy. His reputation. You could have refuted Reno and Benteen and their slanders.

Who'd have believed me?

You were there.

Others said they were. No one believed them.

They'd have believed you, she said.

Allen set his glass down. He looked out at the river. A tug shouldered its way north, dragging a barge. I ran away from the fight, and I've been running away from you ever since, Allen said.

Bosh, Mrs. Custer said.

It's true, he said. I owed it to you to come.

Never mind, she said. You've loved Addie Grace all these years, and there's redemption in that.

She smiled then, and the smile pinched her eyes and recalled the delicate bewitching face that once was.

Afterward, as their train was creeping out of the Pennsylvania Station, Allen said, Everyone wants to find a lesson in it. A cause. They all cast it as a morality play, no matter what their point of view.

She loved him, Allen.

That doesn't make it right, he said.

She loved him, Addie Grace said again.

"Let's go home," Sadie says again.

She gets up and turns and waits for him to rise, which he does slowly, stiffly. She takes his arm and he makes no objection, as he often will, is in fact glad of it on this lengthening day of rambunctious memories and confusion of time. It anchors him: her firm hand, her close presence. They go slowly out the narrow campus road, through a stone arch, and on toward Railroad Avenue.

"I believe we'll go the long way," Sadie says. "Avoid the steps."

"You're the boss," he says.

There isn't a breath of wind and in the stillness and failing light the world of stone buildings and massive old trees is darkly autumnal.

"What does your father do, Sadie?" Allen says.

She glances at him very briefly. He can feel it. "Pennsy Railroad," she says. "Dining car waiter."

"I knew that, didn't I."

"People forget things, Mr. Lord."

"Wesley's shipping out in a few days. I remember that."

Wesley is Sadie's fiancé. Wesley Ewell. A striver, like Sadie. Wants to fight Hitler then come home and go to college on Roosevelt's GI Bill.

"Wednesday," Sadie says.

"That's what I thought."

They turn onto Railroad Avenue. The old black oaks grow up through the sidewalk, warping it. A street lamp comes on, suddenly and magically, as if by the touch of a wand. An automobile passes, headlights ablaze in the gray twilight.

"What you need, Mr. Lord, you need to see more people."

"All our friends are dead," he says.

"Invite some neighbors over," she says. "Cocktails. The Sheffields. Or that nice young couple up the street. They're your friends. I shouldn't have to tell you that."

"You'd have to sit with us, Sadie. Help me with the small talk. I'm not very good at it anymore."

"You're fine at it. You sure keep me alert."

They have come to the quiet leafy corridor of their street. They look both ways and cross Railroad Avenue. Their house is the second on the right. The lawn runs back past the brick terrace, past the rose beds, to Gracie's vegetable garden, which is Sadie's now. They step up the curb and move across the lawn. Sadie keeps his arm until they reach the terrace, shadowy under its shed roof of trellis and grape leaves.

"I believe I'll sit out here," Allen says.

"Will you be warm enough?"

"If I have a highball I will."

He lowers himself into an Adirondack chair and stretches out his legs and crosses his bony ankles. Sadie goes inside, the screen door bangs behind her. Allen looks out through the tattered grape leaves into the deepening twilight. The lights are on in the Whitmans' house next door, and in the Sheffields' across the street. A car hums by out on Railroad Avenue. There is the burnt-leaf smell of autumn, though the air is still summer-warm.

They walked to the river and stood at the wall and looked across at the ochre buildings. The Arno ran brown, turgid, sluggish. The Ponte Vecchio, off to their left, top-heavy with its warren of shops and apartments. Clatter of wagons and carriages, clop of hooves, on the cobbled Lungarno.

I'd have gone to her eventually, he said.

I always thought so, she said.

I was punishing her, he said. For sending me.

I know that too.

His mother's obituary had rated two columns in the Manchester guardian *and* Daily Telegraph, *which you could read at the British Institute. Mary Deschenes had died of a ruptured appendix. Her exact age was unknown, but the consensus was that she was approaching fifty. Her last role was Gertrude, In* Hamlet.

I used to picture her getting the news, Allen said. She'd have blamed Custer, not herself.

Told people he went and got her son killed.

Addie Grace smiled. She took his arm. Aren't we lucky? she said.

The screen door creaks open and swings shut. "Lean forward," Sadie says, and places a sweater around his shoulders and spreads it. She sets a highball down on the arm of the chair.

"Have one with me," he says.

"I have to fix supper."

"Sit a minute."

She drops easily into the other chair and crosses her long legs under her knitted skirt, a loafer suspended in the air. She can talk about *Macbeth,* Donne, William Blake. About Duke Ellington and Langston Hughes. She loves Fats Waller. She will write, teach, who knows? Bigots won't prevent her, she's too smart, too resilient. She's too brave.

"Do you believe in destiny, Sadie?" he says.

She looks out through the arbor, thinking. Her forehead in profile is long, regal. "I believe in luck," she says. "Destiny's just a word for what happens. Or what already did. Luck can go any way, good or bad. There's no plan in it."

Aren't we lucky?

Allen sips his drink. Sweet bourbon, water-thinned.

"That's what Mrs. Lord believed," he says.

"I take that as a compliment," Sadie says.

"Do you think she's with her brother?" he says.

Sadie smiles. "My mamma would say so."

Allen drinks again. "You don't believe in God."

"Put it this way: He's got a lot of explaining to do."

A freight train passes the commuter station, and they are quiet, listening to it, a lonely sound. It rumbles on and on and on; you can picture the endless paint-faded boxcars, then the noise swallows itself and is gone.

"I don't know anymore," Allen says. "God. Destiny. I have no idea." Sadie looks at him. She stands up, jackknifing forward out of the chair. "Let's go in, Mr. Lord. You don't want to sit out here alone."

"I don't?"

"No sir. You want to sit in the kitchen, drink your drink. Talk to me while I cook."

"I'll want a second highball."

"I might have one myself."

He lets her help him up out of the deep chair. He picks up his cold drink. Sadie opens the door for him and stands back and cups his elbow in her long-boned competent hand as he passes. It is a gesture — tender, condoling — and he is grateful for it, grateful, as always, for the miracle that is human kindness.

ACKNOWLEDGMENTS

During the research and writing of this book, I received the help of numerous people whose knowledge of the Little Bighorn battle is, in every case, prodigious. No one who takes an interest in this event, it seems, does it halfway.

I owe an unredeemable debt of gratitude to James Donovan, whose *A Terrible Glory: Custer and the Little Bighorn, The Last Great Battle of the American West* stands with Evan S. Connell's *Son of the Morning Star* as one of the two best books on the battle ever, history or fiction. Jim plied me with books, documents, and answers from beginning to end. I couldn't have written *Little Bighorn* without him.

One of Jim's many favors was to introduce me to Michael Donahue, chairman of the Art Department at Temple College in Temple, Texas, and a seasonal National Park Service ranger at the Little Bighorn. Mike spent a long day off giving me and my wife a tour of the battlefield. He took us to the Crow's Nest, an inestimable gift by itself. Like Jim Donovan, Mike provided prompt and intelligent answers to my endless questions.

Thanks to Al Johnson, frontier military and living history specialist at Fort Abraham Lincoln, who sent me photographs, took my phone calls, and played "Garryowen" on his fiddle for me and my wife in the parlor of the Custer house at Fort Lincoln. There is no more amiable and giving person.

I am indebted, too, to Kim Fundingsland, reporter and outdoors writer for the *Minot Daily News* in Minot, North Dakota, and author of *Bismarck, D.T.,* a vivid and useful portrait of Bismarck in the 1870s.

Thanks to Louise Barnett and her superb biography of George Custer, *Touched by Fire,* and to Staff Sergeant Michael Phipps, author of *Come On, You Wolverines! Custer at Gettysburg* and Iraq War veteran who bled for us over there. Thanks to John Doerner, former superintendent at the battlefield, and to Mike O'Keefe, chairman of the Custer Battlefield Historical & Museum Association.

I owe debts for other kinds of help. Heartfelt thanks to Howard Frank Mosher, most generous of writers, whose work speaks for itself. My good friend Karl Zimmermann, travel and train writer, enabled me to write Allen and Addie Grace's rail journey. Thanks to Margaret and Peter Sherin for Irwin Kohn and the Mezuzah.

Thanks to my old friend Marion Morris of Washington, DC, who helped me write the city as it was in 1876, and to Tim Sprattler, archivist at Phillips Academy in Andover, Massachusetts.

And then there's my wife, Kate, steadfast always, and my agent, B. J. Robbins, as good a friend as she is an agent. Thanks, finally, to Lilly Golden, who is as deft an editor as Howard Mosher said she'd be.

ABOUT THE AUTHOR

John Hough Jr.: John Hough Jr. is the author of five novels, including *Seen the Glory: A Novel of the Battle of Gettysburg* (S&S), winner of the 2010 W. Y. Boyd Award for Excellence in Military Fiction, and *The Last Summer* (S&S), and three nonfiction books. He lives with his wife on Martha's Vineyard, Massachusetts.

The employees of Thorndike Press hope you have enjoyed this Large Print book. All our Thorndike, Wheeler, and Kennebec Large Print titles are designed for easy reading, and all our books are made to last. Other Thorndike Press Large Print books are available at your library, through selected bookstores, or directly from us.

For information about titles, please call:
(800) 223-1244

or visit our website at:
gale.com/thorndike

To share your comments, please write:
Publisher
Thorndike Press
10 Water St., Suite 310
Waterville, ME 04901